MERCY ON TRIAL

Mercy On Trial

Wendell B. Will

Writers Club Press

San Jose   New York   Lincoln   Shanghai

Mercy On Trial

Writers Club Press
an imprint of iUniverse, Inc.

For information address:
iUniverse, Inc.
5220 S. 16th St., Suite 200
Lincoln, NE 68512
www.iuniverse.com

ISBN: 0-595-21214-X

Printed in the United States of America

Dedicated to those who will wrestle with the decision whether or not to end the life of a loved one and to those of us for whom such a decision may one day be made.

-1-

It was the 50th wedding anniversary of Dr. David Neal and his wife, Lu. It was already dark on the late November Saturday afternoon. Bundled in warm clothes and blankets against the gray cold, the honored couple had been invited to sit in the president's box of the colorful Albion College stadium. With a thousand other football fans, the Neals had happily shouted themselves hoarse rooting for Albion. In an exciting game their team had defeated Hope College for the 1992 championship of the Michigan small college conference.

After the game David and Lu mingled among the 200 guests gathered in the Albion College Faculty Room to honor the anniversary of the respected retired psychology professor and his beloved wife. Most of the crowd remained dressed in the same colorful clothing they had worn to the football game. Many still carried pennants and wore Albion College sweatshirts. Animated and excited by the victory, they filled the large room lined with lavish antique book cases that displayed the college's rare book collection.

David Neal looked at his wife, Lu, and marveled that 50 years had passed since their marriage ceremony in her parents' modest Philadelphia home. Lu was radiant as she moved across the crowded room, chatting with the guests that included faculty, townspeople and her husband's former students. Always ill at ease with people, David stayed close to Lu, knowing she would remember everyone's name and something about them, though it had been years since she had seen many of them. He had always counted on Lu's ability to exchange pleasantries and whisper forgotten names to him at reunions and other occasions.

David knew it would be a cliché for him to say that Lu, at 73, was as attractive as she had been at 23, but the cliché was true and he had resolved to tell her so before the day was out. He was proud his wife remained such a beautiful woman. She had never gained a pound. She still wore stylish clothes and kept her hair its original jet black. Just watching her laughing and smiling with the guests made him feel young and almost in love again.

This afternoon was a time to forget that once their marriage was in such turmoil that he had doubted they would stay married 30 years, let alone 50.

It was also a time to forget that only two years ago David had feared she would die. After Lu's second frightening fainting spell she had had surgery to clear out the artery in her neck. Though she looked healthy and energetic as she vivaciously chatted with the president of the college, David would never forget his terrible feeling of panic when he had realized Lu might die before him, leaving him alone in the world. It had been the threat of her death that had driven home how desperately dependent he was on her caring and nurturing.

David was delighted when some in the crowd began chanting:

"Speech!"

"Speech!"

"We want a speech!"

David had already surmised that he would be called upon to deliver remarks for the occasion, but he was not confident he could deliver the words his heart desired. He wanted to tell the assemblage how important Lu had become to him as the years had fled by. To tell them that despite his pretense to the contrary, he had been miserable since he retired, and how Lu, knowing what he was going through, had been there for him. He wanted them to know that when his plans for an energetic, productive retirement had collapsed in a heap, he had become so dependent on her.

However, as David watched the president step to the lectern he was suddenly overwhelmed by a wave of self-doubt. While he was accustomed to speaking in public, it was always about matters of the intellect–neatly arranged lectures and the like. He had never been able to tell people, often not even Lu, about his inner feelings.

Apprehensive, David watched as the president smiled. "I know it's not I you want a speech from," the president said. "But as president of the college I have certain prerogatives, you know."

"We know, but the right to hog the microphone all afternoon is not one of those prerogatives," joked David. Making wisecracks often relieved his tension. He was annoyed at himself for being anxious about making the speech. At 75, it was about time he was able to say what he damn well wanted without getting tied in knots.

"I'll give you the mike soon enough," the president responded. "But first I want to say a few words about you and your wonderful wife." The group had quieted down. "David, you had your day when you retired. We've all admired your extraordinary career. You've brought honor to Albion College and for that we are grateful, but today we're here to celebrate something more important than an academic career. We are here to celebrate something special in this modern society of ours–a long and successful marriage."

The crowd warmly applauded.

As David listened, Lu squeezed his hand. He thought back to the day they met before the war. He was a graduate student at the University of Pennsylvania, completing his Ph.D. She had earned her master's degree from Penn and was teaching high school English in the Philadelphia public schools. They married after he completed Officer's Training School and before he went overseas.

David took his place at the lectern, which stood in front of the lighted fireplace. "I thought you had all forgotten us," he began. "After all, it's been ten years since I retired." David looked and felt fit. He had maintained his weight at 168. He swam daily in the college fitness center and regularly used the exercise room.

"We have forgotten *you*," said a laughing voice. "It's *Lu* we haven't forgotten."

"I know. I know," David responded, smiling. "You'll hear from her in a few minutes."

He was more relaxed now. He felt he could go ahead with what he had planned. "Fifty years is a long time. Lu and I are very pleased that all of you have joined us to help us celebrate. I know many of you have come from great distances. One even from California...and we appreciate it." Drawing himself together, David hesitated. He looked around the luxurious room at the familiar faces. "Many of you think you know me well, but you are mistaken..." David could feel himself begin to quake inside. He took a breath, still annoyed at his nervousness. "You see, I want to be serious with you for a few minutes. Since I retired, you have seen me in my office and around the campus. I'm sure you thought all was well with David Neal." David stopped and anxiously put his hand to his mouth as if to cough. Suddenly he doubted he could continue–at least not without breaking down and for him breaking down was out of the question. He could feel the color drain from his face. His knees grew weak. He saw apprehension on the silent faces in the crowd. The only way he could continue was to change what he would say and finish just as quickly as he could. He gripped the lectern to steady himself. "You see, these years of retirement have not been what I thought they would be. Not at all." David did not know what it was he feared about speaking from his heart. He cleared his throat and looked down at the carpet by the lectern. "Anyway, I want to thank this wonderful lady here for standing beside me." David felt Lu grasp him by the hand.

"All these years you thought I was a decent speaker, but, as you can see, not on occasions such as these." David reached for his handkerchief and pretended to stifle a cough. "I guess the truth is that my public speaking is confined to the classroom, but then you know that Lu has always been the one to send you greeting cards. It's always been Lu on the telephone to see how you are getting along." He pretended to be speaking lightheartedly. "Yes, I guess the truth of the matter is that sort of thing is Lu's department."

David was embarrassed. He wished he had stuck to safe things to say. "So now I guess I'll give you the real public speaker in the family."

The group began applauding—politely at first—but then as Lu kissed her husband on the cheek, a burst of relieved applause filled the room.

As she adjusted the microphone to her shorter height, Lu turned to David. "That may be, dear, but our marriage has been a partnership for 50 years and I don't see why today should be any different. I guess I'll continue to be the social secretary and you'll be the department head." He saw Lu's broad engaging smile, the smile that had originally attracted him and that now captivated the audience.

David stepped back, relieved that his nervousness had receded. "What a pleasure it is to have all of you with us today," Lu began. She had developed her speaking skills in her many civic activities including speaking to garden clubs throughout the county and serving three terms on Albion's school board.

"If I had my life to live again," Lu continued. "I wouldn't change a thing. I would still want all of you as friends, I would still want the same wonderful daughter, the same wonderful son-in-law, and of course the same wonderful grandson." She pointed to their daughter Betty, who stood with her husband, and their teen-aged son, Eddie.

"And above all," Lu continued. "I would not change the man I chose to marry." David smiled as Lu's emphasis of the words "I chose" drew a chuckle from the audience. "Ah, you didn't know that, did you? Yes, it's true. Despite what David may have led you to believe, *I chose* him, not the other way around." David knew the group's laughter was as much at the good time she was having as at her words.

"And now," Lu concluded, "especially you former students, you'll remember how David and I used to have coffee, tea and cookies for you at our house." The crowd murmured its assent as several nodded to one another. "Well, now we have this wonderful room and I want you to stay until the wee hours of the morning. You see, I want to chat with every single one of you."

It was after one o'clock in the morning. David was in bed. By the light on the nightstand he watched Lu readying herself for bed. The sight of Lu's naked body always aroused him. He wanted to make love.

"Joe Held looked good, didn't he?" David asked.

"Yes. Retirement suits him well."

"Imagine his coming all the way from California."

"He seems adjusted to Sue's being gone," Lu commented.

"Yes. I thought he might have remarried by now."

Wearing her nightgown, Lu climbed into bed with him. She turned off the bedroom lamp, but left on the light in the adjoining bathroom. David knew this was a sign that she too wanted to make love. David took her in his arms. "Do you remember 50 years ago tonight?"

"It was our first time for legal sex," she laughed.

He laughed too, remembering how few times they had had sex before they married. "We were so afraid of you getting pregnant."

"We don't need to worry about that tonight, do we?"

He slipped off the straps of her nightgown. Her breasts were still very attractive.

They kissed and held each other for several minutes before actually making love.

There had been times in recent years when David had been unable to perform sexually, but tonight was not one of those times.

✳   ✳   ✳

Afterward they lay together by the dim light, talking for nearly half an hour.

"You know David, you didn't need to be embarrassed about your speech."

"I suppose not."

"Those people have known you for years. They know you have trouble expressing your feelings."

"There were so many things I wanted to say."

"I know."

They were silent for a while.

"Well, it's been a wonderful day, dear," Lu said. "But I'm going to sleep now." She leaned over and kissed her husband. "I love you, David."

"I love you too, dear. That's all I really wanted to tell them."

David lay still for several minutes, thinking, and listening to Lu's steady breathing. It made him feel so good when Lu told him she loved him. For a moment he again thought what it would be like if Lu were dead and there were no one to tell him they loved him. He dreaded that possibility and hoped to God he would be the first to die.

Today had been a happy day. He had been able to forget the dreariness that plagued him since he had retired and seemed likely to hound him until the end. If only there were some way, he thought futilely, that every day could be like today.

-2-

It was Thanksgiving Day of 1993. A year had passed since the Neal's 50th anniversary celebration. While it had not yet snowed, cold winter weather had already come to Michigan. Lu Neal readied dinner, catching glimpses of the Detroit Lions traditional Thanksgiving football game on the small television in the kitchen.

David was in the living room, revising the manuscript of a book he still hoped to get published despite several rejections. He had had such hopes for his book and had been depressed about the rejections. He felt the world had passed him by and was desperate for ideas to keep himself busy. "I miss Eddie," Lu shouted to her husband over the noise of the television. "But it's good to know he's with his dad." Eddie Erickson was their 17-year-old grandson, who was with his father at the Lions game at the Silverdome, north of Detroit. In December the marital problems of Eddie's mother and father had exploded into a fierce divorce struggle. Since June Eddie had been living in Albion with David and Lu. Eddie had driven to his father's apartment last night. His father had recently given him an old car. Contrary to his mother's angry demand that Eddie stay with her, he intended to return to his grandparents' home after the Lions game.

"I miss him too," David called back. The divorce decree had given custody of Eddie to their daughter, Betty, but she had been forced to allow him to live with David and Lu after the youth had run away from her Bloomfield Hills mansion for the third time in as many months, each time hitch-hiking the 100 miles to Albion.

As had been true of Betty since she was a teenager Betty took out her anger at her humiliating failure with Eddie more on David that on her son and certainly more than her mother. David knew very well that the psychological term for this was *transference* of Betty's own anger against herself, but his knowledge was little or no solace. Lu and Eddie had had a special relationship from the start. David recognized everyone concerned considered Eddie to be living with Lu, not with both of them. While he loved Eddie, they lived in different worlds. Two generations was a huge gap. He was out of touch with Eddie, his rap music, long baggy clothes and indifference to school work. Lu had easily bridged the gap. But David had not.

"Look at that!" Lu shouted, excited by the football game. "I'll bet Eddie is having a wonderful time. He's such a sports fanatic."

Lu changed into a good dress and high heels for dinner. David wore a tie and his favorite vest. For over 25 years–since Betty had graduated from Albion College and left for Michigan Law School in Ann Arbor–they had always worn their best clothes for dinner every Sunday and on holidays.

Lu turned on the living room television so they could watch the finish of the game as they ate the traditional Thanksgiving dinner Lu had always prepared.

"I hope his father takes him someplace for decent food after the game."

"I'm sure he'll be all right."

David tolerated the way Lu fussed over their grandson. He knew Eddie had been the light of her life since he was born. Living with his mother in Bloomfield Hills, Eddie's grades had been disastrous. This fall Albion High School had let Eddie enroll as a senior, rather than holding him back a year, only because Lu had pleaded to her friends on the school board that she could help Eddie to change–and, it was working. David was proud that under Lu's magic Eddie's rebelliousness and hatred for his mother had begun to lose their grip. His grades were halfway decent, and there was some hope that the boy might pay more attention to his studies and make something of himself. He certainly had the basic ability.

"Well, I don't care," Lu said. "I'm going to stay up and fix some left-overs for him to eat before he goes to bed."

Long ago David had given up trying to help Lu wash the dishes. The kitchen was Lu's domain. It was getting dark outside as he read the paper in the living room while he waited for her to finish.

"There's another football game, if you want to watch that," he shouted toward the kitchen. Since Eddie had been with them, Lu had been avidly following sports. David knew she did it to have something to talk about with Eddie.

Lu did not answer.

"The next game. Are you interested in that?" he asked more loudly.

Again she did not answer.

Concerned, David went to the kitchen. He saw why Lu had failed to answer him.

In her high heels, good dress and apron Lu was on her knees on the kitchen floor. She gripped her head with both hands.

"Lu! My God, Lu, what's wrong?" David's mind flashed to her last fainting spell three years ago after the concert. Instantly he again experienced his terrible fear of Lu's dying.

"My head. David. I don't feel well. I don't feel well at all."

Lu never complained. David knew she was trying to speak calmly for his benefit, but he could see she was extremely ill.

He rushed to her side, bending down.

"What is it? What's wrong?" He tried to keep panic from his voice.

"This headache. I've never had such a terrible headache. Never in my whole life." She looked pale and shaken. "Oh, look at my hose. These are my new hose."

"Here, should I help you get to a chair?" He put his hands under her arms.

"I guess so, I don't know."

"I'll get you some water."

"The side of my face. My arm."

"What?"

She mumbled something unintelligible and then a word that sounded like "numb."

Lu slumped forward. Panic and pain was on her ashen face. It was only the position of her body on her knees that prevented her from pitching forward.

David did not know what to do. He was terrified, but knew he had to do something. "I'll call 911!"

Again Lu mumbled something he could not understand.

David started for the kitchen phone, but Lu began to slip to one side. She seemed unconscious now.

"Hang on, Lu. I'll get help." He gently lay her on the floor, then hurried to the phone and dialed. Her eyes were open, but she did not look as if she were seeing.

"Don't worry, my darling, I'm calling 911. Please hang on. My God, Lu, try to hang on while I get help!

"Operator, it's my wife. I think she's having a stroke!"

-3-

David held Lu's near lifeless hand as the ambulance rushed toward the hospital.

An all-but-forgotten quotation flashed through his mind. It was first told him by his philosophy professor at Penn over 50 years ago. *We draw to ourselves the very experience we fear the most.* As the siren cut the night air, the truth of the statement suddenly became clear. He had long feared outliving Lu and now the dreaded event seemed imminent. Was the quotation prophetic? Were the very things he so feared–Lu's death–living alone–soon to overtake him?

David looked at Lu's still form and the attendant working over her. Without her he would not want to continue to live. The world had become so unfamiliar with its unwelcome changes and people who lived by such different standards.

"Is she going to be all right?" David anxiously asked the paramedic, dreading the answer.

"She's taking in the oxygen well, Professor Neal."

David wondered how the paramedic knew him. He was too young to have been in one of David's classes. In the more than ten years since he had retired not many people knew him any more. At first he had buried himself in revising his psychology text book, *Neal's Case Studies in Psychology*, that was in use by many Midwestern colleges and universities. After the revision was published, he had written two more psychology books. The first one, *Mass Psychology Under Dictatorships*, had been published, but sold less than a thousand copies. He finished the second,

Psychological Implications of Diversity, after *Case Studies* went out of print. "I'm sorry, Professor Neal," the new editor at the publishing house had apologized. "But Albion is the only college still using your text. While I find your manuscript fascinating, I'm afraid my people don't think there's a market for it."

He had written still another book, *Jung's Archetypes Revisited*. That was the one he had been revising today. But he no longer knew anyone at the publishing house, and, after this latest rejection, his chances of publication seemed remote. His retirement was empty and his life without meaning or purpose. This last year, except for Lu, he had been increasingly alone. So many friends were dying or retiring and moving to Florida. He hated everyone on campus looking so young. He was always mistaking newer faculty for students.

"Try not to worry, sir," said the paramedic. "You'd better take it easy yourself, after what you've been through tonight. We don't want two stroke victims in the same family, do we?"

Try not to worry. What could the young man possibly know about worry? He was not much older than their grandson, Eddie. Lu was lying on that goddamned gurney, looking like death itself, and he was not supposed to worry.

David gently gripped Lu's hand and stared out the ambulance window. It was dark and had begun to snow. David pondered his fear of outliving Lu. Was it the fear of living alone? The fear of having a stroke himself and Lu's not being there to help him? Then it struck him. It was the fear of *dying* alone, not *living* alone. He had known for years that Betty, even as their only child, would never be there for him in his old age the way Lu was. Lu was the only remaining person in his shrunken world. Of course there was Eddie, but they weren't close and he just a kid with problems of his own. David's solace had always been the statistic that most men die before their wives, but now it looked as if fate had planned all along to make his fear come true.

David released Lu's hand and gently slid his fingers up her arm as he had done so often after they had made love. Oh, God, don't let her die! For the first time since she had collapsed, tears welled in his eyes. "You're going to be all right, Lu," he kept saying. "Together we can beat this thing." But he knew she could not hear him.

David thought back to the time Lu had fainted at the college's Goodrich Chapel. They had been chatting with friends at the concert's intermission when Lu passed out. Someone had called for the ambulance as David sat on the floor of Goodrich and cradled Lu's head in his lap. They had been fortunate. Surgery had corrected the artery, but tonight their luck had run out. Oh, God, don't let my Lu die!

The tears streaked his face as he watched the snow increasing in intensity. Before Lu had asked him to leave their house so many years ago—after the discovery of his affair with Jane Taggart—he would have scoffed at any suggestion that he would one day dread being the first to die. In those years the secret truth was that he would have welcomed Lu's death. It would have been the way out of their marriage without hurting her. He had tried to keep the affair with Jane a secret—always insisting on that motel outside Battle Creek 30 miles away, though Jane was more of a risk-taker. He had even fantasized about Lu's dying or maybe her falling in love with some other professor and wanting a divorce. It was not that he wanted to marry Jane. Christ, Jane was half crazy and already married. Besides, even in his need for Jane, he knew she could never be the wife Lu was. Later he realized that what he had really wanted was to be free. Not just free of marriage, but free of all the constrictions in his life.

As they sped toward the hospital, David looked at Lu. She had not moved since he had called 911. As she breathed under the oxygen mask held by the watchful paramedic, he whispered, "Don't worry, honey, you'll be all right."

David recalled that he had become involved with Jane just after his 52nd birthday—his first infidelity in over 25 years of marriage. While he loved Lu, he simply could not imagine staying married to the same mate for the rest of his life–never having sex with another–never running off with someone.

David thought about his colleague, Arthur Mahoney, who had gone through the same thing. He had run off with one of his students at the college–a senior. The young woman was not even pretty, but, as was clear to all who knew him, Arthur's ego craved her admiration. However, Arthur had not been discreet and had ended up resigning from the faculty. David had known he would be discreet with whomever he took to bed. He almost did not care who it was. His yearning, his emptiness, had become that strong.

Here he was chair of the department and the respected head of the psychology section of Great Lakes College Association. Even if he were discovered and had to resign, even if he had to give everything to Lu and write books in his cabin in the Upper Peninsula, it would be worth it. Colleagues said he was on the leading edge of his field. He was published every year, sometimes twice. Yet he was empty inside. How he had wished he could be free in those years. But now, as the paramedic adjusted the oxygen, how he wished to God Lu would be all right.

"Dr. Neal, I think it would be best if I took you to the waiting room," the paramedic said. Two men from the emergency room crew quickly pulled Lu's gurney from the ambulance, exposing her as little as possible to the cold air. "There's nothing you can do for her here."

The affair with Jane had ended tumultuously. He would never forget Jane's husband's pounding on the motel door. "I know you're in there you goddamn tramp!"

David had been relieved the affair had ended. Though his feelings about being married–married to anyone–had not changed–he was at least freed of two years of guilt and scheming.

Lu had taken it hard and had lashed out at him by having a brief sexual liaison of her own. Although he knew he deserved her anger, he could never forget that New Year's Eve. Lu had made sure that David had observed the inordinate attention one James L. Manwearing, Ph.D. on tenure track, was giving her at the party. She was grossly indifferent to David's painful feelings as she and Manwearing slipped into the servant's wing of the college benefactor's mansion, where the party was being given.

Eventually her anger had cooled, and, when she was convinced his affair had ended, they had agreed that they should try to heal their marriage.

He still had been tempted occasionally–he had even succumbed once, to that dark-eyed graduate student the summer he had given a seminar at the University of Michigan over in Ann Arbor. However, these past years, especially since he had retired, he had come to realize how dear Lu was to him. How very much he loved her. How much he wanted to grow old with her. Sadly, fearfully, he watched as they wheeled Lu down the hall.

"Dr. Neal, the waiting room is down this corridor. There's a chapel if you need it."

Reluctantly, but not knowing what else to do, David followed the paramedic. He thought of their house across the snow-covered town and wondered if Eddie had come home from his father's to find them gone. He wondered if Lu would ever be there again to greet him when he came home from another meaningless, listless day–to have dinner ready and to give him a cheerful greeting and a loving hug.

Although he dreaded it, he knew he had to telephone Betty in Bloomfield Hills. Betty had never forgiven him, even hated him, for hurting her mother with his affair. This last year her ill feelings had intensified with the humiliation of having to allow Eddie to live with them.

It was only after staring out the window at the still-falling snow that David realized he was cold. In his haste, the only warm garment he was wearing was the old sweater he had tossed on. He knew he had no choice but to gather his courage and tell Betty the awful news.

-4-

There was a knock on David Neal's bedroom door.

"Grandfather! Grandfather! Wake up! Mother is downstairs!" As Eddie's knocking awakened him, David instinctively felt for Lu's familiar form next to him, as he had done for 51 years. When he realized she was not there, the terrible events of last night rushed to his mind.

"What time is it, Eddie?"

"Almost ten. Mom's just come from the hospital. She told me about Granna."

When David had returned from the hospital after midnight, Eddie was not at home. He saw from a dirty ice cream dish in the kitchen that Eddie had returned from his father's, but must have gone out again. He probably had gone some place with his friends. David knew Lu would have stayed up to confront the 17-year-old. Eddie had agreed to a midnight curfew. But in fact he had been glad his grandson was still out. He always found it difficult to talk to Eddie, and had gone to bed relieved he would not have to tell him the dreaded news until the morning. At least Betty's arrival this morning had spared him that tribulation. David put on his bathrobe and opened his door.

Eddie was wearing his ever-present Detroit Tiger baseball cap with the bill to his back. As usual his long shoe laces were untied. He looked more like a boy than a six-foot near-man. He gazed at the floor, avoiding his grandfather.

"You weren't home when I got back from the hospital. I'm sorry I couldn't tell you…"

"I'm sorry, Grandfather. I was out late."

"Well, what's done is done."

"Grandfather?"

"Yes."

Although the two never showed affection toward one another—Eddie's love seemed reserved for his grandmother—David knew his grandson respected him and was grateful for refuge from the unhappiness of his mother's prestigious but cold Bloomfield Hills residence.

"Is Granna going to be…you know, okay?"

"Yes, Eddie. It's very serious though." David envied Lu for how much Eddie loved her. "Eddie?"

"Yes, Grandfather?"

"I'd appreciate it if you'd do some homework or something. I need to talk to your mother alone for now."

"Okay," answered Eddie. The apprehension in his grandson's voice was apparent to David.

"We'll have a good talk about Granna when your mother and I are finished. Is that all right with you, Eddie?" He did not know what he would say, but he knew he had to say something about their sudden plight.

"Okay, Grandfather." The voice sounded downcast. "Grandfather?"

"Yes, Eddie."

"You wouldn't lie to me about Granna would you? You know, to make me feel better."

"Granna's very sick. Strokes are serious business, but we both need her too much for her to die. I'll talk to you as soon as I can. Now will you tell your mother I'll be there in a few minutes?"

"Okay, Grandfather." Eddie looked bewildered.

"Thank you, Eddie." David closed the door and thought about his telephone call to Betty from the hospital last night. She had been her usual cold, abrupt self. "When did it happen?" she had asked, nearly demanded. "Is she conscious? What does the doctor say?"

Lu was dying and all Betty could do was cross-examine him. Couldn't she for once just be a daughter and stop being the consummate lawyer?

"This couldn't have happened at a worse time," she had said. "I'm in the middle of a very important trial in federal court. It's a good thing court is closed tomorrow. I'll get there when I can."

Betty had hung up without a word of empathy. David knew she had lost all respect for him–even hated him–since she had come upon Lu, crying and upset over his affair with Jane. Betty had been a law student at the University of Michigan then and was visiting home for the weekend. Although Lu had forgiven him, that was something Betty had made clear she would never do. David remembered being so proud when his daughter graduated from law school. She had won such high honors–Law Review–Order of the Coif. He had told her how proud he was–tried to make amends–but it was no use. He knew he had no choice but to accept the relationship, or lack of a relationship, for what it was.

At least Betty loved Lu, David thought. For years she had called her mother every Sunday afternoon, even after she had gained prominence as a trial lawyer in the Detroit area. However, she had not visited Albion in years. Late last year, after Betty had separated from her husband, Lu had taken to periodically visiting the Bloomfield Hills mansion. "Eddie needs me," Lu had told David. "Betty is away so much. The boy shouldn't be staying in that big house with only the servants."

In February Lu had stayed with Eddie for a full month while Betty stayed nights at Detroit's Pontchartrain Hotel during the trial of a major court case.

Filled with anxiety about seeing his daughter this morning, David leaned against the bedroom door and took a deep breath. He thought of Lu as she had been when he left the hospital last night–lying helplessly in Intensive care with all the tubes and the oxygen.

He looked at his image in the bathroom mirror as he brushed his teeth. He looked haggard. His thinning hair had been completely white for ten years. His mustache needed trimming. For a fleeting moment he wondered if he should get a haircut, in case of Lu's funeral, but he pushed the dreadful thought out of his mind. As he descended the stairs, he felt on the verge of tears. *I've got to control myself*, he thought. He knew any feelings he might show about Lu's plight–his plight–would only be met with disdain from Betty.

"I've just come from the hospital," said Betty without greeting her father. He saw she was still wearing her winter coat, as if she did not intend to stay long. "I talked to your Dr. Jacobson. I wish Mother were in a hospital near me. I'd feel much better." Betty had always been critical of Albion–its restaurants–its lawyers–everything about the small town. Her remark was an implicit criticism of her parents' long-time physician as well as the area's hospital.

"Here, Betty, let me take your coat. You're going to stay the night aren't you?"

"No, I've got to get back to Detroit. I'm in the middle of a very important trial–a copyright case in federal court."

"But your mother…"

"There is nothing I can do for her."

"She's going to be all right."

"How can you say that? You saw the situation yourself."

"I did, but…aw, forget it."

David yearned for Betty to call him Dad, but he knew his wish was futile. How he wished she would hug him as she did when she was a child! Instead it was always this cold, analytical, rat-a-tat-tat attitude of hers. She had been that way ever since law school and she was not about to change simply because of Lu's condition.

"At least let me make some coffee," David said. "You must be exhausted. Your mother made some cookies yesterday morning." David knew that sweets were Betty's weakness. When she was a teenager he had once talked to her about being overweight, but she had ignored him. Now she was 49 years old and, at 50 to 60 pounds overweight, a few cookies did not matter.

"You know I shouldn't eat cookies!" Betty snapped. "I lost three pounds. I didn't eat anything at all on Thanksgiving."

Betty took a package of cigarettes from her purse, tapped one, but did not attempt to light it. "I need to talk to you about Eddie, and then I've got to get back."

"Eddie's doing much better. If he keeps improving, they may let him play basketball."

"What if Mom doesn't get any better? What then?"

"She *is* going to get better." David was angry. It was presumptuous of Betty to assume the worst.

"Perhaps Dr. Jacobson wasn't as frank with you as he was with me. After all, he is your friend."

"What do you mean, frank? Exactly what did he say?"

"It was a massive stroke. Oh, she's likely to keep living, but only because of those machines they have in Intensive Care. It won't be much of a life."

"I don't believe it!"

"And even if she does, she probably won't be able to talk or move much."

"I'm much more optimistic than that, I'll tell you."

"The question remains, what about Eddie?"

"Eddie will be all right."

"Eddie will be all right," she mocked. "That's what his father always said, *Eddie will be fine*. I didn't believe it then, and I don't believe it now. Certainly you can't take care of Eddie. He'd run circles around you."

Things were happening so fast David did not have time to know what he was feeling. People saying *Lu might be some kind of vegetable. Eddie his responsibility*. It seemed as if it were happening to someone else, not to him. He knew he should be feeling something, but he did not know what.

"Betty, it's too much for me. I can't think about Eddie. Not at a time like this. Eddie will be all right."

"I think it would be best if Eddie lived with me again, when my trial is over."

Suddenly Eddie came rushing down the stairs. "I don't want you talking like that when I'm not here!" He was shouting at Betty. "You've got no right!"

"But Grandmother is very sick," Betty responded, taken back. "She probably won't come home again. The doctor says—"

"I don't care what the doctor says," Eddie angrily interrupted. "You just want me home with you again. That's all. Well, I'm not going back. No matter what!" The teenager was usually hard as nails–like his mother, but for a moment David thought he was about to burst into tears.

"Eddie," said David. "I'm sure your mother isn't going to make you go with her."

"Just one moment, now," said Betty raising her voice to match Eddie's. "I'm your mother, young man, and until you're 18 you live where I tell you, do you hear me?"

"I'll run away again!" Eddie threatened.

"Now Eddie." Eddie's threat caused Betty to calm her voice. "Your grandmother is very ill, and your grandfather will be in no position to take care of you."

Both turned to look to David, as if he had an answer for them, but David felt confused. Arguments upset him. The truth was he did not want Eddie living with him while Lu was in the hospital. He had only agreed to the youth living with them in the first place because that was what Lu wanted. Until now he had not minded his being there–at least as long as he stayed out of trouble–but Eddie was Lu's responsibility, not his. The idea of Lu's lying in the hospital and his having to make a home for the teenager seemed overwhelming. Yet he did not want to make Eddie go back to Bloomfield Hills. No one should have to live in that loveless half-empty house. Besides he did not like the way Betty was ordering the boy about. "We should wait. I want to see Lu. I want to ask her about it."

"Have you heard a single word I said?" asked Betty sarcastically. "Mother is unconscious. I don't think she's ever going to talk again."

"Stop talking as if your mother is dead! I want to talk to her, do you hear!"

"I can see there's no use talking to you. I'm going to Detroit," said Betty disgustedly. "Eddie, I'll call you tomorrow night at eight o'clock sharp. I want you to be in your room studying."

Eddie walked to the side of his grandfather. He did not answer his mother as she left the house. The two stood side by side as they watched Betty wade through the snow, get in her Cadillac and drive away.

"Eddie," David said softly. "Granna may be sick a long time. I'm not sure I can make it without her."

Eddie looked at the floor. "I can't go with Mom any more, Grandfather. I just can't."

When David went upstairs to dress to go to the hospital, he did something he had not done in a long time. He went to the seldom used chest of drawers in the big closet off the bedroom. He opened the second to the last drawer near the bottom. He reached in and took out a carved wooden case. Inside were two gold-plated Colt pistols. They had been made in honor of the 150th year of Michigan's statehood. Years ago, on an impulse, he had ordered them from a catalog. He removed one of the guns from the case and examined it. Although six bullets were loaded in each gun, neither had been fired.

Holding the gun in his right hand, carefully avoiding putting his finger on the trigger, David sat on the edge of the bed. He thought of Betty's words. "She'll only be kept alive by those machines." It would be so lonely in the house without Lu. What would he ever do without her should the worst happen? A wave of depression came over him. He knew he should be there for Eddie, but he also knew that he could not be. Without Lu, he doubted he could take care of himself, let alone Eddie. It was the first time David Neal had ever thought about killing himself.

-5-

Frederick Cain
Deputy Prosecutor

The lettering was on the glass door of Frederick Cain's cramped office in the Calhoun County Prosecutor's offices. Although Marshall, Michigan was actually the Calhoun county seat, the main Prosecutor's offices were situated in the dingy basement of an outmoded building in nearby Battle Creek, by far the county's largest city.

Fred Cain, not yet 30, with neatly trimmed dark hair, had graduated well up in his law class of '90 from the Detroit College of Law. As a student, he had been a "grinder", earning his undergraduate degree from the University of Michigan. His 3.1 grade point average at Michigan, although very good, was not high enough for the university's highly rated law school. Fred had to accept admission to Detroit College of Law, a perfectly good law school, but one Fred considered second rate.

Gone was the entree to the big firm job opportunities that Fred knew would have been his as graduate from the prestigious Michigan Law School. He was still angry at the fact that a slightly better grade point average and a few more points on the Law School Aptitude Test would have given him a shot at Michigan Law and the big time. It was the big time that Fred had wanted since he could remember.

Not daunted, he had devised a plan calculated to get the success he coveted. Upon passing the bar exam, many of his classmates at Detroit College of Law would take beginning associate jobs with small law firms, but that was not what he would do. He decided he would get a position in a prosecutor's office, because he knew that many successful politicians, even senators and governors, had been prosecutors. Fred had decided that his best shot at leapfrogging his hot-shot competitors who had made it into Michigan Law School was to become a deputy prosecutor in one of Michigan's counties. There he could build a name for himself as a tough prosecutor. Maybe successfully prosecute a headline case. Then he would run for judge. If he won a judgeship, then those same hot-shots would be arguing their cases before him. Fred liked that idea very much.

He liked even better his alternate and still more ambitious plan. He would get elected prosecuting attorney in some county. Make a name for himself. Then run for state attorney general and finally governor. He liked the sound of *Governor Frederick Cain* best of all. That was what he really wanted.

Fred picked up the telephone. "Marge, would you bring the file on the Ferguson case. It's on the docket for next Tuesday." The Ferguson case was yet another drug prosecution. Fred had an appointment in a few minutes to talk to the arresting officer to go over his testimony. "Indoctrinating the officer with the truth," he jokingly called such sessions. There was nothing wrong with that. The officer would not be told to lie, nor even to shade the truth. However, in the tradition of the legal profession, he would smooth out the rough edges of the expected testimony. When the session was over, the witness would be just a little more positive in his recollection, a little more forceful in his manner and would understand he should not volunteer any facts favorable to the defense unless asked a direct question by the defense attorney. Most of all, Fred would have a better idea which questions to ask the officer and which to avoid.

"Here's the file you wanted, Fred." Margaret Wolcott had been a secretary in the Calhoun County Prosecutor's office for over ten years, was 34 years old and divorced with no children.

"Thanks, Marge." When Fred began three years ago he had figured that Marge knew where all the bodies were buried in the prosecutor's office and had cultivated her friendship. At first the two years they had been only office friends occasionally lunching together, then sharing confidences. Although Marge was not particularly attractive, Fred had not found any other woman he was interested in. They had been having sex for the last several months.

Everything Fred had done these past years had been with the sole purpose of advancing his ambitious plans. He tried more cases than any other deputy. Most other deputy prosecutors in the office accepted plea bargains– compromises accepting time-saving guilty pleas to lesser offenses–in order to handle bigger case loads. But Fred spurned plea bargains, though it meant he did not handle his share of cases. He wanted to create an appearance of being a tough law and order prosecutor. He offered plea bargains only when he feared he might look bad if he lost the case.

Out of law school, Fred had deliberately selected Calhoun County because the incumbent prosecuting attorney was just over 60 years old and probably would retire in four or five years. Fred's plan required a smaller county like Calhoun, where he calculated he would quickly get the cases he needed to build his reputation while he was young, and then have a shot at the top job. Frederick Cain was in a hurry.

He leaned his slight frame back in his swivel chair, studying the Ferguson drug case file. He wished the case were less mundane, that there were some angle he could use to further his reputation, but it was like a hundred other cases–a small time drug peddler supporting his own habit. Ferguson had not even sold to high school students. Fred put down the file. There were no special angles here.

Thirty days ago fate had knocked Fred's calculated plan into a cocked hat. Unexpectedly, the governor had appointed his boss, the county prosecutor, to a newly created Circuit Court judgeship. Simultaneously, the governor had appointed Martin Lasser, at 51 a more senior Calhoun County deputy prosecutor, to fill his boss's unexpired term. Lasser, who had assisted in the governor's last campaign, immediately announced that he would run for a full term as County Prosecutor in next fall's election.

Fred feared he had little chance if he opposed Lasser. The big cases he had hoped to use to build his reputation had not come his way. In his three years there had been only one big case that the newspapers had picked up on—a political corruption case. But Lasser had wrangled the assignment away from him. Lasser was a handsome, well-dressed glad-hander who was giving law and order speeches at every Lions and Rotary Club in the county. The worst part was Lasser would be running as the incumbent prosecutor and that would make it tough. On top of that if Fred entered the race, Lasser would certainly see to it that Fred was not assigned any big prosecutions. Lasser was no dummy. He'd never give an opponent a chance to build a name for himself.

If Lasser were elected at only 51, Fred could forever kiss good-bye his ambition to become county prosecutor, yet there was little hope for victory against a smart incumbent.

Downcast, Fred stood and looked out his window—a basement window that let in only a small mount of natural light. He had to find some way to beat Lasser. He would have to do something dramatic and do it soon.

-6-

L u's condition had not improved in the four days since her stroke.

Each day David had visited her three times in the intensive care ward. Each morning, afternoon and again after dinner David was there. Except for her breathing she had not stirred once in that time. The ventilator obscured much of her face. An I.V. drained into her arm. The part of Lu's mouth David could see was twisted and distorted, the way his colleague Bob Helner had looked after his stroke.

"Lu, I'm here with you," David often softly repeated.

"Everything is going to be all right," he would say.

"Soon you're going to be home again."

"It's my turn to take care of you, after all these years."

But Lu never responded.

David had read that stroke victims might hear, though they could not acknowledge you. However, from what he could see, that was not true of Lu.

The second afternoon he thought of the words from Thornton Wilder's play *Our Town*. It had been performed by the students in the drama department about five years ago. He could not remember the exact quotation, but it had struck a chord with him at the time. Wilder has asked whether we ever really enjoy each moment of our lives as they slip by. David thought he had—especially in the past few years. He had always told Lu that he loved her. He had come to savor their life together, their chats at the dinner table. His problems with his writing projects. Her challenges with Eddie. But now, as Lu lay in her bed looking so vulnerable, he was not at all sure he had followed the *Our Town* admonition. These years, especially these recent years, had gone by so swiftly. No, he was not certain at all that he had really savored each moment and he regretted it.

When Lu pulled out of this, he would take care of her. If she could not walk, he would push her wheelchair around the Albion campus. If she could not talk, he would do the talking. And, if it were necessary, he would feed her, even change her diapers, if that had to be. Beyond anything, David wanted Lu to live.

Benjamin Jacobson M.D., dressed in his white smock, put his hand on David's shoulder as David sat watching Lu. "How are you holding up, old friend?"

"Not so good, Ben," David responded.

"Do you sleep? Want me to give you something to help you sleep?"

"No. I don't sleep as much as I used to anyway. Besides with this situation..." David's voice trailed off.

"I understand."

"Ben?"

"Yes?"

"Is there any hope for us...for Lu?" David turned away from Lu to look the doctor in the eyes. "Betty says–"

"David, I think we should step into the other room."

It was ten o'clock in the evening. No one was sitting in the small intensive care waiting room. The nurse was working on charts behind her counter. Ben Jacobson waited until David sat before he did the same, while intently watching his patient and friend of 20 years. David and Lu had been among his first patients when he had started his practice in Albion.

"What is it you want me to tell you?" the doctor asked. His voice was soft–barely above a whisper.

"The truth, I guess." Tears welled in David's eyes. "No, I don't want you to tell me the truth! I want you to *lie*. I want you to tell me Lu is going to be okay. I want you to tell me I can kiss her again. That I can tell her I love her again. Even make love one last time." David was weeping.

Ben Jacobson said nothing. He waited for his friend to gain his composure.

David took a deep breath and stared away from the doctor. "All right Ben, I guess I'd better face it. Face up to it."

"What do you want to know?"

"I already told you. I want to know she's going to be all right. At least that she's going to live."

"David, there's always hope. We doctors know we don't understand everything. There's always hope."

"You mean I've got to hope for a miracle, is that it?"

"I think Lu might keep living. We might be able to keep her alive."

"But she'll be like this." David gestured toward Lu's room. "That's what you mean, isn't it?"

The physician did not reply.

"Will she regain consciousness?"

"It has happened before. But no, I'm afraid it's unlikely that Lu will regain consciousness."

"You're wrong, Ben." David turned and looked resolutely at the doctor.

Ben reached to put his hand on David's shoulder, but David turned away.

"I'm not giving up." David was grim–stern–dry-eyed. "I need her too much. Eddie needs her too much. She is *not* going to die! She *is* going to get well."

"Come on, David. You've had enough for one day. I think it's time you had a decent night's sleep."

Later that night, alone in his bedroom, despite his determined words to Ben Jacobson, David took out his pistol again. He held it in his hand. Guns had always made him uncomfortable, but not tonight. This time he half-hoped it might discharge and kill him.

Instead of undressing for bed, he put on his heavy Mackinaw and snow boots. He tucked the loaded pistol into the inside pocket. The garment was so heavy that the gun made no bulge. He had no intention of shooting himself tonight. He only planned to take a long walk and think. He did not know why he was taking the pistol. There was a comfort involved.

He could see that Eddie's light was still on. It was amazing how hard the boy was studying this week. No doubt he was trying to prove something to his grandmother, David thought.

"Eddie," he said through the door.

"Yes, Grandfather."

"I'm going for a walk. Got to clear my mind."

Eddie opened his door. David could see he was working with his computer. "Was Granna any better?" As usual the youth was wearing his Tiger cap with the bill to his back. The radio was playing unintelligible rap music. The room was a mess.

"No, Eddie, there was no change."

"You'll be careful on your walk, won't you?"

"Sure, Eddie. Sure I will."

David smiled slightly as he left the house. Eddie had never shown concern for him like that before. It was not snowing, but it was a bitter cold Michigan winter night. David walked the mile to the college nature preserve, a hundred or more acres of virgin forest near the river. It was closed at this hour, but he managed to get over the fence, being careful of the gun. He had walked the preserve often and knew it well. He decided to take the trail that led along the river bank. In the darkness he stumbled several times before coming to the familiar clearing near the river. This was where he liked to think.

"What am I to do?" he asked aloud, oblivious to the cold and darkness. He had talked aloud in the forest often. He knew it was not God he was asking for advice. In fact he had secretly come to doubt there was such a thing as God. Yet for some mysterious reason it was comforting to ask for help.

David stood in the cold for 30 minutes, thinking, occasionally touching the pistol. Finally he began shivering and turned back toward the nature study entrance and home. He had no better answer than when he came to the desolate spot, but he knew he would return. There was nothing else he knew to do.

-7-

David's resolve not to give up on Lu's recovery ebbed during the next 30 days of intensive care. Thirty days that seemed like 30 months. Thirty days of talking with Lu with no response. Thirty days of holding her hand and telling her he loved her without her hearing.

The bills were pouring in. David was not sure Medicare covered everything. Irrationally, he worried he might not have enough money to see Lu through. He worried about everything, even that his retirement might be jeopardized. He had never felt such pressure.

Each night David prepared dinner for Eddie and himself. Eddie had offered to help, but David had declined. He needed to do something besides go back and forth to the hospital. He was amazed at how hard Eddie was working. It was as if he were studying to honor what Lu would have wanted. If it had not been for his horrible record in Bloomfield Hills, he might have a chance to be admitted to Albion College next fall. Now he was talking about joining the army and getting an education there. David supposed that was best under the circumstances.

Tonight they watched part of the Pistons game on the Battle Creek station before leaving for the hospital. As he had been doing, Eddie was driving David's car, since the old car his father had given him badly needed new tires. Eddie's school was to break for Christmas tomorrow.

"Eddie, I think you should visit your mother over the holidays." Since that first day after Lu's stroke, Betty had not visited Lu. When she telephoned about Lu, she avoided speaking to her father by calling Eddie on his bedroom

34

phone. David had never felt the need of human understanding more than he did in this crisis, but it was clear his only child still despised him.

"I don't want to go to Mother's," Eddie moaned in protest. "She doesn't want me. I'll just get in her way."

"It'll only be for a few days. I'll come in for a visit on Christmas Day and bring you back then."

"But Grandfather, I don't want to be with her even for a few days. I know how she treats you. I hate her, you know. Really hate her!"

"Don't you see, it's for my sake I'm asking you to go, not yours. I need to be alone for a while. Your grandmother's stroke has been very difficult for me, Eddie. I need some time."

"Besides, there's my tires. I'm was going to work at the post office to earn some money," complained Eddie.

"I'll give you the money for tires."

Although the doctor had instructed the nurses that Eddie could visit Intensive Care, he hated to see his grandmother lying in her coma and usually only joined his grandfather for a few minutes before they drove home. In the meantime, he did homework in the intensive care waiting room.

Tonight he chatted with Ruby Thompson, the nurse usually on duty at the station, adjacent to the elevators.

"You and your grandfather sure are faithful visitors," commented Ruby amiably. "You must love Mrs. Neal very much."

In the past month Eddie had talked with the nurse frequently. Ruby was a very tall, slim, black woman about 30, with an outgoing personality. She was always smiling, showing her remarkable white teeth. She had become the only bright spot in Eddie's dreary days.

"It sure is different at home without her. Grandfather isn't a very good cook, you know."

Ruby laughed. "He may not be much of a cook, but I can tell you, he was one heck of a professor." Her teeth appeared all the more white contrasted against her dark skin.

In previous conversations Ruby had told Eddie that she had taken two years at Albion College before transferring to Michigan State University for her nursing degree.

"I didn't know you had my grandfather for any courses."

"Oh, I did–Psych. He was a whiz, believe you me. Always gave me something to think about. Something besides plain old textbook psychology. He was the best prof I ever had."

"Ruby?" Eddie asked after a pause.

"Yes, Eddie."

"Can I ask you something?"

"Sure you can."

"You've been a nurse a long time, haven't you?"

Eddie was sitting in the reception area with his feet propped on the coffee table, while Ruby remained behind her counter.

"Not too long, but, yes, I guess long enough. Why, what's on your mind?"

"Do you think my grandmother is going to get well?"

"Me? You're asking me what I think?" Surprised, Ruby questioningly pointed at her chest.

"You're a nurse aren't you?"

"Yes, but I'm not a doctor."

"C'mon Ruby. You must have an opinion."

"You listen to me, young man. I may or may not have an opinion, but I leave that sort of thing to Dr. Jacobson. You could get me into a lot of trouble asking a question like that."

"I was only asking…"

Ruby walked from behind the counter and stood near Eddie. "Tell me, Eddie, what does Professor Neal say–about your grandmother, I mean?"

"When I ask him about Granna, he changes the subject right away. I don't think he wants anybody to talk about the truth."

Ruby reached out and touched the youth on his shoulder.

"And you think you know the truth, do you?"

"Sure I do. Granna's not going to get well."

"Now, you don't know that!"

"What's the point of her living, anyway?" Eddie asked, looking at the floor. "She wouldn't want to keep living the way she is."

"I have no answer for you, son. I'm sorry, but I have no answer to a question like that." Sadly Ruby slipped her hands around one of Eddie's hands. "I wish I did."

Eddie thought he knew the truth. Ruby didn't really think Granna was going to get well. She just didn't want to say so.

David and Eddie were home from the hospital. David had made hot chocolate, and idly turned on the television news to see whether the Pistons had won.

"Grandfather?"

"Yes, Eddie."

"Mom says she's not going to come to Albion again unless it's for Granna's funeral."

"There's not going to be any funeral!" David nearly shouted. This was what he would expect Betty to say.

"Why does mother hate you so?" He was sitting with his cup in Lu's chair, staring at the television.

"For something I did. Something a long time ago."

"I see."

"I'm afraid I once hurt your grandmother very much."

"You mean the affair you had?"

David was startled. "I didn't know you knew about that." He looked in Eddie's direction for a moment.

"Oh, sure, Mother used to talk about it all the time. She even drove me by the woman's house once. I'll never forget. I was about 13. She told me to stay away from women like Jane Taggart."

David was embarrassed. "I'm sorry she did that. It wasn't Jane's fault," he murmured.

"Yeah. Like when Mom was mad at Dad, she'd yell and say he was just like you. 'You men are all alike', she'd say." Eddie still looked straight at the television.

"She's a bitter woman. There is a truism I've thought about recently."

"A truism?"

"A truism is a saying, a truth. *We draw to us that which we fear.* Is the truism I was thinking about."

"We do? What does that mean?"

"It means there is a sort of principle of life. When we fear something will happen to us, when it dominates our thinking, there's a tendency for the very thing we fear to happen to us."

"Sort of like magnetism?"

"Sort of, I guess. Maybe that's a good way of putting it."

"Do you think that's true? About getting what you fear?"

"I think so, Eddie. I'm beginning to think that it is true. Look at your mother. Look at me…" David didn't finish.

They did not speak for a while. The sports announcer said that the Pistons had won in overtime. The Tigers had made a trade.

"You see, Eddie, what I think is that your mother always feared she'd have an unhappy marriage and so, in ways she really doesn't see, she's created an unhappy marriage for herself."

The T.V. weather man was on.

"Does Granna hate you for your affair?"

"She didn't like it much."

"But she doesn't hate you any more, does she?"

"No, she just sort of forgot about it. Put it behind her, I guess."

"Then why does Mother still hate you for it?"

"I don't know, Eddie. Your grandfather's supposed to be a psychology professor, but one thing is certain. He doesn't understand your mother. Maybe something about feeling she doesn't deserve love—I don't know." David had never talked this way with Eddie before.

"It's all pretty dumb," Eddie concluded, breaking the silence. "I mean, I don't hate my Dad because he had an affair and hurt my Mom."

"I suppose you're right. It is pretty dumb."

The news ended and it was time to go to bed. It was then that Eddie asked another question—one that forced David to confront the truth he had been avoiding.

"Granna's never going to get well is she?" He asked with the same matter-of-factness as if he were asking whether tomorrow were Wednesday.

Shocked, David put down his can of soda. To hear Eddie say what was obviously the truth got through to him in a way nothing else had. Seeing Lu lie helpless for so long talking to the doctor and all the other obvious facts simply had not penetrated David's inner defenses. Eddie's straightforward remark made him suddenly see that he was wrong in thinking Lu would recover and their lives would someday be normal again. He realized now he had been deluding himself.

"I don't know what to say, Eddie." David felt as if he might choke on his words. "I'm sorry I really don't."

"Do you think she's going to die or just lie there forever?" Eddie asked.

David's mouth felt full of cotton. He was very weary. As if he had been awake for 40 days and nights. "I don't know Eddie. I just don't know."

"You know what I think, Grandfather?"

"No."

"I think it would be best if Granna did die."

Not wanting to answer, David stared at the television screen.

Eddie stood. "Well, Grandfather, I'm going to bed now."

For a moment David thought that Eddie was going to bend over and give him a hug, but he did not.

"I hope you get a good night's sleep, Grandfather."

"You too, Eddie. I'll see you in the morning." David swallowed. He wished that Eddie had hugged him.

David sat for a minute after Eddie left. He wished that he could break down the barriers within himself that held him from going after Eddie and giving him a hug–even telling him he loved him. His eyes moistened. Lu had been the only person he ever had been able to tell that he loved and who had told him that he was loved–the only one.

-8-

Joseph Jefferson rose to his feet to address the jury in the large Detroit courtroom filled with the press. The 66-year-old African-American had argued over a thousand jury trials in his long career as a criminal defense attorney.

Jefferson's client, Dr. Webster Magnuson, a prominent white neurosurgeon, pensively watched as his attorney walked confidently toward the jury. Jefferson was dressed in an expensive but conservative suit.

The case had made the newspapers for months before it went to trial. Jefferson's client had been accused of murdering his wife, Joni Magnuson, a popular personality on a Detroit morning television show. The prosecution had proved that the accused doctor had a girlfriend and that both Dr. Magnuson and his dead wife had taken out $1,500,000 life insurance policies a few months before the murder.

Tall, trim and distinguished, Joseph Thomas Jefferson, Jr. was a handsome man. Although on close examination his face reflected his 66 years, most people thought he was just past 50. Looking at the jury with the witness stand to his back—the same witness stand that, following his advice, the doctor had declined to take—Jefferson fingered one of his gold cuff links.

In his own calculated time, as if he were a prominent violinist indifferently tuning his violin while his expectant audience waited, the seasoned attorney carefully sized up each juror one at a time. The courtroom was his concert hall.

"Ladies and gentlemen, this trial has lasted over a month. You have suffered through a tedious and unsuccessful attempt by the prosecutor to weave a web of evidence that he claims should put Dr. Magnuson in Jackson Prison for the rest of his natural life. To hear the prosecutor tell it, the doctor is lucky Michigan has no capital punishment." Jefferson paused and looked at the prosecutor, Warren Rabowitz, then dramatically turned back to the jury. "The fact is, I agree with Mr. Rabowitz! *If*, and I say *if*, the prosecution had in fact made its case, I would not only agree there should be a death penalty, but I would ask the governor for permission to pull the switch myself, personally!"

Joseph Thomas Jefferson, Jr. had never gotten over his anger at the white dominated legal system–still angry despite 40 years of successful law practice and becoming what many said was the top criminal defense lawyer in the Midwest. He had attended Michigan Law School long before affirmative action, graduating high in the class of 1952–just missing *Michigan Law Review* and Order of Coif. At law school he was a winner in the moot court competition, displaying the debating skills he later mastered. Upon graduation, he had served as a trial lawyer in the Army's Judge Advocate General Corps in Korea.

He knew if he had graduated 20 years later, he would have been courted by large law firms from Wall Street to Los Angeles, each trying to outbid the other. He would have become a top partner in any firm he had chosen. Indeed, if he were 20 years younger he might have been appointed to the federal bench and even to the United States Supreme Court. He might be Mr. Justice Joseph Thomas Jefferson, Jr. But the doors of opportunity were tightly closed to him in 1952 and he had never gotten over his anger at that immovable fact.

However, compared to his father, Jefferson did not know the meaning of struggle and discrimination. His father had been raised in a Kentucky sharecropping family of nine children. Escaping the doom of that existence, his father had come to Detroit at 18 and been hired as a janitor at the huge Ford River Rouge plant. During the summer layoffs he had hung around the old Wayne County Courthouse downtown, getting jobs serving legal papers and collecting debts. He was so persistent that he soon had a small process serving agency of his own and no longer worked at Ford. The senior Jefferson was 45 years old when he graduated from Wayne University Law School and passed the bar examination on the second try. Even then half his work was not really lawyering. He still ran his process serving agency and soon a collection agency, getting work from many white lawyers. His office was in the second story of one of the decrepit buildings from the last century situated between the courthouse and the Detroit River. The only law practice he could develop was representing small-time criminals, some accident cases and the occasional homosexual unluckily ensnared by police surveillance of public toilets.

His father never had the opportunity to try a case of this magnitude, Jefferson thought, as he continued his argument.

"But I would never have to ask the Governor to let me pull that switch! You see, members of the jury, the problem Mr. Rabowitz has is that the web of circumstance he attempts to paint is *defective*. Woefully defective. When you look at his case closely, without all the flowery talk, all you see is *suspicion*. I remind you that the constitution of the United States of America–the same constitution that guarantees your serving on this jury–says we do not convict on *suspicion* in this country." Jefferson overtly looked at the two black jurors seated together, as he referred to the constitution.

"Of course, the prosecutor would never agree to put it the way I am about to put it–put it so that you could see the defect in his case so clearly–but what he argues is this:"

Jefferson turned to the blackboard, interrupting eye contact only briefly.

"Dr. Magnuson was having an affair. All right, let's put that down."

He wrote *1* followed by the single word *affair*.

"A woman is murdered. If the husband is having an affair, he must be the one who murdered her. Right?" Jefferson looked expectantly at juror number one, the owner of a chain of dry cleaners, whom his experience told him might well be selected as foreman.

"Of course not. You would not be so foolish as to reach such a conclusion." The juror's face hinted of a smile in agreement.

Jefferson spoke without a trace of the *Detroit black* accent of his childhood friends–his father had refused to tolerate it in any of his children. His father had always insisted that Joseph be better than he.

"All right then, let's look at Mr. Rabowitz's reason number two." Jefferson told the jury, writing *2* and *insurance* on the blackboard.

"So this is to be our new rule of law, is it? If a successful and respected doctor–and you'll remember even the coroner admitted that Dr. Magnuson is one of the most respected neurosurgeons in Detroit–if this doctor takes out a million-and-a-half dollar policy on his life and his wife does the same, then this Mr. Rabowitz's new rule of law says that such a doctor is intending to murder his wife."

Rabowitz squirmed in his seat, as if he could hardly keep from objecting, but both attorneys knew the judge would grant Jefferson great leeway in his final argument.

"A $250,000 a year television star takes out a million-and-a-half-dollar policy on her life. Watch out, lady, your husband is going to kill you! Maybe we should eavesdrop on his house, because a man is bound to be planning to kill any wife with that kind of money on the line. Is that the new rule?

"Oh, come now. Hasn't Detroit had enough of that kind of thing? Cuff a man around because of the color of his skin. Haul him in for questioning because of the neighborhood he lives in. That's what it comes down to, you know. There is *no* distinction between shooting a black man on the street because he looks suspicious, and dragging a white doctor into court on a murder charge because he has a girlfriend and because his wife has a lot of insurance.

"Ladies and gentlemen, wherever injustice is found it must be stamped out. If you hate seeing anyone pushed around by people who control the system as much as I do, you will seize this opportunity and say *no* to the State of Michigan. You will say no, Mister Prosecutor we will not be a party to such a flimsy case. In this country we will not throw a person in prison, because he is a wealthy doctor, any more than we will allow shooting or throwing in jail a young black male because he is driving through the wrong neighborhood at the wrong time."

When Jefferson took his seat at the counsel table, he looked as cool and confident as when he had begun. He had argued for but an hour, meticulously pointing out the holes in the prosecution's case. As usual, his rage had found its way into his argument. In fact, it was his barely contained anger toward authority and what he considered to be an unreasoning system that made him the effective defense lawyer he was.

It was the same rage he had felt back in 1952 when he had angrily stormed out of the Lawyer's Club dining hall at Michigan's Law School upon hearing a fellow senior telling of the job he had just taken at Detroit's best law firm. The student was no better qualified than he, yet he knew he was condemned to a government job or joining his father in his third-rate practice.

The assistant prosecuting attorney began his rebuttal argument to the jury, hoping to undo the damage that Jefferson had done, in 60 minutes, to the case that had taken 30 days to present.

Jefferson barely listened to his opponent. He knew he had done well–probably better than most lawyers in the country could have done–and soon the case would belong to the jury.

Upon completing his three year hitch in the Army, he had joined his father's practice and ultimately built a reputation second to none. After his father died, he had rejected the offers that had been made. He wanted no part of the big firm existence. They had not wanted him then and he did not want them now. His office, with a fireplace, was on the top floor of one of the Renaissance Center towers, overlooking the river and the new building built on the old site of his father's office.

Now he lived in Bloomfield Hills in a very large house. He served on charity boards of directors with the leaders of Detroit. For five years he had been on the board of one of the big three auto makers, earning over a hundred thousand dollars annually for that post alone. With his other earnings he was well over the million dollar bracket. But the anger of 1952 was still there. He knew it would never go away until the day he died. Long ago he had recognized his anger as a formidable ally in achieving far more in life than he had ever imagined.

-9-

As David stood by the river bank, again huddled in his Mackinaw against the cold night, he mused on Eddie's words. "I think it would be best if Granna did die."

He knew the youth was right. Surely Lu would also agree with her grandson's simple observation. He fingered the pistol inside the large side pocket of the warm greatcoat. As he had done so often, he imagined what it would be like to be dead. Would being dead be any different from what Lu was right now? Unknowing. Unconscious. He removed the gun and in the moonlight felt the glistening fancy work on the pistol. Strange how an instrument of death could be so beautiful. He had always feared handling guns–frightened that he might accidentally shoot himself, but now the fear was completely gone.

He supposed the only difference between himself being dead and the way Lu was now was that Lu was still breathing. She would lie lifeless in the hospital bed and he would lie in a coffin in the ground.

It would be so easy. All he would have to do would be to raise the gun and pull the trigger. There was no need to wait until Eddie went to his mother's. It would be over without the lingering that Lu was going through. It would be quick, with no pain. No longer would he have to think of the agony of continuing to live without Lu and the emptiness his life would be without her.

Perhaps after his suicide Lu would soon die. It would not matter that he would not be alive to visit her. He would no longer have to watch her lie there helpless–useless.

Despite his protestations that Lu would recover, he had thought these same thoughts every night since he had first looked at the almost forgotten gun.

He would be sorry to leave Eddie, but it would be all right. Their wills left everything to him when both were dead. Eddie would be free from his mother when he was 18. He was sorry if he was letting the teenager down, but without Lu he could not take care of himself, let alone handle Eddie.

"Should I do it tonight?" he asked aloud.

The moonlight bathed his steam-like cold breath as he waited.

"For God's sake, didn't you hear me?" he shouted. "I need an answer!"

He heard the scurry of a startled raccoon.

Then it was clear.

No, not tonight. If he were dead, Lu would be lying there alone. There would be no one to decide whether she would live or die except Betty!

"No," he dismayed aloud. "Not Betty. For God's sake not Betty!"

He fired the gun toward a spot on the river where fast moving water had kept the river from freezing. Once! Twice! Three times! The noise of the shots cracked through the icy darkness. Four! Five! Six! The weapon was empty.

When the silence returned, David was aware of a sense of power within him. For the first time in years, he had a feeling of purpose. He would not leave Lu behind. He would not leave her in Betty's hands.

He would see Ben Jacobson in the morning and ask him to disengage Lu's life support system. Once that was done, he would be free to take his final walk by the river.

-10-

David sat by Lu's bedside. After all these weeks it was as if the respirator and tubes were an integral part of her body. Today Ruby had combed Lu's hair, which had grown to half an inch of white at the roots. He found himself wondering what Lu would look like in her coffin. At least she would be freed of the hospital and its smell of sickness.

David checked his watch for the third time in the last 15 minutes. It was 6:50 p.m. and Ben Jacobson usually came by about 6:30. He tried to eat the hospital dinner that Ruby had brought, but he wasn't hungry. He was too nervous about talking to Ben.

"My, my, Dr. Neal, you haven't eaten very much," said Ruby, her smile brightening the dreary room. "Are you all right?"

"As well as could be expected, I guess."

"I think you do very well. Everyone here at the hospital talks about how you visit so faithfully."

"They do?"

"They certainly do. Twice a day, every day. Where's Eddie tonight?"

"I asked him to stay at home. I wanted to talk to Ben about something important." David checked his watch again. "Are you sure he's not been here already?"

Ruby smiled. "I checked with his office. He's had a busy day. He hasn't left for rounds yet."

Ruby looked at Lu's still body as she took David's tray. "I'll wait until you've seen Dr. Jacobson before I move her. We don't want those bed sores to get worse." Ruby paused. "I wish I could color her hair for her."

"Could you? She would like that."

"I'm afraid not. It wouldn't be practical."

"When it comes time maybe the undertaker will do it. She wouldn't want her gray to show for her funeral. She was always so proud of her appearance."

"Why, Dr. Neal," Ruby sat on the chair next to the tray and looked intently at David. "I've never heard you talk this way before."

"I'm afraid I've got to begin looking at reality—tough as it is."

Ruby reached her long sinewy arm across the table and placed her hand on David's shoulder. "I was wondering when that was going to happen. I've seen it with other families before."

"That's what I want to talk to Ben about. I was down by the river last night, thinking."

"I used to sit by the river when I was a student."

"You did?"

"At first I had a rough time of it at Albion—especially as a freshman. I walked the nature study trails all the time." Ruby started to laugh. "Once I nearly tripped over a couple of lovers. They were doing their thing and along comes this six foot black woman out of the woods. They must have thought I was a cannibal or something."

David smiled.

"I'm sorry for laughing."

"It's all right, Ruby. I don't have many laughs any more."

"You were saying you were by the river last night?"

"I decided to ask Ben if we should let Lu die."

Ruby took a deep breath. "That is a difficult decision, Dr. Neal."

"I don't know if I have the right to even be thinking about it."

"If anybody has the right, you do. The way you love her."

"It's not just that I love her; the truth is I need her too."

"But we all need people."

"Eddie needs her too."

"Have you talked to him about this?"

"Actually, he's the one who started me thinking about it."

"He talked to me too," said Ruby.

"She's not doing anyone any good this way." With tears welling in his eyes, David gestured toward Lu lying in her bed. "Tell me, what sort of life is that? She was always so active."

"Would you like me to wait with you until Dr. Jacobson gets here?"

"I'd like that very much."

It was almost eight o'clock when Ben Jacobson finally arrived.

"I'm sorry, David, but I had to admit a patient. Chest pains."

"Ben, I need to talk to you about something important."

"Should we go to the intensive care waiting room? It's empty."

"Maybe we should."

"Ben, I want to know whether we shouldn't just let Lu die. It all seems so hopeless."

"I been wondering when we'd have this conversation."

"Do you think it would be the right thing?"

"It's what you think that matters most—not what I think."

"At first the idea of taking Lu's life seemed terrible to me. I doubted I could ever do such a thing to her, but now there doesn't seem to be any point in prolonging the inevitable. Can you tell me any reason on God's earth why we should go on this way?"

"I can think of only one and it has more to do with you than Lu."

"Me?"

"Yes, you," Ben continued. "You see, the truth is, from Lu's viewpoint, she would clearly be better off if we marched into her room right now and shut down her oxygen. I don't think there is any question about that.

David, Lu is brain dead. She's only breathing because of that ventilator. If this had happened years ago, before we had all these machines, we wouldn't even be having this conversation. She'd have been dead in a few hours. You want me to give it to you straight, don't you?"

David nodded his agreement.

Ben put his hand on David's shoulder. "David, there's absolutely no hope for Lu and even if somehow she did regain consciousness, she'd be just lying there all day. She'd be an empty shell, unable to talk or even to think. I'm sure Lu would want no part of a life like that."

"I know you're right," said David soberly. "She was so involved in life. She never could stand it, being kept alive by machines."

"Lu was an independent woman if ever I saw one. She would never want to be a burden to you."

"Oh, my God, Ben, it would be a burden I'd gladly accept if only she could live. I'd take her to the bathroom. Wheel her around campus in a wheelchair. Cook her meals. She would have done all those things for me. I'd gladly do all those things for her if only she could talk to me, or at least smile at me a little."

"I wish there were some hope that might happen."

"But you don't think there is any hope, do you?" David stared at the floor.

"No, David. I'm sorry, but you're asking me as a doctor and as a doctor I don't think there is."

They said nothing more for some time, letting the words have their effect.

Then Ben spoke. "So that's what I mean when I say it's really a question of how you would feel if we went ahead. You know what Lu would think and I've told you what I think."

"I'm not really sure how I would feel."

"I think I know something about how you'd feel. You'd feel guilty. At times guilty as hell. You'd have this nagging doubt whether you did the right thing. After a while it would ease a bit, but you'd always have that nagging doubt."

"I know I'd feel guilty."

"And you know I think that probably is the way it should be."

Ben pulled his chair even closer to David and continued.

"I've been through this David. When you're letting a life go you *should* have guilt, you *should* worry, you *should* toss and turn. If you take it lightly, you're not much different from the guy at the dog pound who injects a stray nobody wants. No human life should be deliberately ended without going through that agony. It may be the best safeguard we have."

Filled with gloom, David looked down. "You know we never signed any legal papers in case one of us got into this situation."

"You've made out your wills, haven't you?"

"Yes, we have had wills for a long time."

"But nothing about terminal illness?"

"Every once in a while she'd say something like *I'd want to be put out of my misery.* Like with her sister there at the last, but we never got around to signing anything."

"It's called a 'Designation of Patient Advocate.' It's just as important as a will–maybe more important in times like this."

"Does that mean we have to let Lu just lie there until she dies?"

"No, there are other ways, but they're more complicated."

"What other ways?"

"The truth is, for generations doctors have let their patients die when there was no longer any point in keeping them alive. They just kept it to themselves."

"Could you do that?" David asked as if he were pleading. "Just let her slip away?"

"We can't do it like in the old days any more. These days everybody sues everybody. We've got procedures our lawyers make us follow."

"What procedures?"

"In the big cities they have a hospital committee that makes the final medical decision–assuming that's what the families want–but we're too small for that around here. We don't have any such committee."

"What do you do, then?"

"Assuming the family agrees, I call in a second doctor, a specialist, for a second opinion. It's really to protect the hospital and me. Then, if we all agree, we withdraw the life support. That's the practice here in Albion."

"What would happen next?"

"We'd just let Lu die naturally."

"What do you mean naturally?"

"We'd slowly turn her oxygen supply down until she finally expired."

"And that would be legal?"

"There is nothing that says doctors have to keep doing all these heroic measures to keep the patient alive, when there's no hope–when the family agrees. It's a medical decision to remove treatment."

"Ben, I want you to forget you're the doctor for a minute. If it were your Sally, what would you do?"

"I hope I would be able to let her go."

"But how can you be positive it would be the right thing to do?"

Ben pondered before he answered. "You can't be absolutely positive. Miracles do happen. Miracles, misdiagnoses, or whatever the explanation might be. However, I know this. I've never seen a case where I was sure the patient was never going to regain consciousness and it turned out I was wrong."

"And in Lu's case? Do you think that Lu is never going to regain consciousness?"

"There's been too much brain damage–far too much."

"What about Betty? Does she have to be consulted?"

"Yes. We have to talk to the whole family. It's a family decision. She's Lu's daughter, after all."

"But, Ben, I'm Lu's husband. Doesn't 51 years count for something?"

"I'm sorry, but we'd have to have Betty's consent. After all you and Lu didn't sign anything. I cannot risk Betty's suing. They might even prosecute me."

"I can't possibly talk to Betty. You know we don't get along. Could I possibly ask you to do it for me?"

"I guess there is no other alternative but for me to do it."

"I hope she'll agree–after all, she's been counting Lu as dead from the very beginning–but you never know about Betty."

"I'll talk to her, but first I want you to be certain this is what you want. You should consult with anybody and everybody you feel you need to. Take your time. Be as sure as you can."

When Ben left Intensive Care David returned to Lu's bedside.

"Well, Lu," he said softly. "I've got some serious thinking to do. I've got to decide if I should have them turn off your respirator. Sweetheart, I wish you could tell me what you want, but I guess I've got to decide for both of us."

David passed Ruby's nurses' station on the way from the hospital.

"Good night, Ruby."

"Did your talk with Dr. Jacobson help?"

"Some, but I guess I'm the one who has to decide. I've got all this indecision and guilt."

"I can tell you, Dr. Jacobson knows something about that."

"Because of other cases, you mean?" David asked.

"More than that."

"What do you mean?"

"You remember three years ago, his father was in that horrible car accident?"

"Yes, of course I do. He finally died from it."

"Well, it was Dr. Jacobson who had to make the decision to let his own father die."

-11-

For the past month Marge Wolcott had sensed she was losing Frederick Cain. Not to another woman. She was confident there was no other woman in Fred's life. She knew she was not losing him to the pressures of his job either. He had won the Ferguson drug case and had more than a dozen routine prosecutions on his upcoming trial list. There was no particular pressure there. She doubted he was bored with her. When she first noticed his indifference, she began to be more aggressive sexually and, like most men she had known, Fred had responded.

The possibility of losing him distressed Marge. She wasn't in love with him, but then she doubted she would ever be in love again. Fred gave her a sense of being protected. He was bright and reasonably good-looking. She doubted she would find any man she liked better. Not many eligible males had come into her life and her prospects were not apt to get better. Despite her apprehension that a confrontation might bring trouble, Marge decided that tonight she would try to get to the root of what was bothering Fred.

Marge turned off the television. "Fred, we've got to talk." She had prepared their customary Wednesday night dinner and joined him in her living room after doing the dishes.

"What's the matter?"

"Something's gone wrong with us and I don't know what it is. It's driving me crazy."

"Nothing's wrong."

"Fred, it's Marge. Remember? I know when something is wrong."

"Nothing's wrong, I tell you. What makes you think there's something wrong?"

"You're off somewhere else all the time. It's as if you're not here half the time. Lately you act as if you only want me for sex."

"Come on, Marge."

"Is there another woman?"

"*No*, there is *no other woman!* You know very well we don't use any protection. I wouldn't do that to you. Dammit, Marge!"

"Are you tired of me? Is that it?"

"*No, I'm not tired of you.* Come on, Marge, we screw all the time."

"What is it, then?"

"Nothing. It's nothing I can't handle."

"It's the prosecutor's job," she suddenly realized. "It's the election for the prosecutor's job isn't it? That's what has got you so preoccupied."

"You'd be worried too, if your whole future were on the line."

"What do you mean? How is your whole future on the line? Even if you lost to Lasser, you'd still be a deputy prosecutor."

"Do you think I could settle for being a Calhoun county deputy prosecutor all my life? You know damn well I couldn't do that."

"And exactly what's wrong with that? You make a decent salary. People respect you. I respect you."

"You don't understand, do you? Why is it women don't understand? My mother never understood why I couldn't settle for being ordinary."

"I guess that puts me with your mother then. What's wrong with a good safe job? You'll get good retirement. You could do a lot worse you know."

"Dad sure didn't settle for a good safe job and a decent retirement."

"Sure, but look where it got him. Dead of a heart attack. What did you tell me? Dead at 47?"

"Yeah."

"And how old were you then?"

"Thirteen."

"Thirteen. There, you see. He'd have been better off with a regular job."

"My father was a damn good lawyer. He could have been a judge if he had decided to. Marge, I simply can't settle for being a deputy prosecutor in Battle Creek, Michigan. For God's sake, what would my father have thought?"

Marge was silent. Knowing Fred for three years now—sleeping with him for six months—he had never opened up to her about these feelings. Did every man in the whole world keep things to himself until he was ready to explode? Her husband had not breathed a word of his discontent with her until he served her with divorce papers.

"I'm sorry, Fred. I didn't know."

"Well it's true."

Marge sat on the carpet next to Fred's chair. Tenderly she took his hand. If men would only share such things with their women. "What are you going to do?"

"I don't know. That's what I've been trying to decide."

"Please, Fred. Tell me what you've been thinking. I might be able to help. I'd like to try anyway."

Fred began to pace. "I feel I'm damned if I do and damned if I don't."

"Let's go into the kitchen and talk about it. I made your favorite dessert last night. How about a great big piece of chocolate cake?"

They ate their cake at the small table in the kitchen, where Marge had breakfast every morning. She poured their coffee. Fred began to tell of his concerns. She felt she was finally beginning to know the man she had been making love with these months.

"You see, if I decide to file for the race against Lasser and he beats me, I might as well kiss good-bye my career in the Calhoun County Prosecutor's office."

"Why do you say that?"

"You know Lasser. He'd never give me anything but routine cases."

"Of course. He'd be afraid you'd build up a reputation and run against him again."

"Besides, Lasser is not the type to forgive an upstart deputy who had the gall to run against him."

"Do you think he might be appointed judge in a few years?" Marge pondered. "That would leave the top prosecutor's spot open again."

"That's a possibility, but I can't wait those few years. I might not live any longer than my dad."

"Oh, Fred, I don't want you talking that way! You jog every day. You take care of yourself. You're not going to die, for heaven's sake."

"My dad didn't think he'd die either."

Marge knew Fred was an excellent prosecutor, but she had not understood how driven he was. She wanted to be helpful—not to argue with him.

"If you decided to run and lost, you could start your own criminal practice right here in Battle Creek," she offered. "I know you'd be successful. Look at the lawyers who are doing well at criminal law, and they don't hold a candle to you."

"You're right. Criminal defense probably would be my best option."

"Sure. I could be your secretary—if you wanted."

"There would be a major disadvantage to practicing criminal law in Battle Creek, though."

"What disadvantage?"

"You've seen how important plea bargains are to defense attorneys?"

"Sure, lawyers try to get them all the time," she said. "They always come into the office looking for some sort of compromise to avoid a trial."

"Plea bargains are essential if you're going to make the big money. Hell, a good criminal defense lawyer can charge as much for a decent plea bargain as he does for a whole trial."

Marge filled Fred's coffee cup.

"And a plea bargain can take less than an hour," he continued. "A trial can take two weeks, even more."

"Yes, and most would charge the same fee." Her years in the prosecutor's office had made Marge savvy in the ways of criminal lawyers.

"And the clients love it. They serve a shorter sentence–maybe even straight probation–if it's a first offense. They don't risk spending big time in Jackson Prison. No, you must be able to make your share of plea bargains if you're going to practice criminal law. You'd starve to death if you had to try every case you took."

"But what's your point?"

"My point is if I run against Lasser and he beats me, he would damn well see to it that I would never be offered a plea bargain by any of his deputies."

"You figure he would do that to get even?"

"Nothing would give Lasser greater pleasure. He could be a spiteful son-of-a-bitch. It would be tough as hell to practice law with a handicap like that. No plea bargains from the prosecutor's office. When word got around, my referrals from civil lawyers would dry up."

"But you don't make many plea bargains now," Marge protested.

"No, I don't, but now I'm paid by the county. I get the same monthly check no matter what."

"I have heard some complaining that you try too many cases–that you never compromise."

"Sure, Lasser and the others grumble, but I don't give a damn. I'm not going to have a reputation as a weak prosecutor. The only reason I have any shot at all at beating Lasser is that I try most of my cases and I have a damn good conviction rate. I get longer sentences too–a lot longer."

"Then, you think you'll file as a candidate?"

"I'm not positive yet. I've still got another month before the filing deadline."

"Do you want more cake or shall I put it away?"

"No, I've had enough." Fred wiped his mouth with his napkin. "The problem is I need more going for me if I'm going to beat Lasser. The only real case I ever had was that bribery case I won. You know the case the chief wanted Lasser to take? Remember, he ducked it because he would look bad if he lost, and it got tossed in my lap."

"I remember," said Marge. "It was obvious he was afraid he'd lose."

"So it was handed to me, the new kid who didn't know any better and I won the damn thing."

"You could expose all that in the campaign, couldn't you?"

"It's a decent issue, but I need something more."

"Like what?"

"I need to win some kind of really big case. You remember that murder case in Marshall two or three years back?"

"Yes, the husband murdered his wife. He claimed there was some intruder. The chief tried it himself and won."

"That's what I need if I'm going to have a crack at beating Lasser. Some big headline case."

-12-

It was three days after David's meeting with Ben Jacobson. He had finally resolved his doubts about ending Lu's life.

"I'm going home soon," he told the unconscious Lu as he sat by her bedside. Although he knew very well Lu could not hear him, talking to her made him feel she was still a human being and not a freak of medical science. "I'm very tired tonight. You see, I've been debating whether they should shut down your respirator. Well, this afternoon, I decided. I thought I'd better tell you first." He looked at Lu for a sign of comprehension. "You know how much I love the nature study and the river. I went down there this afternoon and prayed. It surprises you, I know, but I've been praying a lot lately. Lu, I think it's best if they do shut it down. Is that all right with you?" David waited for a possible answer. It was an answer he knew she would never give, but he had to ask. "Well, I'll be back tomorrow and we'll talk." David stood and kissed Lu on the cheek. "Good night, dear. You think about it, won't you? I'll see you tomorrow."

What he did not say was that he had reaffirmed his decision to take his own life once he knew she was safely gone from this world.

"Ruby, is there any way you can take your break now? I need to talk."

"Certainly, Dr. Neal. I'll have the front desk send up my relief." David had repeatedly tried to get Ruby to call him by his first name, but she had declined. "I'm sorry, but you were my teacher once," she had told him.

"You'll always be Dr. Neal to me. But thank you for asking." Over these past weeks their friendship had deepened.

The cafeteria was closed, but they got coffee from the dispensing machine.

"I've pretty well decided to have Lu's life support removed." David looked at the table, avoiding Ruby's eyes.

"I thought that would be your decision. I'm sure it's the right one." Ruby reached for David's hand.

David looked up. "Ruby..." He faltered. It was more difficult than he had thought. "Ruby, I want you and Ben to end it for her."

"My, my."

"I want you to turn off the respirator."

"I..."

"Will you? Would you do it for both of us?"

"If it's all right with Doctor."

"Thank you. I can't tell you how much that would mean to me." David faltered again.

"I'm sure it will be all right with Dr. Jacobson. I was with him when–you know when we let his father die."

"You do think I'm doing the right thing, don't you?"

"Yes, I do."

"You see, I know you care about Lu too."

"Thank you, Dr. Neal. You're right; I do care. I care about both of you."

"Have you talked to other people about your decision?"

"Just our minister."

"And what did he say?"

"He wasn't much help. He just told me it was a very serious thing to do. I don't think he wants me to do it."

"He doesn't come here every night like we do."

"He's seen Lu several times. He just had doubts. I had doubts too."

"Have you seen anybody else?"

"No. I've got to talk to Eddie when I get home tonight."

"How about your daughter?"

"No. Ben is going to do that for me."

"Do you think she'll agree?"

"I don't see why not. She never comes to the hospital and I know she thinks her mother will never recover. Ben is going to her office in Detroit tomorrow afternoon. She says she can't come here to talk. Getting ready for another big trial. She's a very successful lawyer, you know."

Although it was late when David arrived home, Eddie was still studying in his room.

"Eddie, I need to talk to you. Could you come downstairs?"

"Is it Granna?" Eddie had apprehension in his voice. "Is it bad?" Eddie was in his pajamas, wearing his Tiger cap. He took the chair usually used by Lu.

"Nothing more has happened to Granna."

"Okay."

"Eddie I've given a great deal of thought to our situation."

"You sound like you've made up your mind."

"Made up my mind about what?"

"About whether Granna should die, I guess."

"I have made up my mind. I'm going to ask them to turn off Granna's oxygen."

"I figured as much. You've been at the nature study so much that I knew you must be thinking about something important like that."

"What do you think, Eddie? You have a voice in this too."

"It sounds awfully final. You know–Granna dead."

"It would be final. Once it's done, it's done forever. Maybe I shouldn't do it."

"No, I think that you should do it. For a long time now, I've thought she would be better off in heaven or someplace–if there is a heaven. Grandfather, do you think Granna will go to heaven?"

"I honestly don't know if there is a heaven, but if there is one I'm certain your grandmother will go there."

"I don't think there is–a heaven I mean."

"Maybe you're right, Eddie. I wouldn't be surprised if you are right."

"Whatever you decide, Grandfather, is all right with me."

"Do you want to think about it and we'll talk later?"

"No. I don't need to think about it."

"Okay, Eddie. Unless you need to talk some more, I'm going to bed. I'm exhausted." David was surprised at the way Eddie accepted his decision.

"I'll go up too. I've got some more studying to do."

When they had reached the top of the stairs Eddie turned to David. "Grandfather?"

"Yes, Eddie."

"When will they do it?"

"I don't know, but soon."

Later, when David got up to use the bathroom, he saw that Eddie's light was still on. As he walked by, he could hear his grandson crying.

-13-

Ben Jacobson was annoyed as he sat in the plush waiting room on the 38th floor of Detroit's Renaissance Center, nicknamed the "Ren Cen" by Detroiters. He had come for Betty Neal's permission to allow her mother to die a natural death. Ben knew of the estrangement between Betty and David, although he didn't know its reasons. He would never have agreed to take the initiative with Betty if it were not for his friendship with David and Lu.

His annoyance was due to Betty's attitude. When he telephoned two days ago, he was told he could deal only through her secretary, as Betty was in a series of depositions. He was damned if he would tell the secretary, an outsider, the delicate reason he had wanted Betty to come to Albion. On top of that, the secretary had told him Betty had said the depositions were very important and, while she could squeeze him in this morning, she could not take time to come to Albion. Ben wondered if this were a case of a high-powered big city lawyer deliberately putting down a small town doctor.

Ben looked at the roster of attorneys listed on the marble wall of the reception room. "Law Offices of Willard, Oates and Schultz." Ben counted 28 names. Betty Neal was in the middle. He decided that only partners were listed, because Lu had mentioned at the 50th anniversary party that Betty's firm had over a hundred lawyers.

"How do you do, Dr. Jacobson? My name is Jackie. I'm Ms. Neal's secretary." Jackie was an attractive woman in her mid-20s, dressed quite casually for such prestigious offices. "I'm sorry, but Ms. Neal is still in deposition. They should be finished in 20 or 30 minutes. Would you like a cup of coffee while you wait?"

Ben's annoyance rose, but he knew it was not the secretary's fault.

"Thanks. I'll have it black. I expect it's difficult for Betty with her mother so ill."

"Is her mother sick? I didn't know. She never mentioned it."

One floor up, on the top floor of the same Ren Cen tower, Joseph Jefferson, Jr. was being interviewed in his law office by a reporter from *Newsweek* magazine. She was doing an article on prominent African-Americans. The spectacular view from his office was down river, with Canada to the left. There was a sensation of the tower's being directly above the Detroit River.

"Don't you get bored doing the same thing over and over?" the reporter asked. "Jury trial after jury trial, I mean. A couple of months ago you got that doctor acquitted of murdering his wife and here you are in another prominent case."

"Hell, no," Jefferson responded. He was sitting behind his huge desk. One wall was covered with awards from civic groups and other organizations. "You've seen those circus performers who climb up hundred-foot ladders to jump into those little tanks of water day after day, year after year?"

"Yes, once when I was a child."

"If you think they get *bored*, you've another think coming. It's the same with me. Trying difficult cases is like jumping from that hundred-foot ladder. Let me assure you, I never get *bored*," he said grimly. "The only difference is that if the circus guy slips up it's his own ass. With me at least it's my client's."

"You must be very proud of these awards," she pointed. "Would you tell me about them?"

"Now, there is something boring." Together they stood near the wall that was covered with plaques and photographs.

"Hmm. 'The President's Commission on the Future of the Automotive Industry'," observed the reporter. "My background check didn't turn up that."

"Of course not. No one ever read the damn report, including the President."

"This photograph. Your family?"

"Yes. I was being sworn in as the first black president of the Great Lakes Trial Lawyers Association."

"Tell me who they all are."

"My wife, Coakie," Joseph pointed to the file. "She died four years ago. A long fight with cancer." He missed Coakie very much. It was only in the past year that he had been able to speak to others about her without being overcome with emotion.

"I'm sorry."

"The tall one on the left is my niece, Ruby. My sister's daughter."

"I'm told you never had children."

"I guess the law has been my children–although Ruby, there" he pointed to Ruby's photograph, "is like a daughter to me. She's a nurse. Works in a hospital near Albion–intensive care."

"I certainly will *not* consent to the death of my mother!" shouted Betty pounding her fist on her desk.

Ben Jacobson was shocked. He had not dreamed that Betty Neal would withhold her consent. "But David told me you gave up on your mother right after the stroke."

"Let me make myself clear, Dr. Jacobson. I appreciate your coming all the way to Detroit, but I'm afraid you've wasted your trip."

Ben was shaken. Surely Betty would change her mind if he could adequately explain everything to her. He could not imagine her refusing. "I was glad to do it. I've known your mother and father for many years. I–"

"It's one thing for me to feel mother is not going to get well, but it's quite another to agree to my own mother's *murder*."

"Now, Ms. Neal, I would hardly call it *murder*."

"Exactly what would you call it? She's alive now and you want to do something that will make her dead."

"We'd merely shut down the respirator. We aren't proposing to *murder* anybody," Ben pleaded. "I'm afraid she's already dead for all practical purposes."

"But not for *legal* purposes. Isn't that quite clear? For legal purposes my mother is very much alive."

"Ms. Neal, you're the lawyer, not me, but I've faced these issues before. May I explain things to you?"

At first Betty did not reply. Nervously she drank from the glass of water on her desk. Ben thought that for an instant he detected a note of vulnerability in the hardened lawyer. "I suppose so, but I'll be honest, you've got a tough sell. I love my mother very much." She choked on the last words. *Yes*, he thought, *there was a human being in that stern body*.

"I'm afraid that it's my medical opinion that Lu is never going to regain consciousness. My consultant, and he's a good one, agrees."

"When I saw my mother that first morning, I knew very well she'd never speak to me again, but I won't allow you to kill her like some old dog!"

"Ms. Neal, Betty, I'm afraid Lu is nothing but a burden to your father. He doesn't look well at all. He's lost considerable weight and–"

"Dr. Jacobson, my mother has taken care of my father for years, it's his turn now."

"It's taken a great deal of courage for him to decide on this. He doesn't want her dead either."

"Good! Then it's settled. She should be allowed to live."

"What I mean is, he would be perfectly willing to take care of her if there were any hope at all."

"Doctor, I don't mean to be impolite, but do you have any idea what my mother has put up with from the *highly respected* Professor David Neal?" The sarcasm in her voice was plain. The momentary vulnerability Ben had seen had disappeared.

"No. I don't believe I do, but all marriages have problems from time to time. We have to accept that in life."

"Not the woman you see across this desk. I'm getting a divorce right now from a man most women would walk stark naked down Woodward Avenue for. However, I'm never going to go through what your professor friend put my mother through."

"Your father loves your mother. This is a very difficult time for him."

"Dr. Jacobson, did you know my mother has family money?"

"Why, no, I did not."

"My grandfather had stock in a business in Philadelphia. There is a trust."

"I see."

"My mother wanted to leave it to me, but in the last will I know about she leaves it to him."

"And you think your father might have designs on this trust?"

"It was when I was in law school that Mother changed her will and left her inheritance to me. I went with her to an attorney in Ann Arbor. She was very upset with Father."

"Betty, I don't believe for an instant your father has any ulterior motive."

"Then after a few years, I was married by then, she changed it back. She didn't want to hurt my father's feelings, she said. Father gets everything. Grandfather would die all over again if he knew. He never forgave my father. You see, Father had an affair. Big and bold as life. Right there in Albion. I don't think he ever understood how much he hurt my mother."

"Surely that was years ago."

"Yes, all these years she has put up with that memory and now he wants me to agree to her murder. Well, I simply will not agree. I trust you understand that."

"I'm sorry you feel that way."

"That *is* the way I feel. You can be rest assured that if my mother dies under any suspicious circumstances whatsoever, you and your hospital are going to find yourselves at the wrong end of a law suit."

"I guess I'd better tell David."

"Yes, I think you'd better. Now if you'll excuse me, I've got to get back to my deposition."

-14-

David's apprehension mounted as he waited in Ben Jacobson's private office. The nurse had called earlier to say that the doctor wanted to see him right away about something very important.

Dressed in his white jacket, Ben looked grim as he entered and sat behind his desk.

"What is it? Has Lu passed away? Is that it?" David asked.

"No, that's not it. For your sake I wish it were."

"You've seen Betty, then?"

"She won't give her consent."

The news sent David reeling. For a moment he thought he would faint.

"David, are you all right?" Ben rushed from behind the desk and took David by the shoulders. "I want you to take some deep breaths. As deep as you can. You've had a bad shock."

David stared uncomprehendingly at the doctor.

"David, look at me. I want you to take a very deep breath," Ben repeated. "Breathe as deeply as you possibly can."

This time David responded.

"That's it. Now hold it as long as you can. Purse your lips and blow the air out through your lips—slowly." Barely understanding, David took in the breath and then expelled it.

"That's it. Now again."

Again David took a breath and expelled it.

"Once more."

When they finished, the color returned to David's face. Ben took his chair, intently observing him.

"I'm sorry I shocked you. I didn't know how to tell you."

As David absorbed the news, the shock was replaced by feelings of dismay and anger. "Why? She hasn't even visited Lu since that first time. My God, Ben, she's the one who said her mother would never recover. Long before I was ever ready."

"I know, David. I know."

"Did you explain it all to her?"

"I did. Believe me, I did."

"And still she…is there a chance she'll change her mind?"

"Not a chance. She's very angry with you. An old wound."

"So that's it. I guess I shouldn't be surprised."

"She thinks you deserve everything you're getting. If she could, she'd condemn you to sitting by that bedside for the rest of your life."

"I'd gladly sit by Lu's bedside for the rest of my life, if only she'd regain consciousness."

"I told her that. I told her you wanted to take care of Lu."

"But she's not thinking of Lu at all."

"Of course not," Ben agreed. "She's only thinking of herself. She thinks she's getting even."

"Did she explain what she was getting even about?"

"Apparently some old affair of yours."

"One I have suffered with all these years. God, if only there were some way, we could undo the past."

"When you find out how to do that, you'll have a best seller on your hands," the doctor reflected.

"What next? Does this mean you'll not go ahead?"

"I'm sorry. I've already called the lawyer at the medical association hot line."

David nodded.

"He says it's too risky, with her being a trial lawyer and making all those threats."

"Threats?"

"She said she'd sue me for everything I've got. The hospital too."

"Ruby too, I suppose," David said.

"Ruby?"

"Yes, I asked Ruby to turn off the ventilator."

"The lawyer said she could win a big judgment."

"She'd do it too. She's been determined ever since she was a kid."

"She looked like one very determined woman today, I'll tell you." Ben paused. "There is more."

"What more could there be?"

"Criminal charges. The medical association lawyer says there's a risk of criminal charges."

"What criminal charges?"

"I don't know; manslaughter, I suppose. Maybe even murder. The law is not clear. They prosecuted Dr. Kevorkian, you remember, and he didn't actually do the act himself. He only helped his patients."

"I remember."

"The lawyer says they would have a stronger case against a doctor who actually did the deed himself–the killing–as he so bluntly put it."

"They wouldn't prosecute you, would they?"

"Probably not, but it would be a risk if the prosecutors found out."

"And Betty would be sure they found out."

"Even if she couldn't get them to prosecute, she would sue for everything I have."

"I can't ask you to take a chance like that."

"I'm sorry. I wish there were something I could do," said Ben.

"What do I do now?"

"There is nothing you can do. Just wait."

"Just wait and hope that Lu dies. Is that it?"

"I'm very sorry, Ben. I did my best."

It was very late afternoon when David arrived at the entrance to the college nature study. He had stopped at home to put on his Mackinaw against the fierce February cold. As he turned onto the path toward his spot by the river, the only tracks he saw were his own. The river was completely frozen. The only sound in the barren forest was that of his feet crunching on the snow. Finally he stood on the river bank, with its bleak trees pointing wildly to the nearly dark sky. He must decide what to do about Lu.

David's ordeal these last weeks had taught him that he had fewer answers to life's problems than he had thought as a younger man he had. He had learned that often he did not know the best course for himself to take, let alone what was best for anyone else.

Until Ben's news, he had thought he had the way out of his dilemma. They would turn off the respirator. Lu would die. He would go to her funeral. Then, one night by the river, he would fire his pistol into his brain. Maybe he would wait until Eddie graduated and turned 18, but he knew one day soon he would take his own life.

Now, with Betty's refusal, he did not know what to do. He only knew he had to surrender his problem to someone or something other than himself. Maybe this was what other people called God—he did not know—but he knew he lacked answers of his own.

David took a few steps along the frozen edge of the river while he contemplated. He had come prepared to stay for a very long time, but no sooner had he quieted his mind than an answer came. The plan came from within himself, not from the thinking part of his brain. Nonetheless, he immediately knew he had been given a course of action that was right for Lu and for himself.

-15-

David left the college nature study for the short drive to his residence. He had made his decision and now there remained the execution of the plan. Tonight he, Doctor David Neal, 76, Albion College Professor Emeritus of Psychology, would kill his beloved wife, Lu, and then take his own life.

He preferred to think of it another way: *David Neal, a desperate man, would terminate the life of Lu Neal, who, in fact, was already dead, and who lived only in a technical sense.* If he did not think of it this way, he would never be able to proceed with his plan.

In his bedroom he carefully wrapped and placed his pistol in his tattered leather briefcase. He loved that old briefcase. For so many years he had carried it to the lecture rooms in Rob and North Halls. He would miss it, as he would miss so many things about the college. He had loaded all six chambers, so that one bullet was bound to enter his brain the first time he pulled the trigger. There would be no error. He would be sure that Lu died, then he would raise the gun to his temple and squeeze the trigger. The plan would then be completed.

David put his briefcase in his car trunk and began the drive to the hospital. Unfocused thoughts ambled through his mind. Thoughts of his mother lying in her casket over 40 years ago. Thoughts of how she had always believed there was a heaven. Although David had never believed in heaven, he hoped he was wrong. Was it possible there was some unthought-of dimension where he would again see his mother? If there were, perhaps he would see Lu, once again healthy and vibrant. He was softly weeping as he parked in the nearly deserted hospital parking lot–visitor's hours were over. He took his briefcase from the trunk and walked resolutely toward the entrance.

The gun was for himself. He knew he could not shoot Lu. He would have to find some way to disconnect the machine that had kept her alive for too long. That way would be more peaceful, more natural, the way Lu deserved to die. He could never fire a gun into Lu's head. His own head, yes, but not Lu's.

"Hello, Dr. Neal." Ruby's happy smile seemed out of place, given David's plan for this evening.

"Hello, Ruby." He tried not to betray his nervousness. "Has there been any change?"

"She looks very nice tonight, Dr. Neal. She would appreciate your coming so faithfully."

"Do you think somehow she knows when I'm with her?"

Ruby smiled. "She might. There are a great many things we don't understand." Ruby glanced at a monitor. "Her pulse rate has been steady all day. Dr. Neal, I want you to know how sad I am that your daughter has refused permission."

"I guess I should have known. Betty has always been difficult." David did not want to be drawn into a discussion about Betty. He hurriedly looked at his watch. "Your shift will be ending before I'm through visiting. I'll see you tomorrow."

"Oh, I'll look in on you before I leave."

David approached Ruby's desk. "No, please don't do that, not tonight."

Ruby looked puzzled.

"I want to be alone with her." He hesitated. "You see I want to pray with her."

Ruby nodded her understanding.

"I brought our Bible from home," David said pointing to his briefcase. "I want to read aloud to her. I hope you understand."

"Don't worry, Dr. Neal, you won't be interrupted. I'll tell Lilly when she relieves me. You'll have your privacy."

Head down, David walked down the hall. At this hour the hospital was so quiet.

"Good night, Dr. Neal."

David turned and looked at Ruby. "If for any reason she doesn't make it through the night, I want you to know how much I appreciate your kindness."

"Oh, come on, now, Dr. Neal. She's going to make it through the night." Although Ruby was black and in her 30s, in that moment she reminded him of his mother.

David started to resume his fateful journey down the hall. "But just in case, will you promise me one thing?"

Ruby looked up, waiting for him to continue.

"Will you come to the funeral?"

The lanky nurse looked as if she were about to cry.

"I'd like you there," David continued. "My grandson will need someone to comfort him."

"Of course I'll be there. He's a fine young man. He'll need you too."

"I doubt very much if I'll be able to help him, but perhaps you would."

With his briefcase in hand David turned and walked purposefully toward Lu's room.

David had not lied to Ruby. At the last minute he had put their family Bible in his briefcase, next to the gold-trimmed pistol. He sat by the edge of Lu's bed and took out the Bible. Then, realizing he had not closed the door, he returned to the doorway. Quickly he glanced up the hallway–Lu's room was the last, six doors down. There was no one in sight. He closed the door tightly and returned to the still bedside.

Ruby was right; Lu did look peaceful. Despite the circumstances, she even looked beautiful. Yes, Lu's hair did show a lot of white. He hoped Ruby would remember their conversation and ask the undertaker to color

Lu's hair. He wasn't sure whether Betty would order an open casket or whether she would want it closed. He had never been able to discuss much about life with Betty, let alone death.

His own death came to mind. No doubt his casket would be closed because of the head wound. He was sure Betty would not allow a double funeral. She might not even give him a funeral. Betty would never attend his funeral, but she might allow one for his friends and Eddie. He really didn't give a damn if she came. He did hope his friends and colleagues would attend, though surely they would disapprove of what he was going to do to Lu. He could hear them now, muttering:

"He should have let God's will be his guide."

"For all we know, she could have pulled through."

"We don't understand these things. Life is too precious for any man to set himself up as God, and take a human life."

Not everyone would talk this way, but most of them. At least that was what he thought.

But all he really cared about was Eddie. He wanted Eddie to come to his funeral. Eddie would come no matter what his mother would say. Suddenly he was angry. Betty damn well better not try to keep Eddie from coming. He hoped Ruby would come to his funeral. Ruby would know that he loved Lu. She would know love was the reason he took her life. The others could take all their goddamn judgments and stick them.

He slipped the gun under Lu's blanket. No. He returned it to his briefcase. That would be better. Once he was sure Lu was gone, he would have plenty of time to use the gun.

David took the family Bible from the briefcase. The cover had come loose from the worn binding. As he had a thousand times since the stroke, he opened the Bible to the pages at the beginning, where the family tree was supposed to be written in. It was all in Lu's handwriting:

David Neal married to Lu Ann Hawthorne Neal in Philadelphia, Pennsylvania on the 20th day of November, 1942 Reverend Donald P. Laker performing the ceremony. Attendants were...

David could not remember most of them. Only their respective parents, his brother, who had been his best man, and Amy, Lu's sister, who had been the maid of honor. God, they were all dead now. Every one of them. Lu had filled in the blanks on the next page.

Born September 25, 1946 Betty Lu Neal. Albion Hospital. Weight 7 pounds 4 ozs. 10:30 a.m. Dr. William Skeeter.

Skeet had been dead at least 25 years now. The half dozen other blanks on the page, the blanks for additional children, were empty. He had noticed only last week that there was no page for grandchildren. He would have liked it if there had been a place for Lu to make an entry for Eddie's birth, but there was none.

He turned to the next page. It was the page for deaths. Lu had made no entries. In the next few minutes there would be two deaths, but there would be no one to make the entries.

David lowered the Bible and looked at Lu's closed eyes. Thank God, they had not divorced. It was amazing how in recent years their love had grown. They both had come to prize their marriage—that they had been married so many years, had shared the same house and the same bed. He remembered when his father had died at 88, and they had slid the casket into his mausoleum crypt and closed the granite slab. His mother had slumped against the wall. He could see then that her purpose for living was over. She was dead within the year. Now he understood how his mother had felt.

David opened the Bible to the Sermon On The Mount. Lu had frequently read it when she felt troubled. It was for his benefit that he would read aloud—he knew that—but perhaps she would know.

"Lu, I brought our family Bible with me tonight. I thought I'd read some of your favorite passages. Would you like that?" As he had done all these weeks of talking to his wife, David looked at her silent face, partially obstructed by the ventilator.

Lay not up for yourselves treasures upon earth, where moth and rust doth corrupt, and where thieves break through and steal: But lay up for yourselves treasures in heaven, where neither moth nor rust doth corrupt, and where thieves do not break through nor steal. For where your treasure is, there will your heart be also.

"And here's another," David continued.

Therefore I say unto you, Take no thought for your life, what ye shall eat, or what ye shall drink; nor yet for your body, what ye shall put on. Is not the life more than meat, and the body than raiment? Behold the fowls of the air: for they sow not, neither do they reap, nor gather into barns; yet your heavenly Father feedeth them. Are ye not much better than they? Which of you by taking thought can add one cubit unto his stature? And why take ye thought for raiment? Consider the lilies of the field, how they grow; they toil not, neither do they spin: And yet I say unto you, That even Solomon in all his glory was not arrayed like one of these.

David stopped reading. He wished he had done a better job of applying these truths to his life, but of course it was too late.

Although he was nervous, he felt at peace with what he was about to do. He should do it quickly, because he might lose his nerve. He was not positive he knew which valve turned the respirator off. It was vital that Lu be dead before he used the gun on himself. He could imagine nothing worse than blundering by killing himself but leaving Lu surviving in that dreadful vegetative state. The time to act had come. David closed the Bible and put it on the table. He checked his gun again. It would only take a few minutes and she would be gone. He took a breath of resolve and reached for the ventilator.

Suddenly, he could not believe what he saw.

Lu's eyes were open!

Still expressionless, still with her mouth distorted by the stroke, she was looking at him!

Shocked, David moved his head to see if her pupils followed him.

They did.

"Lu, can you hear me?" David restrained his excitement, to keep his voice low.

Lu did not respond.

"Lu, darling, if you can hear me, please blink your eyes."

Lu blinked.

David could not be positive the blink was in answer to his question.

"Did you hear me reading our Bible?"

This time it was a good firm blink before she closed her eyes.

David was unnerved by what he had seen. He broke into perspiration.

"Lu, I've been planning to kill you, to kill both of us."

Her eyes remained closed.

"You know that commemorative pistol." He held it up. "Here this one."

Except for her breathing, Lu was perfectly still, her eyes still closed.

"I was going to turn off your ventilator and then use the pistol on myself. It all seems so hopeless!"

David looked desperately for another response, any response, but there was none. His hands were shaking.

"Lu, darling, I don't know if I can do it without its being all right with you."

Desperately he looked across her face for a sign—the slightest sign, but there was none.

"Don't you see? I think it's for the best." His voice was quavering. His strength of will had been cut short by the astounding event.

He wondered if he had imagined the whole thing. Surely what he had seen was impossible. "Sweetheart, I really think it's best if I end it for both of us, here, right now, but I need to know it's all right with you."

Hands shaking David looked at the Bible again. If only there were an answer in the Bible for him—some sort of guidance. Once more he looked at Lu. *Her eyes were open again.* This time they were glistening. Clear blue. He could see compassion, an endless deep compassion for him that came from her soul.

"Oh, Lu, if that's what you want me to do can you blink your eyes? I need to know what you want!"

Lu blinked her eyes once again. Then she closed them. She looked so much at peace that David was not sure she was breathing. He hoped she would look like that in her casket. Probably the undertaker could do nothing about the distortion around her mouth, but at least she would have that look of extreme peace.

He felt renewed resolve as he turned the valve. He could tell from the change in the hissing sound that the oxygen flow had been stopped. He waited as her breathing slowed and then seemed to stop. Finally he bent over her body. He could detect no breathing. He tried to find her pulse, but could feel nothing.

Now he was sure. He reached for the pistol. It was his turn.

As David raised the gun toward his head, Ruby burst through the doorway.

"Dr. Neal…the monitor." Then seeing what he was doing: "What are you doing? Oh, Dr. Neal, you can't do that!" Ruby rushed across the room toward the bed.

David grabbed the gun. "Stand back, Ruby. I don't want to hurt you. I've got to do this." He pointed the gun at Ruby. "Now, you get away, do you hear?" Again he raised the gun to his head.

"I'm not going to let you do this!" Ruby shouted. "You're going to have to kill me first!"

Lilly, the relief nurse, burst through the doorway. "What's going on here?"

Without a word, and like the sprinter she had been in college, Ruby hurtled her body across Lu and her bed, and grabbed David's raised arm. Simultaneously, David squeezed the trigger, but Ruby's daring leap jarred David's firing arm so that the bullet exploded into the acoustic ceiling of the hospital room. The loud bang of the gun seemed to follow, rather than precede, the sound of a chunk of the ceiling crashing to the floor. David had pulled the trigger a millisecond too late.

"My God, Ruby, you must not stop me. *Not now for Gods sake.*" David's shout was like a wail. He started to raise the gun to his head again. Ruby, still lying on Lu's body, quickly reached up and slashed down wildly on David's trigger arm. The gun fired loudly again as it tumbled to the floor and slid under Lu's bed, on the slick linoleum.

"Oh, my God, I'm hit!" exclaimed Ruby.

"Jesus, Ruby. I'm sorry. Oh, my God, I'm sorry!"

Painfully Ruby managed to roll to the side of the bed. "*It's my leg. My thigh.*"

As Lilly rushed to Ruby, an orderly entered the room. "What happened?" he shouted.

"He shot Ruby!" Lilly screamed. "*His gun. It's under the bed. Get the gun! You've got to stop him.*"

"Oh, Holy Jesus, it hurts!" cried Ruby.

"I'm sorry, Ruby. I meant it to happen to me, not you!"

The two police officers were in Lu's room within 15 minutes. Another, Detective Rodgers, soon joined them. David sat on the chair next to Lu's bed, where her lifeless body lay covered by the blanket. One of the police officers had handcuffed David. David remembered the other's reading him his Miranda rights. Ruby, in great pain, had been taken away on a gurney.

"Dr. Neal, my name is Jim Rodgers. I'm a detective with the police department. I'd like to know what went on here."

David did not respond. He barely knew where he was. "I'm not sure," he finally managed. "Is my wife dead?"

"Yes."

"And Ruby?"

"They say she'll be all right."

"Thank God for that. I meant to kill myself, not Ruby."

"We know."

"I guess I really screwed up." David felt destroyed, empty. My God, he had killed Lu, but he was still alive. That wasn't the way it was supposed to have been at all. "May I see her?"

"She's in the operating room right now."

"I think he means his wife," said one of the officers.

"Yes. If you want." The detective motioned to the officer, who slowly lowered Lu's blanket, exposing her face. Lu was still and ashen. Her eyes were closed and her hands placed across her body.

Shakily David stood next to Lu. For several moments he absorbed the fact that she was dead. Then, with his hands handcuffed together, he reached down and took her hand. Tears welled in his eyes.

"At long last, my dear Lu. Your ordeal is over."

-16-

David sat in his cell in stunned silence. He barely recalled the drive to the Albion police station and being interrogated by the detectives. Oddly, the only thing he remembered clearly was the metal security screen in the rear of the big Chevrolet police cruiser jamming against his legs. He vaguely recalled being fingerprinted and being interviewed, but he had no idea what he had told the detectives. Even though he seemed to remember their reading his rights, it had not occurred to him that he should have a lawyer.

The way events and faces faded in and out, he wondered if he was in shock. Wasn't Talison's work on World War II shell shock still in the college library? He would have to read it again someday. But there never would be a someday. Lu was dead and he was in jail for killing her.

He felt another surge of depression come. The black, dark waves of depression had been inundating him since he had been locked in the stark cell. Although he had wrapped himself in the blanket, he was cold. His hands sweated and his body shook. Why was he still alive? What had gone wrong? If only Lu could be alive and he could be in her place in the morgue. The night he fired his pistol into the river, he should have put the sixth bullet into his brain. Why had Ruby tried to stop him? Good God, he had shot Ruby. Was she too going to die instead of him?

David looked through the window of the steel door. He could see only a small anteroom. He was the lone prisoner in the cramped cell. There was a small television camera trained on him. He wished he had another blanket, but he did not know how to summon the jailer. What difference did it make anyway? He wanted to be dead; why should he worry about being cold?

He had no idea whether it was day or night. He felt overwhelmed–forlorn. If only there were some way he could kill himself here in jail, but there was no knife, no fork, nothing; and besides they were watching him.

"Wake up, Neal. Somebody's here to see you. Says he's your grandson."

The gruff voice of the jailer startled David. It took several moments for him to realize where he was. He was extremely cold under the thin blanket.

"Eddie? Eddie is here?" David asked weakly.

"Your grandson. Yeah. I'll let him into the cell with you. I've searched him. No harm, I guess. You're not going anywhere."

As the jailer opened the steel door, David sat up, still not fully comprehending.

Hands in his too large trousers and wearing his familiar baseball cap, Eddie entered the cell. "Hello, Grandfather." Eddie looked at the bare floor, avoiding eye contact. The officer closed the door. David stood, wondering what to do or say.

"You found out?"

"I called the hospital. They told me."

"Did they tell you everything?"

"The nurse said you killed Granna." Eddie looked as if he were about to burst into tears.

"I had your okay, didn't I? Remember?"

"I guess so." Eddie spoke hesitantly.

David looked at the youth, hoping for eye contact, but then he looked at the floor. "Eddie, you said you thought Granna would be better off dead."

"But I didn't know *you'd* do it. I thought you meant the doctors would do it!" With that, Eddie burst into tears.

"Eddie, I'm sorry. I thought I was doing the right thing."

Eddie turned away, facing the bleak concrete block wall. "You didn't have to do it yourself," Eddie sobbed. With anger and dismay in his eyes, he looked at David.

David wanted to hug his grandson. Or do something to relieve the sudden tension between them, to tell him he was sorry for the pain he was going through, but he held back. "I didn't know what else to do. Your mother wouldn't give permission, and so the doctors couldn't go ahead. Eddie, believe me, if there were any other way…" David's mind was reeling with confusion and dismay. He had not expected this reaction from Eddie.

"But I didn't know it would be like this. I loved Granna. Didn't you know?"

"I know you did," David said softly. "But we couldn't go on the way we were. Remember our talk?"

"I guess so." Eddie looked again at the wall. "What's going to happen now? I'll bet Mom's going to try to make me live with her." His face streaked with tears, he had stopped sobbing. "I wish we could go back like before."

"Can't you stay at the house? You're old enough to do that."

"Not with Granna dead. You're in jail. There isn't any place for me any more. There's no place in the whole world that's home for me any more!"

"But Eddie…" David's heart felt as if it would break in half.

"I've got to go now, Grandfather." Eddie banged on the door. "Hey, Mister. Can you get me out of here? I'm in a hurry. I've got to go."

"Good-bye, Eddie," David said after the jailer had let his grandson out.

Instead of answering, Eddie wiped the tears from his face and hurried down the hall.

David sat disconsolately on the hard bed. He knew that in his dismay over his plight, he had not given proper consideration to Eddie's feelings. He should have known that the troubled 17-year-old was in no position to give consent to the ending of his grandmother's life. The depression that had gone with Eddie's unexpected visit returned with all its impact–dark, gloomy depression. He was trapped. First by Lu's, stroke and now by what he had done. He was sorry for Eddie, but he still wished he could find some way out of this nightmare forever.

-17-

Frederick Cain was in his spartan office. He had tried to concentrate on the file on his desk, but his mind was elsewhere. The filing deadline for running for prosecutor in the November election was imminent. He stared blankly out the basement window, thinking.

The talk with Marge on Wednesday had helped clarify his decision. He had to hand it to Marge. She had seen that his preoccupation with the prosecutor's job was ruining their relationship. He was glad she had insisted on talking about it. Their love-making that night had been even more passionate than in the beginning. He could see it was his indecision that was screwing him up. What he ought to do was jump in the race, win lose or draw. On the other hand, his better judgment told him that, as matters now stood, Lasser was sure to whip his ass. Fred slammed his fist on his desk. He was damned if he ran and damned if he didn't!

The intercom buzzed.

"Fred, I've got something here I think you should read." It was Marge.

"Yes. What?"

"It's a report from Al Kitchen at the coroner's office. It's a hospital death he thinks the prosecutor's office should take a good look at. Looks like a mercy killing case. Shall I bring it in?"

"Might as well, okay."

Marge entered his office, and put the one page coroner's report on his desk. "It looks like a professor–retired professor–over at Albion College decided to take matters into his own hands. Seems his wife had a stroke and so he shut off her respirator."

Fred could see Marge's excitement, and quickly read the report. "Deprivation of air–suffocation."

"I got the police report for you too." Marge handed him the thin police file. "Might be something there for you, Fred."

With increasing excitement Fred began reading the police report. "Mercy killing, all right. Tried to kill himself too."

"Sort of remind you of that Royal Oak doctor case? You know, the one who helped people kill themselves. Kevorkian."

Fred's eyes lit up. "Yeah. If those cases had been in Calhoun County, I would have gone after him right away. Could've been the biggie I've been hoping for. Except this case is different…"

"Different? How so?"

"Kevorkian was never accused of actually killing anybody himself. This Albion professor, he did it himself. The guy did it himself."

"I see, but…"

"This case could be even better–a lot stronger–don't you see?"

"Yes, but won't some people on the jury be sympathetic? You know, the wife's terminal and so the husband puts her out of her misery. On top of that they go and keep him from shooting himself. There's a lot of sympathy there, Fred."

"I don't give a damn how terminal she was, it's against the law to kill someone!"

"I know, but some people will think it makes a difference, morally I mean."

"Marge, I'm not in the morals business. That's for the theologians. I'm in the crime business."

"That's why I thought you'd be interested in the report."

"Damn right, I'm interested. Look at this," Cain was reading the police report. "The professor was waving a revolver."

"Yes, I saw. He was going to kill himself right there, but they stopped him."

"Marge," Fred asked excitedly. "Has Lasser seen any of this?"

"No. It just came in. Lasser doesn't know the first thing about it. I brought it straight to you." Fred knew that Marge was fully aware that this violated procedure. As chief, Lasser had directed he see all cases first. In major cases, Lasser was the one to decide whether to bring prosecution. It was then he would assign them out to a particular deputy.

Cain threw his arms around Marge. "Marge, I love you. This may be just the case I need. It's better than the suicide doctor." Cain took his overcoat from the hook.

"Where are you going?"

"Over to the hospital. I want to talk to everyone who was there that night. Don't breathe a word of this to Lasser."

-18-

Morbid as the task was, Betty Neal had forced herself to identify her mother's body at the coroner's office. Betty was resolutely determined not to cry. This woman who had argued cases before the United States Supreme Court had no intention of showing her emotions before some stranger. From the morgue she had gone to the funeral home. There she selected her mother's coffin and made arrangements for funeral services at Albion College's Goodrich Chapel. The casket she chose was in Lu's favorite color–light blue. Again she showed no emotion. She resented the mortician's syrup-laden sympathetic attitude. Her mother was dead. She could not bring her back to life. All she could do was attend to the business of burying her and seeing to it that her murderer was punished.

At the Albion McDonald's Betty nervously gulped down a Big Mac as she studied the computer printed dossier on Calhoun County Prosecutor, Alvin P. Lasser. She had a two o'clock appointment to see him in Battle Creek. She desperately wanted a second Big Mac, but resisted and finished her diet cola. Until now she had always overeaten when under stress, but she was determined to control herself. So far this year she had lost nearly five pounds, under her new diet program. If she kept it up, she would be below 200 pounds before summer.

Betty pulled her Cadillac onto the snow-cleared I-94, westbound toward Battle Creek, and sorted out the facts she had gleaned about Lasser. He was 55, married, had two children in college, was active in Republican politics, had a good reputation as a career prosecutor, had been appointed chief prosecutor by the governor and had announced he would run for an elected term.

Betty intended to do everything she could to assure that Lasser would prosecute her mother's killer to the fullest extent of the law. She anticipated reluctance on his part, because to prosecute would risk alienating many voters–a risk any candidate would be loath to take. But she did not care about Lasser's election problems, nor did she care that her mother's killer was her own father. The simple fact was that despite her refusal to agree to the ending of Lu's life, her father had deliberately murdered Lu in cold blood. Betty was not going to let him get away with this. If Lasser proved to be reluctant, he would learn that she and her law partners were not without political influence.

Half an hour later in Battle Creek, Betty pulled off the interstate toward the civic center and Lasser's office. She was seething with anger over her what her father had done–an anger she knew had been buried in her since his betrayal of her mother and even before that. She would never forget the night she had overheard her father arguing with her mother about Betty gaining so much weight. She was 13 years old. "We've got to talk to her about getting so fat," he had told her mother that night. "She'll ruin her future." They were in the kitchen when Betty had started down the stairs. "Betty will be all right; just leave her alone. She's a very bright girl," her mother had replied. Sometimes it seemed she had always been angry–not only with her father, but angry with all men. Maybe even angry with everyone in the whole stupid world, except of course her mother, who had always loved her no matter what.

Suddenly she spotted another McDonald's. Impulsively she pulled into the drive-up lane. "One Big Mac…and an order of fries."

One-handed, she gulped down a handful of fries as she parked in a far-off corner and began to unwrap her hamburger. But before she could begin eating it, the dam restraining her emotions burst. She had not cried even when she had found her husband was cheating on her and she had filed for divorce. She had not cried when Eddie went away.

She had not cried when her mother was first stricken, nor in all these many weeks. But now, sitting alone in her window-steamed Cadillac with her Big Mac getting cold, she no longer could hold back her tears.

As the sobs came, she tried to control herself. After all, she was a partner in Willard, Oates and Schultz, one of Detroit's major law firms. In 1993 she had earned over $400,000. She was the envy of business and professional women. She had even won 1990 "Woman of the Year" honors, but, despite her success, she was miserable–absolutely miserable. She was fat and undesirable and was helpless to do anything about it. She had lost her husband to another woman. Even her son refused to live with her. For 40 years she had had no father, and now she had no mother. The only person in the world who would ever love her unconditionally lay dead in that cold steel drawer.

Eddie came home immediately after school. His mother had left a message with the principal at Albion High School that she wanted to talk with her son this afternoon before she drove back to Bloomfield Hills.

Eddie sat at the desk in his bedroom wearing his oversized trousers and his baseball cap. He put his book down. It was no use trying to concentrate. He knew the only reason he had done so well at school was because of Granna, but Granna was dead, so what was the point of studying? He just knew Grandfather would never be coming home from that stinking jail–ever. After all, Grandfather had killed Granna, hadn't he? Besides, Grandfather had meant to kill himself too. That would have left him all alone. Nobody cared about him any more. Why should he care?

And there was his mother. What did she want anyway? She probably wanted to take him back to Bloomfield Hills. Well, he wasn't going to do that. Nobody, not even some judge, could make him live with his mother again. Tears came to Eddie's eyes. Oh, how he missed Granna. Who was going to bake him cookies? Who was going to ask him–to ask him nicely–to do his homework? Who was going to love him?

Eddie went downstairs to the kitchen. Grandfather had told him Granna had collapsed there by the refrigerator. He opened the refrigerator. There wasn't much stuff there like there always had been when Granna was well. Why didn't Grandfather buy more stuff for the refrigerator?

Oh, he was mad at Grandfather. Why had he done all this? He hadn't meant for Grandfather to kill Granna himself. He had only meant for the doctor or Ruby to do it. That way, he could have lived with Grandfather. He would have graduated from Albion High. His grades were getting better. He might have gotten into college. Maybe even Albion College. Or if he hadn't, he could have joined the Marines, like Bill James's brother. Now he couldn't do anything. Granna was dead. Grandfather was in jail and his mother wanted to see him. Eddie took Granna's apron off the hook where she had put it weeks ago. It felt *so* soft. Soft like she had been. Now he would never see her again.

Eddie sat at the breakfast table, raised his hands to his face and sobbed. He hadn't cried this hard since the time he had burned his hand on the barbecue that summer when he was ten. Only that time Granna had been there in her apron to comfort him. To put butter on the burn and tell him it would be all right. This time there was no Granna for him to go running to.

-19-

Alvin Lasser barged into Frederick Cain's office without knocking.

"Fred, Marge tells me you've got the file on that mercy killing case–the Neal case. Is that right?"

Fred could see that Lasser was angry. "Yes, I have. As a matter of fact I've just about finished my work-up."

"Your work-up? What the hell are you talking about–your work-up?"

"Look, Al, calm down. All I did was take the initiative to see if we should file charges against Neal. I've interviewed several witnesses and–"

"You what?"

"I think it's clear we should file. I don't know what you're so upset about. I was going to talk to you in the morning. Neal's in jail now and we have to make up our minds whether to file before the deadline."

"What the hell are you talking about *make up our minds*? *I'm* the prosecutor around here. *I'm* the one who makes the filing decisions in this office!"

"I was only making a recommendation to you. In the morning I was going to recommend that we prosecute. That's all. A recommendation."

"How the hell did you know about the case in the first place? You know damn well I make the assignments around here!"

"The coroner's office. I got the report."

"But how did you get the report? That's what I want to know." To Fred it looked as if steam might burst from Lasser's nostrils any moment. "No. Don't bother telling me. Marge gave it to you, didn't she?"

"Al, you're making a mountain out of a mole hill."

"Give me that fucking file. There's a big shot Detroit lawyer due in my office and I'll need to know what the hell I'm talking about." Lasser jerked the file out of Fred's hands. "I want you in my office at nine tomorrow. Nine sharp!"

"But I'm in court in Marshall on a sentencing at nine."

"The hell you are. Get somebody to appear for you or you're going to be looking for a new job!"

With Lasser gone, Fred remained in his plain wooden swivel chair and held out his hand. Steady as a rock. Not one sign of nerves. He smiled to himself. A few days ago he would've been frightened of Lasser's threat, but not today. *I've got you right where I want you, Mr. Prosecuting Attorney,* he said to himself. *Either way. Whether you let me prosecute or don't let me prosecute, it will be you, not me, who'll be the one looking for a new job.*

"Show Ms. Neal in," Al Lasser said on the intercom from his spacious, but spartan office. Lasser wondered why Betty wanted to see him. He had hurriedly read the David Neal file while trying to cool down over Fred Cain's rank insubordination. Damn Cain. What was he up to anyway? Cain knew the office rules. All new cases went through him. Marge and Cain had deliberately defied him. Cain's competitiveness had been obvious from his first day in the prosecutor's office. A month ago Lasser had realized Cain might be thinking about a run at the prosecutor's job, but what in the hell was so special about this case? So some old professor was guilty of mercy killing. The Kevorkian case had proved it was a no-win situation for the prosecutor. No matter what you did, you alienated half the public. Well, no matter. He'd think about that later. For now, he had to figure out what to say to Betty Neal. No doubt she was going to ask him to take it easy on her father. *Poor Dad,* she'd say. *He was so distraught. He didn't know what he was doing. Please, I can't handle the thought of my mother dead and my father's being prosecuted for her murder.*

That would be an easy one for him. He'd pretend to wrestle with the decision for a few days and then tell her, out of a sense of compassion, he had decided not to prosecute.

As Betty entered the room the prosecutor was surprised at her appearance. She must have been 75 to 100 pounds overweight. While he had not heard of Betty, her firm, Willard, Oates and Schultz, was widely known as one of the most politically connected law firms in Michigan. Over the years one governor and two U.S. senators had joined the firm as senior partners upon leaving office. The firm maintained expertise in election and campaign law and its senior partners were known as advisors to the present governor and other high level politicians.

Al rose to his feet. "How do you do, Ms. Neal? Please allow me to extend my sympathy on the death of your mother."

"Mr. Lasser I don't view this as the *death* of my mother. I view it as the *murder* of my mother. And that explains why I'm here. I want to know what you intend to do about my mother's *murder*."

Al was glad he didn't have to sleep with a woman like this one. Involuntarily he crossed his legs and swiveled halfway around in his chair. "Now, Ms. Neal. Don't you think that's being a little harsh on your father? These cases are very difficult."

"Mr. Lasser, I don't know about these cases in general, but I do know about this case. Did you know that my father sent his doctor all the way to Detroit to ask my permission to end my mother's life?"

"Why, no, I didn't." Betty reminded Al of his Grandmother Lasser. When she was having one of her spells, you'd surely better not get in her way or you might not live to tell about it.

"And I turned the doctor down flat. I told him I'd never consent to my mother's murder."

"Now, Ms. Neal," for a moment Lasser thought of calling her Betty, but the thought of Grandmother Lasser changed his mind. "Don't you think that's a pretty harsh judgment? After all, Professor Neal intended to kill himself too."

"And would you mind explaining to me exactly what that supposed fact has to do with anything? Murder is murder, Mr. Lasser. Intended suicide doesn't change that."

Al was glad he had changed his mind about calling her Betty. "For one thing, it goes to intent," he said. "It makes it that much harder to argue first degree intent. Surely, as a lawyer yourself, you realize that."

"Nonsense. His intention that night was to kill her, from the time he set foot in her room."

Al was nonplused. Instead of the expected plea that he refrain from prosecution, this woman was vengeful. "Frankly, Ms. Neal, I don't know what to say. I wasn't expecting…Exactly what do you want?"

"I want to know what you intend to do. I understand you're up for election and I'm sure the people of this county are interested in someone who intends to enforce the law."

"Of course I intend to enforce the law, but surely you realize that there are many cases in which a prosecutor has to exercise discretion as to whether to file charges."

"Oh, really, now. I always had a rather naive belief that intentional killing was murder."

"I'll tell you what, Ms. Neal. Let me think about it for a day or two. I'll get back to you. Is that all right?"

"Mr. Lasser, I'll be in Albion Monday for my mother's funeral. I'll come by your office then about three."

After Betty left, Al sat stunned, as if he had been in an auto collision. His mind leaped about, examining the alternatives. If he decided not to prosecute, Betty Neal would spell trouble in the election. If he decided to prosecute, the jury might be hung. He could imagine Dr. Neal pleading insanity and maybe being acquitted. And what if he made a plea bargain for some lesser charge like manslaughter and a year in jail? If he did that, Betty Neal would raise as much hell as if he hadn't prosecuted in the first place. Dammit, why should he worry about Betty Neal? What harm could she cause him? Her firm's influence in Lansing or Washington shouldn't mean much in a lousy small county prosecutor's race. True, she could give a wad of money to his opponent, whether it be Cain or whomever, but a big shot Detroit attorney was not going to come across too well in Calhoun County. He shouldn't let Betty's threat influence him. Morally, he had always thought mercy killing with proper safeguards was all right. What Dr. Neal had done was not the most heinous of crimes. Although he had never personally faced the issue, he might very well have done the same himself. No, he decided. As soon as he chewed out Cain in the morning, he would assign a staff investigator to look into the matter and give a formal report, but Al's decision was already made. He wasn't going to get involved in this no-win situation. There would be no prosecution.

-20-

Betty retraced the 25 mile drive back to Albion from Battle Creek. She felt the same surge of energy and strength she felt when she defended one of the firm's major corporate clients in the court room. Nobody was going to push her around. That was what she liked about being a highly skilled lawyer. No matter what the field of law, she could become as knowledgeable as any opponent. Few had her tenacity and quick mind. She welcomed a fight and won far more times than she lost. If necessary, she would wear an opponent down with endless depositions and a stream of money-draining motions and maneuvers. That was what she liked about being a partner in Willard, Oates and Schultz. If Lasser decided not to prosecute, he would be sorry. She didn't know exactly what she would do to him, but she'd figure out something. Under Michigan law, the attorney general had the power to prosecute cases in which the local prosecutor was abusing his power by failing to prosecute. Two of her partners personally knew the attorney general and she'd see to it that Lasser was aware of this fact. It wouldn't look good in the election if the attorney general overruled Lasser and directed the prosecution from Lansing. Then, too, the investigator who had prepared Lasser's dossier speculated that one of his deputy prosecutors, Frederick Cain, probably harbored ambitions for the top job. If Lasser proved balky, she would not hesitate to offer a substantial contribution to this Frederick Cain. That might be just what would get him to throw his hat into the ring.

Next on Betty's agenda was her son. Eddie should be waiting for her. She knew she had made a mistake in allowing him to live in Albion, but with her mother dead she was not about to repeat the mistake. Eddie was not yet 18 and still a minor. She had every legal right to force him to live with her in Bloomfield Hills. As she took the Albion exit, she thought about what she would tell the young man. *Eddie, I'm still your mother and I'm insisting you return with me right after Granna's funeral.* She passed the McDonald's at the interstate exit, not even thinking about the dish of yogurt she had resisted when she had her first Big Mac earlier in the day.

She got out of her car in front of her childhood home and paused. There was a time when she had loved this big old wooden frame place, but all it did now was make her angry that her mother had wasted her life living for her father. She was damned if she would ever play housewife to some mediocre man like that. She would never forget the fall when she had started high school. Lu had taken her on a long walk in Victory Park. "Betty, I've loved your father–don't misunderstand–but I don't want you to make the same mistake I did. There's a wonderful world out there for you. I want you to study hard and get the best grades you can. I don't want your happiness to depend on whom you marry." When no one had asked her to go to the senior prom, Lu had found her crying in her room. She would always remember her mother's words. "Don't ever let a man be the one to decide whether you'll be happy. You start at the college this fall. If you get top grades, you can get into Michigan Law School and make yourself an independent woman." Betty knew her mother was a brilliant woman. She had the brains and drive to be anything she wanted, but, because she had been born in the wrong part of the 20th century, she had settled for being on the board of education of this jerkwater town and supporting the career of her unfaithful husband. Betty wanted her son out of this town and when the funeral was over she never wanted to return.

"I don't care what you say, I'm not going to live in that place with you!" Eddie shouted.

The confrontation with Eddie had not gone the way Betty had wanted. "We'll see about that, young man. Legally you're not an adult yet!"

"I'll live with my father first!"

"Your father doesn't want you. All he wants is that girlfriend of his. Do you think for a minute she wants you to break up their little love nest?"

Betty could see that she had hit Eddie where it hurt.

"An occasional Lions game and maybe opening day with the Tigers. That's all you'll ever get from that love-sick wimp. Even if I let you, you wouldn't stand a chance to get him to take you."

"I'll run away then! That's what I'll do!"

"This time there's no more Granna to run to."

"I'll stay with Grandfather. He'd want me."

"You listen to me. Your grandfather's going to be in jail permanently," she said sternly.

To Betty's surprise, Eddie burst into tears. She realized she had gone too far with her trial lawyer tactics. "I'm sorry, Eddie," she said moderating her tone to try to win him over. "I know these days have been tough on you. I loved Granna too, you know."

Still crying, Eddie turned away from her.

"I love you, Eddie. Don't you see we'll be good for each other?" She looked at Eddie to see if her change in tactics had had any effect.

He looked at her like an angry steer who had been roped and knew there was nothing he could do.

"I'll come by for you Thursday. We'll go to the funeral together. Is that all right?"

"I guess so."

"I want you to think about what I said. I'm sure you'll see I'm right. You can transfer back to Cranbrook and graduate from there. We'll get you into a college someplace. I want you to have your things packed before the funeral, because I want you to go back with me."

"I've got my own car, you know."

Betty smiled. She felt she was winning her case. "That's right," she said, smiling. "I forgot for a moment. Maybe we can find a better car for you. What would you think of that?"

Eddie's expression did not change.

It was nearly dark outside as Eddie stood on the front porch. His mother was preparing to leave. He had shoveled the snow off the walk this afternoon, thinking that his Grandfather might be released from jail.

"Well, good-bye, Eddie. Promise me you'll think about what I said, won't you?" Betty asked.

"Yes." Eddie mumbled, allowing his mother to kiss him on the cheek.

When his mother's car had disappeared around the corner, Eddie went inside. He sat in his grandfather's chair thinking, and did not turn on the lights. From experience, Eddie knew his mother better than she thought. He had seen that anger from the time he was a small boy. He well knew the syrupy false kindness she had ended with. He had seen that phony part of her many times too. He wondered if that was how she won her cases in court. One thing he knew for certain. He was resolved there was no way he was going to live with her. Somehow he'd try to get Grandfather to get himself out of jail. Maybe that way the court would let him stay in Albion. If that didn't work, he didn't know what he'd do. Maybe he'd run away to California or someplace, but he was not going to Bloomfield Hills. And that was final.

Betty resisted taking the route to the interstate that would take her by Albion's McDonald's and the yogurt that she suddenly craved, but her resolve failed her as she neared the Five Points convenience store. She bought a large bag of Oreo cookies and retreated to her Cadillac. Fearing she might be recognized in the parking lot, she pulled off on a side street and began eating the cookies.

God, she hated being so fat. As soon as all this pressure was over, she was going to stop eating so much. Maybe just fast for a week.

As it had so many times, her mind flashed to the time she had overheard her father and mother talking about her weight. As long as she lived, Betty would not forget that night. It was the first time she remembered hating her father.

She had dieted once and found herself a husband and it hadn't done any good at all. All he did was start cheating on her as soon as she gained a little weight.

She finished the package of cookies and sped away toward the interstate.

First she'd force Lasser to file charges against her father, and then she'd get Eddie to live with her. Then, she thought, everything would be all right.

-21-

That night as he sat down to her usual roast beef dinner, Fred thought Marge seemed in an unusually upbeat mood. He knew he was right when she began their conversation.

"Mr. Frederick Cain, I wonder whether you realize what an enterprising girlfriend you have."

Fred smiled. "You been up to something, haven't you."

"I think we may have gotten lucky this afternoon." She winked at him across the table.

"Come on, Marge. Don't keep me in suspense like this."

"Well," she said girlishly. "You had a meeting with Al this afternoon. Right?"

"Yes."

"I heard him screaming at you through the door."

"He was really pissed about that Neal case."

"About bypassing him, right?"

Fred nodded. "I've got to see him tomorrow at nine. He may be assigning me to Timbuktu. We are in for one very large collision. So go on, will you?"

"Okay. So then I see this overweight lady in the reception room and I hear Mary Jo tell Al on the intercom that Betty Neal is there to see him."

"Aha. Dr. Neal's daughter."

"So I tell Mary Jo that I'd watch the reception room while she took a break. This is where it starts to get interesting."

"Go on. You're enjoying dragging this out, aren't you?"

"I don't know if I should tell a deputy prosecutor this or not, but I probably committed a crime."

"Oh, you did, did you?"

"Yes. I flipped the intercom switch and listened in on them."

Fred laughed. "That's no crime. That's what a substitute receptionist is supposed to do."

Marge wiped her brow in mock relief. "I was afraid you'd prosecute me, what with your being Mr. Law and Order."

"Come on, Marge. What did they say?"

"She wants him to prosecute."

"Her father? She does?"

"She's evidently got something in her craw. Seems the father's doctor asked her to consent to removal of the old woman's life support system, and guess what? The daughter refused."

"So Neal goes ahead and does it himself anyway."

"Right."

"What happened next?"

"Mary Jo comes back from her break, so I have to shut off the intercom."

"Oh."

"When the meeting is over I see this Neal lady leave Al's office. Was she ever in a huff. Real mad. So I take a chance. I follow her out to her car."

Eagerly Fred listened.

"I catch her just as she's about to get in her car to leave. She's still upset."

"Okay."

"I tell her who I am. That I happened to overhear her name. That I didn't mean to butt in, but that I knew what had happened to her mother and that I was very sorry. Of course I wasn't about to let on I was eavesdropping."

"Sure."

"She thanks me. Then I tell her that one of the deputy prosecutors had done an investigation on her mother's case and that maybe she'd like to talk to him."

"You didn't."

"I told you you had an enterprising girlfriend."

"I can see that." Fred leaned forward in anticipation.

"So I give her one of your cards and ask her if she'd like your home phone number. And you know what?"

"Did she want it?"

"I write it on your card. Then she wants to know if I think it would be all right to call you tonight. Here, she gave me her card." Marge handed Fred Betty's business card.

"Hmm. Willard, Oates and Schultz."

"You've heard of them?"

"Just the most politically connected law firm in the state, that's all. This could be a break, all right. I wonder what she wants."

"I told her I knew you had a meeting tonight, but that I thought she'd catch you about ten o'clock if she called then."

"But I don't have any meeting."

"Oh, yes, you do. Right here with me. I'm not going to be through with you until nine-thirty."

"Is that right, Miss Enterprising girlfriend?"

"As soon as we finish dinner, I want you in my bed. After all, you're apt to get a phone call at ten o'clock."

Fred saw Marge in a new light that night as they made love. Since their affair had started she had been a pleasant enough companion and bed partner; now tonight, for a moment, he wondered whether they should get married some day.

Frederick Cain's telephone rang precisely at ten o'clock.

"Mr. Cain, this is Betty Neal. I'm sorry to telephone you at this hour, but a secretary in your office—a Margaret Wolcott, I believe—gave me your number and thought it would be all right to call you."

"It's perfectly all right. She told me about your little chat. She said you might call."

"Mr. Cain, I'd like to get right to the point."

"Please do."

"The bottom line is I want my mother's killer to be prosecuted and it doesn't trouble me one bit that the killer is my father."

"I see."

"But the problem is that your Mr. Lasser is reluctant to file charges."

"That would be Al, all right."

"Why do you say that?"

"Ms. Neal, you've been frank with me. May I be frank with you?"

"I wish you would."

"Al Lasser has just been appointed chief prosecutor by the governor. He's running for a full elected term."

"So I understand."

"You can understand, then, that he doesn't want to take any chances."

"This case would be a hot potato for him. That's what you mean, isn't it?"

"As hot as you'd ever get in Calhoun County. He'd be damned if he filed and damned if he didn't, and even more damned if he filed and didn't get a conviction."

"I assumed as much. And where do you fit in, Mr. Cain?"

"I've decided to oppose Al in the election. You're the first person I've told." Fred was surprised to hear what he had said. He had the feeling he had joined a poker game without making sure he had enough money in his wallet.

"And where do you stand on my mother's case? Tell me, would you file charges if you were the chief prosecutor?"

"Frankly, if I were Lasser I probably wouldn't, and for exactly the same reasons that Al doesn't want to file."

"But you aren't the chief prosecutor. You only *want* to be chief prosecutor."

"You are exactly right."

"Tell me, what would it take to get you elected? A generous campaign contribution?"

"It takes more than that. By the time I got sworn in it would be too late, as a practical matter, to file charges against Dr. Neal."

"What do you propose then?"

"I want to see to it that charges are filed now and *I want to prosecute the case myself.*"

"Of course, but how can you accomplish that?"

"I'm having a meeting with Al tomorrow morning. At that meeting, Ms. Neal, I want to be able to tell him two things."

"Go on."

"First, I want to tell him that if he doesn't let me prosecute I'm going to make an issue out of it in the campaign. And second, I want to tell him that I have a friend in high places who has considerable influence with the attorney general and that she'll see to it that the attorney general will prosecute the case if he doesn't."

"And your friend is me and the high place is my law firm?"

"Exactly. Your firm's reputation precedes you, Ms. Neal."

"Mr. Cain, I like your style. It's that kind of moxie that can get a conviction, if one can be had.

Fred was in his office before nine o'clock the next morning. He felt an unusual sense of power about the meeting with Al Lasser. This time it was as if he knew every card in his opponent's poker hand.

Al asked Fred to be seated and began. "I've got a busy morning in front of me and so this won't take long."

Fred bided his time, saying nothing.

"I have only two things to say. First, you know damn well you were out of line in taking that file before I saw it. But I've thought about it and I've decided to let you off with this reprimand. Is that clear?"

"And the second thing?" Fred asked, letting his boss have his say before he said anything.

"I've decided not to file in the Neal case."

"No charges at all?"

"No charges."

"Is it my turn to talk?"

"If you want."

"Al, I want you to file murder charges and I want you to assign the case to me."

"And tell me Mr. *Deputy* Prosecuting Attorney just exactly why should I do that?"

"The man killed his wife. He knew very well that what he was doing was wrong. My investigation showed his mercy killing plot had been turned down by his daughter and by his doctor, but he went ahead anyway. You and I both know that's in violation of Michigan law."

"But will twelve members of the jury know?"

"I don't know the answer to that one. Only a trial will tell for sure. But you can't turn a criminal loose just because you're afraid you might lose."

"A criminal? Are you sure he's a criminal?"

"I've only been in this business three years, but I've learned one thing. I'm not supposed to judge whether someone's a criminal or not."

"So cynical in only three years?"

"Look, off the record?"

"Yeah. Off the record."

"If I had been Neal I would have probably done the same thing, right?"

"And that doesn't matter to you?"

"The system says we're the prosecutors, not the judge and jury. It's what the law says, not what we say!"

"I don't look at it that way."

"Exactly what way is that?"

"There's such a thing as prosecutorial discretion. You've heard of that?"

"I've never heard of its being used because the prosecutor thought the crime was an okay crime."

"I can see we're not getting any place here. *I'm* the prosecutor and I say I'm not filing. Besides, we'd never get a conviction."

"Do you want to bet your job on it?" With those words Fred knew he had taken the leap.

"What are you talking about?"

"I'm telling you I'm running for your job, Al."

"Why, you bastard. I'll wipe your nose in it."

"That may be, but you're handing me my campaign issue."

"What? Because I won't file charges against some 76-year-old college professor? Some campaign issue!"

"I'd like to make a suggestion."

"*You* want to give *me* a suggestion? You've got balls, Fred."

"You'd be better off filing charges."

Al looked at Fred as if he couldn't believe the younger man's audacity. Fred's heart was pounding with excitement. The poker bets had been made and the players were about to show their hands. "You see," Fred went on. "If you don't file I have a very good friend of the attorney general–I think you know her–Betty Neal–and she believes she can see to it that the attorney general files this case if you refuse to. File it over your head."

"Why, you dirty son-of-a-bitch. How do you know Betty Neal?"

"That's my little secret, Al. Let's just say she's one of my political supporters."

"You don't miss a bet, do you."

"I try not to, Al. I try not to. How do you think that would go over as a campaign issue? *Attorney general steps in to enforce the law after Lasser refuses.*"

Fred had never seen his boss at a loss for words. This was a first.

"On the other hand," Fred continued. "You let me try the case and I fall flat on my face–as you say I will–you win the election. That's why I said *Do you want to bet your job on it?*"

"So that's it. You want to use this case to get my job."

"No different from you, Al. You want to use it to *keep* your job."

"And the merits of the case have nothing to do with it."

"Now look who's the one being cynical."

An hour later Al Lasser's secretary buzzed him.

"I have Betty Neal on the line; she's been in a meeting."

"Thanks, Teresa."

Al paused a moment before picking up the phone. He hated eating crow, but he had no other alternative.

"Ms. Neal, I'm glad I reached you. I wanted to tell you that I've decided to file charges after all. What's more I've assigned my best deputy prosecutor to the case. I think you know him. Frederick Cain. If anyone can win, he can."

When the brief conversation was over, Al stood looking out his basement window. He could see that it was snowing again. "That cocky son-of-a-bitch," he said aloud to no one. "I hope he gets his ass beat."

-22-

David had no idea what time it was when he awoke. His overwhelming depression remained. The realization that Lu was dead and that he would spend the rest of his life in jail–probably in Jackson State Prison–was unbearable. If only Ruby had not interrupted his suicide attempt.

The jailer had seen to it that there was nothing in the cell he could use to take his life. To eat he was given only hamburgers and other food that did not require knives and forks. They had even taken his belt. When he stood he had to hold his trousers up. He had lost so much weight these last weeks. It was impossible to avoid the ever watchful television camera that swept the cell.

"Can you find out when Lu's funeral is going to be?" he asked when the jailer slid him food through the small opening.

"I'll try to find out, but they won't let you attend. You'll be transferred to the Marshall jail right after your arraignment. You'll be the sheriff's prisoner then–totally out of Albion's jurisdiction."

"Is there anyway at all I could go to the funeral? After all, we were married 51 years."

"I'll tell the chief about your request, but you haven't got a chance in hell. After all, you're the one who killed her."

It was about two hours later when the jailer again appeared. "The funeral is Monday at two o'clock. The chief wants to talk to you now."

"He does? Does this mean maybe I can go?"

"All I know is the chief wants to see you. I'm going to handcuff you before I take you upstairs. Here, you'll need this." The jailer handed David his belt.

When the jailer unlocked the security door at the top of the narrow stairs David was met by two uniformed officers who escorted him down the long hallway to the chief's office.

"Dr. Neal, I'm Harry Benton. I'm chief of Albion's Department of Public Safety—the police department. I knew your wife. She did a lot of good in Albion." Benton was a kindly looking man, about 50. He did not look like a police officer. David remembered meeting him at one of Lu's civic functions.

"These are Officers Ott and Sanderson." The chief nodded toward the officers. "You see, it's against regulations for you to be out of the jail section and so I've asked that you be handcuffed and that my two men be here."

"Thank you, chief, you see I'm pleading to you to allow me to go my wife's funeral. I'm very grateful you are seeing me." David's legs felt weak. It had been so cramped in his cell. "May I sit down?"

"Of course. Bill, pull up that chair for Dr. Neal. Yes, the jailer told me you wanted to attend the funeral."

David sat down. "I killed her; I don't deny that, but I loved her very much." For a moment he was overcome with emotion. "I'd like this one last chance to be with her before…well, before they bury her and put me in prison."

"You give me a very serious problem, Dr. Neal. You're going to be arraigned first thing Tuesday morning. An arraignment is a brief appearance in the District Court down the street—you know the building?"

"Yes, I was there for a traffic ticket once."

"All they do at the arraignment is tell you what charges have been filed against you. If it's murder, there is no bail and you're immediately transferred to the sheriff. They'll take you to the Marshall jail."

"So it's hopeless. I can't go to the funeral then?"

"I didn't say that. The funeral's Monday and the arraignment is Tuesday. You're in my jurisdiction until then."

"I'm not going to run away, if that's what's worrying you."

"I'm more worried about your carrying out your suicide threat. My name could be mud with the prosecutor's office if you tried anything."

"All I want to do is to see her one last time and go the funeral. Is there anything I can do to persuade you?"

"I ought to have my head examined, but I'm going to do it. I've been searching my conscience for the last two hours. Your wife was a fine lady and I know you did what you thought you had to do. The only thing I know for certain is that if my wife took my life under the same circumstances as yours, I'd want them to let her attend my funeral."

"How can I ever thank you?" David was near tears. He was overjoyed by the unexpected decision.

"For one thing you can thank me by not trying any funny business. But these two officers here are going to be with you every minute to see to it that you don't." The chief spoke to the officers. "I want him in cuffs even at the funeral. When he's in the car I want one of you to drive and the other to be cuffed to him. Is that clear?"

"Yes, sir."

"Thank you, chief. You're a compassionate man," said David.

"From the way it looks, there's going to be plenty of press coverage. Don't make me look stupid."

-23-

David's elation over Chief Benton's permission to attend Lu's funeral had been short lived. His depression had returned with a vengeance. What little remained of his spirit would be dead after Lu's funeral this afternoon. There came to his mind a statistical study in one of the Ivy League journals that showed higher mortality rates for those whose spouses had died. He hoped to God this would be true of him. He hoped his years in prison would be mercifully few. He wanted no humiliating trial, with its dreadful recital of facts. Surely there was some way to arrange for immediate sentencing so that he would be in Jackson Prison, where he would not be constantly observed so that he could find a way to take his life.

Half an hour before the funeral, the two officers took him to Goodrich Chapel. Lu's casket would be closed for the funeral, but he would be allowed to view her body beforehand.

Last night the officers had gone to David's home where Eddie had helped them find his good dark suit.

As they entered the back room where Lu's coffin was, David realized he was not in fear of seeing her body. Strangely, he was looking forward to it. There had been such bedlam at the hospital that night. He had been whisked away before he got a good look at Lu's body. Now it would be peaceful. This would be his last time alone with her. His last time ever. He wanted to see her without the respirator and those tubes. He wanted to tell her he loved her one more time. To be certain that she understood his reasons for taking her life. After this he did not care what happened to him.

"Officer, could you possibly remove my handcuffs? I promise I won't pull anything."

"What do you think, Charlie?" the larger man asked.

"I'll stand by the other door. It'll be all right. After all, the chief didn't say we couldn't."

David stood over Lu's open casket, the unfastened handcuff hanging to his side. The gentle tears that flowed down his face came more from relief than grief. "Oh, Lu," he said softly so that the officers could not hear. "You look so beautiful. Your dress is so very pretty." He knew that Betty must have picked it out. It was the dress Lu had bought for their 50th anniversary party in the Faculty Room. He recalled how vivacious she had been that day. That was how he wanted to remember her. David gently stroked the fancy work on her dress. Lu liked fancy work even when it was no longer in style. He noticed the white roots of her hair had been colored. One of the reasons he had always dreaded the possibility of Lu's dying first was he did not want to see her dead body–let alone touch it, but now it was not at all fearful for him. He found peace in seeing her out of that hospital bed and at last freed from her stroke. Lightly he ran his finger across the top of her nose. The dress–the touch–reminded him that they had made love the night of their 50th anniversary. He wondered if they would have made love the night of her stroke. They often did when they dressed up for dinner.

His tears intensified. It seemed as if another part of him watched himself cry. They had had such a beautiful life together. The tears seemed so sweet–so tender. They had loved each other so much. There had been so much happiness. Now it was gone–ended. There was nothing more for him to do. It was so final. So absolutely final.

He looked at the many flowers around the casket. He looked at one of the name tags. The president of the college and his wife. The chairman of the board of trustees. So many loved and respected her. Part of him wanted to stand there forever. To fix the scene in his mind. Another part wanted the scene to end, wanted everything to end.

The undertaker entered the room. "Dr. Neal, it's time now. I must close the casket."

"Can I stay while you do it?"

"It's best if you don't. Here, I'll give you her rings."

Solemnly the undertaker removed Lu's two rings.

"Here you are, Dr. Neal."

David took the old-fashioned rings in his hand. They had bought the engagement ring in a small shop in downtown Philadelphia. He remembered its name—Fogel's. They were so happy that day. All these years Lu had worn her rings. They were part of her. She had always been so proud to proclaim herself as Mrs. David Neal.

David stepped back a few paces. Suddenly he felt exhausted. His knees felt as if they would not support him. Impulsively he rushed forward to Lu and threw himself across her lifeless body. "Oh, Lu," he said through his sobs. "I wish it could have been different. I wish it could have been me first."

The larger officer stepped forward and gently pulled David back. "Professor Neal, don't you think it's time for us to go in now?"

"I'm ready." David stepped back and helplessly leaned against his captor's large body.

David and the two officers followed Lu's casket as it was wheeled into the large chapel through the rear door. He heard the organ playing "Nearer, My God, to Thee." Lu had always liked that song. Betty must have selected it.

A place in the first pew had been reserved for the three of them. David could see Betty, in the second pew, turn her head so as to avoid eye contact. Quickly he scanned the many faces to see if Eddie was nearby. If only he could talk to him—tell him things would be all right—but he could not find his grandson.

He saw people streaming in from the entrance. It looked as if the large chapel would be nearly filled for Lu. He was relieved that he was not permitted to talk to any of them. He did want to face their words of sympathy and the unspoken question he knew was on their minds: *David, how could you?* He would never make them understand he had done it for love. Sometimes even he was not sure he had done the right thing. He would be glad when the funeral was over and he could go back to jail.

David did not concentrate during the funeral. He held Lu's rings in his hand as the young soloist from the church sang. He wondered who would get the rings when he died. He hoped there was some way he could be certain Eddie would get them. Perhaps, though, he ought to send them to Betty. That was probably what Lu would have wanted. He wished things could have turned out better with Betty.

The president of college spoke fondly of Lu. She was always serving the college one way or another, even after David had retired. Next, the chairman of the school board spoke of Lu's service to the Albion community. David wished he could take the lectern and make everyone understand what Lu had meant in his life. He would tell them how Lu could have been something far beyond the wife of a not-very-significant college professor, yet she had devoted herself to being his wife and the mother of his child. He wondered if Betty would ever appreciate that. Probably not, he thought.

When the funeral service was over, the officers took David to the police car parked on the back street. David looked up at the wing of the library where the Faculty Room was located. How often during these past months he had sat in that room and remembered their 50th anniversary party. David took his place in the back of the police cruiser, handcuffed to the officer.

Motor running to heat the car, they waited at the curb until the last of the procession of cars drove past, headed for the cemetery across town and then began following a block away.

"I don't want to go to the cemetery," David said. "All those people. I can't face them."

"Are you sure, Dr. Neal?" the driver asked. "We could just stay in the car if you want."

"No. I don't want to be in some police car at my wife's funeral. I don't want to go."

"All right, Dr. Neal."

"If that's how you feel," added the other officer. "We might as well go back to the jail."

"No, I don't want to go back. Not yet."

"What do you want then? We're supposed to take you back to the jail, you know."

"The river. I want you to take me to the river."

"What do you mean, to the river?"

"The nature preserve. I go there all the time. Can't we go for a walk by the Kalamazoo?"

"What do you think, Charlie? Do you think it would be okay?"

"Why not? We'll be back by the time they're through at the cemetery."

-24-

It was extremely cold as the mourners gathered at Albion's Riverside Cemetery. Even though the Kalamazoo River was very wide at the cemetery, it was frozen over except in the very center. Eddie anxiously looked around for his grandfather, but he was nowhere in sight. He wanted to talk to him. To tell him he was sorry for the way he had acted at the jail. He knew all along Grandfather had done the right thing. It was just that he had been upset over Granna. He missed her so much.

Eddie knew his only hope for staying in Albion was Grandfather. He wanted to keep living with him. They had been fine together since Granna had her stroke. It was true he didn't feel the same way about Grandfather as he did Granna. Grandfather didn't seem able to love people the way Granna always did, but he was a good old guy. He didn't hassle him and he had done his best to make a nice home for them.

One thing for sure, he did not want to live with his mother. Before he did that he would join the Marines, the way his friend's brother had. But he had called the recruiter in Battle Creek, who said a guy had to be 18 to get in without his parents' consent. That was a month off and he knew his Mom would never give consent.

If only Grandfather could get out of jail. He could run away until he turned 18 and then he could live with Grandfather, no matter what Mom said. Surely they wouldn't keep Grandfather in jail very long. They would have to see that he had done the right thing in ending it for Granna.

Eddie looked around at the crowd bundled against the cold. Where was Grandfather anyway? They were all gathering around Granna's casket and

Grandfather was nowhere to be seen. He had to tell him he was sorry and wanted to stay with him in Albion.

Ruby stood next to Eddie near the graveside. Her bullet wound, while painful, had been superficial. She was able to get around with the aid of a crutch, and last night had invited Eddie to her home for dinner. Eddie's mother hadn't come back to Albion until this morning and had made him ride with her in the limousine to the cemetery, but he didn't want to be with her any more than he had to. Eddie thought his mother should have stayed with him at Granna's and fixed his meals, but, no, she had to go off to Detroit. That would be the way it would be if he lived with her. Just like before. Always away on some big case.

At least Ruby had cared enough to invite him to dinner, despite having to use her crutch. She had been a nice lady from the beginning. Why couldn't Mom be more like Ruby?

"We are gathered here to say our final good-bye to our friend, Lu," the minister began. Eddie had decided his grandfather wasn't going to come. They must have taken him back to jail. Eddie wasn't wearing his baseball cap. He thought Granna would have liked his cap, but Mom had made him leave it home.

The minister was reading from the Bible. It was so final. In a little while Granna would be in the cold ground. They would leave and before long she would be alone with dirt over her. He was going to miss her something awful. He began to cry. He felt so bad. So lonely. No more cookies. No reminding him to do his homework. No more loving him when he needed it. He had not cried very much yet—even when he was alone at night—but now he didn't care. Let them all see him cry. He didn't care any more.

Eddie looked at his mother, standing across from him near Granna's casket. She wasn't even crying. He wondered if she was thinking about some big case. He wondered if she was going to try to make him go home with her tonight.

Standing two inches taller than Eddie, Ruby held her crutch with one arm and put her other around him. Eddie liked Ruby's doing that, but it didn't do much good. Granna was dead and nobody could do anything about that. Not ever.

-25-

A few miles up the Kalamazoo River the police cruiser stood empty–parked in the cold at the entrance to the college nature study. Its three passengers had left tracks along the snowy trail leading to the river's edge. The barren forest and the cold gave no hint that buds would pop forth in a few weeks' time. The tracks of a lone raccoon left the all but hidden path and disappeared at the end of a long, fallen tree.

David stopped where the path turned toward the frozen river. "I'd like to go on alone, if it's all right with you." The officers had not handcuffed him.

"What do you think, Charlie?"

"I always come to this spot when I'm troubled," David interrupted. "It's important I be alone."

"I don't think so, Dr. Neal. I'm sorry, but the chief had his reasons. We're too close to the river."

"But it's frozen. Look, all I want to do is be by myself for a minute. You see I'd like to pray."

"I'm sorry the ice is too thin."

"Yeah, I don't think we should," agreed Bill, the other officer. "We'd have one hell of a time fishing him out of the river."

"For God's sake, they're burying my wife. Can't you understand that?"

"I'm sorry, Dr. Neal, we can't take a chance on you. Bill's right. If you made a dash for it, it could mean our badges."

"We're sorry," Bill agreed.

"All right, then." David held out his arm. "Go ahead, handcuff me. I want to stand near the river."

"Sorry, I've got to do this." Charlie handcuffed himself to David.

Stooped and forlorn, David trudged between the two of them to the edge of the river. Their breath steamed against the cold. It was at the spot from which he had fired six shots into the river.

Our Father, which art in heaven...

The officers turned away, giving David a modicum of privacy.

Hallowed be thy name...

David stumbled through the rest of the Lord's Prayer.

When he finished he added final sentences of his own. "Lord, please take care of my Lu. Please help me to join her as soon as possible."

Strange, he thought, for a man who doubted the very existence of God to be asking for divine help. Sometimes in these past months it seemed as if there simply had to be a God. There had to be someone or something that could help–some power that was in charge of what had befallen him. He wanted to scream out for help. He wanted to fire shots into the river. He wanted to do something–anything–to relieve his pain. The agony of his grief was as intense as that of a battlefield amputation. Surely nothing could hurt more than this. Staring at the river, he fingered Lu's rings in the pocket of his Mackinaw.

Impulsively David burst toward the river. The force of his sudden lunge against the handcuffs pulled Charlie off his feet. Trying to drag the large policeman with him toward the icy edge, David pulled as hard against the cuff as he could. The metal dug violently against his wrist.

"For Christ's sake!" Charlie cried out. "What are you trying to do?"

"Hold on, there!" Bill shouted, tackling David and knocking him onto the ice near the shore.

The ice did not break as David furiously tried to somehow free himself from the sharp grip of the cuffs and the officers who held on to him. But he was unable to move.

"Hold him, Bill!"

"I got him!"

"For God's sake, hang on! We've got to get him back to the cruiser!"

"Goddamn, I don't want the chief to hear about this!"

As the men got to their feet forcing David to stand with them, he began to sob. "Please let me go," he cried. "I've got to get out of here! I can't stand it any more."

"Dammit, Neal! We take a chance on you by bringing you to the river and you pull a stunt like this!" Charlie shouted.

"That doesn't do any good, Charlie. Can't you see? C'mon, let's get him back to the jail where he's somebody else's problem."

-26-

"Do you want me to give you a ride home?" Ruby asked as she and Eddie walked from Lu's grave toward the long row of parked cars. It was slow going for Ruby with her crutch and the snow-covered thick grass.

Eddie saw his mother busy talking to the president of the college. "Yeah, thanks, but if it's okay with you, I'd like to leave right away. I don't want to have to ride back with her."

But it was too late.

"Eddie!" Betty called out. "I want to talk to you!"

Betty left her conversation and hurried toward Eddie, her fur coat doing little to hide her obesity. "You wait for me! Do you hear?" she commanded.

"I'm sorry, Ruby, but I guess I've got to talk with her."

"I understand. Good luck, Eddie." Ruby squeezed Eddie's hand. "You take care now. Give me a call."

"Okay. If I can, I will."

"You can come over for supper again if you want. Love to have you." Ruby walked toward her car as Betty rushed up.

"Who was that woman?"

"Granna's nurse. She got hit by one of the bullets. If you had come around to the hospital, you'd know."

"Don't get smart with me. Your grandmother's lying in that box over there. What did she want?"

"She was going give me a ride to the house."

"Well, I'm going to take you there. We've got some serious talking to do."

"About what?"

"About you living with me."

A man and woman in their 50s whom Eddie didn't know came up to them. The woman spoke. "Ms. Neal, I'm Billie Bancroft. This is my husband Arnold. I was in Lu's garden club."

"How do you do, Mr. and Mrs. Bancroft," Betty said. "I'd like you to meet my son, Eddie."

"Yes, we've met at high school football games. Our son's in Eddie's class. Eddie, we're all going to miss your grandmother very much."

"Thank you. Thank you very much," responded Betty, not giving Eddie a chance to speak. "I know everyone loved my mother."

"We certainly did. All the people of Albion did," the woman went on. "Eddie, we'd like to have you over for dinner sometime soon. This is a difficult time for you, I'm sure."

Eddie started to answer, but Betty interrupted. "I'm afraid that will be impossible. Eddie's going to live with me in Bloomfield Hills. Now, if you'll excuse us, Mr. and Mrs. Bancroft, we've got to be getting along. I'm sure you understand. There is so much to do."

"Oh yes, we understand. Well, our sympathy to you."

Eddie sat in the Cadillac with his mother.

"Why did you tell them that?"

"Tell them what?"

"You know. That I'm going to live with you." Eddie was angry.

Betty started the car.

"Because you are. We're going to Granna's right now and pack some of your things. We'll come back this weekend and get everything else. We can pick up your car then and get the rest of your stuff."

Eddie exploded. "I'm not packing anything! I'm sick and tired of you trying to tell me what to do. That's all you've done today, is tell me what to do!" Eddie started to open the car door, but Betty was accelerating onto the highway.

"Eddie, you're my son and you're still a minor. I've got certain responsibilities and I intend to fulfill them." She was driving too fast as she approached downtown.

"I can take care of myself!"

"We've been over this before, young man. My house is the only place you've got."

"I don't care! Grandfather will be out soon. He'll let me stay."

"Your grandfather is going to jail! Do you hear me? To jail for a long time."

They were interrupted by the brief wail of a siren. It was a police car.

"Damn!" Betty shouted. "Now look what you made me do!" She pressed the button to lower the driver's window.

"You were going pretty fast there Ma'am," said the officer. "May I see your driver's license?"

"I'm sorry, officer, we were just coming back from the cemetery. We just buried my mother. I guess I wasn't concentrating."

Seizing the opportunity Eddie opened the passenger door.

"And just where do you think you're going?"

"I don't know. Anywhere away from you!"

"You get back in this car! Officer, he's my son. Make him get back in the car."

"Ma'am I don't have any jurisdiction to make somebody stay in your car."

Eddie stormed down the street–Superior Street, the bricked main street of Albion. He had no idea where he was going. Maybe home. Maybe over to Ruby's. Maybe to the jail to see Grandfather. He didn't know. He only knew that no matter what, he was not going to get into that car with his mother.

-27-

Eddie trudged down Superior Street, blankly staring into the shop windows. He was seething with anger at his mother. He never wanted to see her again, let alone live with her!

What a difference there was between Albion and Bloomfield Hills. The kids in Bloomfield Hills would look down on Albion, with its unsophisticated shops and boarded-up movie theater, but he liked the small town. He knew the people were plain and simple, but they were not phony and didn't put on airs. What's more, he liked the college being in Albion. He still hoped he could attend there someday.

Eddie didn't want to go to Bloomfield Hills. Even with Granna dead, he wanted to stay in Albion with Grandfather. He had to persuade him to fight these stupid murder charges. There had to be a smart lawyer someplace who could get him off. Like some of them he had seen on TV.

Eddie crossed the wide red-bricked street and headed for the jail. The cops must have taken Grandfather back to the jail and that's why he hadn't been at the cemetery. He wanted to talk to him right now.

"I'm sorry, but the chief had your grandfather transferred to the Marshall jail," said the clerk behind the glass. She was watching the jail cells on her television monitors. "It seems he tried to kill himself a few minutes ago. They'll keep him in Marshall until his trial."

"My God!" Eddie exclaimed. "He tried to kill himself?"

"I'm afraid so. He tried to jump into the river, but they stopped him."

Eddie decided to get home as fast as he could. He'd get his car and drive the ten miles to Marshall. He had to see his grandfather right away. He had to stop him from trying to kill himself. He had to tell him to get a lawyer and fight.

Eddie was out of breath from running, as he approached the house. His mother's Cadillac was parked behind his car. As he got nearer he could see that she was sitting in her car. He didn't want to get into another argument with her, but he couldn't avoid her if he were going to see Grandfather.

"Eddie, I want to talk to you!" Betty shouted as he hurriedly opened his car door.

"Well, I don't want to talk to you any more! There isn't anything you can do to get me to go with you!"

"But, I've been thinking…"

Quickly, Eddie was in his car and started the engine.

Betty pounded on his window. "Please, Eddie, I want to talk to you."

She sounded conciliatory to Eddie, but he knew very well it was just one of her tricks. He knew she would never give up. His heart was racing as he pulled away without even looking at her. He almost brushed her with his car. She'd better watch out, because he wasn't going to stop!

As her son's car picked up speed, Betty stood back. Eddie could see her standing in the street, as he turned the corner and headed for the interstate. For a moment he felt sorry for her, but ever since he was a child this had been one of her tricks. First, to act tough, and then to put on her helpless, deserted act. It wasn't going to work this time.

Eddie had a tough time finding the Marshall jail. The traffic circle was confusing. Then he found it. It was to the rear of the modern two story courthouse. He hoped this was the right place. He must talk to his grandfather.

There were printed signs giving visiting hours in the reception room. Eddie peered through the dark glass and could see a woman talking on the telephone. She sat some ten feet away from the glass partition and he couldn't tell for sure that she was the receptionist. He doffed his baseball cap in order to get a better look.

"Yes?" said a voice coming over an intercom device.

"You mean me?" It didn't seem to Eddie that the voice belonged to the woman, yet he couldn't see anyone else.

"Yes, I mean you," said the voice. "What is it that you want?"

"I didn't know you could hear me," Eddie said. He figured he was talking into a hidden microphone. "I came to see my grandfather. The police at Albion said he's been transferred here."

"You mean he's a new prisoner?"

"Yeah, I guess so."

"What's his name?"

"Dr. Neal. David Neal. He's a professor…"

"Yes. He's just been processed. We have him here." She was looking at a computer screen. "But you can't see him."

"Can't see him? But he's my grandfather. I have to talk to him. It's very important!"

"You're not 18, are you? You don't look 18 to me."

"No, but I will be next month."

"You've got to be 18. See that sign to your left."

Eddie looked. "Visitors must be 18." He hadn't noticed it.

"But I don't know what to do. I've got to see my grandfather."

"I can't make any exceptions. That's the rule."

"Isn't there some way? I'm almost 18."

"The only one is Lieutenant James and he's in Lansing today. You'll have to try him tomorrow."

"But–"

"That's the rule, young man. Now, if you'll step away from the window. You'll have to try tomorrow, and even then I'm not sure what the Lieutenant will say."

"But—"

"Please step back."

Eddie was angry. He slammed the door as he left. He knew he might get a ticket as he sped away from the civic center parking lot toward Albion, but he didn't give a damn. He was going home and pack his stuff. He was doing 85 the minute he entered the interstate. "I'm getting out of here!" he said aloud. "They're not keeping me in Michigan any more. I'm through with this goddamned state!"

-28-

The next morning on her way to her office in downtown Detroit, Betty nearly rear-ended the car in front of her. The fast lane had slowed suddenly as it neared the interchange with the Walter Reuther Expressway. Mercifully, there had been room for her to skid into the next lane, avoiding the imminent collision. She realized she had been thinking about her trouble with Eddie and not concentrating on her driving.

She was still shaking inside when she pulled into the huge underground garage in the Renaissance Center complex. As she got out of her car, she realized she had strained her ankle from the force of suddenly applying her brakes. For several steps she could hardly put her weight on her right foot. The problem with Eddie seemed unsolvable.

For many years Willard, Oates and Schultz had refused to handle divorce cases, thinking them undignified, but in recent years, with so many top executives of their important corporate clients getting caught up in the tidal wave of divorces, the firm had bowed to the necessity of not referring such important clients to outside divorce lawyers. Charlie Flint had become the partner specializing in the firm's divorce work. That department had flourished so well that the firm now had a second partner who, along with three associates, handled mostly domestic relations matters. Betty had insisted that Charlie handle her own case, although originally he had expressed reluctance to take on the divorce of one of his partners.

The first thing that Betty did after collecting herself in her office was to telephone Flint. "Charlie. I need to talk to you. May I come over right now?" Betty liked Charlie. He brought the same unrelenting professionalism to domestic relations that marked the firm's work in other matters. Also he was a practical, straight-talking man. At first she had not liked it when Charlie had frankly told her she was pushing too much in her case against her husband, but she had learned to respect him and to prize his counsel in matters that might not be considered strictly legal. Charlie had become the one partner with whom she felt she could confide without fearing an effect on her standing and progress within the firm.

Charlie's office was on the 38th floor, the same as Betty's, with a view back up Woodward Avenue toward the northern suburbs. They were about the same in age and seniority and had virtually the same number of points–the system by which profits were divided. "Betty, I'm truly sorry to hear about your mother. I wish there were something I could say or do to help you."

"Well, maybe there is, Charlie. I'm in such a state of mind I don't trust my own judgment any more."

Betty told Charlie how Eddie had run away to her parents and how, since her mother's death, he refused to return to live with her.

"At first I thought I should have you get a court order–making him live with me, but now I'm not so sure."

Charlie had tried to give up cigarettes half a dozen times, but the best he could do was to refrain from smoking until noon. Although he still consumed a pack a day, because it was Charlie, the firm winked at its no smoking policy. It would look foolish for a three-hundred-dollar-an-hour attorney to go to the employees' smoking room every time the urge got the best of him. Although it was only just past nine o'clock he took a cigarette from the silver box on his desk and put it in his mouth, but did not light it.

Betty knew it was his habit to do this until it was finally noon. "It's okay by me if you light up," she said. Charlie's compulsion gave Betty a feeling of kinship with her partner. She felt confident he would never criticize her behind her back for her eating being out of control–a fact she doubted to be true of the other firm members.

"Thanks, Betty, but I'll wait until after lunch."

She told him about recent the events "What do you think I should do about Eddie? I really want your advice."

"I'm not sure what you should do, but I am sure what you should not do?"

"Oh. And what's that?"

"You shouldn't push Eddie so hard."

"But I want him with me!"

"It'll backfire. I'm telling you, Betty, you've got to let go of him."

"You could get a court order, couldn't you? You know he's not legally an adult and I've got custody."

"I suppose I could get an order, but he already ran away–how many times?"

"Three."

"So what good is an order. When is he going to be eighteen anyway?"

"Next month. March 27."

"There you have it. If he got an attorney he'd have a chance of stopping me. At least slow me down. What good would it do anyway? He's already ignored the custody order. Besides, by the time I got the order he'd be 18."

"But what's going to happen to him? My father will be in jail. Eddie's father has his girlfriend. He won't want Eddie. She would never hear of it."

"I don't have an answer to that any more than you do. When Eddie's 18 he'll be legally an adult. He'll be responsible for himself."

"Charlie, sometimes I think the law is a fool. Suddenly a boy totally unable to handle the world becomes an adult and is supposed to be completely responsible for himself."

"There has to be some age as a dividing line. You know that, Betty, as well as I do. The law's full of dividing lines."

"I feel so helpless. When he kept running away he was slapping me in the face. And now this. He's just defying me."

"All you can do is help him. And then only when he asks."

"He'll never ask."

"That's his problem. He's got to mature enough to be able to ask for help."

"Never. He'll never ask me. I've lost him, Charlie. First my mother and now my son." Betty's voice faltered and tears came to her eyes.

Charlie matter-of-factly reached for a tissue and handed it to her. "What about your father?"

"He's in jail."

"They've decided to prosecute him, have they?"

"Yes. He's been charged with murder."

"First degree?"

"Yes."

"Dirty bastards. You'd think the prosecutor would show some compassion, wouldn't you? What county is it? Maybe Jim would have some influence there."

"Calhoun. Not this prosecutor. He's out for blood. I've already talked to him. There will be no changing his mind."

As Betty returned to her office she hoped to hell Charlie never found out what had really happened in that prosecutor's office.

-29-

Having left the cemetery, Ruby impulsively stopped at a pay phone and telephoned Detroit. She was connected to her Uncle Joseph's secretary.

"He's in a meeting, Miss Thompson. Shall I interrupt him?"

"I've got to see him. I can get there by five-thirty or six o'clock. Do you think he could see me then? It's an emergency."

"He'll always make time to see you, Miss Thompson."

Next, Ruby tried to reach Eddie. She wanted to tell him she couldn't have him over for dinner, because she was going to see her uncle about defending Dr. Neal. But there was no answer. She'd call again from Detroit.

Two hours later Ruby took the elevator to Joseph's office in the Renaissance Center. She had been there only once, five or six years ago, when the entire family had been invited to the opening of his lavish new law offices. The occasion, which was also her uncle's 60th birthday, had been a celebration of his reaching the pinnacle of success as a lawyer. Ruby had just graduated from Albion College. He was simply Uncle Joseph to Ruby–the kindly uncle who, having no children of his own, had paid for her education. But that night she became fully aware of the heights Joseph Thomas Jefferson had attained. The mayor of Detroit had proposed a toast, but, since the mayor was black, what really had impressed her was the chairman of one of the big three car makers–of course white–announcing that her own Uncle Joseph had accepted an appoint-ment to his board of directors. Since that night, she had followed with great pride the legal career of her illustrious relative. "The best trial lawyer in the Midwest," the newspapers said.

Ruby paused before the huge wooden doors. "Joseph Thomas Jefferson. Lawyers," announced the bronzed letters. The names of half a dozen associates were listed below. Ruby said a brief silent prayer to herself. Uncle Joseph had done so much for her. She hoped she could ask another favor.

"Ruby, it's so good to see you. Your mother told me about your getting shot. She said it wasn't serious, but I'm amazed to see you up and about so quickly."

"It turned out the bullet only grazed me."

"Thank God for that. Is that why you're here to see me?"

"Only indirectly."

"Here, sit down. Can you manage with that crutch or do you need me to help you? Joseph motioned for her to sit in one of the two large easy chairs flanking the fireplace.

"No, I can manage, thanks."

Wearing a colorful vest, Joseph sat in the other chair, looking at her with obvious affection.

"Your mother always keeps me posted on you. You must tell me all about this shooting."

"I will, but first tell me how you've been. Mom's always sending me clippings about your cases. I particularly liked the one about the talk show hostess and her doctor husband. Do you always win?"

"You flatter me," he laughed. "If I can just win the ones where I'm in the right, I'm doing all right."

For the first time in her life, Ruby was nervous about talking to her uncle. Somehow, she had to get him to defend Dr. Neal.

"Uncle Joseph, are you free for dinner tonight? I'm afraid I've got a very special favor I want to ask you."

"I've got a trial lawyers' meeting, but we can go for drinks and then to dinner. I'd love to show you off, that is, if you feel up to it."

Ruby flashed her bright smile. Of course; I feel fine, but first I've got to call Albion to cancel my dinner plans."

"A young man, I hope."

"Well, he's young all right, but he's only a teenager. His name is Eddie Erickson."

Ruby called Eddie from her uncle's phone, but again there was no answer. "I'll have to try later," she said.

"Come, let's make our appearance at the lawyer's association and have that dinner" he said. "You can tell me all about this favor you're going to ask."

At dinner in Detroit's Greek Town Ruby told the story of Lu's hopeless stroke—of David's agony and indecision—of his taking of Lu's life—and of Ruby's befriending Eddie. "They're charging Dr. Neal with murder. Can you imagine that? He did it because he loved her and now they're calling it murder."

"Ruby, you've had the heart of a nurse since you were a child. I don't know if I ever told you how you bandaged my hand when I cut it at your house when you were a child."

"No. You never have."

"Come on, now, we both know you're lying," he laughed. "I've told you that story a million times. Ever since I can remember you've wanted to rescue people."

"Now, Uncle Joseph, isn't that what you do? Rescue people in trouble?"

"Perhaps, but I'm not as noble about it as you. I do it for the money. You may have noticed my house and my office are a little on the luxurious side"

"Come on, I don't believe you defend people just for the money."

"Maybe not. At least not as much as I used to, but money still gives me great happiness."

They both heartily laughed.

"I'm worried as much about Eddie as anybody."

"Tell me more about Eddie."

"Well, he's almost 18. A senior in Albion High. He kept running away from his mother to live with his grandparents. The woman who died was his grandmother. In fact, you may know Eddie's mother–she's a lawyer with some big firm here in Detroit–Betty Neal."

"Sure, I know of her. Hell, she's only one floor down." Joseph was silent for a moment. "You keep what I'm going to tell you confidential, do you hear?"

"Yes, of course."

"Clinton is thinking of appointing her a federal judge. I serve on the bar's judicial committee that's checking her out right now."

"Poor boy."

"What do you mean 'poor boy?'"

"That's the whole trouble. Eddie's mother is totally into her career. She doesn't really care about Eddie."

"And so you want me to defend this Eddie's grandfather? And exactly why should I do that?"

"Because I asked you to?" Ruby's grin showed her out-sized beautiful teeth.

Joseph laughed. "You've already gotten across the point there's not much of a fee to be had–retired college professor and all. Tell me, Miss To-the-rescue Nurse Thompson, exactly why I should interrupt my entire practice for a case like this? And 'because you asked me' doesn't quite cut it–although I must confess it goes a long way."

Ruby could tell by the twinkle in her uncle's eye that she was making progress. "Uncle Joseph, you should have seen what Dr. Neal went through. He was at the hospital every day twice a day for two months while his wife was in a coma. You know what that's like. You did it yourself when Aunt Coakie died."

"But I didn't kill her."

"Dr. Neal never gave up hope until the very end. We all knew it was hopeless, but he wouldn't give up."

"Evidently he did give up."

"Only when it became obvious."

"I don't know about this one, Ruby."

"I thought lawyers weren't supposed to pass personal judgment on their clients."

"He's not my client, at least not yet."

Ruby smiled inwardly at the crack she saw in her uncle's shell. "Dr. Jacobson is the best doctor in Albion. He wanted to turn off the respirator and let her go. There was no hope for her."

"Why didn't the doctor do it, then? Why did Neal do it?"

"Because of his daughter. This daughter you say may be a judge."

"What do you mean 'because of her?'"

"She wouldn't give permission. Dr. Jacobson drove all the way to Detroit to ask her. She practically threw him out of her office. Said it would be murder."

"Betty Neal said that?"

"You've never seen such a tough lady in your life."

"I know she's a tough one all right." Joseph put his hand to his chin. "So they filed murder charges?"

"Good Lord, they can't convict him, can they?" Ruby asked.

"That's a very good question. I'll tell you what. I'll go to Albion as soon as I can. I'd like to talk to a few people and meet this Professor Neal."

"Oh, would you? You'd be doing a wonderful thing if you would!"

Joseph smiled as if indulging a child. "Mind you, though, no commitment. I'm just going to talk to him."

Ruby was elated on the drive back to Albion. In her heart she knew Uncle Joseph would not turn down the case once he had talked to Dr. Neal. It was well after midnight when she entered her kitchen. She thought about calling Eddie, but decided it was too late. She'd call in the morning.

-30-

Fred was having dinner with Marge at their favorite Battle Creek restaurant. February's raw weather had moderated a bit as they entered March, but they knew it was likely there would be more bad weather before spring arrived.

"I've never seen such tension around the office," Marge commented. They were having cocktails in their booth before ordering. Since Fred had forced Lasser to allow murder charges against David, Fred and Marge had been spending much more time together.

"I've refused to take any new cases, so I can concentrate on the Neal case."

"Has Al complained about it to you?" Marge asked.

"He wouldn't dare. He knows damn well he'd better give me all the time I need to prepare. I'd turn any interference from him into a campaign issue in a minute." Increasingly Fred had been discussing the case with Marge. He had learned she had a keen mind and had come to value her opinions. A trial date had been set for late March and Fred often ran his strategy ideas by her.

"You know, my biggest worry, is that Neal will plead guilty," Fred continued.

"Plead guilty?"

"My contact in the sheriff's department says he told one of the guards he didn't want a trial. Just wants to go to straight to Jackson Prison. I hear he's refused to be interviewed by the public defender."

"Why would he plead guilty?"

"Don't forget, the guy had planned to kill himself when he finished off his wife. Maybe he feels guilty. How the hell do I know what goes through an old man's mind?"

"Wouldn't that be good for you? A guilty plea, I mean."

"I'd get a conviction, but there wouldn't be much voter pizzazz in it for me."

"I see what you mean. Lasser would say anyone could have gotten a guilty plea. A real no-brainer."

"That would leave me without the campaign issue I need."

"Do you think the judge would allow a guilty plea instead of a trial? That's pretty serious stuff."

"In the last analysis, I don't think he'd have much choice. Judge Hoskins is a damn good judge. He knows if Neal is sane, he has a perfect right to waive a trial. Oh, sure, Hoskins will appoint an attorney for the guy. He has to in a murder case. But if a competent defendant wants to plead guilty, he can't very well stop him."

"Wouldn't you offer him some sort of a plea bargain?" Marge inquired. "Maybe reduce it to second degree. Something like that?"

"Normally I would, just to get rid of the case. Save the expense of trial. Especially in a mercy killing. But not this one, Marge. Not this one."

"I'm not sure I get your reasoning."

"Look, if Neal wants to plead guilty, I've got to stop him."

Marge's face brightened. "Of course. If you refuse to offer him a deal—"

"If I insist on a first degree—"

"—then he's not apt to plead guilty."

"Precisely!" Fred agreed. "If I stick to my guns, the public defender would tell him he'd be a fool to plead guilty to first degree."

"Sure. I see. He might as well go through a trial. He wouldn't have anything to lose."

"That's what any attorney would tell him. Neal may have murdered his wife knowing damn well he'd get caught, but he can't be an absolute fool."

"No, not a fool." Marge agreed. "But he may be playing by different rules than you usually see."

"What do you mean, 'by different rules?'"

"He may *want* to go to jail for the rest of his life. And the surest way to do that is a guilty plea to murder, even if it is first degree. After all, as you say, he wanted to kill himself that night."

"Aw, spur of the moment stuff. When it comes right down to it, he won't want to go to that stinking hell hole at Jackson Prison. Nobody would."

"I hope you're right," Marge replied.

"Trust me. I'm going to get my murder trial. Marge, my dear…" under the table Fred ran his hand up his girlfriend's leg "…you're looking at the candidate who's going to be the next prosecuting attorney."

-31-

Joseph Thomas Jefferson walked briskly from the Detroit Federal Building toward his waiting limousine. This morning's trial had ended before it began. While the jury was being impaneled, the deputy United States Attorney had capitulated and thrown in the towel on his RICO prosecution. Jefferson's client, the chairman of a securities firm, pleaded guilty to a minor offense for which it was agreed he would get no jail time. Joseph took satisfaction in knowing that the plea bargain would not have been offered except for his reputation for gaining acquittals in difficult cases. Joseph, with his staff, had spent hundreds of hours in preparation and was thoroughly prepared for the expected six week trial, facts which the U.S. Attorney well knew. Joseph felt that his fee of one million dollars—up front—was completely justified and, by the smile on his client's face after court there was no doubt he agreed.

The client, together with his wife and two teenaged children, again happily expressed his gratitude as Joseph entered his stretched black Lincoln. This was what it was all about, Joseph thought. There was no doubt in his mind that his client had bent the securities statute too far, but there was also no doubt that he did not deserve to go to jail. A lot of people had done a lot worse and were sitting untouched in high places. Besides, he knew his client had learned a lesson. What was more, Joseph resented the holier-than-thou attitude of the U.S. Attorney's office in trying to apply the RICO anti-racketeering statute to this type of case.

If it had been summer, Joseph would have taken off the afternoon and headed for the yacht club and his boat—he had been admitted to membership nearly ten years ago–but in the chill of March that luxury still was many weeks off. For a moment he thought about his condominium in Florida. He knew one of the corporate jets of the auto company could be his for the afternoon and that by twilight he could be on his patio overlooking the Gulf sunset. But he thought about his promise to visit Ruby's Albion professor. Besides, Florida wasn't the same after Coakie's fight with cancer and her death.

On the car phone Joseph punched his secretary's direct line. "Willa, they caved in. Offered me a plea bargain I couldn't refuse."

With a smile, he listened to his secretary's congratulations. She had been a loyal employee for nearly 20 years.

"You remember, Ruby has that retired professor. The one charged with mercy killing. I've decided to see him this afternoon and not come in to the office. Are there any calls that need answering?"

He listened as she told him of the morning's activities.

"They all can wait. Call me here in the car if you need me."

At expressway speeds, the trip to the Marshall jail was less than two hours. With this morning's trial blowing up, he felt pulled in two opposite directions. The part of him that had thought about Florida felt like stretching out in the seat and sleeping the whole trip. In fact, since he had turned 65 Joseph had been indulging in short afternoon naps in his office when he wasn't in court. However, as it had been his whole life, his more dominant drive was to work. He pulled the lap top computer from the back seat compartment in front of him and began typing–jotting down his thoughts on each of his pending cases. He had completed perhaps 20 pages of rough notes as they neared Jackson.

Prison Area. Do Not Pick Up Hitchhikers, said the highway sign.

Joseph zipped down the chauffeur division window. "Edward, if you see any of my former clients hitchhiking, don't stop–unless they owe me money." He was laughing, still elated over this morning's victory.

"That isn't likely, sir," answered Edward, the only chauffeur he'd ever had–over ten years now. Edward reminded Joseph of the chauffeur in the movie *Driving Miss Daisy.*

"Which isn't likely, Eddie?" Joseph asked, teasing. "That we ever see a client of mine in Jackson Prison or that we never see a client who still owes me money?"

"Well, neither, I guess Mr. Joseph," Edward chuckled.

Joseph read again the bar association report on Betty Neal's qualifications to be a federal judge. What a coincidence that he was on his way to see her father in jail at the same time as being asked for his opinion on her possible appointment by President Clinton. If he took this case perhaps he'd decline to give an opinion. Possible conflict of interest. Yet the president wanted the opinions of lawyers who had fought against their nominees. No, he would simply disclose the possible conflict.

Soon he saw a sign announcing the Albion McDonald's. "Edward, if you want to stop for lunch, it's all right with me. I'm just going to have one of these Diet Cokes from the refrigerator." Mindful of his tendency to gain weight, Joseph seldom ate lunch.

"I am rather hungry, sir, if you don't mind."

"I don't mind."

As Edward ate his Big Mac in the car, Joseph thought about Betty Neal and the fact she had been born and raised in Albion. He remembered seeing her on the Ren Cen elevators from time to time, and seeing how fat she was. The report he was reading expressed concern about her excess weight–the effect it might have on her life expectancy. Joseph simply could not understand someone like Betty. Good God, if he had a weight problem like that, he would stop eating. That was what his father had taught him. If something was wrong with you, fix it. Don't bellyache. Fix it. On the other hand, he thought, he couldn't very well vote against recommending her to

the President because she was overweight. After all, he wouldn't want someone to vote against him for being black. On the other hand, she could
change being fat, he debated, and there was nothing he could do about
being black. He certainly remembered a time 40 years ago when, if he
could have changed his color, he would have. Today's African-Americans
would never forgive him for once having such thoughts, but they hadn't
been there. They would never know what it was like back then. Well, hell,
fat or not fat, the woman was qualified and so he'd vote for recommending
her to President Clinton.

It was two o'clock when they pulled off I-94 at the Marshall exit and
found their way to the sheriff's headquarters and jail. As he waited for the
receptionist to get off the telephone, Joseph thought about his father. Next
week was the 20th anniversary of his death. He had lived to be 81. He
thought about the many times his father had waited at jails as a bail
bondsman. Even after passing the bar examination after so many years
part-time at law school, his father still had had to write bail bonds to support his family. All those years as a lawyer, and he never had represented a
white man. It was only in later years, after Joseph had joined the practice,
that the senior Jefferson finally earned enough money to give up the bond
business. Joseph thanked God that his father had lived to see his son's success. God, he missed that grizzled old man. Sometimes he ached to talk to
him. If only there were some way his father could have ridden in the limousine with him and shared his triumph today.

"I'm Joseph Jefferson. I'm here to see Dr. David Neal." Joseph handed
his card to the receptionist, who had left her desk to come to the window.

"Yes, sir, Mr. Jefferson. Your secretary called. The paper work is all
ready for you to sign." Joseph loved it when his reputation preceded him
like this. This too was something he wished his father could have seen.

Joseph was shown to David's cell rather than being directed to an interview room. "Dr. Neal is considered a suicide risk," explained the deputy. "We're keeping him under very close scrutiny."

"I see."

"Yes, sir. He's made two attempts."

"Does he seem prone to suicide now?"

"Only that he's very depressed. Eats practically nothing."

It was no wonder Neal was depressed, David thought as they walked along the corridor. The whole stinking place was depressing. Bars. Few windows. Colorless. Even though the jail was for prisoners awaiting trial and those serving short term sentences, the inmates were sallow-skinned and bordering on animal-like.

Noisily the deputy sheriff slid open David's cell door.

"Dr. Neal, my name is Joseph Jefferson. I'm Ruby's uncle. She's asked me to look into your case." Joseph tried to picture what the whiskered gaunt man who stood before him would look like as the defendant in a court room. He was used to seeing inmates who had been yanked from their everyday lives and accused of crime. After a few hours in a jail and wearing prison garb, they rarely looked like the corporate president they had been a few hours ago, or like the securities promoter arrested in his office or the prominent civil lawyer charged with drunken manslaughter after an auto crash. Being jailed did something to people. Facing the criminal justice process instilled fear. It had a leveling effect on all but the most hardened criminals, knocking out from under them any sense of control over their lives. However, David Neal looked different. Joseph detected no fear in the man. He looked as if he had been in jail ten years and expected to remain there until the day he died. Furthermore, he looked as if he didn't care.

"Mr. Jefferson, I appreciate your coming here all the way from Detroit. It must be very inconvenient for you, and I'm sure you're very good at what you do, but I told Ruby I don't want an attorney. There's no point."

"Please, Dr. Neal, I want you to call me Joseph and I'd like to call you David. Is that all right with you, sir?" For a moment Joseph felt as if he were talking to his father in the hospital, just before he had taken that final turn that had resulted in his death.

"Of course it is. I wish I had a better chair for you."

Joseph drew the uncomfortable chair close to David, who sat on his bunk. "The law gives you the right to have an attorney. Indeed it comes close to insisting that you have an attorney. Especially in a case such as this. Do you realize that you could spend the rest of your time locked up in a place even worse than this hole?"

"Mr. Jefferson...Joseph, I don't know if they told you, but I had planned to kill myself that night I killed my wife."

"I know."

"It was only your niece that prevented my doing it."

"I understand that, but that was three weeks ago. Emotions fade. That was spur-of-the-moment."

"I tried suicide a second time at the river the day of Lu's funeral. You see, I'm simply not interested in living any more."

"David, I can understand how you would feel guilty about your wife's death, but it's the law that decides guilt, not you. You may have half a dozen possible defenses. Good Lord, man, they're going for first degree murder."

"This isn't a legal matter. I don't want lawyers quarreling over me. Can't you understand it wouldn't make any difference to me if some jury said I was guilty or innocent? You're wrong about feeling guilty. I don't feel guilty. What I did was the right thing. It's just that I have no interest in defending myself."

"You're depressed. You shouldn't be making decisions in your frame of mind." Joseph had never encountered such a client. The others were eager to get off.

"Certainly, I'm depressed. My wife is dead and I had planned to be dead along side her. Now they're trying to make me keep living. First they wouldn't let Lu die and now they won't let me die. That's what makes me depressed."

"Depressed is one thing, but I can't understand why anyone would want to die."

"Why would I want to live?" David had a grim smile as he looked at the lawyer. "I've had no reason to live for these past years."

"Ruby tells me you had everything a man of your age could ask. Retirement after an illustrious career at a prestigious college. Respect. Enough income. Good health."

"When I retired I thought all that was going to be true. I had painted this magnificent picture in my mind. I would write books that would be received with great acclaim. I would research all the subjects I never had time for. I would give lectures. Maybe the Carl Jung Lectures at the University of Michigan. Oh, it was a real ego trip."

"Perhaps your expectations were too high."

"Too high? Perhaps," David pondered, "but no higher than I've always had. One doesn't control these things."

Joseph was frustrated. He didn't like trying to persuade someone to defend himself. Furthermore, he felt any attempt to convince David would be fruitless.

"What happened to all those plans of yours?"

"My books were outdated before they were written. No one cared about them. Oh, my publisher was polite enough, but publishing is a business and they're not in the business of making some has-been professor feel good."

"But you had your life on campus. You had your family."

"I had Lu, yes. Thank God, I had Lu. She was the only thing that kept me going for years and now she's gone."

"My own wife died almost five years ago. It was a terrible blow, but I never thought of giving up. Do you mind if I tell you a bit of what I feel about life?" Despite his frustration, Joseph liked David. He wished he could find a way to help him.

"Of course not. You've come all this way." David smiled a grim smile.

Despite his feeling that arguing with David was a lost cause, Joseph waded ahead. He had tried too many lawsuits to give up when it looked as if he were going to lose. "My father always told me that life is for living. Simple as that. 'Life is for living.' I'm 66 years old and I've discovered my father was correct. Life is not for philosophizing. It's not searching for some insightful purpose that everyone else has missed. Frankly, I don't have much patience with people who are always seeking the so-called meaning of life. You see my father's grandfather was born a slave. My ancestors never had the time or the inclination to worry about such nonsense as the purpose of life. For my father, life was nothing but struggle against odds, but that man absolutely loved life. Oh, I grant you he didn't love every minute of it. He didn't love being barely able to support his family and he certainly didn't love doors being slammed in his face because of his color, but he loved life, the struggle included. He taught me that the struggles *are* life."

"He sounds like a wonderful man."

"He was. Do you know what he'd have said to me if I had told him what you've been telling me? That I was tired of life? That my life might as well be over?"

"No."

"He'd call me crazy—absolutely crazy. I can hear him now. 'Joseph,' he'd say with that patronizing tone he'd get, 'Why don't you get off your ass and get out there and live? The most money I ever made in a year was $10,000,' he'd say. 'A lot of times you make that much money in one *day* for Christ's sake.' And he'd be right. Plenty of days I do make $10,000. I would be crazy to complain about life."

"But you can't argue that money is the purpose of life."

"I'm not trying to argue that. All I'm saying is you don't find a man who is struggling to keep his family alive wondering about the meaning of life. He'll tell you the purpose of life is to stay alive and to *live* and I don't think I could disagree with him no matter how much money I had."

"Well…"

"I think it's in the Bible someplace, "Revel in the day the Lord has made" something like that. Man, that's the absolute truth. That's all there is to it. Revel in each day. Every day is unique–a day to be lived to its fullest. I didn't use to believe that myself. I thought I could only be happy on the good days–not the bad ones, but as I've gotten older I've learned that each day is for living. There is no other purpose. No deep meaning. Just living, until it's over."

"Well, I suppose thinking that way serves you well."

"Let me tell you something," Joseph continued. "Something I've never told anyone before."

David nodded his assent.

"The day of my wife's funeral I was happy. It was a bad day all right, but I was happy. Can you believe that? Oh, there was a part of me that was totally destroyed–wondering what I would do without her. But there was another part of me–a wiser part: that her suffering was over–that I was alive–that I still had the opportunity to live and that I could choose to make it only one bad day. I could have moped around for the rest of my life, but there was no other real choice except to *live*."

"There was a time in my life when I would have told my students exactly that," David responded. "But in these past years I discovered I've been lying to myself."

"Lying to yourself? In what way?" In all his years of practice Joseph had never been party to such a strange conversation.

"Look, I can understand it when you say a person should live one day at a time and enjoy it. I'm sorry, but to me that's surface. Simplistic. Lying to ourselves to make ourselves feel better."

"Feel better? Feel better about what?"

"Feel better about the truth of the universe."

"And this truth of the universe is…?" Joseph braced himself for more pessimistic jargon.

"That life is quite unimportant."

"Unimportant? Try saying that to a dying man! He'd give anything to live another day."

"That's because he's frightened."

"Maybe, but…"

"My point is, we are all much too preoccupied with living," said David.

"What's wrong with that? Life is living!"

"Joseph, look," David continued. "Look around the world. We've made the world evolve around the life of man. Our novels are about man. Our paintings are about man. Our movies. Our plays. Our religion is about life after death, because what people really want from religion is to keep from dying."

"What could be more natural?"

"But you see, when you're dead you're dead. Except for a few people, you might as well have not existed in the first place. And soon those few people will be dead. What difference does it matter whether any of us lived? I look around the campus. Every building, most of the rooms are named after somebody. Do you know why people want things named after them?"

"I have an idea, but why?"

"Because they want to keep living. Well, I've got news for them. When they're dead, they've become nothing but a plaque. In a few years nobody will remember them, plaque or no plaque. They'll be just as dead as anyone else—reduced to some meaningless lettering.

"Have you always been this pessimistic?"

"I don't call it pessimism. I call it realism. Look at Abraham Lincoln. Everyone loves Abraham Lincoln, right?"

"Of course."

"Came from a nervous breakdown to be President."

"So I've read. A remarkable man."

"But he's as dead as everyone else. In a million years, do you think it will matter whether Abraham Lincoln lived or died?"

"Well, sure, a million years."

"A million years is nothing. Take prehistoric man. We have a few bones left. That's all. Do their lives really matter? Of course not. No one cares whether they loved their women, loved their children."

"It mattered to them," Joseph argued.

"A million years from now it's not going to matter whether the South was allowed to break away from the Union. Whether some ruler freed the slaves."

"That's my very point. All that's left to us is to revel in each day. Enjoying it. Living it. Each day is our day and we should make it special. You talk about Lincoln. It was Lincoln who said he'd found a man is about as happy as he makes up his mind to be." Joseph paused to let David absorb what he'd said. "Well, I believe that. That's what we've been talking about. You're saying each day is meaningless. Well, I'm saying it's not. I'm saying life is more important than anything in the world."

"I guess I'm saying nothing in the world is very important. You see I'm ready to die. I've had a decent life, but now it's over. I just want it to end. It doesn't really matter whether it ends in jail ten years from now or whether it ends tomorrow by my hanging from the ceiling of this cell."

Joseph did not know what more to say. Perhaps he had said it all. "Well, my friend, I'm certainly not in the business of convincing people to continue living."

"I'm sure I'm a very strange man to you, but that's the way I feel." David said. "Ruby has told me all about you. I'm certain that if any lawyer could do anything for me, it would be you. But even if I wanted to fight, I couldn't afford you."

"Who said anything about money? I came here because of Ruby. Your case intrigued me. Mercy killing is an unsettled area of the law."

"Well, somebody else is going to have to settle it. I appreciate your seeing me, but I don't want an attorney. I don't want a trial. I simply want to get it over with."

"David, I can't imagine anyone's not wanting to live. You know the possibility of taking my wife's life occurred to me too—or helping her to take her own. Those last few weeks were extremely unpleasant, to say the least."

"It took me a long time to make the decision about Lu."

"But I made the opposite decision. I guess when it comes down to it I don't believe in mercy killing."

"Then why did you come here at all?"

"Because I believe you had the right to disagree with me without going to jail for it."

In the limousine on the way back to Albion, where he would dine with Ruby, Joseph pondered his conversation with David. He felt a melancholia which he couldn't escape. The professor's ideas could not be simply shrugged off as the rambling of an intellectual nearing the end of his life. He had to admit the possibility that David was correct. It was true that in the very last analysis life might be meaningless. But Joseph thought of himself as a practical man. He would never accept David's philosophy—even if he were living a hopeful lie. To him, life was not meaningless. He enjoyed life and he intended to keep living it to its fullest.

The limousine left the interstate and turned onto Ruby's street. Joseph shook his head ruefully. He wished David wanted a legal defense. He knew it was just such challenges as this that made his life count for something.

-32-

Kalamazoo Avenue in Marshall, Michigan, lined with beautifully restored 19th century homes of near-mansion size, had experienced the first thaw of March, clearing the cityscape of snow. Looking out the window of her home of 15 years, Billie Croft noticed her large lawn still had vestiges of green left over from last year. It wouldn't be too long before the barren stately trees showed signs of spring.

Her husband, John, would be returning from New York tonight. She was to pick him up at the Battle Creek airport. Billie could see the postman delivering the mail next door. She was in charge of the church board of trustees' meeting at Schuler's Restaurant today, but she'd look at the mail before she got ready for the meeting.

"Good morning, Paul." Paul had been their postman their entire 15 years in Marshall. When John had started at the advertising agency in Battle Creek, they had dreamed of someday owning one of these fine homes, where they would raise their daughters. They loved Marshall's small town atmosphere.

"Morning Mrs. Croft. Won't be long 'til April's here. Mr. Croft comes home today, doesn't he?"

"Yes. Tonight." Billie took the offered small packet of mail. Although it was a 20 mile commute to Battle Creek for John, they had bought their home in Marshall as soon as he was awarded a partnership. Billie had quit the insurance agency where she had worked since college and devoted herself to her family and restoring their home. "We'll see you tomorrow, Paul," Billie called after the postman as she thumbed through the mail.

She immediately noticed the official-looking envelope with the return address *Calhoun County Circuit Court.*

Billie sat at the breakfast bar that had been built from a timber hewn in the last century. "You have been summoned for jury duty...Report to the Circuit Court in Marshall, Michigan..." A few years back she had received a jury notice, but had managed an excuse. She couldn't remember the reason she had given, but it had bothered her conscience that she hadn't served. Now that the girls were living away, maybe she should serve, she thought. She had been a little bored lately. Maybe it would do her good. She'd have to speak to John about it.

"I think it would be a great idea," said John at breakfast. "You've always been a law-and-order person. This will give you a chance to see how the system actually works."

"I think I will," Billie responded. "If it won't interfere with you too much."

"Don't worry about it. This New York thing is going to keep me hopping for at least a couple of months. It'll give you something to do. You know I've always wondered what it would be like to be on a jury."

"Oh, they'd kick you off. I hear the defense will kick you off if you've got too much intelligence."

"Come on, Billie, you were a Phi Beta Kappa yourself," her husband protested.

"I'll send in the questionnaire. Maybe I'll get to serve on some murder or something. That would be exciting, wouldn't it?"

"I'd hate to be the defendant. Knowing you, you'd lock him up and throw away the key."

Billie chuckled. It was true she'd been vocal about the way the crime rate had been increasing these past years. She supposed she might not be permitted to serve, but she ought to send in the questionnaire anyway. If some defense lawyer kicked her off, at least she would have done her civic duty.

-33-

The sun was just coming up to Eddie's back as I-94 crossed from Michigan into Indiana. His old Chevy was filled with hastily packed belongings.

Ruby's words of last evening repeated in his mind. "Eddie, my Uncle Joseph saw your grandfather in jail today." Ruby had come by the house. The minute she entered the living room he could tell she had bad news. Last week Ruby had told him her uncle would look into the possibility of taking the case.

"Uncle Joseph says he's never seen a case like this. Your Grandfather simply does not want anyone to defend him. In fact, he's fearful Dr. Neal will take his life if they give him a chance."

The news did not come as a surprise to Eddie. From the time he saw him in jail, Eddie had given up any real hope his grandfather would do anything to try to get out of jail so they could go back to their old way of life.

As soon as Ruby had left last night, Eddie had begun to fill the Chevy with his things. All he could think of was getting out of Albion as fast as he could, before his mother got some kind of court order making him live with her. He was fed up with Michigan. With Granna dead, no one really wanted him any more. Grandfather had deserted him. His Dad didn't want him—he knew that. And his mother didn't love him—she only wanted to make him do what she wanted—like it had always been.

He had not shed a tear since Granna's funeral, but as he crossed the Michigan border he began to cry. Except when he was little, he'd never been outside Michigan. He didn't know where he was going, except he was headed west. He didn't have much money and his car was not in good condition. Although he was determined, the truth was he was frightened. He didn't know what was going to happen to him and he didn't care as long as they didn't find him. He hoped they never found him. He was so mad at Grandfather. Didn't Grandfather know he needed him to be out of jail? That attorney was good. Ruby said he was best in the state. He could have gotten him off somehow.

Eddie saw a police car on the on ramp and slowed down. The last thing he wanted was a ticket.

He wished Grandfather hadn't killed Granna. Things would have been all right if he'd just have let Granna alone–to just die on her own. They would never have put Grandfather in jail and everything would still be all right. It was a stupid thing to do–killing Granna that way. Sometimes he hated his grandfather. Like right now. Maybe he shouldn't, but right now he absolutely hated him!

It was dark in Iowa when Eddie stopped at the roadside park to get some sleep in the car. He had bought a map of the U.S. Interstate System and had been looking at it all day on the seat next to him. California. That's where he would go. He calculated he would still have some money when he got there and then he would decide what to do. San Francisco sounded like a good place. He'd always liked the Giants. They'd never be like the Tigers, but he could root for them too. After all the Giants were in a different league. He was still scared, but he felt better now that he was out of Michigan and his mother couldn't get him. He'd figure out something after he got to San Francisco.

*   *   *

Michigan seemed a million miles away as Eddie crossed the Bay Bridge into San Francisco. Eddie was agape. The city was spectacular. A lot more tall buildings than Detroit. He'd had to get two new tires in Utah and his money was getting low, but he figured he had enough for at least a week–maybe ten days–if he was careful and stayed at the Y. The first thing he wanted to do was see Candlestick Park. He put on his Tiger cap that had been on the seat beside him. Maybe he should get a Giants cap, he thought. It wouldn't be long before the season started.

It had been an exciting day for Eddie. He had checked into the YMCA. It was okay, but he knew he'd have to find a cheap place to park his car. Candlestick Park was just like on TV. He found a sports shop on Fisherman's Wharf and bought a Giants cap. He went to the top of Coit Tower. He drove out to the Golden Gate Bridge, but when he found out there was a toll he did not actually drive on the bridge.

Four days had passed. Eddie had gotten a job doing dishes at a seafood restaurant, but he wouldn't be paid for a while yet. He figured he had just enough money to last. The Y was okay, but especially at night he was lonely. He missed his grandfather. He missed Ruby. He wondered if they worried about him or even thought about him. He wasn't so mad at his grandfather any more. After all he had done what he thought was right. It couldn't be much fun being in jail. If it was lonely at the Y, think how lonely it must be for Grandfather in jail. Maybe he should write home. Yes, he'd think about writing. He really ought to. Maybe they were worried.

-34-

Initially David had not intended a hunger strike. It started simply because of a case of the flu. On top of his depression, he felt lethargic and his stomach was too upset for him to eat. The flu lasted only three days, but he still had no appetite. It was when the prison guards insisted that he must begin eating that the idea of deliberate starvation occurred to him.

Since the meeting with Joseph Jefferson, no one had visited him. He was aware of a dim hope that Eddie might come by. Perhaps even aware of a wish that Jefferson would want to see him again. But his primary emotion was clear–he wanted to die.

As in the Albion jail, out of fear of suicide the guards here in the Marshall prison provided him with no utensils of any type. If he were to eat it, had to be with his hands. He had been assigned a special cell for would-be suicides, where there was no way he could kill himself. They kept his belt and there was nothing high enough, such as a fixture, from which he could hang himself using his bed covers. He wondered if his permanent cell in Jackson Prison would have the same safeguards. Surely once he was there he could find a way to take his life.

It had been one full week since he had eaten when the guard told him he had a visitor–Ruby.

"Dr. Neal, you must begin eating again." Ruby was wearing her nurse's uniform and no longer used a crutch.

David tried to stand to greet her, but was too weak to rise from his uncomfortable bed. He managed a smile on his gaunt and unshaven face.

"They thought they could force me to keep living, but I've fooled them. I've found a way out."

Ruby had tears in her eyes as she bent over him. "At least take some liquid. If you don't do something, they'll put you in the hospital and pump you full of fluids. They're not going to let you die."

"They can't do that, can they?"

"I'm sure they can."

David frowned. This was a possibility he had not thought about. "Your leg. Is your leg all right now? I wish you hadn't tried to stop me."

Ruby took David by his hand. "I'm nearly as good as new. You can see I'm already back working."

"I want to thank you for having your uncle see me. I don't mean to seem ungrateful, but I just don't want an attorney."

"He feels he could help you—maybe get a jury to give you a lesser charge."

"I'm sure he's very competent. I liked him too. I wish I had something to live for, the way he does." David was so weak he felt as if he had to force out the words. He was glad for Ruby's visit, but he didn't want to talk about lawyers and trials.

"His wife died too, you know."

"He told me. Don't you see, Ruby? You younger people, even your uncle, your lives are still ahead of you. Mine is behind me—gone." He knew he could never make her understand.

Ruby started to say something more—as if to argue with him—but released his hand and sat on the lone simple chair.

"I'm afraid I have some bad news for you."

"More bad news?"

"Eddie's disappeared—gone."

"He's with Betty, I'm sure."

"No. I called her. She didn't seem too much concerned. Said he'd run away before."

"He's not at our house?"

"I've tried every day for the last three days. His car's gone."

"He must be staying with one of his friends."

"I don't think so. The parents would have called," Ruby said.

"Who would they have called? There isn't anybody to call."

"I don't know, but I'm worried."

"Have you tried his father?"

"I don't know how to reach him."

"He's listed in the book. You could call him."

"I'll do that. That's probably where he is. I didn't think of that."

"Even if he's not with his father, I'll bet he'll call you any day now."

"Could your daughter be right? Would he have run away?"

"I don't think so. Where would he go?" David asked.

"He was so afraid the court would make him live with his mother. Did you know she's being appointed a federal judge by President Clinton?"

"A federal judge?"

"That's what she said. She's wrapping up her law practice."

"Lu would have been proud. I wish I could be." David paused. "Betty–a federal judge." He shook his head. "I wish she would want me to be there when she's sworn in. Wasn't she at all worried about Eddie?"

"She said she's given up on Eddie. He's going to be 18 in a few days. She said there's nothing she can do."

"It figures. That's the way she is. It never would occur to her to tell Eddie she loves him and wants to help him. All she would think about is threats. I don't think she ever wanted a child in the first place. Where do you think he might be?"

"I just wish I knew he was all right," Ruby said.

David was angry with Betty. She would rather be a federal judge than a mother to her son.

As Ruby left the cell, David felt alone and defeated. He had been right in telling Joseph Jefferson there was nothing in the world left for him. With Eddie gone, it was even worse. He would find it easy to continue fasting. They could take him to the hospital. They could try every trick they could think of, but they could not force him to keep living.

-35-

It was March 27, 1994, Eddie's 18th birthday. San Francisco had been much more expensive than he had ever expected. He had just collected his pay in cash. Not quite $200. He knew he wasn't earning enough washing dishes, but had no idea what else to do. He made a deal with a guy who owned a gas station south of Market Street. He parked his car there free for pumping gas Saturday nights. He hadn't driven his car, because it was too expensive. Besides, he walked to the restaurant every day. San Francisco was a pretty small place.

It was midnight as he walked home from work to the Y. It had been a very lonely 18th birthday. He hadn't even mentioned it to anyone. Maybe he could get one of the guys at the Y to go with him to the movies tomorrow. He wanted to do something to celebrate.

Turk Street was only one block from the Y, but he had never walked there at night before. At the Y they had warned him that Turk Street had a lot of tough characters, but he knew he could handle himself, so he decided to walk that way.

"Hey, good-looking," the woman near the closed store front called out to Eddie. "For a guy as cute as you, I'd give you a really good time. If you like girls."

She was sexy in her very short skirt, high heels and seamed stockings. Eddie figured she was a prostitute. He had seen a woman dressed that way on Sutter the other night when he had walked home that way. A guy had picked her up in his car.

"Sorry, but I don't have any money." Eddie figured that was a good way to say no. The guys at the Y had told him prostitutes were serious AIDS risks. Eddie wanted no part of AIDS.

"What's the matter, cutie? Don't you like girls?" she asked.

"I'm sorry, maybe some other time."

Eddie was relieved that she hadn't given him any trouble. There were no cars coming, so he crossed against the signal. He decided he should cut over to Golden Gate Street where the Y was and get off Turk earlier than he had planned. He'd heard there were a lot of drugs done on Turk.

"Hey, young fella, can you spare a buck so I can get something to eat?" San Francisco had quite a few beggars asking for money. Eddie figured most of them were using the money for drugs, but at least they were polite when you said no.

This guy was an old guy. Almost as old as Grandfather. It must be awful to be that old and have to beg for money. Eddie reached into his pocket and pulled out all his money. He gave the old man a dollar.

"Thanks, young man. I appreciate it."

It was then that Eddie felt the gun against the back of his neck.

"That's not very generous for a guy with a roll like that," said the voice behind him.

Eddie whirled around to confront the gunman, but before he could raise his fist he took a sharp blow from the gun barrel on the side of his face. The blow staggered him, but he did not fall.

"Now, I suggest that you be a nice little boy and give me that roll of money, or do I have to hit you again?" It was too dark for Eddie to see much of the man. He was white and kind of small. His clothes were scruffy.

"Jeez, man," Eddie replied, feeling the blood on the side of his face. "I worked hard for this money. Why don't you get a job like the rest of us?"

The force of the second blow knocked Eddie to the sidewalk. He cried out in pain and for a moment thought he was going to lose consciousness.

"Smart ass. I'll just take that, if you don't mind," said the gunman grabbing Eddie's money from his outstretched hand. The gunman rifled though the money and flipped a bill toward the beggar. "Maybe this will teach you to be more generous next time."

"You son-of-a-bitch!" Eddie screamed after the gunman, who ran down Turk and disappeared at the corner. The blood was gushing from the side of his face.

"You'd better get some help, young fella," said the beggar.

"Yeah. I'd better get to the Y right away."

"Here," said the beggar. "Take this money he gave me. I don't want no part of money like that."

-36-

March 27, 1994 had been a special day for Betty Neal. She had been sworn in as a United States District Court Judge for the Eastern District of Michigan. Although the position meant a substantial cut in income from her law partnership, for her it was her ultimate achievement.

When she was in law school she had been a moot court judge, triggering a dream of one day becoming a real judge–perhaps a Wayne County Circuit Court Judge. But being a *federal* judge was beyond anything she had imagined. Federal judges held lifetime appointments. Few, if any, positions held as much prestige in the Detroit area. She would have a magnificent courtroom. She would have the privilege of knowing her written opinions would be in every law library in the land. One day she might be appointed to the United States Court of Appeals or even the Supreme Court itself.

This afternoon her law firm had given her a party at the firm's offices. All of her partners attended as well as various leading attorneys from the city, such as Joseph Thomas Jefferson, the prominent criminal attorney who officed up one flight. Betty had heard Jefferson was on the American Bar Association Committee to which President Clinton, following custom, had submitted her name. Obviously the committee had rated her "qualified."

It was now past one in the morning. United States District Judge Betty Neal lay alone, sleepless, in her bed in her Bloomfield Hills mansion, going over the events of the day.

She was not unmindful of the fact that her several partners who were Democrats were also personal friends of two of President Clinton's cabinet members, and that her partner, Jack Snyder, often invited Michigan's Democratic United States Senator to golf at Birmingham Country Club. The Senator's endorsement had been vital.

As Betty decided to take a sleeping pill, she also was not unmindful of the fact that the four people who had once mattered most to her had not been present at the day's events.

First there was her husband—actually now her ex-husband—who, no doubt, was sleeping like a baby in the same bed as his skinny slut girl-friend.

Second, there was her mother. She would have given anything if her mother could have been there. She knew that without her mother this day would have never happened.

Next, there was her father. Betty knew he deserved to be in jail for defy-ing her wish that her mother remain on the life support system, but, for the first time that she could remember, she wished her father had been with her today. She wanted him to be proud of her.

Finally, there was Eddie. How she wished she could have handled him better. Last week she had hired a private investigator to try to locate him, but so far there was not a trace of her son. If only Eddie could have kissed her on the cheek today in front of everybody and said, "I'm proud of you, Mom." Maybe even, "I love you, Mom."

The fact that today was Eddie's 18th birthday added to her misery. Her little boy had become a man today and she had no idea where he was. In fact, she had no idea whether he was even alive.

Crying, Betty knew she would never get to sleep. She found her way from the bedroom to the kitchen. She opened the freezer and took out the unopened package of ice cream. As she dipped the spoon into the ice cream she did not feel much like a United States District Court Judge.

It was not until an hour later that the tears completely stopped. The whole quart of ice cream was finished. She climbed the stairs to her bed, knowing at last she could get to sleep.

-37-

The doctor at the hospital emergency room took three stitches to close each of two wounds caused by Eddie's pistol-whipping. The bandages wrapped completely around his head under his chin, leaving his face, ears and the back of his hair exposed. Eddie thought he must look a sorry sight as he walked into the police station to report the robbery.

"I'm sorry, Mr. Erickson," the police officer said. "But this sort of thing happens all too often, especially on Turk Street. I wish you hadn't flashed your money in public that way."

"Do you think there's any chance I'll get it back?" Eddie asked, angry that he couldn't give a dollar to a beggar without being mugged.

"No chance at all. He's already spent it on drugs. You can count on it. If we catch him at all, it'll be when he robs again...somebody else. If you move from the Y please let us know, because if we're lucky we'll have him in a line-up someday."

"What am I supposed to do for money? I won't get paid for two weeks."

"I'm sorry, young man, but this sort of thing happens all the time. Maybe the welfare office can help you. There's an agency over on Gough Street that might lend you a hand–and you could try the welfare office."

Christ, Eddie thought, as he stormed along the street toward the Y. To think I thought San Francisco was a beautiful city. What was a guy supposed to do anyway? Even though it was daytime, this time he steered clear of Turk Street. An idea hit him as he walked down Golden Gate. If he could get a little money, say a hundred bucks, he could drive down the coast. He'd heard there were plenty of small towns between here and L.A. He'd get some kind of job and be away from all this mugging shit. But where to get any money? Grandfather was in jail. His mother was out of the question. Maybe his father.

From the pay phone at the Y he got his father's number and called collect.

"Mr. Erickson is in New York, but I'll accept the call." Eddie recognized the voice of his father's girlfriend. Eddie had only met her once. He guessed she was living there now. "Yes, operator, I'll take the call," she repeated.

"When will Dad be home?"

"I don't know, Eddie. He went to New York and he wasn't sure whether it would be tomorrow or the next day. Is there something wrong?"

"Yeah. I got robbed. I'm stuck here in San Francisco with no money."

"Oh, Eddie, I'm so sorry. Here, I can give you the number of your father's hotel. Do you want that?"

"Yeah, I guess so." Dammit, Eddie thought. If his mother and father hadn't gotten a divorce he wouldn't be in this fix.

"I'm sorry, but Mr. Erickson doesn't answer the phone. He must be out, but I'm allowed to leave a number if you wish," the long distance operator told Eddie.

"No," Eddie answered feeling discouraged. "I'm calling from a pay phone."

Eddie could think of only one way out of his mess. He would have to sell his car. There was no other way out. Maybe he could get a thousand for it.

It took him half an hour to walk to the gas station where he kept his Chevy. He didn't know what he would do after he sold it, but with the money he'd have a while to think. Maybe he should keep his job and keep living at the Y. Not everybody in San Francisco could be a mugger.

"Hi, Eddie. What the hell happened to you?" Said the gas station owner, pointing to Eddie's bandages.

"I got mugged. He took every dime I had. I've decided I've got to sell my car. Do you know where there are any used car lots?"

"Sell your car?"

"Yes."

"I figured it was you who had taken your car."

"What do you mean?"

"Your car's been gone a couple of days now. I figured you had taken it."

"I didn't take my car! The last time I saw it was Saturday. Right there where I've been keeping it."

"Well, I'm sorry, kid, but it's been gone. Like I said, two days. I figured you took it."

"Well, I didn't. Goddammit, where's my car? What kind of city is this anyway?" Eddie was dismayed and angry.

"Look, Eddie, don't blame me. I didn't steal your goddamn car. You have to expect things like this in a big city. That's why insurance is so fucking expensive."

"I don't have insurance."

"You don't have insurance?"

"You heard me right. I don't have insurance."

"Christ, Eddie. I don't mean to rub salt in your wounds, but you got to have insurance in this day and age."

Eddie didn't know what to do. He was mad and ready to cry at the same time. He loved that car, and some bastard had stolen it. Probably for drugs too. What was he going to do now?

Eddie felt desperate when he got back to the Y. His rent was due in three days and he couldn't think of what to do.

"I'm sorry, sir, there still is no answer at Mr. Erickson's room," said the operator.

"Do you have any idea when he'll be back?"

"I'm sorry, sir."

Eddie decided to try another idea. He would try to call his grandfather in jail. It was after six o'clock in Michigan. Maybe he would get lucky and that grouchy receptionist would not be on duty.

It took forever to get the telephone number for the jail from Information. Eddie had not known that the Marshall, Michigan area code was different from Albion's. Finally he got the right number.

"I have a collect call for Dr. David Neal from his grandson," said the long distance operator. She was very understanding when Eddie explained he'd been mugged. "It's very important."

"I'm sorry, operator," said the person at the jail. "This is a jail and Neal is an inmate here."

"But it's vital that my party reach him."

"Look, operator, inmates aren't allowed to take calls, let alone collect calls." The voice sounded disgusted.

"But can't you help? My party says it's an extreme emergency."

"I don't doubt that it is, but we have rules here. There's nothing I can do." The receptionist hung up abruptly.

"I'm sorry, sir, but you heard."

Suddenly Eddie had an idea. Ruby. He would try Ruby. Maybe Ruby could get in to see Grandfather. The only other possibility was his mother and he would go begging on Turk Street before he did that.

"Eddie, where are you?" asked Ruby.

"San Francisco."

"I've been worried about you."

"Things haven't been going so well, Ruby. Some guy pistol-whipped me."

"Are you all right?"

"Yeah. I will be in a few days. I've got bandages all over my head."

"Have you called either of your parents?"

"I couldn't get hold of Dad and there's no way I'll call Mom."

"Now, Eddie, you really should tell your mother. She's bound to be worried–disappearing like that."

"Has she called you?"

"No, but some private investigator she hired called me."

"Yeah, well she just wants to get me to come back. You've got to promise me you won't tell her I called."

"All right, Eddie, but…"

"Listen, Ruby I'm in a bad way here. Can you go see Grandfather and see if he'll send me some money? See, I was going to sell my car, but it's been stolen too."

"Oh, Eddie, I'm so sorry."

"Yeah. I'm dead broke. Can you go see Grandfather?"

"I'm afraid I've got bad news. Dr. Neal is fasting. He hasn't eaten anything for over a week now."

"Why's he doing that?"

"Well, Eddie, I'm afraid he wants to kill himself."

"Can he do that?"

"I don't think so. They'll take him to the hospital first. It's a crazy system, Eddie. They want him to be alive so they can put him away for the rest of his life."

"Yeah. It's crazy all right."

"He won't let a lawyer defend him. You know my Uncle Joseph—the one who is such a good lawyer?"

"Yeah."

"He went to see your grandfather, but he doesn't want to be defended."

"And when I need him too."

"Listen, Eddie, I'll go see your grandfather if they'll let me, but I've got a few dollars in my account. Give me your address. I'll wire you one…no, make that two hundred dollars."

"Ruby, you'd do that for me?"

"Of course I would. Now give me your address."

-38-

The next morning Eddie walked up Golden Gate from the YMCA on his way to Western Union to get Ruby's money. He felt guilty about taking money from her and resolved to pay her back just as soon as he could. He didn't know what he was going to do about his plight. He wanted to be away from the mess in Michigan. He wanted to make his own way–his own life–but should he stay in San Francisco? Should he find some small town like he was thinking yesterday? He certainly didn't want some dead end job like he had now. He felt trapped. He had to find a way out.

As he neared Van Ness, he noticed a sign he had missed before. It was on the first floor of the tall building. *United States Marines*, said the sign. He walked into the lobby. The suite contained separate recruiting offices for each of the armed services. He recalled his high school friend talking about his brother who had joined the Marines. Eddie had met him once and had been impressed by the uniform.

The Marine recruiting officer at the main desk interrupted his conversation with another young man to speak to Eddie.

"Are you interested in the Marines?" he asked.

"Yes, I'd like to talk about it."

"It'll be about 15 minutes before I'm finished here. While you're waiting take a look around."

Eddie saw that the offices were businesslike and efficient. There was a setup to watch videotapes, and displays about Marine history and famous battles. Eddie was impressed. He took several brochures from the table and sat down to read them. They explained the educational benefits available–college and vocational opportunities while in the Marines and college benefits after serving four years. Eddie recalled how striking his friend's brother had looked in uniform. He was glad he had stopped by. The Marines were something he should look into.

The recruiter told him he would have to pass a stiff test. The starting pay was about $800 a month. He had to pay for his own uniform. Basic Training would be 13 arduous weeks at the Marine Corps Recruit Depot in San Diego. Many men–the recruiter always called them men–not guys or young men–did not make it through Basic Training. If he made it, he would be entitled to be called a United States Marine and his specialty training would begin. Ultimately, he would be assigned overseas–perhaps Okinawa or maybe even some hot spot like the Persian Gulf or Somalia.

"How long would it take before I could join?" Eddie asked.

"Normally it's two or three months before we have an opening."

"That long? I need to do something right away."

"The Marines don't want you to be in a rush. The Corps invests a lot in you and we don't want you dropping out. It will be tough. You're going to go from being a kid to a man. We don't like second thoughts. Besides, I think you need to wait until those stitches come out." Eddie had told him about the mugging.

"Let me think about it, okay? I'll come back tomorrow."

"Sometimes we have openings for immediate filling. Somebody might drop out at the last minute–that sort of thing. I'll check it out if you'd like."

"I'd like that."

"Be here at ten o'clock tomorrow all right?"

"I'll be here."

-39-

The guard escorted Ruby down the depressing corridor of the Marshall jail to David's cell. As she was on her way to work, she was wearing her nurse's uniform. She was shocked when she saw him. He looked as if he had lost nearly 15 pounds from his already lean frame.

David did not attempt to get up from his bed, but acknowledged Ruby's visit with a wan smile. She thought he looked like death itself. She was surprised they had not taken him to the hospital by now.

"I'm glad you came," David croaked out.

"It's very upsetting to see you this way, Dr. Neal. You belong in a lecture room or a faculty office–not in this stinking place, starving yourself to death." Ruby had not planned to come on strong like this, but she was miffed at her former mentor's attitude, despite all she had done to help him.

"You're as bad as your uncle," David chuckled weakly. "Don't want to give up on me, do you?"

"You're darn right I don't want to give up on you. I took a bullet in the leg so you wouldn't kill yourself. Remember?"

"I suppose I have been ungrateful."

"I spend every day helping people who want to stay alive. I swear I just don't understand you."

David smiled as if he didn't expect her to understand. "Don't you see? I simply don't have any reason to keep on going–especially if I'm going to be in jail."

"Don't have any reason?" Ruby raised her voice. "What about your grandson?"

"He hasn't shown up yet?"

"Oh, he's shown up all right, but he's in trouble–deep trouble."

"What you mean *deep trouble*?"

"He's been mugged. He's in San Francisco–all alone."

"San Francisco? Mugged? What do you mean *mugged*?" With a look of shocked concern David managed to sit up.

"He was robbed. Some robber took all his money–every last dime–and on top of that he pistol-whipped him."

"Oh my God, I can't believe this would happen!" David's voice was stronger.

"They took a bunch of stitches–sewed him up and bandaged him."

"He's going to be all right, isn't he?"

"I'm really not sure–poor kid. He was going to sell his car to make ends meet."

"He must be desperate. That car is everything to him."

"It gets worse. On top of everything, somebody went and stole his car. He called me yesterday. He's flat broke. Eddie is across the country with no money, no one to turn to except you!"

"This is terrible. Poor Eddie." David's voice was stronger.

"He needs you more than any person has ever needed you and here you are on a starvation kick! I'm sorry, but I'm really angry."

"He could've called me. Why didn't he call me? I would have sent him money." David shook his head in disbelief.

"You're in jail. He didn't even have money to make calls. He tried to call you, but they don't let people charged with murder take collect calls from their grandchildren no matter how broke they are."

"My God, what is he going to do? I don't know if they'll let me send any money from here in jail."

"I already sent him some, but I only had $200."

Ruby watched as tears formed in David's eyes. It was sad to see him looking so old and forlorn, but maybe this would finally arouse him. He struggled to his feet.

"You're right, Ruby. I've been a selfish old man. I've been only thinking of myself, haven't I?"

Ruby did not answer.

"I'm the only family Eddie's got left any more. There's nobody left for him to count on."

"I'm afraid that's true. I can be his friend, but I can't be his family. You know very well Mrs. Neal wouldn't want you in jail like this when Eddie needs you so badly."

"You're right."

"I know I'm right."

A new spark of life appeared in David's eyes. "Ruby?"

"Yes, Dr. Neal."

"You know that uncle of yours?"

"Of course. Uncle Joseph."

"Yes."

"What about him?"

"Maybe I'd better talk to him again. Do you think he might take my case?"

"He told me he wasn't interested if you didn't want to really give it a fight."

"Well, maybe I should try." A new look of determination appeared on David's face. "You tell him I'd like to talk to him again. Please tell your uncle I don't see how any lawyer can help me, but tell him I'm ready to fight if he is. I've got to do it for Eddie. It's what Lu would want."

Ruby could hardly contain her joy. "That's what I was hoping you would say! If anybody can help, it will be my Uncle Joseph."

"I hope so, Ruby; I hope he's the miracle man you say he is."

-40-

Eddie returned to the Marine Recruiting Office at ten o'clock that morning.

"Well, Mr. Erickson," said the recruiter. "Have you decided whether to see if you're good enough to be a United States Marine?"

"Yes, sir, I have. I want to join. I'd like to take the test right now if I could."

Eddie had made the decision last night. He had walked down to the Union Square area, thinking. He had thought about Michigan, about Bloomfield Hills and Albion. He thought about his father and about his mother. He thought about his grandfather sitting in jail—probably for the rest of his life. As he was walking back to the YMCA, he had wondered what Granna would tell him to do. Before he went to bed he had made his decision. He would join the Marines.

"I've got good news for you," said the recruiter. "There's been a cancellation. If you pass the test, you can leave for San Diego the day after tomorrow if you want."

Eddie smiled. He couldn't remember being this happy since Granna got sick. "Sir, I'd like that very much."

-41-

The magnificent giant trees in front of Billie Croft's 19th-century home were filled with spring leaves. The birds had returned from the South. Tonight Billie's husband would be playing golf into Michigan's late twilight. When her jury duty was finished they would spend a few weeks at their place on Lake Michigan—John commuting to Battle Creek in mid-week as his business required. This morning Marshall's Kalamazoo Street was small-town Michigan at its best. Billie backed her two-year-old Buick from her driveway and headed for the courthouse, five minutes away. Fulfilling her civic duty was important to her. Today she was pleasantly happy.

As Billie walked from the parking lot to the courthouse she passed the county jail. A shudder went through her. What sort of people must be locked up in a place like that? She was glad that kind were off the streets. She wished they would keep the prisoners in Battle Creek, where most of the courts were, but then Marshall, as small as it was, was still the county seat. She supposed they had to have a court and a jail here.

As Billie entered the building to find where prospective jurors were to report, she was surprised to see television crews taking their equipment up the stairs. She did not know there was anything of interest to TV—but then she paid little attention to the news—it was the same crime stories night after night—most of it, thank God, from the big cities.

Billie was directed to report to the second floor courtroom of Circuit Court Judge Philip R. Hoskins. She found she had to make her way around the television cameras and crews that obstructed the hall. Was she to be on some big case? She hoped she would not be on television. What if it were some mobster or someone like that? Didn't people like that sometimes retaliate against jurors?

Like the building, the courtroom was modern. The sign inside the door said the occupancy was limited to 200. Billie sat in the portion of the spectator section reserved for prospective jurors. There were about 40 of them. The other spectator seats were filled–some with people who looked like newspaper reporters. Evidently it was a big case of some sort.

Billie wondered what would happen next. Soon a well-dressed young man entered the court room from a back door near the judge's bench. The question in her mind as to whether he was the prosecutor was settled when he sat at the table marked "People."

Next came a pale white-haired man about 75, wearing an out-of-date conservative suit. He was accompanied by an expensively dressed black man carrying a briefcase. When the black man directed the older man to be seated at the table marked *Defendant,* she realized the white man was the defendant and the black man his lawyer. She was surprised, because, as far as she knew, Marshall didn't have any black attorneys. Maybe there were some in Battle Creek, but John knew a lot of attorneys and he had never mentioned any black ones. Maybe the defendant was from Detroit. Perhaps that would explain it. Could this be some kind of Mafia case they had sent to Marshall for trial? Once John had remarked they sometimes sent cases to distant cities so as to get impartial jurors. Well, she was certain she could be impartial, even though she had to admit she was surprised to see a black attorney representing an elderly white man. She knew she was free from racial prejudice–this was the 1990's and she was an educated woman–but she couldn't help but wonder if the same were true of all the prospective jurors. After all, this was still a small middle-American town.

"All rise, please," the bailiff said. "This Circuit Court for Calhoun County is now in session. Judge Philip R. Hoskins, presiding."

Billie did not know Judge Hoskins well, but she had met him at two or three fund raisers and social events. He was a good-looking, dark-haired

man in his late 40s. Billie thought he lived over near Battle Creek. If he
had a wife, she had never met her. She'd ask John if he knew.

"The clerk will call the calendar," Judge Hoskins said.

"People of the State of Michigan versus David Neal"

"Ladies and Gentlemen of the jury panel," the judge began. "The case
we have before us this morning is one wherein the people allege the defendant committed a violation of the Michigan Penal Code–a violation called
murder. The defendant, David Neal–would you stand, Dr. Neal?" The
thin white-haired man stood and turned toward the prospective jurors.
Billie wondered what kind of a doctor he was.

"Ladies and gentlemen, the defendant denies this charge." The judge
continued. "The Calhoun County Prosecutor's office is represented by
Frederick N. Cain, Esquire, who is the deputy prosecutor in charge." Cain
stood and turned toward the panel. "The defendant's Counsel is Mr.
Joseph Thomas Jefferson, Esquire. Mr. Jefferson, if you please." The black
attorney stood briefly. Jefferson, Billie thought, looked confident in the
courtroom setting. He radiated a sense of power. She wondered exactly
what his client had done.

"As I will instruct you in detail later," the judge continued, "the mere
fact that charges have been brought against Dr. Neal are in no way evidence that he committed any crime. Every defendant is presumed innocent unless and until he or she is proved guilty beyond a reasonable doubt.
You are not to assume the defendant did anything wrong just because he is
charged here today. If any of you has any problem with that principle, I
would ask you to raise your hand at this time." Billie knew she would not
have any such difficulty, although she was curious to find out what Dr.
Neal had actually done to bring about these charges. She looked around.
No other potential jurors raised their hands.

"Ladies and gentlemen, the clerk is going to draw twelve names. If your
name is called, you should take a seat in the jury box." The judge pointed
to his right. "The rest of you will stay where you are until we've settled on
the final twelve who will actually serve on the jury. The court and then

each Counsel will have questions of you. This process is called *voir dire.* Each side has twelve peremptory challenges. That means that each attorney has a legal right to excuse up to twelve potential jurors without offering any reason or explanation. You should not draw any conclusions for or against either attorney or his case when he exercises his peremptory challenges." Billie wondered if either of the attorneys would kick her off the jury without explaining why. She couldn't think of any reason why they would. After all, she was certainly an open-minded person.

"Mrs. John Croft," intoned the clerk. Billie was pleased. She had been the sixth name called. This sounded like it might be a case that would be interesting. With all the media, it must be out of the ordinary. It would be fun to tell John and her friends about it. She hoped it hadn't been too gory a murder though. There must be something strange about it. Why would someone well into his 70s commit murder? And why was there all this media attention?

The judge asked them as a group a series of questions. Billie had never seen this part of a trial on television or in the movies. At first it didn't seem very dramatic. Questions about their families. "Are you married to anyone connected in any way with law enforcement?" "Have you ever been a victim of a crime?" Questions like that. When juror number two said her father had been a policeman, the judge asked whether she would still be able to be an impartial judge of the facts.

"I would have no trouble with that," the juror answered. "My father always said his worst nightmare would be to send an innocent man to jail." The juror was a woman in her 30s who was a pharmacist's assistant from Battle Creek.

Billie was surprised at the casual attire of the jurors. Only one man wore a tie and suit jacket. She had worn a fairly new dress—conservative, with a longish skirt. She was the best dressed of the twelve. She found herself a trifle annoyed that the others would not dress up more to be in court. Soon it was Billie's turn to answer the judge's questions. She had lived in Marshall over 15 years, she told him. Her husband was a partner in an advertising agency. She had two grown daughters. She had gone to Kalamazoo College for two years and quit to get married. She was very active in the community. There was no reason why she couldn't be a fair and impartial juror. Billie certainly hoped neither attorney would use one of those peremptory challenges on her. It had become a challenge to stay on the case—especially one like this.

When Judge Hoskins finished questioning all twelve, he dropped a bombshell. It was the first real clue as to what the case was all about. "Ladies and gentlemen, the attorneys in this case—Mr. Cain, here, and Mr. Jefferson—have agreed that I can tell you certain undisputed facts in this case. This will facilitate the court and the attorneys in asking you *voir dire* questions—both to see if there is any reason why you should be excused from the jury for cause, and also whether either counsel wishes to exercise a peremptory challenge. Again, I caution you against coming to any conclusion—even a tentative conclusion—about this case before you have heard all the evidence in the course of the trial. I admonish you to be absolutely open and straight forward in answering the *voir dire* questions." The judge took a sip of water from the glass on the bench.

"It is nothing to be ashamed of to be excused from a jury. If you are excused for any reason, you will have done your duty. But you will not have done your duty if you fail to disclose any reason why you should not serve, even if you think the reason is insufficient to disqualify you. It is not for you to decide whether you should serve. It is for the attorneys and the judge to make that decision. Your job is to be completely forthcoming in answering the questions." Billie could hardly wait to hear what these *facts* were that the judge was going to tell them.

"Ladies and gentlemen, the defendant, Dr. David Neal, is a retired professor at Albion College." The judge was reading from a sheet of paper. "He had been married to his wife, Lu Neal, for over 50 years." The judge looked up. "Did any of you know Lu Neal?"

Juror number seven, a telephone company supervisor, raised her hand. "I think I heard her give a talk once."

"A speech? What sort of speech?"

"It was about gardening. My hobby is gardening."

"Did you know her in any other way?"

"No. It was the first time. The only time. I admired her for being able to get up and give a speech–especially at her age."

"Is there any reason why you could not give a fair and impartial verdict? You see, it is Lu Neal that the defendant is accused of murdering."

Billie felt as if she had lost her breath. A murmur swept the prospective jurors–both the twelve in the jury box and the others in the audience. So that was it! Billie thought. My God, Dr. Neal had killed his wife!

"Why, no," answered the juror. "She was a fine lady. Like I say, I admired her."

"But can you be an objective juror?"

"Why, certainly. I'd need to know more about what happened. It must have been terrible, but I can serve, all right."

Another juror, number eleven, raised his hand. "I didn't know Mrs. Neal, but I think I may have read something about this case in the paper. Isn't this the mercy killing case?"

Judge Hoskins addressed the attorneys. "Would counsel approach the bench, please?" Cain and Jefferson walked to the side of the bench farthest from the jury and conferred in whispers. After three or four minutes they finished. "Ladies and gentlemen, as those of you who are finally selected for the jury will undoubtedly see, counsel and I will frequently have these little meetings. They are called sidebar conferences. There are many matters under the law that should be discussed outside your presence. You should not infer anything from these conferences nor draw any conclusions

against or in favor of any party because of these conferences. They are common occurrences in trials. Now it has been decided that until the attorneys
begin their part of the *voir dire* questioning there will be no further refer-
ences to what you may or may not have read in the newspapers about this
case. I'm going to leave those questions up to the attorneys."

So it was a mercy killing case, Billie thought. She was sure she'd remember if she had read anything about it.

Judge Hoskins resumed reading from the paper before him. "On
Thanksgiving Day of last year Lu Neal suffered a severe stroke that put her
into an immediate coma. She was in that coma for over 60 days. Dr. Neal
constantly visited his wife in the intensive care unit of the hospital, where
she was on a life support system. Mrs. Neal had not signed a living will
nor a power of attorney respecting terminating her life in the event of a
terminal illness. On the night of February 28, 1994 the defendant entered
his wife's hospital room. While he was there Mrs. Neal died. You will hear
testimony about the facts and circumstances surrounding her death. After
hearing all the testimony and at the end of the closing arguments, I will
instruct you as to the law on the subject of murder. The people of the state
of Michigan through the deputy prosecutor contend the defendant is
guilty of first degree murder. The defendant contends that he is innocent
of all charges. You should not infer from the giving of instructions that I,
as the judge in this case, have any belief as to the guilt or innocence of the
defendant. Under our system of justice you, the jury, are the sole persons
to determine the facts."

Frederick Cain then began questioning the various jury members, commencing with the first juror. "Would you be able convict the defendant of
first degree murder, even though you might be sympathetic to the pressures he was under, if under the law as given to you by Judge Hoskins you
felt that he was, in fact, guilty?" Billie listened attentively as the deputy
prosecutor asked a dozen questions of the first juror and then posed nearly
identical questions to the second juror. Billie thought the lawyer appeared
very professional. He was a good-looking young man–smooth–but not

too smooth. Well-dressed, he appeared very talented and self-assured. She found herself thinking that the chief prosecutor must think a great deal of Cain's ability to entrust him with such an important case. Soon it was Billie's turn to be questioned.

"Mrs. Croft, have you or your husband made legal provision as to whether you should be kept alive by artificial means in the event of terminal illness?"

"Why, no, we haven't. I suppose we should, but we haven't discussed it." This was a question Cain had not asked the others.

"Do you believe a husband has the right to take his wife's life because she is being kept alive only by heroic means?"

"Why I don't know. I wouldn't think so. At least unless she had signed something. I don't know. Isn't there a law about something like that?"

"Very good, Mrs. Croft. And if you were instructed by the judge that the law was that it was murder for a husband to take the life of his terminally ill wife in the absence of such a directive by her, would you be able to vote for conviction though you might be sympathetic to the husband's motives?"

"Well, yes…if that's what the law is."

"In other words, Mrs. Croft, do you feel a man should be able to take the law into his own hands?"

"No. Of course not."

So that was what this case was about, Billie thought. Dr. Neal had taken his wife's life without permission. If the circumstances were bad enough, she guessed she could understand a man's doing that, but as Cain had said, wasn't that taking the law into his own hands? How could she ever vote for that? She'd always been taught that we had a system of law, not men. Anything else would be chaos. Anyway, she imagined the judge would explain to them what the law was. She could see why this would not be an ordinary case. She hoped she hadn't said something that would make them want her off the jury. She wanted to be careful about that. Still the judge had told them they should be honest in their answers.

The rest of Cain's questions seemed to be the same as he had asked the previous jurors. As he moved on to question the remaining jurors, her mind was still on what Cain had asked her: "Do you think a husband would have the right to take the law into his own hands?" She didn't see how she could vote to allow that.

Finally, Cain finished with all twelve of the jurors and it was Jefferson's turn. Billie felt the defense attorney might unload on her when it was her turn. She wished she hadn't been so quick to answer Cain's questions the way she had. She supposed there could have been some sort of extenuating circumstances explaining what Dr. Neal had done. Jefferson's questioning of the first jurors was rather perfunctory. From the previous questioning everybody already knew a lot about each of the jurors. Their names, their occupations, their families, that sort of thing. Billie thought about the jury's make-up so far. There was such a wide variety of people. Three were black. She had counted five women and seven men. All the women except Billie and one who was a retired supermarket supervisor worked at jobs. One man ran a clothing store, another was a gas station attendant and one woman was a secretary at Kellogg's. Still another man was a factory worker. There was even Mr. Dempster, who was an assistant minister. None, except the one with a suit coat and tie, held a position anywhere near as important as her husband. The man with the coat and tie, Mr. Banning she thought was his name, owned some kind of a small busi-ness—something to do with representing plastics companies—she wasn't quite sure what it was. She always thought a person was supposed to be tried by a jury of their peers. She hoped she wasn't being snobbish, but somehow this group didn't seem at all to be Dr. Neal's peers. Jefferson fin-ished his questioning of the first five jurors and turned to her. Her palms were moist.

"Mrs. Croft. I want you to know that I appreciated your answers to Mr. Cain's questions."

Billie was surprised. "Thank you," she managed.

"According to my recollection, you said two main things. You said that you didn't think a person should be able to take the law into his own hands. Did I understand you correctly?" Billie wondered if Jefferson were setting her up in some way.

"Yes. That's what I said."

"I quite agree with you, Mrs. Croft. You have two grown daughters. Do I recall correctly?"

"Yes, I do." Billie was surprised Jefferson would remember such a detail. Perhaps also a little flattered–after all, there were twelve jurors.

"And you raised your daughters to believe the same? That they shouldn't take the law into their own hands?"

"I'm certain I did–my husband and I–but I don't actually remember its coming up."

"I'm certain you did too, but let me ask you another question along those same lines."

"All right."

"Every lawyer knows that the law isn't always clear. What if the law in a given case weren't clear? What would you tell your children to do in those cases?"

"Well, I don't know exactly."

"Would you tell them to do what seemed to them to be the right thing in such a case? The case where the law was muddled?"

"Yes I would. That's what I'd do."

"But not to do the thing that was right only for themselves? Would that be correct?"

"Yes."

"Not just what was best for themselves, but what was right for all of mankind."

"Yes. I don't recall ever facing such a situation, but that's what I'd try to do myself."

"Mrs. Croft, have you ever read the book *Les Miserables*–or seen the musical?"

"Yes. We saw it in New York."

"Do you remember the basic plot of *Les Miserables?*"

"Yes. I do. Jean Valjean steals bread to feed his starving family."

"What happened to him?"

"He was hunted down and finally went to jail."

"Had he taken the law into his own hands?"

"Yes, I suppose he had."

"Mrs. Croft. If when your children were young, your husband had lost his job and your children were starving–"

"Yes."

"–and your husband had stolen bread to feed his family, as in *Les Miserables.*"

"I see where you're going."

"Would you have voted to convict him of theft?"

"I don't know. It would be a tough one wouldn't it?"

"It certainly would. It certainly would."

Jefferson, who had been standing, walked to the other end of the jury box and looked at all twelve. "I commend you, Mrs. Croft. You seem determined to follow the law to the best of your ability."

"Thank you."

"Now I'd like to turn to another aspect of this case. Reasonable doubt. Have you heard of the principle of finding the accused not guilty unless the state has convinced you of his guilt beyond a reasonable doubt?"

"Yes, I've heard of that."

"Mrs. Croft, if the judge told you that you should follow that historic principle, do you think you could in good conscience follow it?"

"That the defendant must be convicted beyond a reasonable doubt?"

"Yes. In other words. You have stated that a man should not take the law into his owns hands."

"Yes."

"Do you think you could vote to acquit that person if you were left with a reasonable doubt as to whether the man had taken the law into his own hands?"

"Yes. I believe I could. Vote for acquittal, as you say."

"What if all eleven of these fine people disagreed with you–thought you were crazy for thinking there were a reasonable doubt. Would you still vote not guilty because of your reasonable doubt?"

"Yes. I think so."

"Of course you'd listen to what your fellow jurors had to say?"

"Yes. Of course."

"You'd weigh very carefully why they felt that way, wouldn't you?"

"Yes."

"But–and this is the big question–you'd still vote not guilty if you personally had a reasonable doubt as to whether the defendant did in fact take the law into his own hands?"

"Yes, I would."

"In other words you'd follow Judge Hoskins' instructions that you are entitled to vote not guilty if you and you alone had this reasonable doubt?"

"Yes."

"Even if the other eleven thought you were crazy? Even if the television people we see all around here thought you were crazy?"

"Yes."

"Even if your husband thought you were crazy? Is that right?"

"Yes."

"Thank you, Mrs. Croft."

With that, Jefferson started to go on to the next juror, but he stopped. "Mrs. Croft?"

"Yes."

"This may be a trifle embarrassing–embarrassing to both of us–but I have one more question."

"All right."

"It's a question I might be afraid to ask many jurors, but the fact is that I have found you to be very frank and open with your responses."

"Thank you. I've tried to be."

"And I hope you won't think I'm trying to butter you up–I know that would surely backfire." Jefferson looked up and down the jury box and then returned his attention to Billie. "Mrs. Croft, are you bothered by the fact that I am an African-American?"

Billie nearly choked. That was the last question she had expected. "No. Of course not," she managed to blurt out.

"You see, Mrs. Croft, I've been an African-American all my life. Oh, once before that I was called black. And before that I was called a Negro, but I've been this color all my life." Nervous laughter broke out here and there in the courtroom. Jefferson smiled–a warm, toothy smile–and waited for the tittering to stop before he continued. "You see I've discovered over all these years–66 of them–that most people in a public situation like this won't admit the fact they might have a prejudice."

"I suppose so."

"Now I can deal with prejudice. I've dealt with it all my life. My father before me dealt with it. But what I can't deal with is when that prejudice affects my client. You see, my client deserves a trial free of prejudice. If I thought for one moment that you or any of these fine jurors might not give Dr. Neal a fair trial because of my color, I'd resign from this case immediately. Do you understand?"

Billie gulped. Jefferson certainly laid it on the line. "Yes. I understand."

"Now, the reason I'm asking you these questions is that I have found you to be so frank and honest with me on these other subjects."

He paused to give Billie an opportunity to respond, but she didn't know what to say and said nothing.

"Now, what I want to know is whether you are troubled that I'm an African-American?"

"No, not troubled."

"But something bothers you?"

"Not bothers me exactly, it's just…"

"Yes?"

"I must confess I had wondered about why an African-American was representing a white man in Calhoun County, Michigan. Not prejudiced–I just had wondered–even though I know it's none of my business."

The attorney folded his big arms across his chest and smiled broadly, showing his teeth. "Mrs. Croft, I like that answer. I cannot tell you how much I like that answer. Do you know why?"

"No," Billie said weakly.

"Because it was absolutely honest. An absolutely honest answer. Of course you wondered why I was representing Dr. Neal! If you didn't wonder, you'd have to be blind, dishonest or living in some fairyland. Mrs. Croft, you're exactly the kind of person I want to judge my client. I thank you very much for your honesty."

Billie was relieved. Evidently she was not going to be challenged. Jefferson certainly was a dynamic man. She liked him.

Jefferson went on to question the other jurors. When the day was over Cain had exercised one peremptory challenge and Jefferson four. Billie could only guess why the challenges had been used. The juror Cain had excused had himself been charged, but acquitted, of some sort of embezzlement. The jurors Jefferson had excused were all men. One had served on a number of juries before and had always voted for conviction. Why the other had been excused, Billie didn't know. Mr. Banning, the man in the suit coat and tie, was left on. The excused jurors were replaced by others and eventually the questioning ceased.

"The people accept the jury as constituted," Cain announced.

"The defense also accepts the jury," said Jefferson.

"Very well," said Judge Hoskins. "The hour is late; we will adjourn for the day. The trial will resume tomorrow with opening arguments. The jury is admonished not to discuss anything about this case with the media, their family, each other or anyone."

Billie was elated. She had survived the cut. She still had a buzz on from the elation she felt when Jefferson had finished with his questions and she realized she would remain on the jury.

John had come home from playing twilight golf and Billie was telling him about her day as a prospective juror. "The defense attorney really put me through a grilling. I thought sure he would kick me off."

"Why would he do that?"

"I had said I didn't think a man should be able to take the law into his own hands. You know, decide for himself whether he had the right to kill his wife just because she was in a coma."

"Is that what this Dr. Neal did? Kill his wife?"

"I guess he did. That's what the judge said." They were in the breakfast area of their kitchen, eating a salad that Billie had prepared. "John, if you had a stroke—say a really bad one…"

"Yes?"

"Would you want me to have them let you go—disconnect the ventilator or whatever they do?"

"I don't know. I've never thought about it."

"We should do something, you know. We should see a lawyer or something."

"It would be a tough decision—what to do."

"Yes, but let's say we hadn't gotten around to seeing a lawyer and I had a stroke."

"I shot a 41 today with a ball in the lake. We only played nine."

"John, I'm serious."

"I'm sorry."

"Let's say I were in a coma for two months. You'd come to see me every day and I had not gotten better."

"Were you able to speak to me?"

"Let's say I could not."

"And you want to know whether I'd pull the plug."

"Yes."

"I don't know. I really don't know. Maybe it would depend on whether you would have died soon anyway. Look, can we talk about something more pleasant?"

Billie couldn't get to sleep. She kept thinking about the day's events. Even while they had made love, thoughts of the case came into her mind. She knew John loved her and would never deliberately harm her, but she didn't know if she would want him to have the say of life or death over her if she were like poor Mrs. Neal.

Billie kept thinking about the questions the attorneys had asked her. She agreed that no one should take the law into his own hands. That would be all too dangerous. Yet what about *Les Miserables*? Maybe Jean Valjean was justified in stealing the bread for his family, but then maybe society had no alternative but to treat him as a thief. She was beginning to think she had made a mistake in wanting to be on the jury.

She remembered her promise to Mr. Jefferson. If she had a reasonable doubt about Dr. Neal's guilt, she would stick to her opinion even if the other eleven disagreed. She knew she would do just that, and that she had answered Jefferson correctly, but how could there be a reasonable doubt in a case like this. After all, wasn't murder still murder?

John was sleeping soundly. She was glad he could get away to play golf. They had made such a good life together. She hoped neither one of them would ever have to decide when the other should die.

-42-

Apprehensively, David sat next to Joseph Jefferson at the defense table and studied the faces of the jury. The reality was that these twelve citizens would be deciding whether he would spend the rest of his days in Jackson Prison or whether he'd be free. It was awesome to realize his fate was vested in these strangers sitting before him.

Ruby had visited him in jail to report that she had been unable to find a trace of Eddie. He had checked out of the San Francisco YMCA, leaving no clue to his whereabouts. David was terribly worried about his grandson. He knew he had let him down. Eddie's disappearance had driven home the painful realization that, even before Lu's stroke, he had been totally self-centered–completely possessed with his failed retirement and dismay over Lu's sickness. He was ashamed for giving such little thought to his grandson. Somehow Eddie must be found. He needed to put his arms around him and tell him he loved him. He needed to assure Eddie he would be there for him. What good would it do Eddie for the only person in the world who genuinely cared for him to be locked up in prison? Somehow these twelve people before him had to be convinced to free him.

In jail last month Joseph had conferred with David for a full day. The attorney had brought his secretary, who took extensive notes and tape-recorded the entire session. Joseph had elicited every fact and circumstance that conceivably could affect the case. David's marriage to Lu, his career at Albion College, his estrangement from Betty. David had bared his soul. He had told of his old affair and its effect on Lu and Betty. Joseph had closely questioned him about the day of Lu's stroke and, step by step, his agonizing decision to take Lu's life and to end his own. If Joseph had yet evolved a defense strategy, he did not divulge it.

"Why are you asking me all these personal questions?" David had complained.

"I'm the attorney. You're the client," Joseph had said. "Your job is to tell me the facts–all of the facts. My job is to defend you. If I decide to put you on the witness stand, which I doubt, I need to know everything there is to know about you."

"Why wouldn't you have me testify?"

"Because you'd have to admit what you did, and what you did could land you in jail for the rest of your life."

"All rise, please," the bailiff intoned. "This court is again in session. The honorable Philip R. Hoskins, judge presiding."

The judge took his seat behind the bench. "Mr. Cain, you may now present your opening statement."

Smartly dressed in a suit different from yesterday's, Frederick Cain walked to the corner of the jury box. "Ladies and gentlemen of the jury, it is now my duty to outline the case for the State of Michigan against the defendant, David Neal."

This was it, David thought. This was no Perry Mason television show. This was real. The *defendant* Cain was talking about was he, David. Cain was trying to keep him in jail for the rest of his life, and so far it looked as if he were likely to succeed.

"This is a case where I am saddened to have to fulfill my duty," Fred continued. "I take no pleasure in the prosecution of Dr. Neal, but when a violation of the law has occurred it is my duty to prosecute. When you have heard the evidence you, like me, will be saddened to have to fulfill your duty. However you, like me, will have to do your duty.

"Yesterday when I questioned you, I listened very carefully to your answers. It is clear that each of you has made a commitment to uphold the law. It is clear that each of you will fulfill your duty to apply the law as it is explained to you by the judge. It is equally clear that, however saddened you may be about the circumstances of this case, after hearing the evidence each and every one of you will find beyond a reasonable doubt that the defendant committed the crime of murder, as murder is defined by the state of Michigan.

"I have used the words *as defined by the state* deliberately and carefully. For it is the state legislature that makes the determination of what is murder and what is not murder. This means–and please listen to me carefully on this point–that the defendant, Dr. David Neal..." Fred turned and pointed to David, "...is not the one who defines murder in this courtroom. He is not the one to say when a killing is legal and when it is not. The law determines that. The law says that what the defendant did is murder. It is your sworn duty to apply the law to Dr. Neal, no matter how much you may understand why he did what he did."

Despite himself, David was impressed by the prosecutor. The young man knew how to state his case. He was bright, articulate, impressive. Fred Cain was a formidable adversary.

"Now, for the same reason that David Neal is not the one to decide when it is legal to kill his wife, so ladies and gentlemen, you are not the ones to define what is murder and what is not murder. In your deliberations at the end of this case some of you may be tempted to redefine murder, so that what the defendant did can be found to be legal. You can be expected to hear evidence explaining that this was a so-called mercy killing case. Let me point out to you again that you have been sworn to apply the law. You have no right to define mercy killing as anything else than murder. No matter where your sympathies may lie, no matter how understandable, even compassionate, the killing may have been, that–may I be so bold as to say–is none of your business. Your business–your responsibility–is to apply the law, not to make the law. You have not been elected to the legislature. You are jurors. You have not been elected governor with the power to veto legislation. You have no right to violate your oath as jurors, which is simply to apply the law.

"When the evidence is in, you will have no legal, ethical or moral alternative but to find the defendant guilty of first degree murder."

David put himself in the position of the jurors. How could he possibly argue with the logic of the prosecutor? Legally, he would have to vote for conviction. He didn't know if there were any way the jury could be made to understand what he had gone through in making his decision. The agony of seeing Lu lie comatose for so long. The feeling of hopelessness about her condition. But should that make any difference? When he turned off that respirator, he knew it was a violation of the law. He certainly ought to have realized he was committing murder and yet he had gone ahead with it. He was in fact a murderer, was he not?

"We will show that on Thanksgiving Day 1993 Lu Neal, the wife of the defendant, suffered a stroke. That she was taken to the hospital by ambulance. That she was constantly and continuously in a complete coma through to the date of her murder on February 28, 1994. She never regained consciousness. It is true that she was kept alive only by a respirator and by intravenous feeding, but, ladies and gentlemen, Lu Neal was in fact alive until her life was deliberately and unlawfully ended by the defendant. We will show that she never had executed a document–power-of-attorney–any document authorizing anyone to take her life in the event of terminal illness. The defendant is an educated man–a Ph.D. and retired head of the Psychology Department of Albion College. From the beginning he maintained that his wife would recover." Fred coolly walked to the other end of the jury box, moving his eyes from one juror to the next as he spoke.

"We will show that after some 60 days, the defendant decided upon a plan–a plan to kill his wife. At first he tried to gain permission of the attending physician, Doctor Benjamin Jacobson. In fact he wanted Dr. Jacobson to commit the final act. Dr. Jacobson went to the office of the defendant's daughter, Betty Neal, to attempt to obtain her consent. At that time his daughter was a practicing attorney in a major law firm in Detroit. Only recently Betty Neal has become Judge Betty Neal, by virtue of her appointment as a United States District Judge by the President of the United States. Judge Neal will sit in that witness chair..." Fred pointed to the witness stand. "...and will testify that she refused to give her consent. In fact she called the proposed killing of her mother *murder*. She told Dr. Jacobson she would do all in her power to see to it that anyone who caused the death of Lu Neal be prosecuted for murder." Cain stepped back from the jury box toward the prosecutor's table. Briefly, he glanced outside, where the American and Michigan flags gently flapped in the breeze.

"Failing to gain the assent of Dr. Jacobson and his daughter, the defendant decided to murder his wife himself. On the night of February 28 he paid his final visit to the intensive care unit. Said, *Hello* to the only nurse on duty in the immediate vicinity, and entered Lu Neal's room. By now this was an everyday experience, except for two things. First, David Neal had decided to unlawfully take the life of his wife. And second, he carried with him a loaded pistol.

"Next, for reasons known only to himself the defendant decided not to use the pistol on his wife, but to turn off her respirator. Perhaps so he could not be heard. Perhaps for some other reason. We do not know. But, in fact, he did take the life of Lu Neal.

"The nurse, Ruby Thompson, will testify before you." Again Fred pointed to the witness chair. "Ms. Thompson saw from her monitor that her patient was not breathing. She rushed into the room. Seeing the defendant about to fire the gun–perhaps on himself–perhaps to be certain his wife was dead–we do not know for certain–Ruby Thompson attempted to intervene by taking the gun from the defendant. For her trouble she took a bullet in her thigh. Thank God, she now has recovered.

"We will have the testimony of a hospital orderly to whom defendant admitted he had killed his wife. You will also hear from an Albion police officer who will testify that Dr. Neal admitted to him he had murdered his wife.

"That is it, ladies and gentlemen. The facts are indisputable. The defendant killed his wife, Lu Neal. You will be instructed that the law is clear. The defendant had no legal right to take the victim's life. You will have no alternative but to find the defendant guilty of first degree murder. I expect you to do your duty, no matter how distasteful. The people of Calhoun County have every right to expect the prosecutor of this county to do his duty, no matter how distasteful, and they have exactly the same right of you."

As Fred sat down David felt lost. It seemed there was no other possibility than a murder verdict. David knew if he were on the jury he would have no alternative but to convict. How, he wondered, could Joseph possibly do anything to help him?

"Mr. Jefferson, do you wish to make an opening statement at this time?" the judge asked.

Slowly Joseph rose to his feet. "The defense does not choose to make its opening statement at this time, but reserves the right to do so at the close of the state's evidence. Your Honor, we respectfully request the court to admonish the jury not to draw any adverse conclusions from this action."

"Yes, ladies and gentlemen, as Mr. Jefferson rightly says, the defense has every right to reserve or even to waive an opening statement. From this you are not to draw any conclusions, tentative or otherwise, that are adverse to the defense.

"I see that the time is 11:45. At this time the court declares a recess for lunch. We will resume at 1:45, at which time Mr. Cain should call his first witness. Again, the jury is instructed not to discuss this case with anyone."

After the judge and jury left the courtroom, the buzzing reporters quickly moved into the hallway. David could see the television cameras outside the doors. He felt a sense of dismay. He didn't know what he had expected Joseph to say, but he certainly had anticipated some sort of an opening statement. Despite what the judge had said about not drawing any adverse inferences, David knew that he himself couldn't help but assume his attorney must feel his case was impossible. As David started to go with his jailer, Joseph whispered to him.

"They've still got to prove their case. It's easier said than done. Besides, this old attorney is not about to roll over and play dead."

-43-

Marine Corps Basic Training was much tougher than Eddie had imagined. There were times when he was so angry he could have killed all three of his drill instructors. Gone were the days of his baggy pants and backward Detroit Tiger cap. His hair was cut very short and he wore Marine fatigues most of the time. Six weeks had gone by since he had enlisted. Seven more to go. He had lost over ten pounds. Twenty-four hours a day, seven days a week, his life was in the hands of one of his drill instructors. The three took shifts, taking turns sleeping in the barracks, watching the recruits' every move and taking delight in humiliating them. The D. I.'s always called him Recruit Erickson, never a Marine or a private.

"The Marines will make a man out of you if you have the guts to stick it out," was the favorite saying of his toughest D.I., a guy named Benson. He must have said that a thousand times. Always shouting at the recruits.

"Well, I'm already a man and I don't need your help to do it," Eddie had wanted to holler in return. "How in the holy hell does humiliating a guy 24 hours a day make him a man?" Eddie yearned to ask. Sometimes it was all he could do to keep his mouth shut. So far, thank God, he had restrained himself. Sammy Bernstein, a guy in his outfit from L.A., hadn't been so lucky. He had mouthed off to the D.I. and had gotten extra marching duty for his trouble. Bernstein had quit the Marines in his third week. Eddie didn't know they allowed quitting, but they let Bernstein out. A couple of other guys had talked a lot about quitting, but they hadn't as yet.

Marching. Marching. Marching. It seemed all they did was march while the D.I.'s yelled at them–that and cleaning their rifles.

Eddie had spent two weeks at Camp Pendleton, up the coast from the Marine Corps Training Depot in San Diego where they were stationed. At Pendleton they had lived in tents in the mountains. It was really cold at night. The guys from California had never been that cold, but he hadn't found it so bad.

The training at the obstacle course at MCTD had been especially tough. Eddie's muscles had really ached until he got used to it. He had to climb tall obstacles, jump down slides into water and crawl on his belly while live ammo was shot over his butt. One guy, Timkins, from some place in New Mexico, had chickened out when they had to jump off the tall building-like steel structure. It was six stories high and they had to slide down a rope from the top, bouncing their feet against the wall on the way down. Eddie was scared too, but when he saw the other guys jumping, he just jumped. Timkins had lost his nerve and couldn't jump. When he talked about quitting like Bernstein had, the D.I. said he could try the jump again. The next time Timkins got up his nerve and jumped while the whole platoon cheered. When he was finally at the bottom Timkins had a grin a mile wide. He didn't talk about quitting any more.

Maybe the best thing about the Marines was all the guys. Everybody was going through the ordeal together. Eddie felt they were a big family. Everybody's griping together about their chow and the D.I.'s made him feel better.

Probably the worst thing was the loneliness. There wasn't much time for anyone to write letters or do any personal stuff. On Sundays they let everyone go to chapel. That's when most guys took advantage and wrote their families or girlfriends. But Eddie didn't have anyone. The last thing he wanted to do was write his mother and he doubted if his father cared where he was. Grandfather was in jail and he didn't know how to address a letter to him. They probably wouldn't let Grandfather have any mail in jail anyway. He still was mad about that stupid jail receptionist not letting him see Grandfather.

Eddie's worst loneliness was at night. Sometimes he'd be exhausted, but still couldn't sleep. The San Diego airport was right next door and the planes made a lot of racket. A lot of nights he felt like crying, but he didn't want the guys in his barracks to hear, so he held back. God, he missed Granna and being home. The other guys got cookies in the mail from their mothers and grandmothers, but his mother didn't give a damn about him and Granna was dead. He sure wished he could see Grandfather. Talk to him. Tell him about the Marines. Tell him how tough it was.

Although he knew better, he always checked to see if there was any mail for him. Of course there never was. Most of the guys got lots of mail. That made him feel even more lonely.

"All right, recruits, the Marine Corps has a special treat for you." It was late afternoon. They had just finished marching for about two hours. The asphalt made the sun even hotter. "You get to call home!" continued the drill instructor. "Free—on the Corps!" The entire platoon let out a spontaneous yell of joy. "Here's how it works. You each get five minutes—no more. You know where the phones are. Form separate lines by each phone. Remember, if you take more than five minutes it comes off the time of your buddy."

Eddie watched as the entire platoon made a mad dash across the yard to the phones. They had not been allowed to make phone calls or see anyone from the outside for all these weeks. Slowly, Eddie followed in the direction of the phones. There wasn't anyone for him to call. Without getting in any of the lines, he hung around. It made him feel even more lonely to hear the young men talking to their families. Then he got an idea. He would call Ruby! Ruby had turned out to be a friend. Maybe she could tell Grandfather he was in the Marines. He raced back to the barracks to get her telephone number.

He waited almost an hour before it was his turn.

"Ruby, this is Eddie. You know, Eddie Erickson."

"Eddie!" Ruby exclaimed. "Where are you? Are you all right?" Ruby's enthusiasm made him glad he had called.

"I'm in San Diego. I've joined the Marines. They're only giving us five minutes to talk."

"You've joined the Marines! In San Diego! Wait until your grandfather hears this."

"How is Grandfather?"

"About as well as could be expected, I guess. He's in the middle of his trial right now. He's been worried sick about you, young man. We didn't know where you were."

"I didn't think anybody cared where I was."

"Well, I do and Dr. Neal certainly does."

Eddie didn't know what to say. He supposed he should have written Ruby to tell his grandfather where he was, but he hadn't seen any point. Grandfather hadn't seemed to care much what happened to him.

"You got the money I sent?" Ruby asked.

"Yes. It came in the nick of time. I'm paying you back when I get my pay check."

"There's no hurry."

"I had to pay for my uniforms and stuff out of my first month's pay."

"That's all right. I'm just glad to know you're all right."

"Is Grandfather holding up okay?"

"At least he's defending himself. You remember my telling you about my Uncle Joseph in Detroit?"

"Yes."

"The one who's the famous defense lawyer?"

"Sure, him."

"He's defending your grandfather."

"Is there much of a chance?"

"I don't know, Eddie. I sure hope my uncle has some tricks up his sleeve."

"I wish I could be there."

"Oh, Eddie, I wish you could too. Your grandfather needs you. It's quite a mess."

"Tell him I love him." Eddie gulped. He'd never told anyone he loved his grandfather.

"Oh, I will, Eddie. I will! Imagine, you in the Marines!" Eddie could just see Ruby–the friendly, tall black lady with the big happy smile. It made him happy just to talk to her.

"Tell him I'll write him a letter and mail it to you. Would you give it to him for me?"

"Of course I will! He'll be so happy!"

"My five minutes are up. I'll write. Tell Grandfather I'm writing."

Eddie walked back to the barracks. He felt sorry for Grandfather. He had learned how it felt to be under the gun and be all alone. He had felt that way himself for months now. He'd write the letter as soon as he got a few minutes.

-44-

Looking businesslike and professional, Frederick Cain stood to call his first prosecution witness. Outwardly he radiated complete confidence, but inside he was nervous. This case was the test of his lifetime and he was desperate to win.

His thoughts returned to last night when, with Marge, he had prepared for the trial the final time. In her den they had gone over the instructions that Judge Hoskins would read to the jury before their deliberations. Marge and he isolated each legal element of the crime of murder and once again went over which witnesses he would use to prove each essential fact. Marge read aloud the printed jury instructions. By now she knew them nearly by heart. *Murder in the first degree is a willful, deliberate and premeditated killing of a human being, with malice aforethought.* With her stylish reading glasses perched on her nose, she read, *Willful means intentional. Deliberate means as a result of careful thought. Premeditated means considered beforehand.* She paused to push up her glasses. *Malice aforethought means intentionally killing.*

Together they reviewed the extensive witness and fact chart they prepared last month. When they had finished they had no doubt that Fred could methodically prove David Neal had committed murder in the first degree.

Satisfied, they had gone upstairs to her bedroom. Fred relaxed on the bed, watching her while she undressed and poured two brandies. He took two quick sips. "You know, Marge, the main point I've got to get across is that the case is really a simple one. See how this sounds. *Ladies and gentle-*

men, this case is really quite simple. If a man kills a woman after thinking about it, considering it beforehand, and intentionally doing it, he is guilty of first degree murder. There can be no ifs, ands, or buts. He took another sip from the generous glass. *There is nothing in the law that requires a murderer to be evil or malicious. Kindly men with kindly intentions can commit murder. The law does not excuse a killer because he commits his deed from compassion for his victim. In short, ladies and gentlemen, nothing in the law permits mercy killing. Murder is murder.* Fred had looked at Marge "Well, what do you think?"

"I think you've got him." Naked, she had unbuttoned his shirt while he spoke. "And I think I'm about to make love with the next Calhoun County Prosecutor."

When they had finishing having sex, Fred could not sleep. Despite his painstaking preparation, he was worried. After all, Joseph Jefferson knew the law as well as he did. He knew very well his client had committed murder. Jefferson's only possible defense would be to get the jury to ignore the law. Fred listened to Marge's easy breathing as she slept. Hoping it would help him sleep, Fred poured another brandy. He remembered his criminal law professor telling the class, "One reason the constitution gives a right to a jury trial is so the jury can choose to ignore the facts and the law if it wishes. The founders wanted to retain the British system whereby the jury could refuse to convict a defendant even if the judge told them they must." Fred knew that just as for centuries English juries were free to defy the crown, American juries were free to acquit guilty defendants. That was what worried Fred.

"I call Lieutenant James Rodgers to the witness stand." The same worry hung over Fred as he spoke the first words of the trial.

Joseph Jefferson's reputation was legend. Fred knew he was in for a battle royal. Ignoring the law, the shrewd defense lawyer would try to convince the jury that Lu Neal's killing was justified and compassionate–an act the members of the jury might very well take against their own loved one, given the same circumstances. Fred had to convince them that the killing was murder, no matter what the circumstances–that the law was the law and no man could take the law into his own hands.

The clerk administered the oath to the witness. "Will you state your name and occupation?"

"I am Lieutenant James Rodgers of the City of Albion Department of Public Safety."

"Albion's police department?" Fred asked.

"Yes."

"On the night of February 28, 1994, were you called to the hospital?"

"Yes. There had been a disturbance–a killing."

"And what did you see and hear on that occasion?" With the opening few questions, Fred felt more at ease–like a football player after the opening kickoff.

"I went to Room 236 in Intensive Care. Two of my men were already there." The lieutenant spoke as if the events of that night were routine and that he recalled them perfectly. "As I entered the room, I saw the defendant, David Neal." He pointed to David. "I saw the patient, Lu Neal–she was in the hospital bed and appeared to be dead. I saw two orderlies." For the first time Rodgers referred to the note pad he held in his hand. "Garcia and Wilmot. I saw a nurse, Ruby Thompson."

"Do you see the nurse in the courtroom?"

"Yes, that's Ms. Thompson in the first row, the African-American female in the nurse's uniform. And there was another nurse present, a Lilly McCoy. She's the other nurse, next to Nurse Thompson. Shall I go on?"

"What further did you observe?"

"Nurse Thompson had been shot in the thigh. She was in pain. The scene was one of total disarray."

"Did you talk to the defendant?"

"Yes."

"Tell us that conversation."

"First, I had one of my men read him his Miranda rights. His right to remain silent."

"Yes."

"Then I asked him what had happened."

"Before you go on, tell us exactly where the defendant was when you talked to him."

"He was sitting on a chair next to his wife's body. He had an open Bible on the bed."

"Very well. Now what did he say?"

"He asked me if his wife was dead. I told him she was."

"And then?"

"He asked about Ruby–the nurse, Ms. Thompson–whether she was dead. I told him I thought she was going to be all right."

"What, if anything, did he say next?"

"He said he hadn't meant to shoot Ruby. That he had intended to commit suicide." Rodgers looked at his note pad. "He said, 'I guess I really screwed up.'" Rodgers looked up. "Then he asked if he could see his wife. I told him he could."

"What happened next?"

"He said something to his wife. Actually to her body–she was dead."

"What did he say?"

Lieutenant Rodgers looked at his note pad. "He said, 'At last your ordeal is over.'"

"Is that all he said?"

"In my presence, yes."

"Did you question Ruby Thompson?"

"Not at that time. She was being taken to Emergency."

"Did you question her later?"

"Yes. I took her statement the next day in the hospital. It's in my report."

"And would you tell us the gist of that report?"

Jefferson rose to his feet. "Objection, Your Honor. Calls for hearsay. Mr. Cain knows perfectly well any statements made by Ruby Thompson are hearsay and inadmissible. If the deputy prosecutor wants to question Ruby Thompson, let him bring her to the witness stand."

"That's exactly what I intend to do. That's why she has been subpoenaed."

"Your Honor," Jefferson argued. "Mr. Cain persists in doing what he knows very well is improper. He–"

"Gentlemen," said the jurist sternly. "I want you to approach the bench."

The two advocates approached the edge of the judge's bench outside the hearing of the jury. The court reporter moved into a position to take notes on her shorthand machine.

Judge Hoskins continued in a low voice. "Gentlemen, I will not have this conduct in my court. Fred, I haven't a doubt in my mind that you knew you could not ask the officer hearsay questions. Your only purpose was to force Joseph…May I call you by your first name, Mr. Jefferson?"

"Certainly Your Honor."

"I like to do that in my court. Outside the jury's presence of course."

"That's fine with me."

"As I was saying, Fred, I know very well your only purpose was to force Joseph into objecting to the question. Making him look bad in front of the jury. On top of that, you managed to bring in that you had been forced to subpoena her. You've been in my court many times and you know I will not tolerate that sort of behavior. Are you clear about that?"

"Yes, Your Honor."

"As far as you are concerned, Joseph, I want you to understand that in this court we don't allow arguments in the presence of the jury that in any way might prejudice them. If you have an objection, you make it, but I do not want you to be making your arguments in support of your objections in the presence of the jury. I expect you to ask for a bench conference. I know you have a superb reputation as a defense lawyer, but in my court I don't permit squeezing in prejudicial material before the jury in the guise of legal arguments. Have I made myself clear?"

"Yes, Your Honor," Jefferson responded.

"And by the way, Fred," the judge went on. "I'm perfectly aware you've announced for prosecutor. I don't care who wins, but I expect you to keep the campaigning out of my courtroom. Have I made that clear?"

"You have, Your Honor," Fred answered. "I assure you it will not happen."

The conference over, the attorneys returned to their counsel tables. Fred had never seen Hoskins come on so strong. He assumed it had to do with the media attention. Doubtless Hoskins wanted to come across as an in-charge judge. After all, this case would not go unnoticed in the governor's office and could lead to an appellate appointment for Hoskins.

"I have no further questions of the lieutenant," Fred concluded.

"Cross examination, Mr. Jefferson?"

Jefferson rose to his feet. "So Dr. Neal did not say how his wife had died?"

"No, he did not."

"And, of course, he did not say that he had killed her."

"That is correct."

"I have no further questions. I reserve the right to recall this witness."

"So noted."

"I call Lilly McCoy," said Fred.

"I was on duty that night," Lilly testified. "I was the relief nurse for Ruby. Ruby Thompson–the intensive care nurse."

"Did you go to Lu Neal's room?"

"Yes. I did"

"Where were you?"

"I was rushing after Ruby–down to Mrs. Neal's room, you see."

"And then?"

"Well, when I got into the room Dr. Neal was pointing a gun at his head–his own head."

"What did you see and hear?"

"They were screaming at each other."

"Who?"

"Ruby and Dr. Neal."

"What were they saying?"

"Ruby was saying something like 'You've got to stop. Your life's too valuable.'"

"What happened next?"

"Ruby—she used to be a runner, I think—she jumps right over the bed—right across Mrs. Neal—and she knocks at his gun."

"Yes."

"She says, 'You're going to have to kill me first. Words to that effect.'"

"Then?"

"The gun went off and I think—it all happened so fast—I think there were two shots."

"Yes."

"The first hit the ceiling."

"And the second?"

"The second hit Ruby. Hit her in the thigh. I'm not sure about the first shot, but some stuff came down from the ceiling."

"Did Dr. Neal say anything?"

"He said he was sorry. He meant to shoot himself."

"Did he say anything else?"

"I don't remember much. The cops came. He talked to them, I guess. I remember I got the gun from under the bed and gave it to one of the cops. I went back to the nurses' desk, I think."

"I have no further questions."

"Mr. Jefferson. Cross examination?" Judge Hoskins asked.

"Thank you, Your Honor. Miss McCoy. Did you hear Dr. Neal say anything about how Lu Neal died?"

"No. He didn't talk about that. Not that I heard anyway."

"What caused you to run down the hallway after Ruby, Ms. Thompson?"

"I was just coming on duty. Ruby shouted something about the monitor–trouble in Mrs. Neal's room–and started running."

"I see."

"So I ran after her, but she's so fast she beat me to the room."

"Again, how many gun shots did you hear?"

"I think it was two."

"One in the ceiling and one in Ruby's leg?"

"I think so."

"Was Mrs. Neal hit by a gun shot?"

"Not that I know of. I don't think so."

"I have no further questions, but, again, I reserve the right to recall the witness."

"So noted."

Finished, Jefferson sat down, and Fred stood to call the next witness for the prosecution.

"I call Ruby Thompson." Fred was worried about Ruby's testimony. Ruby had refused Marge's request to come in for an interview with Fred, so he had called her himself. However, she had flatly refused to discuss the case. "I've talked to Dr. Neal's attorney–he's my uncle, you know–and he says I don't have to speak to you if I don't want to," she had said. Fred knew a cardinal unwritten rule of trial practice was never to ask witnesses a question unless you knew what they were going to say. They could surprise you and you could be stuck with what they said. However, Fred felt he had no choice but to put Ruby on the stand. According to Lieutenant Rodgers' hospital interview with her, she was simply too vital. Although Fred had virtually memorized the report, Marge passed him a copy from her seat in the first row. "Your Honor, before I begin my questioning, may we approach the bench?"

"Very well," Judge Hoskins replied.

"I have every reason to believe this witness is an adverse witness and I would like to treat her as such," Fred said in a low voice.

"Mr. Jefferson?" asked Judge Hoskins.

"I think it only proper to advise the prosecution that Ruby Thompson, is my niece. I advised her she need not speak to anyone about this case, unless properly subpoenaed."

"And she talked to you?" the judge asked Jefferson.

"Yes, she's the one who interested me in taking the case in the first place."

"Have you interviewed her about the facts in the case?" Fred asked.

"She told me what happened, yes."

"So you get to talk to her ahead of time and I don't. Is that it?"

"Fred, you know there's nothing wrong with that," Hoskins commented. "That's her right."

"And you're not going to let me point that out to the jury?"

"I certainly am not," the judge replied.

"At least I ought to be able to treat her as an adverse witness." Fred was referring to the legal principle that allowed an attorney to treat an unfriendly witness differently from his own witness. He could ask leading questions and even cross examine her—tools very necessary with reluctant witnesses.

"Only if that proves to be the case," the judge ruled. "If she turns out to be evasive or isn't forthcoming, then I'll let you treat her as an adverse witness, but not until that happens. You're premature."

"I don't think you'll find it necessary to treat her as an adverse witness," Jefferson said.

"Sure, she's your niece and you've talked to her."

"That's my ruling," concluded the judge. "Now let's get started with her."

Fred took a deep breath as he returned from the bench conference. He had no choice but to take a chance with the witness. He hoped she wasn't going to surprise him.

"Ms. Thompson, first let us establish your relationship to Mr. Jefferson."

"I'm his niece."

"And your relationship with the defendant?"

"Dr. Neal was my psychology professor at Albion College."

"Do you consider yourself a friend of Dr. Neal?"

"Oh, yes, very much so. Especially since his wife had her stroke."

As he questioned her, Fred carefully weighed the effect Ruby might have on the jury. She looked efficient in her nurse's uniform. Although perhaps a little tense when she first took her seat, she had flashed an engagingly broad smile as she spoke of her friendship with Dr. Neal. He felt the jury would find her a believable witness. That could be dangerous to the prosecution's case if he left an opening for her to defend Neal. Fred's challenge was to get the facts without giving her such a chance.

"How long was Mrs. Neal in the hospital before she died."

"About 60 days."

"And you were her nurse all that time?"

"Yes. One of her nurses."

"Directing your attention to the night of February 28th last."

"Yes."

"Were you on duty that night?"

"Yes."

"Did Dr. Neal come to visit his wife?"

"Yes. It was later than usual."

"Did he go to her room?"

"Yes."

"Did you have a conversation with him before he went to his wife's room?"

"Yes."

"What did you say to one another?"

"I remember he said he wanted to be alone with his wife–not to be interrupted."

"Was that unusual?"

"I don't remember its happening before. Although he did spend a great deal of time each day alone with his wife."

"Did Dr. Neal have a weapon with him?"

"I now know that he did."

"But you didn't then?"

"No."

"Miss Thompson, had Dr. Neal ever discussed with you the possibility of his wife's life being ended by artificial means? By that I mean turning off her life support system." Fred felt ill at ease asking this question because Lieutenant Rodgers' report was unclear on the point and he wasn't certain what her answer would be.

"He had finally come to the point where he was considering it."

"Considering taking her life himself?"

"No. Asking Dr. Jacobson to do it. Actually if Dr. Jacobson approved, Dr. Neal wanted me to do it."

Fred was elated. He hadn't expected Ruby to be so candid. "Let me get this straight. The defendant asked you to remove turn off his wife's respirator?

"Not exactly that. No."

"Exactly what then, Ms. Thompson, if you please."

"He wanted to know if I would do it, if Dr. Jacobson agreed that it was appropriate to let the patient go."

"'To let the patient go?' You mean to *kill* the patient don't you?"

"Objection!" Joseph nearly shouted as he stood. "Argumentative!"

"Gentlemen. Please approach." Hoskins was plainly perturbed.

"Fred. I have warned you," Hoskins continued when the attorneys met him at the bench. "You know that was an improper question. The next time you do such a thing, I'm going to admonish you right in front of the jury. Now I think you will agree that that will do your case no good. No good at all. And if that doesn't work, a contempt citation might do it."

"I'm sorry, sir. I got carried away."

"Well, see to it it doesn't happen again or my bailiff might carry you away to the jail overnight. Clear?"

"Clear, Your Honor." Fred had not minded what had happened a bit. No matter what the judge did, he had successfully made his point to the jury–his point that Lu Neal's death should be characterized as a *killing* and not merely a *letting go*. To Fred, the judge's threats were not frightening, but merely a part of a high stakes cat-and-mouse game.

"The objection is sustained," Hoskins pronounced within hearing of the jury after the attorneys had returned. "You will ignore Mr. Cain's question, as if it had not been asked."

"Your Honor," Ruby unexpectedly asked.

"Yes, Ms. Thompson."

"Could I please answer the question?"

"No, you may not."

"Your Honor," Joseph spoke. "I withdraw my objection."

"In that case I withdraw my question," Fred responded. The last thing he wanted was to get into a debate with a witness who had an axe to grind.

"Gentlemen. Ms. Thompson. This is a court of law. The sign on the door says I'm the judge here. The question that was asked was objected to and I sustained the objection. The witness will not answer the question." Judge Hoskins was clearly angry. "Ladies and gentlemen of the jury, I apologize for this episode and I ask that you not let it affect you or your deliberations in any way. Mr. Cain, if you would proceed with your next question."

"Now, Ms. Thompson, I believe you had testified that Dr. Neal had asked you, in your words *to let the patient go?* Is that correct?"

"Yes. If Dr. Jacobson would order it."

"By *letting go* I take it you mean letting Mrs. Neal die?"

"Yes."

"You'd turn off the ventilator?"

"Yes."

"And consequently Mrs. Neal would die?"

"No. Not consequently. She would die because she was so sick."

"Now, you are a nurse, are you not?"

"Yes. I am."

Fred knew he was about to ask a leading question, but he felt the judge would agree that he could do so under the adverse witness rule. "Isn't it a fact that in such a case, if you turned off Mrs. Neal's ventilator she would die? Now, isn't that a fact?"

"I object, Your Honor," Joseph said. "That's speculative. There's no evidence that Ms. Thompson turned off the respirator."

"Sustained."

Fred did not intend to back off because of some technicality. "Ms. Thompson, let me ask it this way. You said that the defendant asked you to turn off the respirator?"

"Yes. If Dr. Jacobson issued the order."

"Now, did your friend, Dr. Neal, indicate in any way that he knew that if you did that his wife's life would end?"

"Yes. That's why he wanted me to do it. He knew I loved them both."

It was that sort of answer Fred knew Ruby would try to slip in, but he knew it would be unwise strategy to ask the judge to ignore her gratuitous remark. The jury had heard what she said. He didn't want to embed it in their minds any more.

"Ms. Thompson, we are still talking about the night Mrs. Neal died."

"Yes. I understand."

"Before Dr. Neal went to his wife's room, did you have any further conversation?"

"Yes."

"What did the two of you say?"

"I told him I was sorry to learn that his daughter had refused to give permission."

"Refused permission? Permission to do what?"

"I had heard that his daughter, Betty Neal–she's a lawyer in Detroit–or was…"

"She's a judge now, is she not?"

"Yes. So I've heard."

"A federal judge?"

"I don't know about that."

"What did you tell the defendant that you had heard about his daughter?"

"I told him I was sorry that she had refused to agree to turning off the respirator."

"What did he say?"

"He said he wasn't surprised. Words to that effect."

"Did you discuss anything else–anything else before he went to his wife's room?"

"Not that I can remember. Oh, he said he wanted to be alone so that he could pray with her. Pray with her and read the Bible to her."

"Mrs. Neal was in a coma, wasn't she?"

"Yes."

"Unconscious?"

"Yes."

"Yet the defendant wanted to read the Bible to her?"

"Yes. He thought perhaps she could hear him."

"Ms. Thompson, you're a professional nurse and you observed Mrs. Neal for 60 days."

"Yes."

"In your opinion, could she hear someone speak to her?"

"Mr. Cain, sometimes loved ones need to believe things."

"I understand, but I'm asking for your opinion."

"I don't know."

"Your professional opinion, please."

"No, not in my opinion." Ruby's head was down.

"What happened next?"

"Well, Dr. Neal was in his wife's room a long time."

"Yes."

"I figured he was talking to his wife. He did that a lot. Maybe reading the Bible, like he said."

"Did anything unusual happen?"

"Yes. I noticed the monitor."

"You have television monitors for your patients?"

"Not a picture of them. It shows vital signs—all sorts of information."

"What did you notice?"

"I noticed Mrs. Neal was not breathing."

"Not breathing? Was she dead?"

"I didn't know. I was worried."

"What did you do?"

"Like Lilly testified—she was coming on duty—I had just told her that Dr. Neal didn't want to be disturbed…"

"Go on."

"I yelled to Lilly that something was wrong and she should follow me."

"What did you do?"

"I ran down the hall to the room."

"What did you see when you entered? Was Mrs. Neal dead?"

"I don't know. All I saw was Professor Neal had a gun raised to his head. I figured he was going to kill himself."

"Why? Because of the gun?"

"Yes. He was pointing it at his head."

"What did you do?"

"I told him not to. He was too valuable a human being." Ruby began to sob. "And then I jumped across Mrs. Neal's bed."

"Was she in it?"

"Yes."

"Was her respirator still functioning?"

"I don't know. It all happened so fast." Ruby was still crying.

"Of course you didn't turn off the respirator?"

"No."

"And it was on when Dr. Neal entered the room?"

"Yes." Ruby dabbed at her tears with a tissue.

"Did anyone go into the room besides Dr. Neal, before you saw she had stopped breathing?"

"No. They would have had to go by me–my station."

"Now, you knocked the gun from the defendant's hand, did you?"

"I guess so. I think I did. It all happened so fast. The next thing I knew I'd been shot in the leg and Dr. Neal was apologizing."

As Fred returned to the counsel table to take a last look at his notes, he looked up. The doors to the courtroom had opened. It was Betty Neal.

"Your Honor, I have no further questions of this witness at this time. I see that it is time for the noon recess…"

"Yes. I had noticed that. We shall resume at 1:45."

Fred felt very good about this morning's work. He had proved two essential elements of the crime. That a murder had been committed, and, through a witness friendly to the defense, that the defendant had committed the crime. The only reservation he had was that he needed to do better on the sympathy factors, but he had a few aces up his sleeve on that point and one of his aces had just walked through the courtroom door.

David had not been surprised by what any of the witnesses had said. It was all accurate enough. But hearing the events of that night related here in the courtroom, struck him with the stark reality of his plight. How could the jury help but convict him? As far as he could see there was nothing–absolutely nothing–he could do but to watch and listen as the prosecutor sent him permanently to Jackson State Prison.

-45-

Betty Neal had lunch with Fred Cain and Marge at Schuler's Restaurant, where they went over her testimony one last time. As they were leaving for the short walk back to the courthouse, they held back while the jury filed out of the private dining room that had been reserved for them throughout the trial.

"How do you feel about the jury?" Betty asked Fred.

"I think it's as conservative as the community as a whole. Pretty law-and-order. We've got a hell of a shot for a conviction."

"What sort of sentence will he get?" Betty inquired.

"Did you do any criminal work?" Fred asked Betty.

"No."

"The judge doesn't have any discretion really. If it's first degree, it'll be minimum 25 years," Fred said.

"And if second degree?"

"Fifteen years minimum," Fred answered. "At his age that's as good as life."

"It's not as much as he gave my mother."

"What's that?"

"Death. He gave my mother death."

"Judge Neal, are you testifying for the prosecution?" the television reporter outside the courtroom asked.

"I'm not testifying for or against anybody. I'm here to tell the truth." Betty was annoyed, and wanted to get inside the courtroom, where she'd be away from the media. She hated being seen on television. Despite her new diet, she hadn't lost a pound.

"How do you feel about your own father's being on trial?"

"I have no comment." Betty knew that the case was on the news every evening. Thank God, the judge had decided against allowing live TV in the courtroom.

"Ladies and gentlemen," Betty heard the reporter saying to the television audience as she rushed toward the courtroom door. "That was newly appointed Judge Betty Neal, daughter of the…"

Betty was angry. The publicity was one thing she hadn't counted on when she had pushed the prosecutor into charging her father. It was just something she'd have to face. She knew very well that millions of television viewers would dislike her for what they thought she was doing to her father. Wouldn't they ever understand it was something she had to do? Her father had taken the life of the only person who had ever really loved her.

It was 1:35 as Betty took her seat in the courtroom. Until now she had felt no nervousness, but the episode with the TV reporter had upset her. She realized that she would be on trial every bit as much as her father. Suddenly she felt hungry for a chocolate bar or some ice cream. The psychiatrist she had been seeing had explained that her cravings were a result of tension. Betty knew he was right. The psychiatrist had pointed out that diets were never going to work unless she did better with her anxieties. With her appointment as a judge she thought she would be better, but after Eddie's disappearance she had gotten worse. The private investigator she had hired had traced Eddie to San Francisco, but he had disappeared from there. It had come out in her therapy that she had originally resented Eddie's being born, because she feared the child would interfere with her career. With therapy, she had come to realize that for years she had been carrying around a heavy load of guilt over that. Eddie's disappearance added to her guilt. When this trial was over, she would get things straightened around. Eddie would turn up. Maybe even come home again. She'd lose a lot of weight. All it took was losing a pound a week, then she'd have some measure of happiness.

"This court is again in session," announced the bailiff.

"Ms. Thompson, if you will retake the witness stand, it's Mr. Jefferson's turn to cross examine you."

"Miss Thompson, so there is no confusion in anyone's mind, you are my niece, are you not?"

Ruby's smile showed her remarkably white teeth contrasting against her dark skin. "Yes."

"In fact, you introduced me to Dr. Neal, did you not?"

"Yes. I did."

"And you are Dr. Neal's friend and former student?"

"Yes."

"In fact, you would like to see him acquitted of this murder charge?"

"Yes, I would."

Betty could see Jefferson's tactic. He was taking from Fred's hand the ammunition he might otherwise use against the witness. Betty had used the same tactic herself in civil cases.

"But you have sworn to tell the truth."

"Yes."

"And you will tell this jury the truth regardless of the consequences."

Ruby looked very serious. "Yes, sir."

"You first knew Dr. Neal when you were a student at Albion College?"

"Yes. He was my psychology professor."

"Did you know Lu Neal in those years?"

"Yes. She had a couple of student teas at their house. Albion is a small college."

"After those teas and prior to Mrs. Neal's stroke did you ever see her again?"

"Well, yes. I went to MSU for my nurse's training. When I graduated I decided to live in Albion. I'd see her around town once in a while–class reunions–that sort of thing."

"What was Mrs. Neal like?"

Betty wondered if Fred shouldn't object to the question. What her mother was like was hardly relevant to whether she had been murdered. She supposed Fred felt the jury would resent an objection.

"She was an example to me every bit as much as Dr. Neal had been."

"What do you mean *an example?*"

"She was a successful person. She was on the Board of Education. She was always giving speeches, mostly on her hobby–gardening–that sort of thing."

"I see."

"But mostly she was a wonderful lady. I always wanted to be like her."

"When you went to those teas–as a student–did you have an opportunity to observe Dr. and Mrs. Neal together?"

"Yes."

"How did they seem to feel toward one another?"

"Objection," Fred said, rising to his feet. "Lack of relevancy and calls for opinion, not fact."

"Overruled. This is a murder case, Mr. Cain," said Judge Hoskins. "I'll allow it."

It was clear to Betty that the judge was bending over backward to be fair to her father. She hoped he treated her the same way when she was on the stand.

"You may answer the question," Jefferson continued. "How did they seem to feel toward one another?"

"Respectful. They appeared to admire one another. They were very kind to each other."

"Any arguments–disagreements?"

"None."

"When was the last time you saw them together–before the stroke?"

"At the Faculty Room. I think a couple of years ago."

"And what was that occasion?"

"It was their fiftieth wedding anniversary."

Betty hadn't realized Ruby had attended the anniversary party. She thought she would have remembered her. Six feet tall–black.

"They invited quite a few former students. I was privileged to be one."

"What happened on that occasion?"

"Basically they celebrated their fiftieth anniversary. There had been a football game. Albion had won the MIAA."

"What was Dr. and Mrs. Neal's demeanor toward one another?"

"Very loving."

"In what way?"

"Well, you know it was their fiftieth. Dr. Neal spoke about how important Mrs. Neal had always been to his success as a professor. How important she was to him."

"Anything else?"

"Yes. I remember he faltered. Dr. Neal faltered at the lectern."

"Faltered?"

"Yes. Right in the middle of his speech he choked up. He couldn't seem to go on."

"What happened next?"

"Mrs. Neal came to his rescue, sort of. She took the microphone and really saved the day. I've never seen anything so loving. That's what I meant about my wanting to be like her. She was really a cool lady."

"And Dr. Neal toward Mrs. Neal?"

"Your Honor…" Fred interrupted.

"Overruled, for the same reason." Hoskins waved at Fred, stopping his objection in mid-sentence. "Go on, Ms. Thompson."

"It was obvious to everyone in the Faculty Room that he loved her. I'd say he was even dependent on her."

"Dependent?"

"Well, yes. I'd seen Dr. Neal a few times since he retired. I'd drop into his office."

"Go on."

"He was kind of depressed. His retirement hadn't been going the way he had hoped."

"I see."

"His textbook was not being used. The publishers didn't like his new books. Dr. Neal didn't talk too much about his feelings. That's why I remember so well something he said once."

"What was that?"

"He said he hoped he died before Mrs. Neal did. He said men just weren't equipped to be alone the way women were. He seemed very depressed."

"When was the next time you saw Dr. Neal?"

"The day after his wife's stroke."

"What was his apparent state of mind?"

"Objection."

"I withdraw the question. Let me ask it another way. Would you describe his behavior?"

"He was decimated, but from that first day he was convinced Mrs. Neal was going to get well."

"Did he visit her often?"

"Twice a day, always–sometimes three times. He'd stay by the hour. Many times I'd go into her room and he'd be talking to her or reading to her. You know, telling her what they were going to do when she got out of the hospital."

"Did that frequency of visits continue right through February 28th?"

"Yes. Sometimes his grandson Eddie would come with him."

"Eddie?"

"Yes. Eddie lived with them. He and I became good friends."

"You Honor," Fred moaned starting to make an objection. "I've been very patient, but…"

"Yes. Mr. Jefferson, the witness is getting somewhat far afield. Please confine yourself to answering the questions."

Betty was annoyed. She could see very well what Jefferson was up to. He wanted to make her father appear as human as possible to the jury. She had seen savvy defense lawyers do that in the criminal cases that had come before her as a judge. Some jurors were more sympathetic to the defendant once they felt they knew him.

"You said that in the beginning Dr. Neal was hopeful that his wife would recover?"

"Yes."

"All this time she was in a coma?"

"Yes."

"Never spoke?"

"No."

"Had to be fed artificially?"

"Yes."

"Never responded to stimuli, such as sound–talking and the like?"

"Correct."

"Yet Dr. Neal felt she would recover?"

"No one could tell him otherwise."

"Because?"

"Because he wouldn't hear of it. He simply knew she would recover."

"To your knowledge, did there come a time when Dr. Neal spoke otherwise?"

"Yes."

"When was that?"

"As I recall, it was about two weeks before she died."

"And what did he say or do?"

"He asked me if I thought Mrs. Neal should–you know–be let go–allowed to die. I forget his exact words."

"Did he say why he was asking you?"

"He had begun to doubt her recovery. He had begun to think she'd be in the same vegetative state for years to come."

"And what did he ask you?"

"He wanted to know what I thought about it."

"What did you say?"

"I said I was afraid it was for the best. I knew how hard it was for him."

"You told him that?"

"Yes, as I recall."

"Did he say whether he had talked to anyone else about it?"

"Yes, to Dr. Jacobson. He was going to ask Dr. Jacobson to talk to their daughter, Betty Neal, there." Ruby pointed at Betty.

"Did he say what Dr. Jacobson was to ask her?"

"To ask Judge Neal for her okay."

"Is that what he said?"

"I think so. Yes, although I don't remember his exact words. It was a very upsetting occasion. Upsetting for both of us. I don't remember exactly. Except that I was very relieved he had come to that decision."

"Now, Ms. Thompson, I believe you already covered this under Mr. Cain's questioning, but I want to get it straight. Before the night of the 28th, did you discuss with Dr. Neal whether his daughter had given permission?"

"Yes. I told him Dr. Jacobson had told me she had refused and I was sorry."

"And what again did Dr. Neal respond?"

"He said something to the effect that he wasn't surprised. I knew he had a bad relationship with his daughter."

"Move to strike, Your Honor," Fred said rising to his feet. "Non-responsive and—"

"Motion granted," Judge Hoskins said. "The jury will disregard the reference to the bad relationship."

"Thank you, Your Honor," said Fred.

Betty wished Fred had refrained from what he had done. While he was technically correct, all it had done was to fix the jury's focus on the very fact they were supposed to ignore.

"Again directing your attention to the night of the 28th, did Dr. Neal say he intended to kill his wife that night?"

"No. Certainly not."

"Now you testified that later that night you saw something that caused you to rush into the room?"

"Yes."

"Exactly what did you see?"

"I saw the screens–the monitors. They showed that something was dreadfully wrong with Mrs. Neal."

"What did they show?"

"She had stopped breathing and there was no heartbeat."

"How long did you study the monitors?"

"Not long."

"Just a second or two?"

"Yes."

"You just saw something was wrong?"

"Yes."

"But you didn't study the data carefully?"

"No. I just rushed to the room."

"Did you examine Mrs. Neal in the room?"

"No. I saw Dr. Neal with the gun pointed to his head and I wanted to stop him."

"Stop him from killing himself?"

"Yes."

"And you did stop him, did you not?"

"Yes."

"And took a bullet in the thigh for your trouble, did you not?"

"Yes. I did."

"So after you were shot, you didn't examine Mrs. Neal?"

"No. I was in pain."

"Of course. So you don't know why the monitors showed Mrs. Neal wasn't breathing and had no heart beat, do you?"

"No."

"Then you don't know what caused the death of Mrs. Neal, do you?"

"No. I do not. Not for a fact."

"Well, in fact you simply do not know, isn't that so?"

"Yes."

"When they took you away for treatment, you weren't even sure Mrs. Neal was dead, were you?"

"No."

"And of course you didn't know why she died or even if she had died?"

"No."

"Let alone if anyone had caused her death?"

"No. That's right."

"As a matter of fact, for all you know, Dr. Neal could've seen his wife die and decided to take his own life for any number of reasons, including that he could no longer be of assistance to her, isn't that right?"

"Objection, Your Honor. That's an argumentative question, if I ever heard one."

"I quite agree," Hoskins said angrily. "The objection is sustained and the jury will ignore the question. Gentlemen, I wish to remind you of our earlier conference. I'll have no more of this."

"I have no further questions," Jefferson said, sitting down.

Christ! Betty thought. Was Jefferson going to argue that her father hadn't killed her mother? That was ridiculous! It was perfectly obvious that he had turned off her life support and then tried to kill himself, but from her experience as a lawyer she realized what Jefferson was trying to do. He was raising any question he could in the jury's mind. She didn't like it–you never knew what crazy theory might appeal to some jurors.

"Mr. Cain. Do you have further questions?"

"I certainly do." Fred rose to his feet and approached the witness stand.

"When you entered Mrs. Neal's room, was her life support system removed?"

"I'm not sure. It happened so fast."

"You remained conscious, did you not–despite your wound?"

"Yes."

"Did you see anyone disconnect Mrs. Neal after you got into the room?"

"No."

"Was she disconnected when they took you away?"

"I'm not positive. I was in considerable pain."

"Ms. Thompson, you've already admitted you are a good friend of Dr. Neal. Is that right?"

"I'm proud to say I am."

"Would you lie for him here in this courtroom?"

"No. I know better."

"But you say you don't know if the ventilator was removed or turned off."

"I don't know."

"Put it the other way. Do you know whether it was still operating when you entered the room?"

"No. I don't know. It happened too fast."

"So if the other nurse–Ms. McCoy–testifies that it had been turned off, you wouldn't disagree, would you?"

"I simply don't know."

"Well, we'll see what she has to say when I recall her to the stand. I have no further questions of this witness at this time. Your Honor I request permission to recall Nurse McCoy."

"Permission granted."

The nurse again sat in the witness chair. "Ms. McCoy, did you hear Ms. Thompson's testimony?" Cain asked.

"Yes."

"Do you recall whether Mrs. Neal's ventilator was turned off when you entered the room?"

"I don't recall the situation the exact moment I entered the room. My eyes were on that gun."

"Of course. Tell me, after you retrieved the gun, can you tell us whether the ventilator had been turned off?"

"The first time I remember seeing it, it had been sort of knocked away."

"Did you see anyone knock it away while you were in the room?"

"No, sir."

"Thank you. I have no further questions," Cain concluded.

Betty was relieved. For a moment she had thought Fred was going to have trouble showing her father had been the one to turn off the ventilator. The nurse had seemed to nail it down, but you never knew about juries.

"One moment, please, Ms. McCoy," the judge said as the nurse started to leave the witness stand. "Mr. Jefferson do you have any further cross examination?"

"One or two questions Your Honor," Jefferson smiled and walked toward the witness.

"Nurse McCoy, let me be certain I understand your testimony on the point of the ventilator's being knocked away. You say when you followed Ruby Thompson into the room, you didn't notice one way or the other."

"Yes. The gun was being fired."

"But later you noticed it had been, as you put it, knocked away."

"Yes."

"Did you see Dr. Neal touch the ventilator in any way?"

"No."

"Did you see anyone else touch it?"

"No."

"And of course since you can't say whether it had been knocked away before you went into the room, you don't have any idea whether Dr. Neal did it while he was alone with his wife?"

"Objection," interrupted Cain. "The question is argumentative. Asks for a conclusion."

"I allow it. It might have been phrased better, but he's asking whether she knows it to be a fact that Dr. Neal did something to the ventilator. Go ahead, Ms. McCoy, you may answer the question."

"I'm sorry," said the witness. "I'm confused."

"You'd better rephrase it, counsel."

"Yes. Of course," Joseph responded. "I'll try it a different way. Ms. McCoy, you say that Ruby Thompson leaped across Lu Neal to get at the gun?"

"Yes."

"And knocked it away, so it shot wildly?"

"Knocked the gun away, yes."

"Was she lying on top of Lu Neal?"

"Yes, she was."

"Is it possible that Ruby accidentally knocked off the ventilator trying to get at the gun?"

Lilly looked upward, thinking. "Yes, it's possible. It all happened so fast."

"Do you know whether, when you entered the room, Lu Neal was dead?"

"No. I didn't have any way of knowing that."

"Of course not. So as far as you know, Nurse Thompson might have accidentally knocked away the ventilator, and then Mrs. Neal died?"

"I hadn't thought of that."

"Objection. The question is argumentative and the answer is nonresponsive."

"Well, I think it's a little too late to object to the question. It's already been answered."

"Your Honor," Fred asked. "May we have a bench conference?"

"Yes. Counsel will approach the bench."

Betty could guess what the argument was about. Jefferson was cleverly implanting in the jury's mind his wild arguments and speculations. The proper legal purpose of questions was supposed to be to ascertain facts and not to make arguments. However begrudgingly, Betty had to concede that Jefferson was good at slipping in his arguments.

Shortly the spirited conference ended with the judge nodding his head and the attorneys returning to their posts.

"Ladies and gentlemen, Mr. Jefferson is going the rephrase the last question. Meanwhile you are directed to ignore the witness's response as the question had been previously phrased. Mr. Cain will have one last question when Mr. Jefferson is finished with the witness."

"Ms. McCoy, did you observe any facts inconsistent with the possibility that Ruby Thompson was the reason for the ventilator's being disconnected?" Joseph asked.

"No, sir. I did not. For all I saw, it could have happened that way."

"Mr. Cain, your question please."

"But you did not see the ventilator become disconnected by Ms. Thompson's leap across the bed?"

"No. I did not."

"If there are no further questions of this witness, Ms. McCoy, you are excused," concluded the judge.

Betty cringed. Damn it, this should be an open and shut case. There was no doubt in her mind that her father had turned off the ventilator, yet look at what had happened! Jefferson had implanted in the jury's mind the impression that there could be a reasonable doubt how her mother's death had actually occurred. This was ridiculous. Any sane person would know perfectly well that her father had gone to the hospital intending to kill her mother. Well, she was going on the witness stand next, and she'd point out a thing or two to the jury.

-46-

"I call Judge Betty Neal to the witness stand." Fred Cain spoke in a firm and confident voice.

"Do you swear to tell the truth, the whole truth and nothing but the truth?" asked the clerk.

"I do," Betty Neal answered. She wore a conservative loose-fitting dress that covered her knees. Her heels were of medium height.

"What is your occupation?"

"I'm a United States District Court Judge in Detroit."

"And your relationship to the deceased, Lu Neal?"

"I was her daughter. The defendant is my father."

Sitting in her juror's chair Billie Croft was taken aback. She never would have expected that the overweight woman on the witness stand was a federal judge, let alone Dr. Neal's daughter! What on earth was she doing being called to testify by the prosecution? Billie supposed it had to do with something technical, such as identifying the body.

Billie felt honored to have been selected to serve on the jury. She knew this was the most famous case ever to be tried in Marshall. With all the publicity, she knew the verdict would reflect on her town's reputation. She didn't want the rest of the country to think that small-town Michigan jurors could be crazy like some of those California juries. While she knew she shouldn't make up her mind before she heard all the evidence, so far it certainly looked damning for Dr. Neal. Billie had listened carefully to Mr. Jefferson's cross examination of the various witnesses, but she didn't think he had really shaken any of them. So far it looked pretty cut-and-dried.

While she believed that Dr. Neal had loved his wife, it seemed clear he had given up on her recovery and had turned off her respirator. This despite the smoke screen that Mr. Jefferson had cleverly tried to put up. The fact that the poor man had tried to kill himself didn't have much to do with anything. Clearly he had killed his wife. That was what counted. Billie was making no final decision yet, but it would take some pretty tall explaining to convince her to vote not guilty. So far it looked, as the prosecutor had said in his opening statement, that Dr. Neal had taken the law into his own hands. Despite Jefferson's talk about *Les Miserables*, people had no right to do that.

Billie listened attentively as the questioning began.

"Judge Neal," Cain began. "You were raised in Albion, where your parents resided?"

"Yes."

"Where were you educated?"

"I went to the Albion public schools. I graduated from Albion College. I was a pre-law. Then I went to Ann Arbor and graduated from the University of Michigan Law School."

"What degrees do you hold?"

"A Bachelor of Arts from Albion–I was Phi Beta Kappa–and a J.D. from Michigan Law School. That's a Juris Doctor. I was on Law Review."

"Did you practice law?"

"Yes, for many years–I was with a big firm in Detroit–until I was appointed a federal judge by the president earlier this year."

"Judge Neal, when did you hear about your mother's stroke?"

"The morning after it happened."

"That would be the day after Thanksgiving last year?"

"That's correct."

"Who told you?"

"My father."

"What did you do upon hearing the news?"

"I was in the middle of a very important trial–I was still practicing law–but I was able to get away. I saw my mother in the hospital."

"Was she in a coma?"

"Yes."

"Could she see you?"

"No. She was unconscious."

"Could she hear you?"

"No. She was in a complete coma. It was obvious she would never recover."

"Move to strike the last remark. Nonresponsive and opinion," said Jefferson.

"Motion granted. The jury will disregard the witness's remark about its being obvious her mother would never recover. The witness is not a doctor."

"I'm sorry, Your Honor."

"Yes," Judge Hoskins admonished her. "Please remember you are a witness. You should be responsive to the questions asked and should not venture your opinions."

Throughout the trial Billie had been impressed by Judge Hoskins. Even with a federal judge on the stand, he certainly made it clear he was in charge of the courtroom. Billie wondered whether Judge Hoskins thought Dr. Neal was guilty.

"Judge Neal," Cain continued. "Did there come a time when you discussed with her doctor the subject of whether your mother's life support system should be removed?"

"Yes."

"And when and where was that?"

"It was a day or two before her death. Dr. Jacobson–Ben Jacobson–he's been their doctor for years–came to my office in Detroit."

"What was the substance of that conversation?"

"He said my father had asked him to approach me."

"What about?"

"My father had asked him to take my mother off her ventilator. He wanted my consent."

"Your consent to do exactly what?"

"They wanted my consent to let my mother die. That's why my father had sent him. In what they thought was their infinite wisdom, they had made the decision that my mother should die. They wanted me to agree to it."

"And how did you respond?"

"I told Dr. Jacobson in no uncertain terms that I would not agree to my mother's murder."

"You used the word *murder?*"

"I certainly did. I told him I would not agree to my mother's *murder.*"

"How did he respond?"

"He argued that it would not be murder in a medical sense. I remember him saying she was dead for all practical purposes."

"What did you say in response?"

"I said she certainly was not dead for *legal* purposes. I told him I would never consent and that my consent was legally necessary."

"Did Dr. Jacobson try to get you to change your mind?"

"Yes. He told me that my father was reluctant to make the decision, but that he had finally faced the fact that she wasn't going to get well."

"And what did you say?"

"I told him I had known from the beginning she wasn't going to recover, but that I didn't want her dead and my consent was legally necessary. I told him if she died under suspicious circumstances, I would bring a law suit. His responsibility was to keep my mother alive not to kill her."

"Go on."

"I told him that after all she had been through with my father, he owed a duty to take care of her. I also told him that my father knew he stood to inherit from my mother's estate. She had a substantial inheritance from my grandfather and her latest will, as far as I knew, left it to my father."

"Did you tell Dr. Jacobson that your father's motive was to get that inheritance?"

"I told him it might be. I also told him my father just didn't want to take care of my mother."

"You told him that?"

"Yes. I told him that."

"I have no further questions."

Betty Neal's testimony had taken Billie Croft's breath away. She sank back in her juror's chair. Could Dr. Neal possibly have murdered his wife for an inheritance? It didn't seem likely, but you never knew. Some men had done exactly that, she was sure. She thought of the time she learned of John's affair with that woman in New York. Now she was glad she had never confronted him, and it had blown over. At the time she had wondered whether John might have her killed if she had filed for divorce and had asked for alimony and a property division. People did awful things for money. You never knew.

On top of that, the testimony from the nurse, and now the daughter, made it perfectly clear that Dr. Neal knew he had to have his daughter's consent–yet he had gone ahead without it. There didn't seem any escaping the fact that it was murder. When this case was over, Billie decided, she would have a talk with her daughters. She'd tell them she didn't want John to be pulling the plug on her unless her daughters agreed in writing.

"Mr. Jefferson, do you wish to cross examine?" asked Judge Hoskins.

"I have a few questions." Billie watched as the dignified black lawyer stepped toward the witness box.

"Judge Neal, you and I know one another, do we not?"

"Yes, Mr. Jefferson. I've seen you in the elevator many times. We office in the same building." Betty Neal smiled warily.

"Indeed. Your former law firm is one of the most respected firms in Detroit. You were a partner there for many years before President Clinton appointed you to the bench?"

"Over 15 years."

"You graduated with honors from the University of Michigan Law School, did you not?"

"Yes. Order of the Coif." While her answers still showed a certain guardedness, Judge Neal appeared to relax a little.

"You are now Judge of the United States District Court for the Eastern District of Michigan?"

"Yes."

"Was that something you always wanted?"

"Well, yes. I suppose so."

"Did you ever talk to your mother about your dreams to hold such an honored position?"

"Not exactly, no."

"But you did talk to her about wanting to get ahead?"

"Oh, yes, many times. She was an example to me." Judge Neal choked up at the mention of her mother. Billie sympathized with her.

"An example to you? Your mother never held a high position, did she?"

"Your Honor, I object. The witness's relationship to her mother has nothing to do with this case."

"Mr. Cain, this is cross examination."

"No. She never held a high position—unless you'd call the Albion School Board a high position—but she could have, except that my father's career was her career."

Billie found herself wishing she had known Lu Neal. She must have been an admirable woman.

"Did you ever talk to your father about your dreams for a high position—the high position your mother never had?"

"No. My father and I never talked about such things."

"Did your father pay for your going to Albion College?"

"Tuition was free for children of faculty."

"Did your father pay for your education at Michigan Law School?"

"Yes."

"Did he do so willingly?"

"As far as I know, yes."

"Judge Neal, you loved your mother, didn't you?"

"More than I can say, Mr. Jefferson."

"It saddened you when she had her stroke, didn't it?"

"Of course. I was very saddened."

Judge Neal seemed determined not to let her emotions show. Billie didn't see how she could manage to do it.

"You didn't want her to die?"

"Of course not."

"How often did you visit your mother in the hospital?"

"Just the once. She didn't even know I was there. It was obvious she was going to die."

"Going to die? When was she going to die?"

"I don't know. How could I know? Doctors don't even know such things."

"Soon?"

"I told you I don't know."

"Did you know your mother was only being kept alive by artificial means?"

"Of course, I could see that."

"Did you ever think it might be just as well if your mother would be allowed to die? If the life support system were turned off and she be allowed to just slip away?"

"Never!"

"Did you talk to your father about whether your mother was going to die?"

"I only talked to my father once after my mother had her stroke."

"When was that?"

"Right after I'd been to the hospital."

"What did you say to one another?"

"He insisted she was going to get well."

"And what did you say?"

"That she was never going to regain consciousness again—never speak—never hear."

"As a matter of fact you called him a fool didn't you?"

"I don't remember."

"Your father told you your mother was going to recover, and you called him a fool. Isn't that right?"

"I told you, Mr. Jefferson. I don't remember that."

"Judge Neal, I'm going to ask you what may be a difficult question, but I know that as a judge you will do your best to answer it in a straightforward manner. Why do you hate your father so much?"

Billie watched as the witness seemed to lose her breath. It was a question that no one had expected. Everyone looked intently at the overweight woman in the witness chair. She did not answer.

"You do hate your father, don't you?"

Cain took to his feet. "Your Honor, I must object to this whole line of questioning. Whether the relationship between the witness and the defendant was good, bad, or indifferent is irrelevant to this case."

"Your Honor," Jefferson replied. "These questions go to the credibility of the witness. The jury is entitled to know—"

Judge Hoskins held up his hand, interrupting. "The objection is overruled. The witness will answer the question."

Judge Neal seemed to be gathering herself together. "Of course I dislike my father. Anyone would under the circumstances. But Mr. Jefferson, I'm a judge. I know what it means to be sworn to tell the truth."

"Move to strike the last portion of that answer as non responsive", said Jefferson..

"Motion granted," Judge Hoskins ruled. "The jury will disregard the witness's reference to telling the truth."

"And just what are those circumstances you mentioned that cause you to dislike your father so?" Jefferson asked.

"He killed my mother!"

Billie again marveled at the way the witness kept her composure under the circumstances.

"Now, Judge Neal, you hated your father a long time before that, did you not?"

"I don't know."

"Isn't it true that you hated your father because your son, Eddie, preferred to live with your father rather than you?"

"Eddie wanted to be with my mother, not my father."

"Eddie did in fact live with your father, did he not?"

"Eddie lived with both of them."

"You didn't like that, did you?"

"I wanted what was best for Eddie. It seemed to be best that he live in Albion when Eddie's father and I separated."

"Did you like the fact Eddie wanted to live with his grandparents?"

"Any mother would prefer her son live with her."

"Is that why you hated your father?"

"No. I told you I hate–there you've got me using that word–I don't hate my father. It's just that I hate the fact that he killed my mother."

"Over your objection. Right?"

"Of course over my objection. I would never consent to his killing my mother."

"If you had agreed to Dr. Jacobson's request that the respirator be turned off, would you have hated your father?"

"How can I answer that? I didn't agree. I most strongly objected."

"Judge Neal, did you refuse to agree to ending your mother's artificial life because of your hatred for your father?"

"No. That wasn't the reason at all."

"What was your reason then?"

"My mother was still alive. You don't just kill someone because they are terribly sick–just because they are going to die–just because they are in a coma. Not even if the coma might last for the rest of their life. It's still murder."

"Unless the family agrees?"

"And, if there is no power of attorney, the family must agree–and I didn't agree. I made that clear."

"Judge Neal, did your mother ever talk to you about what she would want if such a tragedy ever struck?"

"No."

"What would you have advised her if she had told you, she would not want to be kept alive under such circumstances?"

"I probably would have told her to see her lawyer and have a power of attorney drawn up."

"Would you have tried to talk her out of it? Talk her out of her decision?"

"No. That would have been her decision."

"All right. Now, Judge Neal, what if Dr. Jacobson had told you–told you when he visited your office–that your mother had briefly regained consciousness and said she wanted her life ended?"

"Your Honor, that question is purely hypothetical," objected Cain. "How is this witness to know ?"

"Overruled, Mr. Cain. This is still cross examination. Please answer the question."

"If she had told him that?"

"Yes. Told him she wanted her life ended. Would you have agreed to her request?"

"And she didn't have anything in writing?"

"Nothing in writing. First of all, would you have believed Dr. Jacobson, if he had told you that?"

"I've never known him to lie."

"All right then, would you have agreed to your mother's respirator being turned off, if that's what she wanted?"

The courtroom was absolutely still. All eyes were watching the witness struggling to find an answer.

"Yes. I believe I would have. If that's what my mother wanted."

"If you were in the same situation that your mother was in and you told your doctor that's what you wanted, would you want him to follow your wishes?"

"Now, Your Honor, I think that question is definitely too far afield," objected Cain.

"Yes. I'm inclined to agree. The objection is sustained."

"That's all right, Your Honor, I am nearly finished with this witness."

Billie watched as Jefferson returned to the counsel table, where he remained standing. She felt confused by the cross examination. It seemed that Jefferson had been making some points, but she was not sure he had done much to change anything.

"Now, Judge Neal, you have testified that your father stands to inherit the trust fund your grandfather set up?"

"Yes."

"How much money is that?"

"I don't know. Years ago it was about a quarter of a million dollars. It's probably much larger now. Maybe a million."

"Did your father know about this trust?"

"I'm sure he did. They would have had to report the income on their tax return."

"Your mother wanted your father to inherit this in the event of her death?"

"Once I was the beneficiary, but she was afraid of hurting his feelings, so she put him back on. As far as I know that was her last will."

"Now, do you actually think your father is capable of murdering your mother so that he could inherit your grandfather's money?"

"People have murdered for much less than that."

"Your father is a respected retired professor at Albion College, is he not?"

"People in high positions in life can commit murder, Mr. Jefferson."

"I suppose so. I suppose some people in this world would do anything for money, or even for revenge for some real or imagined wrong. Judge

Neal, do you know, under Michigan law, whether a man who is convicted of murdering his wife is permitted to inherit from her?"

"That's a bar exam type of question. Such a person cannot inherit under Michigan law."

"I see. So if your father is convicted in this case, he would not inherit your grandfather's trust?"

"That would be correct."

"Judge Neal. If that should be the case, if your father were convicted, who would inherit the million dollars?"

"Well, I would. I would be the next in line. I suppose I would be the one to inherit."

"Objection, Your Honor. Irrelevant."

"Overruled counsel. It goes to credibility of the witness."

"Let me be certain I understand. If your father is convicted of murder, you will inherit your grandfather's million dollars. Am I right?" Joseph continued.

"Mr. Jefferson, I don't know what you are insinuating."

"I'm not insinuating anything at this point. I'm merely asking whether your testimony here today will assist you in inheriting one million dollars."

"Mr. Jefferson, I'm a Federal Judge. I am financially secure. I resent your insinuation that I would perjure myself for money."

"Let me remind you of your testimony a few minutes ago. Did you not tell this jury that you believed that people were capable of committing murder for much less than your grandfather's million dollars?"

"Yes, but I was talking about some people."

"You were talking about your father, weren't you?"

"Objection. Counsel is arguing with the witness."

"Sustained."

"Didn't you tell this jury that people in high places can commit murder?"

"Well, yes, I believe I did."

"Would you consider a Federal Judge *a person in a high place?*"

"Yes, I would, but I'm not being accused of murder."

"Do you believe that if persons in high places can commit murder that persons in high places can also commit perjury?"

"Objection. Argumentative. Counsel persists in arguing with the witness," said Cain.

"Sustained."

"Judge Neal. Did you cause the prosecutor in this case to bring this case against your father?"

"What do you mean *cause?*. How could a private citizen *cause* a prosecutor to do anything?"

"Judge Neal, pursuant to a subpoena *duces tecum* served on the prosecutor's office, I have a copy of a log of visitors to the prosecutor's office commencing with the date after your mother's death. I can show it to you if you wish."

"Why would I want to see that?"

"Because of what it shows, Judge Neal. Is it not true that you visited the offices of the prosecutor for this county?"

"I remember visiting his office."

"You saw the prosecutor, Al Lasser, on the very day of your mother's funeral, did you not?"

"Yes."

"That must have been very difficult for you."

"I was very busy. I was in the middle of a trial."

"Why did you see Mr. Lasser?"

"I wanted to see what he was going to do"

"What he was going to do?"

"About my mother's murder–her death."

"You wanted to see if he was going to prosecute your father isn't that correct?"

"I had every right to do that."

"And was he going to prosecute your father?"

"As I remember, he was."

"Al Lasser told you he was going to prosecute?"

"Well, as I recall, he didn't have all the evidence in yet–the coroner's report–that sort of thing–but when I left it was clear to me he was going to prosecute–yes."

As the questioning continued, Billie, for the first time in the trial, found her attention wandering. She felt divided and confused. At first she was sympathetic to Judge Neal. Here was a very accomplished woman who obviously loved her mother. Billie could understand why she would be reluctant to consent to ending her mother's life. She hoped her own daughters would be reluctant under such circumstances.

Yet how could a daughter testify against her own father in his murder trial? After all, this wasn't a case where Dr. Neal had killed her mother for another woman or something like that. Not only was she testifying, but apparently she had been involved in seeing to it that the prosecutor had brought charges. Under the circumstances, Billie found this unseemly. She couldn't believe Dr. Neal would kill his wife for the trust fund. That, too, seemed unseemly for his daughter to suggest.

Billie realized she shouldn't be thinking this way. She was supposed to wait until all the evidence was in before reaching a judgment. Still, she couldn't help wondering.

"Mr. Cain, do you have any redirect?" Judge Hoskins asked when Jefferson had finished his questioning.

"Just one or two questions, Your Honor. Judge Neal, Mr. Jefferson has been quite wide-ranging in his cross examination. I would like for a moment to get back to basics."

"Very well."

"Dr. Jacobson asked you to agree to ending your mother's life. Is that correct?"

"Yes."

"And you told him that you considered it murder and that you would not agree?"

"That's right. I told him I would take legal action if my wishes were not respected."

"Did you refuse to agree to ending her life because of ill feelings toward your father?"

"Absolutely not."

"Why did you refuse?"

"Because I loved my mother and wanted her to live as long as she could."

"And no other reason?"

"No other reason, Mr. Cain."

"Thank you, Judge Neal. I'm sure this has been very difficult for you. I have no other questions."

"There will be a fifteen minute recess," declared Judge Hoskins. "The court will be in session at 11:15."

David remained at the counsel table with Joseph, as the courtroom emptied.

"Do you think Betty was the one who made them bring charges against me?"

"They might have filed the case anyway, but I feel sure she put the arm on Lasser," Joseph answered.

"That makes me very sad," said David.

"How about angry? If it were me, I'd be mad as hell at her."

"I'm not really angry. Just numb that it has come to this."

-47-

"Damn, that guy is good," Marge lamented, referring to Joseph Jefferson's cross examination of Betty. "He made her look like a hard-hearted bitch."

During the recess Fred and Marge were having coffee in the basement of the courthouse.

"She is a hard-hearted bitch, but don't worry about it."

"Don't worry about it?"

"Yeah, Jefferson is good. There's no doubt about it." Fred sipped his coffee. "But he's being forced to use one of the oldest tactics in the books."

"And what's that?" Marge lit up a cigarette. She had taken up smoking again until the trial was over.

"If you don't have a good case, do your damnedest to make the other guy's witness look bad."

"But what if they don't like her? Dammit, Fred, I didn't like her and she was supposed to be a good witness for you."

"Look, Marge, I never liked the woman from the very beginning, but whether you like her, I like her, or no one on the whole damn jury likes her, doesn't matter. The only thing I needed her for was to show that she didn't consent to her mother's death."

"Oh, you can bet they'll believe that all right. It was obvious she had some axe to grind with her father. She never would have consented in a million years."

"That's all I had to prove. She didn't consent and that's that. If she does-n't consent, the doctor isn't going to pull the plug. Neal had no legal right to do what he did. He killed his wife. With the coroner, I will have made my case."

"The coroner is your last witness, then?"

"Yes. He'll establish the time and cause of death and we'll have proved our case."

"It's funny," Marge said, looking at the clock and finishing her coffee.

"What's that?"

"I always thought of a murder trial as lasting days and days."

"All I have to do is prove the legal elements of the crime, plain and simple. The coroner will button that up. Soon it'll be time for my summation. I just need to convince the jury to do their duty."

Fred had been pushing his election campaign for weeks now–speeches before Lions and Rotary Clubs–radio talk shows. After the trial was over he was going to go after it full bore. Marge had lined up speeches for him nearly every night until the election. Several debates with Lasser were scheduled. The publicity the case had been getting had made him famous. He thought more people knew him than knew Lasser. The mercy killing issue had people stirred up. There was a chance that he might get so well-known that he'd have a shot of winning the election even if he lost the case.

They walked up the stairs to the courtroom. Fred felt good about the case. Jefferson was going to be left with nothing but an emotional argument, trying to justify the killing. It was true that there might be someone on the jury who would hang it up. All it took was one juror who would defy the law and fact that a murder had been committed, but Fred had known that risk from the beginning. It was a chance he had to take to have his shot at winning the election.

"State your name and occupation," said the clerk.

"William Foley. Special Deputy in the coroner's office." Foley was a fiftyish balding man wearing a conservative suit.

"You conducted the autopsy of Lu Neal, the victim in this case."

"I did. I had been brought in from Lansing that week."

Foley explained that he was a pathologist practicing with a Lansing hospital, who had been brought in because the coroner's office had been short-handed the week of Lu's death.

"Did you arrive at an opinion as to the cause of death?"

"Yes."

"Would you state that opinion, please?"

Foley opened a folder that he held before him as he testified. "In layman's terms, Lu Neal died as a result of suffocation."

"Can you be more specific, please?"

"Having read the hospital records, it is clear that her life had been sustained by a ventilator."

"What is the function of a ventilator?"

"Mrs. Neal was in a coma. Her ventilator artificially supplied oxygen to her. That source of oxygen had been terminated–removed–and so she suffocated."

"She died as a result of oxygen starvation?"

"Yes–lack of oxygen."

"I have no further questions."

Fred sat down with a sense of relief that his portion of the trial was over. Jefferson would take his best shot, but it was a prosecutor's job to present the facts showing a conviction and Fred knew he had done a solid job of doing that.

"Mr. Jefferson. Cross examination, if you wish," said Judge Hoskins.

"Thank you, Your Honor," said Joseph, rising to his feet and approaching the witness stand. "Dr. Foley, I shall not take long. I'm sure this was a routine case for you, and you wish to get back to Lansing."

Foley did not answer, but smiled warily. Fred had warned him to be careful in answering Jefferson's questions.

"How long could Mrs. Neal have survived without her ventilator?"

"Not very long. In most cases a very few minutes, if that."

"You say that the ventilator was removed?"

"Yes."

"And that is what caused her death?"

"Yes. In my opinion."

"Dr. Foley do you know who removed her ventilator?"

"Well, I assume–"

"No," Jefferson raised his hand to stop the witness. "Perhaps you have misunderstood my question. What I asked was whether you–Dr. William Foley of Lansing Michigan–know who removed Mrs. Neal's ventilator that night."

"Of course not. I was not there."

"Exactly."

"You don't even know whether in fact her ventilator had been turned off?"

"No. Not of my own knowledge."

"Precisely. You were not there. Could she have died from some other cause?"

"Some other cause? Not in my opinion."

"Dr. Foley, prior to performing the autopsy, did you confer with anyone?"

"No. Except, of course, the attending physician, Dr. Jacobson."

"Did he tell you the ventilator had been turned off?"

"Yes. At least I remember his telling me about the husband being there and all of that."

"Had he told you that Dr. Neal had wanted him to turn off the ventilator?"

"Yes. Apparently it was a sad case."

"And he told you that he had not done so?"

"Right. The rest of the family had objected."

"So when you commenced the autopsy, you thought that probably the defendant had turned off the ventilator?"

"No. I didn't think anything. It was my professional task to determine the cause of death."

"Of course, Doctor, but if the cause of death turned out to be suffocation. Wouldn't it be natural for you to assume that the defendant had turned off the ventilator?"

"Perhaps so, but who had turned it off was not my function."

"Who had turned it off was not medically relevant?"

"No it was not."

"But isn't it fair to assume that before you commenced the autopsy you at least had a tentative opinion, perhaps only a thought, that the deceased had died from her ventilator's being turned off?"

"No. I had no such assumption."

"But Dr. Jacobson had told you what had happened."

"I made no such assumption."

"Not even tentatively?"

"Not even tentatively."

"Now, turning to Mrs. Neal's condition. Did you note that she had had a massive stroke?"

"Yes. Some 60 days earlier. She had been in a coma."

"Did your autopsy confirm the stroke?"

"Certainly. She had had a massive stroke."

"Did she die from the stroke?"

"No."

"No?"

"Well, I suppose one could say that it was a contributing cause."

"Yes, Dr. Foley, but what do *you* say?"

"Mr. Jefferson, without the stroke's having occurred she would not have been on the ventilator. So of course the stroke contributed to her death."

"I see, but you think turning off the ventilator was the primary cause?"

"Yes. I do."

"Dr. Foley, if the ventilator had not been turned off, how long would Mrs. Neal have lived?"

"Oh, I don't know. I have no way of knowing that."

"Would she have lived ten years?"

"Certainly not. She was in her 70s. Although I've read of some cases…"

"Ten months?"

"I don't know."

"Ten minutes?"

"Mr. Jefferson, there is no way of knowing that. You or I might not live ten minutes."

"But this patient had had a massive stroke."

"Yes."

"Was in a coma."

"She really could have died anytime without its being a surprise. Isn't that a fact?"

"Yes. I suppose."

"You suppose. Dr. Foley, you are a man of science. Isn't it a fact that that night Mrs. Neal could have died at any time without it being a surprise?"

"Yes. That is so."

"Is it not true that she could have possibly died of natural causes ten seconds before the ventilator was turned off?"

"That's not likely."

"I didn't ask what was likely. I asked what was possible. Now I'll repeat my question. Is it not a medical possibility that Mrs. Neal might have died ten seconds before the ventilator was turned off?"

"I suppose anything is possible."

"Thank you for your candor Doctor. Now turning to another area of inquiry."

"Very well."

"Dr. Foley, you say that Mrs. Neal was in a coma for 60 days?"

"That's what the records show. Of course I wasn't there."

"Agreed. Dr. Foley is it possible for stroke patients–patients in comas–to regain consciousness?"

"Certainly patients do come out of comas on occasions."

"And when patients occasionally come out of comas, is it possible that they can speak or otherwise communicate–such as fluttering their eyelids or squeezing hands–that sort of thing?."

"I've heard of such cases."

"Thank you, Dr. Foley. I have no further questions."

Fred Cain verily jumped to his feet. He had expected the coroner's testimony to be routine, but Jefferson was cleverly trying to implant some sort of doubt, however unreasonable, in the minds of the jury.

"First of all, Dr. Foley, let us discuss this theory of stroke patients regaining consciousness. Are you aware of any evidence whatsoever that Mrs. Neal regained consciousness?"

"No."

"Even for a moment?"

"No. I was only speaking of some patients."

"But not this patient?"

"No."

"Dr. Foley, in performing your autopsy did you examine the damage the stroke had caused to the victim's brain?"

"Yes. I did."

"To what extent was it damaged?"

"There was severe damage. Very severe damage."

"In your opinion, was it possible for Mrs. Neal to have regained consciousness?"

"No. It was not."

"Was it possible for her to have heard someone speak?"

"No."

"Was it possible for her to communicate in any way such as squeezing her hand or fluttering her eyelids?"

"No."

"Now, you said you've heard of cases where this has happened to some patients."

"Yes, but they were not persons with such extensive brain damage. Furthermore…"

"Yes?"

"Furthermore, there is another phenomenon at work."

"And what is that?"

"The psychological."

"Would you elaborate, please?"

"It is not unheard of for the loved ones of such stroke victims to think they detect signs of consciousness, where, in fact, there are none. Sometimes people want to believe something so desperately that they see things that are not so."

"They imagine them?"

"Yes."

"Now, turning to another area of inquiry by Mr. Jefferson—this ten-seconds-before-death theory."

"Yes."

"Dr. Foley, did you detect any evidence whatsoever that Mrs. Neal had died before the ventilator was turned off?"

"No. I did not."

"In your medical opinion, did Mrs. Neal die by suffocation?"

"Yes, she did."

"And not from her stroke?"

"Not from her stroke, except as I indicated."

"That is, she had had a stroke, and so was dependent on her ventilator?"

"That is what I meant."

"And she did not die from some other cause?"

"No."

"Thank you clarifying your testimony. I have no further questions."

"Mr. Jefferson? Anything further?"

"Yes, Your Honor. Dr. Foley, let's set the record straight. Mrs. Neal could have died at any time without its being a medical surprise. Isn't that what you said?"

"Yes."

"Ten minutes before the respirator was removed?"

"Yes. I would have to agree to that."

"As you said, even ten seconds before."

"Theoretically."

"Someone that sick could drop off at any moment. I have no further questions."

"Mr. Cain?"

"Thank you, Your Honor. Dr. Foley theoretically I might die in ten seconds. Isn't that correct?"

"Yes. That is correct."

"No further questions."

"Any further questions, Mr. Jefferson," asked the judge.

Joseph rose to his feet. "But Mr. Cain, here, has not had a severe stroke and been in a coma for 60 days. Has he?"

"Objection. Argumentative. Asked and answered," said Cain.

"Gentlemen," Judge Hoskins interrupted. "I can see you each want to be the last to speak, but I think we've had enough. Quite enough. Mr. Cain, you can call your next witness."

"The people have called their last witness, Your Honor. The people rest."

"Very well. I see that it is nearly five o'clock. We will start tomorrow at nine o'clock with the defense. Will you be ready, Mr. Jefferson?"

"Yes, Your Honor."

"Very well, until nine o'clock tomorrow the court is adjourned."

-48-

David pushed away his half-finished tray of jail food. The reality was he had little real hope of ever getting out of jail. It was true that part of him thought how wonderful it would be to live and eat at home, but that seemed more a fantasy than a genuine possibility. After all these months the stark routine of jail had become his reality.

Joseph had told him that he had learned from Ruby that Eddie had enlisted in the Marines. It was a relief to know Eddie was safe. Lu would be proud. If a miracle occurred and he were acquitted, he could talk to Eddie on the telephone. He was eager to know more of his grandson's story. Why had he joined the Marines? How did he like it? Did he plan to make the Marines his profession?

These past few days David was in something akin to a dream state. It was as if the trial were happening to another man and he knew the other man had little chance of victory. While Joseph had been brilliant at cross examination, the fact was he had killed Lu. He had to admit that before his ordeal with Lu's stroke, he would have voted guilty, if he were on the jury.

He wished he could feel optimistic about the trial. He knew from his own experience in the service in the war that Eddie needed a place to call home—a place he would want to be on leave—a place where he could yearn to be. If only he could provide such a place for Eddie, but he didn't know how.

"Your lawyer is here," said the jailer.

Jefferson had worked out a plan with the authorities whereby he was allowed in David's cell for consulting his client. They were far from the guard station and were assured of privacy.

David knew his lawyer had been staying at the nearby bed and break-fast, reading testimony transcripts and preparing until late at night. He saw that Joseph looked dispirited–his vigor drained. A trial like this would exhaust a younger man. He was grateful to Joseph for defending him.

"David, I've made an important decision." Joseph sat in the customary wooden side chair, while David sat on his small bed.

"You look tired."

"I must admit I am," said Joseph. "Maybe murder trials are for younger men, all full of piss and vinegar."

David sensed it was his turn to do the cheering up. "You're the only lawyer I'd ever want. Younger men just don't know what life is about." He felt good being able to help this man who was doing so much for him.

"Maybe I need my second wind."

"Maybe I do too," said David. "Maybe that's what the last years of a man's life are about. Getting his second wind."

"It's really all I know to do–defend my clients." Wearily Joseph let his briefcase drop beside his chair.

"You're very good at it, you know," David said.

"You know, back when we first met, we were talking about a man's pur-pose? You got me to thinking about that."

"I was pretty depressed then."

"Hell, David, I don't know what my purpose is. I don't even know if I'm supposed to have a purpose. All I know is that I wouldn't know what to do with myself if I stopped trying criminal cases. I never feel better than when I'm in the middle of a rousing court fight. I know the arena. It's *my* arena. Sometimes I lose, but I know no one could do better." Joseph paused. "I know something else too."

David smiled, waiting for his lawyer and now his friend to go on.

Joseph looked back at David. "I know my daddy would be proud. And that's important to me. To know my daddy would be proud."

"Maybe I need to know Lu would be proud of me. Now that she's gone, there's no one else to be proud of me any more. Funny for a 76-year-old man to admit, but I don't know that I've ever been particularly proud of myself."

"Well, I'm going to give you a chance to be proud tomorrow."

"How?"

"I'm going to have you take the witness stand"

"Take the witness stand?"

"Yes. I've given it a lot of thought. That jury's got to be dying to know what you're like. To really know you. To hear your story. To know why you did what you did."

"But I killed her. I told you that. Wouldn't I be digging my own grave by admitting that on the witness stand?"

"I can't gamble that I've raised a reasonable doubt in their minds. It's a better gamble to have you take the stand. They're going to wonder why you didn't explain yourself to them. Sure the judge is going to tell them you have every right not to testify, but our best shot is for them to see you as a human being. I'm going to bet there will be at least one juror who won't have the guts to send you to Jackson Prison."

"What will I say?"

"The truth. All I want is for you to tell them what you told me. Tell them exactly what happened. I'm going to put Ben Jacobson on the stand and then I'm going to finish with you."

"Joseph, I know you're the lawyer and I'm the client. As far as I'm concerned, you're the best lawyer in the whole country; but I can't help think that when I tell the jury that I killed her, I won't have a chance."

"You may be right," Joseph pondered. "Reading juries is tough, if not impossible, but I've got to be candid with you."

David leaned forward intently.

"I've cross examined a million witnesses and I've gotten pretty damn good at it."

"You sure have. You made them look foolish–especially that coroner."

"I may have scored some points, but the truth of the matter is that most of it was pure bullshit."

"But..."

"All I was doing was kicking up a bunch of dust. Cain is going to point that out in final argument."

"Well, I didn't think so. I thought you raised a good many points."

"What? That your daughter hates you? All Cain needed her testimony for was to show she did not consent to have Dr. Jacobson turn off the respirator."

"Well it's true, she didn't consent."

"There you have it!" Joseph pointed out. "It doesn't matter a whit that Betty hates you. The only legal point is she didn't give her consent."

"But the coroner."

"The coroner was a fool, but do you think any juror is going to think Lu died ten seconds before you turned off the respirator? I think not."

David nodded his understanding.

"Oh, sure, I might conceivably raise a reasonable doubt in the mind of one juror, but I'm not willing to bet on it. No, David, our best shot is you taking the witness stand. I think once they hear the plight you were in, we have a better chance at it."

"Okay, Joseph. You're the lawyer. I'm worried, though."

"Of course you're worried."

"I just hope I can explain things to them."

Joseph stood up as if to go.

"You can if you do one thing."

"What's that?"

"Don't rehearse. Don't think about what you're going to say."

"Okay."

"And one thing more." The lawyer looked intently at his client. "When you're on that stand I want you to stop being a professor for once in your life. For God's sake, man, don't hold back your feelings. Be like you were with me when I came in here tonight. Let them see what you're really like."

David knew what Joseph was talking about. He had always had trouble telling people about his feelings. "I'll try. I'll do my best."

"If you feel like crying when you're on that stand, then for God's sake cry. There are no prizes given for hiding what you went through."

David took a deep breath and sighed. "I know you're right."

"Oh, and one other thing." Joseph opened his briefcase. "Ruby gave me this. It's a letter to you from your grandson. It came today. I guess he figured he couldn't write you in jail."

As soon as Joseph left, David eagerly opened the envelope. It was postmarked San Diego.

> *Dear Grandfather,*
>
> *Ruby says you are in the middle of your trial. I know it must be tough. I tried to see you before I left for California, but the lady at the jail said I wasn't allowed. I'm sorry I haven't written, but they don't give us any time to ourselves. Besides I didn't know how to write to you in jail. Right now I'm in Chapel. It's the only time any of the guys have to write.*
>
> *I've been having a really tough time too. I don't know if I would have joined the Marines if I had known how tough it would be. We've had a couple of guys drop out and some others talk about it. I'm going to stick it out though. I don't know what else I would do. I can see why you and Granna kept telling me I should get the grades to go to college. The Marines do have a good program to help get a college education. I'm going to look into it more.*
>
> *I'm sorry to be writing about myself so much when you are in such trouble. I think it's terrible that they claim you murdered Granna. I've thought a lot about what you did and I know it was for the best. I wish I could help you some way.*
>
> *You know what, Grandfather? When guys ask me about my family, I tell them you're my family. I never realized how important my family was until I got into the Marines. I guess all I can really*

say is that you are very important to me. I really hate to think of
you in that jail. Please do your best to win your case.
I love you, Grandfather. I'm sorry I never told you before, but you
know how hard it has always been in our family to talk about
things like that. I wish I could see you even for a few minutes.
Well, Chapel is over now.
Love,
Eddie

David had begun crying halfway through the letter. *I love you too,*
Eddie. Damn, he wished he had been able to tell Eddie that all along. How
ironic it was. Here he was 76 years old and Eddie was only 18, yet Eddie
had been the first to be able to express his love. If he ever got out of this
jail, the first thing he was going to do was tell Eddie he loved him. In fact,
he decided, he would write him a letter right now.

Dear Eddie,
I can't tell you how much your letter meant to me. I was afraid
you were still upset about what I did to Granna. Even if the jury
convicts me, I now know that you will go through life feeling that
I did the right thing.
You are right, our family had always found it difficult to tell each
other how we felt. I'm supposed to be a psychology expert and I
can't tell you why. It seems to run in families. Maybe it's a
Midwestern attribute. Anyway, I'm glad you told me you love me.
Now let me tell you some things about my feelings that I've never
told anyone—not even your grandmother. I loved you from the day
you were born—even before you were born. I can't explain to you
what it means for a man to have a grandchild. Perhaps it is
because you are a man's chance to live beyond his own years.
Some say that, but I think it's more. Somehow it's a chance for the

generations to connect up. It gives a man a chance to see that he's a part of a chain of people that stretches from the beginning on into the future. Maybe that's it. Maybe it gives a man a chance to feel that he matters. Someday maybe we will be given an opportunity to talk about these things. There comes a time when the future of a man's grandchild is more important to him than his own future. Maybe someday you will be lucky enough to have a grandson of your own and you will understand what I am trying to say.

It always hurt me that your mother felt so antagonistic toward me, but I'll let you in on another little secret. When you left your mother to live with us, I was secretly glad. It gave me a chance to be with you and maybe have an effect on your life.

You say that you tell your friends that I am your family. Eddie, you are my family. I am proud of you being in the Marines. I know it is difficult, but you will always be glad if you stick it out.

Well, Eddie tomorrow is a big day in court for me. My attorney says I shouldn't think about it, but get a good night's sleep. I'll sleep better having received your letter. Maybe if things go well, we can really be a family again. I would like that. Having a family with you would be worth living for. Thank you for reminding me, when I feel so discouraged.

Remember, no matter what happens, your grandfather loves you.

It was an hour before David fell asleep. He kept thinking about Eddie's letter and how important it was to do a good job tomorrow. All he could do was his best. As Joseph had said, he shouldn't even think about it. His job was simply to answer the questions and explain to the jury why he had done what he had done. From then on, his fate would not be in his own hands.

-49-

Joseph displayed confidence as he rose from his place next to David at the counsel table. Years of experience had taught him that how the jury perceived him was as important as the evidence he presented. "I call Dr. Ben Jacobson to the witness stand."

After Dr. Jacobson was sworn in, Joseph began questioning.

"Dr. Jacobson, you were the family physician for David and Lu Neal?"

"Ever since I started practicing. Over 25 years now."

"You were the doctor in charge when Mrs. Neal had her stroke?"

"Yes. Thanksgiving last year. It was a long, sad struggle."

"Mrs. Neal was in a coma?"

"Yes. Until the day she died."

"Dr. Jacobson, have you treated many stroke patients?"

"Oh, yes, many."

"Have you seen them in comas?"

"Yes."

"Many?"

"Yes, many."

"Did you have an opinion as to the likelihood of Lu Neal regaining consciousness?"

"Yes, I did."

"What was that opinion?"

"It was extremely unlikely. No, I would say more than that. I was of the opinion that it was impossible. Well, of course, we all know nothing is impossible, so I'd say virtually impossible."

"And why is that?"

"Because of her condition. Her stroke was so massive."

"Now you said it was *virtually* impossible for her to have regained consciousness?"

"Yes."

"Do you mean that in your opinion there was some–however slight–some possibility of her regaining consciousness?"

"Yes. However slight. I have read or heard of a case–perhaps a case or two–where a patient did regain consciousness–surprising everybody."

"So in your opinion it is possible that Lu Neal could have regained consciousness before she died–however briefly?"

"Possible. Yes."

Joseph was satisfied. He had established in the jury's mind a medical possibility that Lu Neal could have regained consciousness enough to have signaled David that she wanted him to end her life.

"Now, Dr. Jacobson, did you tell Dr. Neal that his wife was likely to be permanently in her coma?"

"Not at first. He wasn't ready for that."

"But later?"

"Yes. More than once."

"Tell us about the first time."

"Well, I remember his asking me–it was maybe a month after the stroke–whether she would ever recover even a little bit–you know, regain consciousness. Shall I go on?"

"Yes. Please."

"You see, in the beginning David was so optimistic about at least a partial recovery that I didn't have the heart to tell him the truth. But then, in this conversation I'm telling you about, his original optimism had faded. We talked about Lu's condition and I told him the truth–that she wasn't going to recover."

"How did he respond?"

"He was still somewhat in his state of denial. However he had no alternative, but to begin to accept the truth. And then later…"

"Yes. Tell us about the next conversation on this point."

"It was more gradual over a period of time. The next main conversation I recall is when he asked me what I thought about allowing Lu to die."

"What did the two of you say?"

"Well, he wanted to know what I thought. First whether it would be morally wise to let her go, and second, legally. Whether legally we could let her go."

"And what did you say?"

"You see, they had nothing in writing. No power of attorney–no will–nothing designating anyone to make the decision to allow her life to end. I told David as far as I was concerned Lu's life was over–it was very difficult for me to say–that she would never recover even in the slightest." Dr. Jacobson sighed and went on. "That she should be allowed to go, but I also told him that it was his decision morally, not mine. I suggested he think about it. Maybe ask the opinion of others–like his minister."

"What did he say to that?"

"He said he would think about it. I think he said he'd pray about it. I know he often went down to the river…to pray, I guess."

"Now, you also told us you discussed whether it could be legally done."

"Yes. I told him that for generations doctors have had to make decisions like this. But I told him we would not do it without permission of the family. I'm talking about cases where there is nothing in writing."

"I understand."

"David is a long-time friend. I knew he didn't get on well with his daughter. I told him his daughter's permission would be necessary. I can't remember whether it was this time or the next time, I volunteered to see Betty–to see if she would grant her permission."

"Now, let me go back and be sure we're understanding you. You told Dr. Neal that even without something in writing, there are cases where doctors remove life support systems—in effect allowing terminally ill patients to die?"

"Yes. It's done all the time. In fact I remember his asking me if I had to go before some hospital committee to get permission."

"Do you?"

"No. Not in this part of the state at least. Some big hospitals have committees—some call them ethics committees. Doctors go before these committees, but we don't have them in the smaller towns. Oh, I would probably get the opinion of a consultant."

"A consultant?"

"Yes. In many cases it's too big decision to make all on your own. So even if there's a power of attorney, we call in another doctor—a consultant—to get his opinion. This is especially true where there's no power of attorney. "

"Did you do that in this case? Call in a specialist?"

"No, Betty wouldn't agree, so there was no point."

"We'll get to that in a moment. Did you have another meeting with Dr. Neal on this subject?"

"Yes. This time he wanted Lu to be allowed to die. He had thought about it—he may have talked to others—and he had made his decision. He even wanted Ruby, the nurse, to do it with me."

"And what would you have done?"

"Simply turned the ventilator way down and allowed her to die."

"But of course that didn't happen."

"No. Betty refused."

"Now, doctor I wish to move on to another subject." Joseph took a deep breath. So far he had made the exact points he wanted the jury to hear. He had expected some objections here and there, but, evidently for strategic reasons of his own, Cain had held back. However, Joseph knew very well Cain would object to the next question. He also knew very well Judge Hoskins would sustain the objection. But he would ask it anyway.

"If Lu Neal had regained consciousness and had asked you to *let her die* as you put it, would you have needed to get Betty Neal's permission?"

"Objection. Incompetent, irrelevant and immaterial." Cain had jumped to his feet. "Furthermore, it is purely hypothetical."

"I agree. The objection is sustained," Hoskins ruled.

Joseph inwardly smiled. The question didn't need answering. He had no doubt that the jury would conclude that Dr. Jacobson, given the chance, would have honored Lu Neal's request to die.

"I have no further questions."

"Mr. Cain?" asked the judge.

Joseph resumed his place next to David as Cain rose to begin his cross examination. "It went well," he whispered to David. Yes, he was pleased with the points he had made, but, as a seasoned trial lawyer, Joseph never became elated when the trial's momentum went his way. He knew exactly which points he would try to make if he were Fred Cain, and he had seen enough of his ambitious opponent to know he was not likely to miss a trick. This very uncertainty of outcome was why Joseph never tired of trying criminal cases. He was almost impassive as he leaned back to watch Cain's effort at reversing the elusive momentum of the trial.

"Dr. Jacobson, I was listening carefully to your testimony," Cain began. "But there are one or two points that I need to clarify. Do you mind if I ask you to repeat yourself?"

"No." Dr. Jacobson looked apprehensive–as if he were a prey being stalked.

"I believe you testified the defendant told you he wanted you and the nurse, Ruby, to end his wife's life? Is that correct?"

"Yes. Eventually. Let Lu die. Yes."

"Well, Doctor, let's get at that issue first. Is there some difference that is escaping me between *letting someone's life end* and *ending their life?*"

"I've always thought so. Yes."

"Exactly what is that difference?"

"Letting someone die is not doing something that would keep them from dying."

"Like not giving an asthmatic his medicine when he's having an attack?"

"Objection, hypothetical," Joseph said reflexively.

"Overruled. This is cross examination. It will be allowed."

"You can answer the question," Cain continued. "Like not giving an asthmatic his medicine when he's having an attack?"

"Yes. I suppose so."

"So if someone sees an asthmatic in the middle of an attack and withholds his medicine that's on the table next to him, that is *letting him die?*"

"I've not thought of it that way."

"Well, what way do you think of it?"

"Deliberately not giving him medicine that is right there, that's more than I mean by *letting a person die.*"

"It sounds more like killing him, doesn't it, Doctor?"

"I suppose so, yes."

"Deliberately killing him?"

"Yes."

"Dr. Jacobson, you've practiced medicine a good many years in this area, haven't you?"

"Yes, over 25 years."

"And your purpose is to save lives, is it not?"

"Of course."

"I'm sure there has been many a night when you went without sleep in order to save lives."

"Yes. That's true."

"And I applaud you for it."

Dr. Jacobson did not respond. Joseph could see the apprehension on the doctor's face.

"When you treated Mrs. Neal for her stroke, was not your purpose to save her life?"

"If I could, yes. That and to make her comfortable."

"You prescribed all the treatment known to modern medicine to save Lu Neal's life, did you not?"

"Yes, of course. But it wouldn't do–didn't do–any good."

"But your purpose–your goal–in fact, your oath–was to try to save her life?"

"Yes."

"Certainly not to end it."

"No. That's true."

"Certainly not to kill her?"

"Objection. Argumentative," said Joseph.

"No. I'll allow it," Judge Hoskins ruled.

Immediately Joseph regretted the objection. Like his own question a few minutes ago, the damage was done in the asking of the question.

"No. I never wanted to kill her."

"But if Betty Neal had never been born, if Lu Neal's daughter had not been there to say *no*, you would have killed your patient, isn't that so?"

"No. I would have allowed her to die."

"Now, just a minute Doctor. You just said that withholding a dying asthmatic's medicine is not what you mean by *letting someone die,* isn't that so?"

"Yes, but the asthmatic could have kept on living. Don't you see?"

"Oh, so Lu Neal could not keep on living? Is that what you're saying?"

"There was no hope for Lu."

"Let's look at that issue for a moment. Lu Neal had lived for two months after her stroke?"

"Yes."

"Isn't it true that she could have lived another two months? Isn't that entirely possible?"

"She was in a coma."

"Please Doctor, I mean no disrespect, but isn't it true that your patient could have lived another two months?"

"She could have."

"Actually, she could have lived another year couldn't she?"

"Yes." Joseph could see a look of resignation in Dr. Jacobson's eyes—as if there were no way he could explain himself.

"Isn't it true that there are cases where patients have lived in comas for years?"

"Yes. I've read of them."

"Yet, you would have killed her, knowing she might have lived on?"

"I didn't kill her."

"Because Betty Neal objected."

"I never planned to kill Lu. I would have merely ordered the ventilator to be turned off."

"Which would have killed her?"

"She would have died."

"Tell me, Doctor, if Lu Neal had not been in a coma, but had been severely paralyzed…Let's say that she could not walk or talk, but was conscious; would you have considered *letting her go* by, say, depriving her of food so that she would die?"

"Of course not."

"Even if her husband had asked?"

"No."

"Even if her daughter had asked?"

"No."

"Even if Lu Neal herself had asked?"

"No. I would not have."

"So the distinction is being unconscious. Is that the distinction?"

"Lu Neal had been in a coma for 60 days. She was never going to regain consciousness."

"So her life should be ended?"

"We have to draw the line someplace."

"Do we Doctor? Do we really? And just who are the *we*? Is it the doctor? Is it the husband who stands to inherit from his wife?"

Joseph sprang to his feet. "Objection. The question is grossly argumentative. I–"

"The objection is sustained." Judge Hoskins was clearly annoyed. "Mr. Cain, you know better than that."

"I'm sorry, Your Honor. I do apologize."

Cain returned to the counsel table, as if to collect himself.

"Doctor Jacobson, would you have agreed to *let Lu Neal go* as you put it, if she had been in a coma for only, say, ten days?"

"No."

"Thirty days?"

"I don't know. Probably in this case, yes."

"But you would have brought in a consultant?"

"Yes. It's the practice."

"What if the consultant had pointed out something to you–something you might not have considered–and had said there was a possibility that Lu Neal might have regained consciousness?"

"I would have waited."

"Given her more life?"

"Yes. At least until the possibility could be resolved."

"Very well. If there's a possibility she might regain consciousness, you would wait?"

"Yes."

"Dr. Jacobson, did you not tell this jury, when Mr. Jefferson was questioning you, that you thought there was a possibility that Lu Neal might regain consciousness?"

"Well, yes, I did, but…"

"So in one case, where there is a possibility that she will regain consciousness you would let her go, but in another case, where a possibility exists, you would not let her go?"

"When I said there was a possibility, all I meant was…" Dr. Jacobson stumbled, trying to collect his thoughts. "All I meant was I couldn't deny the fact that somehow she might have regained consciousness, despite our scientific knowledge." The doctor was clearly frustrated.

"So even in cases where science can be wrong, and you admit it can be wrong, *we let them go.* Yet in other cases where another doctor says it might be wrong, we don't *let them go.* I'm confused. Is that what you mean?"

"We have to base our decisions on something."

"Do we? When all we have to do is do nothing, and let a higher power make the decision for us?"

Joseph had to admire Cain's performance. For as with Joseph, the courtroom was Cain's playing field.

"I would like to shift gears, now, to another area of questioning. You said that you discussed the legal aspects of mercy killing with the defendant?"

"Yes. He and Lu had no legal documents."

"I think you said that it is the practice in this community to *let people go* despite the fact they have not left the proper legal documents."

"Yes. If we all agree."

"You told Dr. Neal that?"

"Yes."

"Again, what did you tell him in that regard?"

"I told him that, if in my medical opinion the illness were terminal, I would call in a consultant. Then if we both had the same medical opinion, we could go ahead, if we had the consent of the family."

"Did you tell him what you meant by the *family?*"

"Yes. He and his daughter."

"So the daughter's consent was necessary?"

"Yes."

"Why the daughter?"

"Well, I knew that Betty and David didn't get along. We both knew that. So we had to get her consent."

"Because she could raise trouble if she hadn't agreed? Isn't that right?"

"I suppose so."

"What about their grandson?"

"I hadn't thought about Eddie. He was a minor. Besides Betty was Eddie's mother."

"Eddie had lived with the Neals there in Albion. Is that right?"

"Yes."

"So Eddie didn't count? Is that it?"

"Well, I didn't think we needed his consent."

"We can both agree that you are not a lawyer?"

"Yes. That's right."

"Do you know what the law on this subject is?"

"No. Not really. I've heard some lectures. I know what the practice is. I guess it's sort of a combination of law and medicine."

"Doctor, have you ever *let a patient go* when there was no power of attorney, yet the family and the doctors agreed?"

"Yes. Of course. Probably most doctors have. Years ago plenty of doctors didn't even consult the family if the case were clear enough."

"But here you clearly told the defendant that Betty's agreement was necessary?"

"Yes."

"And he asked you to go to her office to get her consent?"

"I volunteered, yes."

"And Betty Neal told you she would never agree–that it was *murder?*"

"Yes, she did."

"And you told the defendant of this conversation with his daughter?"

"I did."

"That his daughter called it *murder?*"

"Yes."

"And yet Lu Neal was dead the next time you saw her?"

"Yes."

"I have no further questions, Dr. Jacobson. I appreciate your candor. I know it must have been difficult under the circumstances."

Joseph thought of objecting to this attempt to play to the jury, but he knew the judge could do nothing to erase the remark from the jury's mind. Joseph mentally noted that now he too would be able to get away with a few ploys of his own.

David looked downcast as Judge Hoskins declared the noon recess, and the bailiff approached to take him to his cell. "It doesn't look good, does it?" he asked.

Joseph patted him on the back. "It's all right, David. Things are going exactly how I expected. You just relax for a while. I intend to put you on right after lunch."

Joseph stopped at the desk at the bed and breakfast. "Would you send my usual salad and iced tea to my room? I've got some preparation to do."

"Certainly, Mr. Jefferson. How did the trial go this morning?" asked the clerk.

"Just fine, Millie. Couldn't be better. Couldn't be better."

"I'm rooting for you. They shouldn't even be prosecuting Dr. Neal."

"Millie, you're my kind of woman. Too bad it's too late to get you on the jury," Joseph chuckled.

"All I've got to say is they'd better acquit him if they want to show their faces around this town again."

On his cellular telephone Joseph dialed the number of the automobile manufacturer on whose board he had served for these past few years.

"Chairman Donnelly's office," greeted the cheery voice.

"Hello, Bonnie, is he in? This is Joseph Jefferson. I'm calling from Marshall."

"Yes. He having a luncheon meeting in his office. I'll ring him."

"Thank you, Bonnie. It's important."

"Joseph. How's the mercy killing case going? You're on television all the time."

"It's got its ups and downs, thanks. I need your help desperately."

"Name it, Joseph. I'll do what I can."

"Listen, I'll reimburse the company, but I need one of the company jets to do something–right now, if possible."

"What's that?"

"There's a very important witness. I need him here tomorrow morning."

"Where is he?"

"He's a Marine. He's stationed at the Marine Training Depot, right next to the San Diego airport."

"Consider it done."

"And one other thing."

"Yes."

"I'd like you to call the Pentagon. He'll need special permission. Tell them this Marine's testimony may be my only hope to keep a Marine's grandfather from spending the rest of his days in jail."

-50-

avid was extremely nervous as he took the witness stand.

"Do you promise to tell the truth, the whole truth, and nothing but the truth, so help you, God?"

"I do." David hid his trembling hands from the jury. How could he ever explain the agony Lu's stroke had visited upon him? How could he put the jurors in his place, so they would understand why he had ended Lu's life? Could he persuade them he should not spend the rest of his days in Jackson Prison? Could he possibly convince them that when Eddie came home from the Marines to visit it should be at his Albion house and not behind prison bars? Could he make them believe he should be free to spend his last years making a new life–not wasting them in jail?

Joseph stood to one side of the jury box, so that David's face could be fully seen by the jury as he testified. Although his hands continued their tremor, the presence of his imposing attorney provided David with a degree of assurance.

"You are Dr. David Neal, the defendant in this matter?"

"Yes."

"Doctor Neal, did you murder your wife Lu Neal?"

David was startled. He had gone over his testimony with Joseph, but he had not expected the blunt question. He could see the same surprise on the faces of some of the jurors as he took a breath before answering. "I used to think that what I did was murder, but I no longer believe so."

"You did end her life, did you not?"

"Yes. At least I thought I had."

"Then why do you believe it was not murder?"

David searched for words. "I'm not sure I can properly explain it to another person–at least a person who hasn't been through what I have. I used to think no killing was justified under any circumstance and that it was murder. I guess I'm a wiser man now."

"Dr. Neal how long had you been married to Lu?"

"Fifty-one years."

"Happy years?"

"Most of them." For a moment David choked on a wave of emotion. "Many years ago we had some problems...but mostly we had a happy marriage."

"When did you move to Albion?"

"Nineteen fifty-two. When I began teaching at the college."

"Did your wife work outside the home?"

"Not for money, no."

"What do you mean by *not for money?*"

"Lu was always active in everything. Her garden clubs–the Albion Board of Education–giving speeches–you name it."

"She was a very active woman, then?"

"She was until–well..." David forced out the words. "Until she got sick."

"You had one child–a daughter?"

"Yes. Betty."

"I assume Lu was very busy raising Betty."

"Yes. Lu was always very close to Betty."

"Dr. Neal, you are estranged from your daughter?"

"I'd say she is estranged from me. I've tried, but...it's just been impossible." David turned his head to look at Betty in the front row, but she averted her eyes. "Apparently it's hopeless."

"But Lu kept a close relationship with your daughter?"

"Yes, although they didn't see each other that much. Betty had her career, you know. We both were very proud of her career."

"You are proud that she is a federal judge now?"

"Yes, I am. I didn't know of her appointment until recently."

"She didn't tell you?"

"No. You were the first to tell me."

Joseph looked at the jury before proceeding. "Did there come a time when your grandson lived with you?"

"Yes. Eddie."

"Betty's son?"

"Yes."

"And when was that?"

"Eddie kept running away from home. Betty had separated from her husband, you see. Eddie always came to our house when he would run away."

"They didn't get along?"

"That's right. Then finally we decided Eddie should live with us and go to high school in Albion."

"How old is Eddie?"

"He's 18. He's in the Marines. Still in Basic Training."

"How long had he lived with you before Lu's stroke?"

"Several months. He was doing much better in school. He loved his grandmother." Again David choked on the words.

"Was Eddie home with you Thanksgiving night of last year?"

"No. He was with his dad at the Lions game. Lu and I were watching the game on TV."

"Please tell the jury what happened that night."

"Lu had her stroke. I was in the living room watching the game and she didn't answer." With the recollection of the fateful evening David lost his composure. Tears came down his cheeks. He put his fist to his mouth catching his breath. "I'm sorry, I hadn't meant for this to happen." He made no attempt to wipe away his tears. It actually felt good to lose control. It eased his tension.

Joseph waited until David composed himself.

"I know this is difficult, but it is important that you tell us what happened."

"I went into the kitchen. Lu had collapsed on the floor." David struggled to tell the story.

"What did you do next?"

"When I couldn't get her to talk, I called the ambulance. I went with them to the hospital. I'll never forget that night. The ambulance. The hospital. The whole night."

"Dr. Jacobson has testified Lu was in a coma."

"Yes, for two months."

"I assume you visited your wife at the hospital."

"Always twice a day–at first three times."

"You are retired from teaching at Albion College?"

"Yes. Lu had been encouraging me to write another book, but it wasn't very good. I guess I was out of touch."

"You'd written books before?"

"Oh yes. My psychology textbook. Other books on psychology. But after I retired…well, I had plans to write, but they didn't work out." David knew he could not successfully convey the sense of futility he had over his retirement years.

"Going back to the stroke. At first did you expect Lu to recover?"

"I had no doubt of it. Lu's a fighter. I kept encouraging her. Telling her she could make it."

"I thought you said she was in a coma."

"She was, but I thought she might be able to hear me. I talked to her every night. Sometimes read to her. You know poetry. She liked poetry. I'd tell her how Eddie was doing in school."

"Do you think she heard you?"

"I had no way of knowing, but I kept hoping. Talking to her made me feel I still had her–that she was still alive." As he went along it was becoming easier for him to talk about his ordeal. He saw one of the jurors wipe her eye. Maybe he was making them understand, at least a little.

"Did there come a time when you despaired of your wife's recovery?"

"After a while–maybe a couple of weeks–I realized she probably would not completely recover. I guess what people were telling me had finally sunk in a little."

"What people? What did they tell you?"

"Objection. Calls for hearsay." Cain had not gotten to his feet to make the objection.

"No, Mr. Cain. Overruled," said the judge. "It's not being introduced for the truth of what people told him. It's to show his state of mind. It will be allowed."

"Go ahead. Who told you, and what did they tell you?" Joseph continued.

"Well, Betty for one."

"What did she say?"

"She told me I was a fool to think Lu might recover. I guess she was right."

"Did you agree with her at the time?"

"Oh, no! I told her she was wrong. I told her Lu would recover."

"Who else?"

"Dr. Jacobson. After a while he told me it looked pretty grim. I'm talking about those early couple of weeks. He was even more frank with me later."

"Did you believe him?"

"Not at first. I had these visions of wheeling Lu around in her wheelchair. You know, around the quad at the college when the weather was decent. I knew she might not be able to talk, but I always thought someday she'd come out of her coma–that she'd be able to hear me read to her–maybe even talk to me. Lu was such a wonderful conversationalist. Maybe I'd take her to the Faculty Room for coffee. I didn't know."

"But your visions never came true?"

"No. They did not."

Joseph moved a step closer to David, carefully not obstructing the jury's view. "Did there come a time when you became convinced that Lu was never going to come out of her coma?"

"I finally realized I'd been in denial. That she was never going to regain consciousness."

"You were a professor of psychology. What do you mean by *denial?*"

"Denial is a state of mind where one denies an obvious truth. It's a defense mechanism where the mind simply cannot accept the truth."

"So you were in a state of denial when you thought Lu would get better?"

"Yes. I see now that the possibility of her death or a permanent coma was simply too much for me to bear."

"What caused you to come out of your state of denial?"

"I could see with my own eyes. Lu hadn't moved in two months. Then there was Ruby."

"The nurse."

"I had a long talk with Ben too."

"Dr. Jacobson? What did he say?"

"Ben leveled with me. He thought it was hopeless. We discussed the whole situation."

"Go on."

"We both knew that Lu and I had never prepared for this situation. We had wills all right, but we had nothing about what would happen if we became terminally ill."

"Had Lu and you discussed the possibility?"

"No, we hadn't. I wish to God we had."

"What did Dr. Jacobson tell you besides the fact that it was hopeless?"

"He told me what the medical procedure—the practice—was. That in circumstances like this doctors would turn off the ventilator, provided they agreed medically it was the right thing to do, and provided the family agreed."

"And he wanted Betty's agreement?"

"Yes. He knew my situation with Betty and he volunteered to go to her office in Detroit."

"And if Betty agreed?"

"Then they would turn off the ventilator and Lu would die. I asked him if it was all right if Ruby did it."

"Why Ruby?"

"Ruby had become a friend. She knew how difficult it was for me. We had many good discussions over those two months."

"So you decided Ben Jacobson should get Betty's permission?"

"Not right away."

"Oh. What happened?"

"I have a spot down by the college nature study. I go there by the river to meditate. To pray."

"Did you do that?"

"Yes, I did. It was there I decided Dr. Jacobson was right about ending Lu's life. It was very difficult."

"And you told Dr. Jacobson of your decision?"

"Yes."

"And then he agreed to see Betty?"

"Yes."

"But ultimately he reported that Betty would not agree?"

"That's right. He told me all about his talk with Betty. I must say I wasn't particularly surprised."

"Why?"

"I object, Your Honor," said Cain. "Surely why the defendant was or was not surprised is not relevant."

"I'm inclined to agree," Judge Hoskins said. "It is too far afield. The objection is sustained."

"Did Dr. Jacobson tell you he would not turn off the ventilator, in view of Betty's refusal?"

"Yes. He said Betty had threatened to sue him if he did. To sue Ruby, the hospital, everybody. He just couldn't run the risk."

"What happened next?"

"I was very depressed. I couldn't see any way out. My life was already over–ruined. That was true no matter what happened with Lu. The only thing I had to live for was Lu and she was only alive in a technical sense. Both our lives had ended–were meaningless–and there was nothing I could do about it."

"What happened next?"

"That night I took my gun down to my spot by the river."

"Why?"

"I was going to kill myself. I couldn't end it for Lu, but I could for me."

"Move to strike the reference to suicide!" Cain jumped to his feet as he spoke. "The reference to suicide has no relevance to this case."

"Mr. Jefferson?" Judge Hoskins asked.

"It goes to the state of mind of Dr. Neal, Your Honor," Joseph responded. "The prosecution has charged murder in the first degree. The state of mind of the defendant is essential."

"It will be allowed. Motion denied."

"But you obviously did not commit suicide," Joseph continued.

"No. I decided against it for the time being."

"For the time being?"

"Yes. I decided I morally couldn't leave this earth and leave Lu in her condition. It wouldn't be right."

"So what did you do?"

"I decided the only right thing to do was to take Lu with me."

"What exactly do you mean?"

"The next night I took my gun with me to see Lu. I was going to turn off her ventilator. Then, when I was sure she was gone, I was going to use the gun on myself."

"And why did you decide to do that?"

"As I say, I couldn't leave Lu behind. No one to visit her. No one to talk to her. No one to hope she'd get well."

Joseph paused as he took a step to his right. "Now, Dr. Neal, tell us what happened the night Lu died."

"I deliberately selected a time of night when the hospital was quiet. This was later than my usual time. I told Ruby I wanted to be alone with Lu." David struggled with telling the events of that last night. "That I wanted to read to her."

Joseph waited for few moments. "Did you have the gun with you?"

"Yes. It was in my briefcase. I told Ruby I had brought our Bible."

"And what did you do when you went into your wife's hospital room?"

"I read some of her favorite Bible passages."

"Aloud?"

"Yes. Aloud."

"Even though she was in a coma."

"Yes, she was still in the coma."

"What passages did you read?"

"Some of the passages from the Sermon on the Mount. You know *lay not up your treasures on earth. Take no thought for your life, for taking thought adds not one cubit to your stature.* David could feel the intensity of the jurors watching him.

"What happened next?"

"It was the most amazing thing."

"What?"

"I was trying to get up my nerve to end it for her, when I could see that her eyes were open." Someone in the audience gasped. The jurors watched him intently.

"Wait a minute. Let me get this straight. Lu was in a coma?"

"Yes."

"She had been for two months."

"Yes."

"Yet you tell us she was looking at you?"

"I was astonished, but she was looking at me. I asked her if she could hear me, but she didn't answer. She just looked at me."

"Go on."

"I moved my head and I could see her pupils follow me."

"And then?"

"I asked her to blink, if she could hear me."

"Did she?"

"Yes, she did. It was amazing." David saw the mouth of one woman juror drop open.

"What happened next?"

"I told her I had been struggling over what to do. I told her how hopeless it all seemed and that I had decided to kill her and then kill myself. I told her I had brought my old pistol."

"Did she respond?"

"Not at first."

"Was she unconscious?"

"I don't think so, but she had closed her eyes. I told her I had to know what she wanted. I couldn't go ahead unless she wanted me to."

"Then what happened?"

"I told her to blink if that's what she wanted. Then she opened her eyes again and looked at me. I could see that she loved me. I could see the compassion in her eyes. They were so clear. Her eyes were blue you know."

When David paused there was not a sound in the courtroom. "Then she blinked her eyes once...then once again. I guess it was her gift to me."

"Go on."

"Then she closed her eyes. She had this look of peace on her face. I've never seen anything like it."

"What happened next?"

"I turned off her respirator. Mr. Jefferson, I killed my wife." David looked at the jury. "I took the life of the person most dear to me in the world."

"And then?"

"You've heard Ruby's testimony. It was just as she said. I tried to kill myself with my pistol, but Ruby stopped me. She jumped across Lu and knocked my gun off-line."

"And took a bullet in her thigh?"

"Yes."

"Thank you , Dr. Neal. Thank you very much. I have no further questions."

"Mr. Cain, cross examination?" asked Judge Hoskins.

"Yes, Your Honor." David watched apprehensively as Cain stood at the prosecutor's table and took a place near the jury box. David took a deep breath. Now would come the test of his life. He knew very well Cain would try to make him out to be a cold-blooded murderer.

-51-

Cain stood next to the jury box, staring intently at David. Dramatically, he said nothing for several moments. David knew he was the mouse, and Cain the cat.

"Mr. Neal–or do you prefer *Doctor* Neal?"

"Either one will do." David knew very well Cain's question was designed to make him look egotistical if he had opted to be called *Doctor*.

"Dr. Neal, when you killed your wife, you knew it was against the law, didn't you?" Cain was aiming smack between the eyes.

"I don't know. I wasn't thinking much about legal points at the time."

"Tell me, do you consider murder a mere legal point?" Cain's tone was sarcastic.

"No, Mr. Cain, I do not."

"Isn't it true that Dr. Jacobson advised you he could not proceed to kill your wife because Betty would not give her consent?"

"He didn't put it that way."

"Oh, didn't he? Just how did he put it? I must have heard incorrectly."

"He said he couldn't turn off Lu's ventilator."

"I see. Would turning off the ventilator terminate your wife's life?"

"Yes. Of course."

"Tell me then, wouldn't turning off her ventilator be the same as killing her, or have I missed some distinction?"

"I guess it's just a kinder way of putting it."

"A kinder way of killing someone?"

"Objection, Your Honor," said Joseph, rising to his feet. "The prosecutor is arguing with the witness. He should save his sarcasm for final argument."

"The objection is overruled in this instance. After all, it is cross examination, but, Mr. Cain, you are very close to the line."

"Yes, Your Honor. I'll rephrase." Cain turned back to David. "Dr. Neal, why did Dr. Jacobson need your daughter's consent?"

"Because Lu and I had signed no powers of attorney–he needed the family's consent."

"Meaning your daughter's consent?"

"Yes."

"But why did he need her consent?"

"Because she would sue if she didn't agree."

"But what would enable her to sue?"

"I'm sorry. I guess I don't understand your question."

"I think you do, but I'll rephrase it. Dr. Neal the reason your daughter's consent was necessary was because it would be unlawful to take your wife's life without that consent, isn't that true?"

"I guess so."

"Why else would Dr. Jacobson want her consent, unless he thought it was legally necessary? After all, you were her husband and you had consented."

"I don't know. All he said was he needed Betty's consent."

"Come now, Dr. Neal. Isn't it true that you thought it was against the law to take your wife's life unless Betty agreed?"

"All I knew was that Ben wouldn't do it unless Betty agreed."

"Why didn't you change doctors then? Why didn't you find a doctor who would go ahead?"

"Ben was our doctor. I assumed he knew what he was doing."

"You assumed the next doctor would require Betty's agreement too, did you not?"

"I suppose so. I didn't even think about getting another doctor."

"So if I understand you, you thought it was perfectly legal to kill your wife, despite your daughter's protest, but for some reason–perhaps medical red tape–Dr. Jacobson wanted her to agree?"

"Objection, Your Honor." said Joseph. "The witness didn't say that at all. The question is argumentative."

"Overruled. The question, although, I must admit, rather vigorously put, is to find out exactly what the defendant thought. You may answer the question."

"As I say, I don't know what I thought. I was dealing in morality and medical procedures. I wasn't thinking about legalities."

"Oh, so you thought it was moral to kill your wife?"

"You keep saying *kill* my wife."

"You did *kill* your wife, didn't you?"

"I turned off her ventilator."

"Which caused her to die?"

"Yes."

"But you object to my use of the words *you killed your wife*. Is that correct?"

Joseph jumped to his feet. "Objection, Your Honor, I…"

"Yes," Judge Hoskins ruled. "I think you've made your point, Mr. Cain. I suggest you move on."

"Thank you, Your Honor," Cain responded. "Dr. Neal, you said it was the moral thing to do–you prefer to say *to turn off her ventilator*–I prefer to say *to kill her*–but you contend it was the moral thing do to. Is that right?"

"Yes. She was going to be in that coma forever. There was no hope."

"I'll get back to the coma in a minute, but first, you contend that you had a moral right to break the law?"

"I don't know that I broke the law."

"Come now, Dr. Neal, did not you realize it was against the law to take your wife's life?"

"As I said before, I wasn't thinking much about the legal aspects."

"You said you were not thinking *much* about the legal aspects. Do I take it you thought *some* about the legal aspects?"

"I suppose I was aware there must be some legal aspects, but I was primarily trying to do what I thought was right."

"And my question is, What did you think those legal aspects were?"

"I suppose I thought it was against the law."

"Finally! I thank you, Dr. Neal." Cain moved back a step as if to emphasize David's admission. "But you had determined to go ahead with your plan anyway?"

"I guess the legal part didn't matter much. I was going to kill myself anyway."

"So you didn't much care if it was illegal or not. You were going to have your way."

"I was going to try to do the right thing," David paused. "I still think I did."

"Do you believe a man has the right to take the law into his own hands?"

"I did not used to think so."

"But you've changed your mind, now that you are on trial for murder?"

"I changed my mind because of what happened to Lu. When Ruby stopped me from killing myself, I didn't much care whether I went to jail. I wanted to be dead. It wasn't at all your bringing these criminal charges that changed my mind."

"So you'd do it all over again—if the same circumstances arose?"

"Yes. I would—especially since Lu came out of her coma long enough to tell me it was okay with her."

"That helped, did it?"

"Yes."

"But you would have ended her life even if she hadn't regained consciousness, as you contend she did?"

"That was my plan. Yes."

"Now, getting back to the coma, do you still want this jury to believe your story that Lu regained consciousness?"

"I'm just telling you what happened. I can't control what others believe."

"All right, Dr. Neal. You taught psychology at Albion College?"

"Yes."

"Then you wouldn't be surprised if some people did not believe your story, would you?"

Joseph jumped to his feet. "What kind of a question is that, Your Honor? I–"

"I take that to be an objection, Mr. Jefferson," Judge Hoskins interrupted. "Mr. Cain, you are going too far." He had a weariness in his voice.

"I'm sorry, Your Honor." The judge's admonition did not seem to bother Cain, who hardly paused before asking his next question. "Dr. Neal, something has troubled me about this case. You say the victim, your wife, blinked her eyes when you asked her approval of your plan to end her life?"

"Yes. I'll never forget it."

"You also testified that the reason you decided to end your wife's life was that she was hopelessly in a coma. According to my notes you said, *she never would recover consciousness.* Is that correct?"

"Something like that."

"Let's be certain. Isn't that *exactly* what you previously testified as being the case?"

"Yes." David wasn't sure where Cain was going with these questions, but he sensed trouble.

"So, as I understand it, the long-awaited–even prayed for–event finally occurred. She in fact regained consciousness. Isn't that correct?"

David was confused. "I don't understand."

Joseph quickly rose to his feet. "Objection, Your Honor." The fact that his attorney so vigorously objected confirmed David's fear that Cain was getting into an area filled with danger.

"On what grounds?" Hoskins asked.

"The question is ambiguous. Dr. Neal obviously doesn't understand the question."

"I don't know. It appears clear to me. Dr. Neal, do you understand the question?" Hoskins asked.

"No, not exactly."

Cain charged ahead. "I'll try to clarify this for you. You said you had hoped and prayed that your would wife regain consciousness."

"Yes."

"You also testified you asked Dr. Jacobson to turn off the ventilator, because it was clear she never would regain consciousness. Right?"

"Yes."

"Good. You also contend that your wife agreed to your plan to turn off the ventilator?"

"She blinked her eyes. Yes."

"Her eyes were open?"

"Yes."

Cain looked at his yellow pad. Her eyes were *Very clear. They were blue you know. Filled with love and compassion.* Correct?"

"Yes. I vividly remember."

"So, she had regained consciousness? Is that not the fact?"

"Yes. She looked right at me." David saw the pained expression on Joseph's face and sensed he was in trouble, but there was no time to think. No time to anticipate. All he could do was tell the truth.

Cain walked from the edge of the jury box to the counsel table. Still standing, he put down his yellow pad and placed his knuckles on the table. "Dr. Neal, what you had longed for had happened. Your wife had come out of her coma. The very reason for ending her life had evaporated before your eyes. Your wife had regained consciousness, yet you went ahead and killed her anyway. Isn't that true?"

Collectively the eyes of the jurors moved from Cain to David. Judge Hoskins looked intently at David. Joseph's eyes remained riveted on his yellow pad, as if he did not want to watch. David now saw the trap that Cain had carefully laid, but he did not know what to say–how to avoid the trap. Before this moment he had never thought of the now obvious inconsistency that Cain was driving home.

"But she wanted me to end it for her. She heard me and she agreed."

"Clearly, she was no longer in her coma. Isn't that true?"

"Objection!" Joseph had stood to make his point. "Dr. Neal is not a medical doctor. He had no way of knowing whether she had permanently come out of her coma."

"Overruled!" said Hoskins sternly, without offering an explanation. He turned to David. "The witness will answer the question."

"I didn't think about it. I only knew she had agreed."

"Answer my question Dr. Neal," Cain continued. "You were there at her bedside. Had she or had she not come out of her coma?"

"She had. Her eyes were open."

"She was conscious?"

"Yes."

"Not in her usual coma."

"That's right."

"Thank you, Dr. Neal. As confusing as you contend it to be, it's a relief to get that point nailed down." Triumphantly, Cain walked back to the edge of the jury box.

David knew he had dug himself into a hole. Although there was no question pending, he had to explain himself to the jury. "But, you see, Mr. Cain. I knew it was only temporary. She fell right back into her coma," he blurted out.

"Oh, so *now* you're a doctor of medicine. Is that it? You *knew* she was never going to regain consciousness again? You *knew* she would not come out of her coma a second time and tell you she wanted to live!"

"Your Honor, I must protest!" Joseph had jumped to his feat. Counsel is badgering the witness."

"Yes, Mr. Cain," agreed Judge Hoskins. "You are getting carried away."

"I'm sorry, Your Honor. I'll rephrase my question."

"Do that, please," Hoskins said sternly.

"How did you know your wife was not going to regain consciousness once again?"

"If you had been there, you would have known it too."

"So I suppose you want us to believe your wife came out of her coma of 60 days for the sole purpose of telling you it was all right to murder her?"

"Objection!"

"Mr. Cain!" said Hoskins. "I have warned you several times. I do not want to have to warn you again!"

"I apologize, Your Honor. I withdraw the question." Head held high, Cain walked closer to the witness box. "Dr. Neal, I take it you have studied psychology extensively?"

"Yes. It has been a lifelong study."

"You have written on the subject?"

"Yes, I have."

"Are you familiar with the reasons for hallucinations?"

"I am familiar with some theories attempting to explain hallucinations."

"And what are those theories?"

"I suppose the most credible theory is that when the subject is disturbed he or she tends to see what he wants to see, psychologically speaking."

"Even though the hallucination is not factually true?"

"Yes. By definition hallucinations are not fact."

"Dr. Neal, in your professional opinion isn't it likely that you were hallucinating? That you thought your wife agreed to be killed because you so desperately wanted her to agree?"

"Absolutely not. Lu did regain consciousness! Her eyes were open. She blinked them."

"Dr. Neal, if you had been called in to consult on a case like yours—a case where the attending physician said it was medically impossible for his patient to regain consciousness–wouldn't you immediately suspect the loved one had suffered a hallucination?"

"I don't know. I would have to know more of the facts."

"All right. Let's assume the facts were exactly like yours. Hallucination or real? What would you say?"

"A lot would depend on the subject. If he appeared to be sincere I couldn't dismiss his claim willy-nilly."

"Dr. Neal, isn't it a fact that all victims of hallucinations sincerely believe that what they saw was factual?"

"Yes, at one level, although their logical minds may tell them they were wrong in their perceptions."

"Therefore…"

"You see, I have the advantage. I *know* Lu said *yes*."

"And you *know* you are different from all other victims of hallucinations who also *know* they were not hallucinating?"

"I guess you had to be there, Mr. Cain. I know of no other way to convince you."

"One other question on this subject, Dr. Neal. Prior to today, had you told anyone about your claim that your wife regained consciousness?"

"Only my attorney."

"Not Dr. Jacobson?"

"No."

"Not the nurse, Ruby."

"No."

"Not the police?"

"No one except Mr. Jefferson."

"Yet your wife's alleged assent was extremely important to you?"

"Yes."

"Now, turning to another area of questioning. Did you hear your daughter testify that your wife had assets in her own name worth perhaps a million dollars?"

"I heard her. I don't know where she got that figure."

"You think a million dollars is an exaggeration?"

"I would think so, but I don't know. Lu's inheritance from her father was largely a private matter with her."

"But you agree the value is substantial?"

"I'm sure it is."

"Over half a million?"

"I really don't know. Lu and I seldom discussed it."

"But you knew you inherited under her will. She had told you that?"

"Yes."

"Tell me, Dr. Neal, what were you earning when you retired as a full professor?"

"Objection"

"Overruled."

"A little over forty thousand dollars per year."

"What is your present pension?"

"Half that."

"Any book royalties?"

"Not any more. It never was very much."

"How much was your taxable income last year?"

"I didn't file an income tax last year. I've been in jail."

"All right. The year before that?"

"About a hundred thousand, if I remember."

"So, if I calculate correctly the income from Lu's trust was what? Seventy or eighty thousand or so?"

"I suppose so. I never paid much attention to Lu's income. She spent it as she saw fit. It was really none of my business."

"You don't know how your wife spent $70,000 a year?"

"Well, she paid income taxes. I know that. She gave much of it to charity. She had loaned $150,000 to Betty when she bought her house in Bloomfield Hills. I know because she was upset when Betty never paid it back."

"The point I'm trying to establish, Dr. Neal, if you would simply answer the questions, is that you knew that with Lu dead you stood to have extra income of some $70,000 per year, is that not true?"

"I never thought about it."

"I'm asking you to think about it right now, Dr. Neal. Isn't it true that your disposable income will triple?"

"If that's what it figures out to be."

"That's what it figures out to be. And, if what you say is true about the loan to your daughter, your daughter would owe you $150,000. Isn't that true?"

"Yes. That would be logical."

"You'd like that, wouldn't you? You'd like to be in the position where your daughter owed you $150,000."

"Why would I like that? She's my daughter."

"Come now, Dr. Neal. Your daughter has testified for the prosecution in your murder trial. Do you mean to tell me you wouldn't enjoy every moment of being able to force her to pay you $150,000?"

"No. Not particularly. I've never thought about it."

"Never thought about $150,000?"

"No."

"It would appear we have another issue of fact for the jury to decide."

Jefferson leaped to his feet, but Judge Hoskins held up his hand silencing him. "You will persist, won't you, Mr. Cain? On its own motion, the court strikes the last remark. You know very well, Mr. Cain, that such gratuitous statements are improper. The jury will disregard the remark." Judge Hoskins was plainly exasperated with Cain. "Mr. Cain, I see that we have less than an hour left in the day. Could you advise the court how much longer you expect your cross examination to take?"

"Not long, Your Honor I have only a point or two left."

"And Mr. Jefferson. How many more witnesses do you have after Dr. Neal?"

"One more, Your Honor. However I'm not sure whether he'll be here today. I may have to ask that the court continue the case until tomorrow."

David wondered who the additional witness could be. Joseph had not discussed anyone else with him.

"Very well. Proceed, Mr. Cain."

"Dr. Neal, you visited your wife two times every day for 60 days. Is that right?"

"Three at the beginning."

"I must say, I admire your loyalty—your dedication."

David's first thought was not to respond. He knew Cain was setting David up for something, but he did not want to appear ungracious before the jury.

"Thank you," he said.

"There must have been times when you wanted to stay home. When you hated to drag yourself out. This was winter, wasn't it?"

"Yes, it was winter."

"Times when you'd rather stay home. Times when you were sick and tired of that trip to the hospital and wished your wife would finally be done with it and you could start on your new life?"

"No sir. I always wanted to be with Lu. You don't understand. Lu was my life."

Momentarily, Cain hesitated; and for the first time in the cross examination, David felt he had scored a victory of sorts over Cain.

"Dr. Neal, I would like to review some of your testimony with you to be certain I have it straight."

David made no comment. He wondered what tack Cain was going to take now.

"You say your wife was completely unconscious for 60 days?"

"Except for that last night."

"Of course you were not with her 24 hours every day. Did anyone else tell you she had ever regained consciousness? A nurse? A doctor? Perhaps an orderly?"

"No. She was always in her coma. That's what made that last night so miraculous."

"Dr. Neal, since she was unconscious, did she feel any pain?"

"No. No pain, thank God."

"Did she feel depressed?"

"No. Of course not. She was unconscious."

"Precisely. Tell me, did she despair of her condition the way a cancer victim would?"

"No. She was totally unaware."

"Very well. Thank you for clarifying the situation. That is the way I understood it." The jury watched as Cain returned to the counsel table.

"Now as to yourself," Cain asked, pointing his finger. "Were you in any physical pain during this time?"

"Just some of my arthritis, but that hardly mattered."

"I'm sure, however, that you were in considerable emotional distress. Could you tell us about that?"

David was surprised. Why was Cain asking him this? He thought back to Thanksgiving night. "When she first had her stroke I was in shock. Mild shock. I couldn't believe this had happened to Lu. I always thought I would be the first to go. Most men do."

"And then?"

"I was depressed. I began to realize Lu was never going to make a full recovery."

"You would have to attend to her? Wheel her around?"

"I would have been glad to do that. At least it would have been some sort of a life together."

"Then what made you depressed?"

"It was Lu. She'd always been so active. I realized that was never again to be."

"And then I think you said you ultimately realized she never was going to come out of her stroke. What effect did that have on you? Emotionally, I mean?"

"More despair. She was just going to lie there in that hospital bed. Maybe a month. Maybe a year. Maybe ten years. There was no way to know."

"And this caused you great psychological pain?"

"Yes. It was awful. The thought of her always being in a coma."

"But she would not know it. She would not even know she was in a coma, isn't that so?"

"That was even worse. She might as well be dead."

Cain raised his voice. "Might as well be dead!" He took three steps toward the witness box. "Dr. Neal, for whose benefit was it true that she might as well be dead? Hers? Or *yours*?"

"Well, hers, of course."

"Dr. Neal, your wife was totally unconscious. Feeling nothing. Aware of nothing. No physical pain. No mental pain. The plain truth is it was for your benefit that you killed your wife. Isn't that true? Not her benefit?"

"No! That's absolutely not true! I loved Lu!"

"She had nothing to gain by death. It's *you* who were suffering! It was *your* pain that you wanted to end. You couldn't stand to see her lying there. You didn't want to go through that any more. One hundred thirty visits to the intensive care ward. One hundred thirty times talking to her with no response. Sixty days of having a wife who, as far as you were concerned, might as well be dead. The prospects of ten more years of the same grind. Ten years of no life for yourself."

"Objection. Arguing with the witness." Joseph had not gotten to his feet.

"Mr. Cain, what is your question?" Judge Hoskins asked, again appearing perturbed with Cain. "I would suggest you save your argument for the proper time. If you have a question, please ask it."

David was grateful for the interruption. He was stunned by Cain's accusations. How could he explain that he had wanted to take his own life the night before by the river, but he didn't want to leave Lu alone with no one to visit her no one to care for her? He couldn't leave her to that fate. That would have been the ultimate immorality.

"Very well, Your Honor," Cain continued. "I will put my points in the form of a question, and I expect it to be my final question. Dr. Neal, isn't it true that when it comes right down to it, you killed your wife because it was you who simply could not stand it any more?"

"*EDDIE?*" David shouted, looking at the figure who had come through the door. "*EDDIE, WHAT ARE YOU DOING HERE?*"

In the colorful full dress uniform of the United States Marines, Private Eddie Erickson had walked into the courtroom. Everyone, judge, jury, attorneys, reporters watched in amazement as the ramrod straight handsome figure of a boy-turned-man strode toward the counsel tables.

"Grandfather!" Eddie cried.

David broke into tears of joy. Nothing mattered any more, except to touch his grandson. He jumped from the witness stand, his legs hardly working from having sat so long, and hurried to Eddie.

"Your Honor, I object!" Cain shouted.

"There will be order in the court!" Judge Hoskins commanded. "Mr. Jefferson, you must control your client. He must return to the witness stand immediately."

"Eddie, how did you get here? You're in San Diego!" David continued, not even hearing what the judge had said.

The two threw their arms around each other, Eddie removing his Marine dress hat.

"I'm sorry, Your Honor," said Joseph. "As you can see, this is a very emotional moment for my client."

Judge Hoskins banged his gavel, but then shrugged his shoulders in a sign of helplessness. "This court will resume at 9 o'clock tomorrow morning. The jury will discuss the case with no one. Mr. Jefferson, you will tell your client that this court will tolerate no further such outbursts." Hoskins quickly slipped through the door leading to his chambers as news reporters rushed for David and Eddie.

"What are you doing here?" David asked.

"They sent a private jet for me." Eddie was smiling. "They want me to testify in your case."

"Sorry, Dr. Neal," interrupted the bailiff. "I know you want to talk, but we've got to take you to your cell now. I can arrange for your grandson to visit you after hours if you like."

A mob of clamoring reporters surrounded David and Eddie.

"I'll come right after dinner," Eddie called out as the bailiff led David away. "I'm staying at a bed and breakfast. I'll have some chow and be over as soon as I can."

-52-

It broke Eddie's heart to see his grandfather. The strain of the past weeks had obviously taken its toll on the older man. He had aged so much and looked pitifully forlorn. It was ridiculous that they were trying Grandfather for murder. God, how he hoped his testimony would persuade the jury to let his poor grandfather go free.

As he left the courtroom Eddie was greeted by the television lights and cameras. A television reporter stuck a microphone in his face. "They say that David Neal is your grandfather," she asked. "Is that true?"

"Yes." Eddie tried to get past her, while still being polite.

"How do you feel about what your grandfather did?"

Eddie worked his way through the crowd and equipment.

"He didn't do anything wrong."

"But he killed your grandmother," the reporter persisted.

"Granna might as well have been already dead." Eddie broke away and leaped down the steps three at a time. He was upset with the questioning.

During the long plane ride from San Diego he hadn't imagined the bedlam he was now experiencing. What a shock it had been when this morning at 0600 hours he had been called before the commanding officer of the Marine Corps Training Depot. He had stood at attention as the CO spoke.

"Recruit Erickson, I don't know what's going on or who you know, but I was dragged out of the sack by the Pentagon less than an hour ago. There will be a private jet at Lindbergh Field at 0730 hours. You are to be on that plane. Report here in one hour and my car will drive you. You'll be back in San Diego by tomorrow morning."

Standing in his fatigues. Eddie was confused. "But, sir, what's happened? Where am I going?"

"They want you in Michigan. Apparently your grandfather is on trial for murder. Is that right?"

"Yes, sir. I think so, sir." Awed by the gruff officer, Eddie barely comprehended what he was being told.

"They want you to testify. You are to wear a dress uniform on the trip."

"But, sir..." Both knew recruits were not issued dress uniforms until graduation.

"You are to be in a dress uniform! Am I clear on that, recruit? They'll issue it to you in five minutes. Now, I suggest you hightail it over there before somebody in Washington changes his mind."

Joseph Jefferson's secretary had been on the plane with him, and had explained that her boss wanted Eddie as a witness. She had arranged for Eddie to stay at the same bed and breakfast that Jefferson was staying at. They would talk about the case tonight.

Eddie bounded through the outside courthouse door to get away from the reporters. He was taken aback to see Betty waiting for him. During Basic Training he had not written, nor even considered telephoning her. The few times he had thought of her was when he had compared her dictatorial attitude to that of his drill instructors.

"Hello, Eddie." Betty stepped toward him. "You look so handsome in your uniform." He recognized the mode she was in. He had learned to mistrust her compliments. When she did that, she always wanted something. "Thank you, Mom." He held back from touching her. "It's my new dress uniform."

"Can we have dinner together?" Betty asked.

"I guess so, but we have to make it fast. I promised Grandfather I'd see him in jail, and then I've got to see Mr. Jefferson."

Dress hat on the table, Eddie sat upright as he ate dinner with his mother. It was as if they had an agreement not to talk about Grandfather's case.

"I can't get over how good you look," she said uncertainly. It was obvious to Eddie that she was ill at ease with him. "You're not a teenager any more. You look like a man."

"I'm a Marine now, Mom. Or at least I will be soon."

"Did you know President Clinton appointed me to be a judge?" It was as if she were trying to make conversation.

"That's great, Mom. Does that make you happy?" Eddie could plainly see she was not happy. She looked puffy, as if she had gained more weight. Tired, too. The circles under her eyes looked larger. It was a strange feeling. One he wouldn't have expected. Even though she was a judge now, he no longer feared her. It was as if she were the one who was afraid, not him.

"You know, Eddie, I'm really shocked that you're in the Marines. I mean there's nothing wrong with being a Marine. It's just that I always thought you'd have a better career."

Immediately Eddie saw what she wanted. She wanted him to quit the Marines and maybe live with her in Bloomfield Hills. "Look, Mom, I don't have be a judge to have a good career. Besides, the Marines have a good education program."

"I'm sure they do, son, but I want you to listen to me, please."

"Okay. I guess it won't do me any harm to listen." Eddie realized that for the first time in his life, he felt free of his mother's control.

"I know lots of powerful people."

"Look, Mom—"

"Now, you promised you'd listen. I am still your mother."

"Okay. I'll listen."

"I can get you out of the Marines, if you want. I'm sure I can. You can go to college and–"

"Look, Mom. I don't want out of the Marines. I like the Marines. They'd let me out tomorrow if I asked. It's not like being in a jail." Eddie folded his napkin. He'd had enough of her attitude.

"I only want what's best for you."

Eddie had a flash of anger. She was not being sincere–he knew that. She had never wanted what was best for him. What she had always wanted was to control him. Now, for the first time, he understood that she really thought she loved him, but he decided to let it pass. There was no point in telling her the truth. She was his mother. He would show her respect, the same as he did his Marine superiors, but there was nothing in the Marine Basic Training Skills manual about loving your mother. Maybe someday he would, but not now and not for one hell of a long time.

"Look, Mom, I've got a busy night. I promised Grandfather I'd see him. Then I've got that meeting with the lawyer."

"Eddie, are you going to testify in your grandfather's defense?"

"I'm going to tell the truth tomorrow. That's all. Look, you go ahead and order your dessert. I've got to go. Excuse me, please."

Eddie could feel his mother's eyes on him as he left the dining room. It sure felt good being a United States Marine and out from under his mother's thumb.

"My name is Eddie Erickson. I'm here to see my grandfather."

"Yes, sir. I've been expecting you." The jail receptionist was not the one who had given him such a hard time before he went to San Francisco.

The guard accompanied Eddie to David's cell. He was dismayed at the cramped quarters his grandfather had been enduring. When they were alone, Eddie put his arms around his grandfather. He seemed so thin and frail. When David returned his hug, he realized he did not remember his grandfather's hugging him before.

"It's so good to see you," said David, his eyes filled with tears. "You look so handsome. Tell me all about the Marines."

Eddie sat on the chair while David sat on the edge of the bed, intently listening. "San Francisco was a bitch. I got a decent job all right, but then I got mugged."

"Mugged?"

"Yeah. They took my pay and then they stole my car. I didn't know what to do."

"Eddie you should have called me. I would have helped. That is what grandfathers are for."

"You had enough trouble of your own. Besides I didn't know how to reach you."

David nodded. "Well, tell me. How do you like the Marines? Are they treating you well?" I can't get over how great you look. You're a man now—not a teenager!"

Eddie smiled. It made him feel good. "There were some rough times, but two more weeks and I'll be through with Basic."

"What happens then?"

"I put in for school. Artillery School, I think."

"Will you get some leave?"

"Yeah, I get leave after I graduate from Basic."

"You'll have to come and see me."

"I will. You'll be out of here by then."

"I don't know about that. It looks pretty grim to me. The prosecutor really made me look bad today."

"How could he do that?"

"I don't know, Eddie. Sometimes he even has me convinced I did the wrong thing. Maybe I deserve to be in a place like this."

"But you didn't do anything wrong."

"Don't you remember? Even you were angry with me at first."

"Well, yes, but that was because I wanted Granna to be the way she always was."

David looked at the gray cement floor. "And that was impossible wasn't it?"

Eddie looked down too. "I wish there had been some way she could have been well again, like she used to be, but there wasn't."

They were silent together for some time, each looking at the floor.

Finally, Eddie spoke. "You know, Grandfather, like I said in my letter, when Basic was so rough, we were in the mountains one time and I realized you are my family. What's left of it. You know, I don't think I ever told Granna I loved her."

"She knew, Eddie. Don't worry. She knew." David was still looking at the floor.

"Well, I know one thing, Grandfather."

David looked with pride at his grandson.

"With you, I don't want to wait until it's too late. I want to tell you *I love you.*"

Tears came to David's eyes. They both stood, then held each other. Eddie could feel the warmth of David's body through his jail clothes. He wondered if the next time he came to Michigan his grandfather would be in another jail cell–in Jackson Prison–or whether he could once again sit with him in the family room and talk while they watched the Tigers on television.

-53-

Billie Croft thought of herself as a good juror. At the close of each session, Judge Hoskins admonished the jurors not to discuss the case with anyone. Except for her husband, she had followed that instruction religiously. John and she always discussed everything. Surely talking about the case with him couldn't do any harm. Besides, she only mentioned the case to John when something really important came up. Today was one of those days.

"Just when the afternoon session was over, this young Marine showed up. It was amazing. I'll bet he's Dr. Neal's grandson—the way they hugged."

"He is the grandson. It was on the news," John affirmed.

Following Judge Hoskins orders, Billie never watched the news. Every night John used the television in his den to find out what had happened in court that day. Billie knew that John thought mercy killing could not be justified under any circumstances. She had felt the same way at the beginning, so she had not told him about the mixed feelings she had been experiencing as the case unfolded. Sometimes she could completely understand why Dr. Neal had done what he did, and felt she could never send him to jail. But on days like today, when Cain had made Dr. Neal admit that he had killed his wife for his own good and not so much hers, she found herself swinging the other way. Maybe this case demonstrated why people shouldn't be permitted to take the law into their own hands. She wasn't so sure she wanted John or anybody pulling the plug on her. What if she still had a chance at life? Perhaps another person should not have the right to make a decision like that.

"The TV says the Marine used to live with Neal and his wife in Albion," John continued. "He's stationed in San Diego."

"Really?" asked Billie. "I wonder why he's here? Probably to lend his grandfather moral support."

"How much longer do you think the damn case is going to last? We've already missed out in the couples tournament."

"I'm sorry, John. Maybe I should have tried to get out of jury duty."

"I guess it is your duty. I really don't care much how it turns out. I just wish it would end so we could get on with our summer."

"Today they said there would be only one more witness. You don't suppose it's the Marine, do you?"

"They didn't say anything about that on television. What happens after the last witness?"

"Closing arguments. Then we decide the case."

Billie watched an old movie on cable that night after John went to bed. She was too keyed up to sleep. This was going to be a tough decision. She wanted to do the right thing, but it was difficult to know what the right thing was.

-54-

"Do you swear to tell the truth, the whole truth and nothing but the truth, so help you, God?" asked the clerk.

"I do."

"State your name."

"Recruit Eddie—I should say Edwin—Erickson, United States Marines."

David was proud as he watched Eddie in his dress uniform. He still couldn't get over how much Eddie had matured. His hair cut short, Eddie sat ramrod straight in the witness stand. He placed his dress hat on the ledge of the witness stand. David remembered the time when Eddie had slouched in his chair and had worn his Tiger baseball cap backwards.

"Eddie—do you have any objection if I call you Eddie?" began Joseph.

"No, sir."

"Lu Neal was your grandmother?"

"Yes, sir."

"Eddie, there's no need to call me sir."

"I'd feel more comfortable calling you sir, if that's all right."

"That's fine with me," Joseph smiled.

"And Dr. Neal, here, is your grandfather?"

"Yes, sir."

"You lived with your grandparents for some time before you joined the Marines?"

"Yes, sir."

"And why was that?"

"I didn't get along with my mother, especially after she and my father separated."

"Where did you live with your parents?"

"Bloomfield Hills, Michigan. Outside Detroit."

"Could you describe your house in Bloomfield Hills?"

"Well, it was lonely. Empty and lonely."

"I'm sorry. I mean could you describe it physically?"

"It was very large. Eight bedrooms. Very large. We lived on the golf course."

"Did you play golf?"

"No. I don't like country clubs."

"I see. So there came a time when you moved in with your grandparents in Albion?"

"Yes. I kept running away to Granna's, so they finally decided I should finish high school in Albion. I was having a lot of trouble then. Bad grades. I guess I was mixed up."

"Granna was your grandmother?"

"Yes. I always called her Granna."

"How long had you lived with your grandparents before Granna's stroke?"

"Let's see, she had her stroke on Thanksgiving and I had moved there in about April."

"So about six months?"

"Yes, sir. I lived with them a lot as I was growing up. It always made me happy to be around Granna—and grandfather of course"

"You mean in summers?"

"Yes, sir. Mom never wanted to go to Albion, so Granna would come and pick me up. I spent a lot of time with them in the summer. We'd go to the cabin up North. She'd come get me for part of my Christmas vacations, you know."

"Did your grandmother ever come and live with you in Bloomfield Hills?"

"Yes, sir. Sometimes when Mom was in a trial or away on business."

"I take it that you loved your grandmother?"

"Yes, sir."

Eddie's answer, "Yes sir," stated it so simply, David thought. Eddie had loved Lu every bit as much as he had.

"How were you getting along, living with your grandparents?"

"Much better. I moved in with Granna near the end of that school year and when school started in the fall I was starting to do better. Grandfather said maybe I could go to Albion College if I could get my grades up."

"Then there came a time when your Granna had a stroke?"

"Yes, sir. Thanksgiving of last year. I'll never forget." Eddie looked unblinkingly at Joseph.

"Were you at home?"

"No. I was at the Lions game with my dad."

"When did you hear about the stroke?"

"When I got home, Grandfather wasn't there. He told me about it when he got home."

"Was your grandfather upset?"

"Yes. Grandfather really needed Granna. We all could see that."

"What do you mean, *really needed* her?"

"I don't know if I can explain. Grandfather had been very unhappy for a long time. Granna was the only good thing in his life."

"Why was he unhappy?"

"I don't know. He never talked about it, but Granna told me he felt his work was over. She thought he was just living out the rest of his days. Something like that, I guess."

"How did you feel when your grandfather told you about Granna's stroke?"

"I don't think I understood at first. I knew it was serious, very serious. But grandfather thought she was going to be okay. He never gave up hope, of course, until the end."

Sadly, David reflected upon those days–days when he still had hope for Lu.

"What did you think about your grandmother's condition?"

"I saw her the next day. I could tell it was very bad. I don't know much about strokes, but right away I thought she wasn't going to make it."

"You mean that she was going to die?"

"I didn't know about dying, but she was never going to be my Granna again. I knew that right away."

"Did you tell that to your grandfather?"

"Oh, no. Not right away. He thought she was going to get well. I could tell he had to think that way or he'd go nuts or something."

"Did you talk about your grandmother's condition with anyone else?"

"There was Ruby."

"The nurse?"

"Yes, sir. She and I became friends."

"What did you say to Ruby?"

"That Granna was never going to come out of her coma. That she might as well be dead."

"I see. Did you go to the hospital often?"

"I would usually go at night. Grandfather doesn't see very well at night." Eddie looked at David apologetically. "So I used to drive him over. But I wouldn't usually go into her room."

"Why not?"

"I couldn't stand to see her that way. She was dead as far as I was concerned. I mean–well, you know what I mean."

"Perhaps you could explain."

"Well, sir, she was in her coma for week after week. Never even moved. The only thing that kept her alive was all that equipment. Everybody could tell she was never going to come to. Everybody but Grandfather. It was very depressing. So I talked to Ruby all the time. Ruby always had good advice. She's a very smart woman."

"Did there come a time when your grandfather and you discussed whether your grandmother's life should be allowed to end?"

"Yes, sir. Near the end he asked me what I thought and I told him."

"What did you tell him?"

"I told him Granna might as well be dead. That it was best if Dr. Jacobson would take away all that stuff and let her die."

"What did your grandfather say?"

"I don't remember exactly, but he was beginning to think that way too. He wanted to think about it–to think about whether to ask Dr. Jacobson and Ruby to do it. I knew what he meant."

"What do you mean you *knew what he meant?*"

"I knew he wanted to go down by the river and meditate about it. He did that all the time."

"You mean pray?"

"I don't know exactly what he'd do, but he used to go down to the nature study a lot–no matter how cold it was. He had a favorite spot by the Kalamazoo. He used to take me there when I was a kid."

"Did he finally reach a decision?"

"Yes, but Doctor Jacobson said he needed Mom's permission."

"Did your grandfather ever ask your permission?"

"He didn't need to. He already knew how I stood."

"And how did you stand?"

David saw that Cain was ready to make an objection, but evidently thought better of it.

"The same as I do now. Granna's life was already over. All they were doing was making it official. I mean you don't accuse the undertaker of murder, do you?"

"I'd like to explore that a little more deeply, if you don't mind. Do think what your grandfather did was right?"

"Really, I must object, Your Honor," said Cain. "I've been very patient with this line of questioning, but what this witness thinks about whether this was a crime is quite immaterial to this case."

"The objection is sustained," ruled the judge. "The questions must go to what this witness saw and heard."

"Very well, Your Honor," Joseph responded. "Eddie, would you describe the condition of your grandmother at the end–the last time you saw her?"

"There wasn't much change since the first time I saw her in the hospital. She was unconscious. She had been unconscious all that time. Sixty days. She was very pale. Like death warmed over, I guess you would say. It was tough to take. Granna had always been so happy." For the first time on the witness stand he showed the depth of his emotion. Although Eddie paused only briefly, David could see he had nearly been overcome. "She looked almost as she did when she was in her coffin. Except the undertaker had done something to take the twist out of the edge of her mouth."

"Her mouth was twisted?"

"By the stroke, yes."

"Go on. Tell us what you saw that last time."

"There isn't much more to tell. She looked like she might as well be dead. Except for that damn equipment, Granna was dead. She looked like she had been dead a long time."

"And your grandfather? What was he like the last time you saw him?"

"He looked almost dead too. He had given up all his brave talk about Granna's getting better. He finally knew what I had known from the beginning."

"Anything else?"

"Just that he told me what he was going to do was the right thing to do. I could tell he was in great pain–you know, emotionally."

"So you knew he intended to end Granna's life?"

"Yes. I knew that."

"Did you object to that?"

"No. I didn't."

"Thank you for coming all the way from San Diego. I have no further questions, Your Honor."

"Very well. We'll take the morning recess. Will you be ready for cross examination in 15 minutes, Mr. Cain?"

"Yes, Your Honor. I'm ready right now."

"I'm sure you are, but we'll take that recess now."

David felt good about what Eddie had said. Even if it didn't help with the jury, and he had to spend the rest of his life in jail, he would always know that Eddie had been on his side.

-55-

Fred Cain took his customary place by the jury box to begin the cross examination of Eddie. He knew Eddie had hurt his case. The young man's very presence in his striking Marine dress uniform–his show of support for his grandfather–no doubt had impressed the jury. But Fred knew that Eddie's appeal had been more to the heart of the jury than to its the mind. Eddie had not added one whit of real evidence to the case. Neal had taken the law into his own hands and had killed his wife. The mere fact that his grandson supported him in the crime should make no difference–Marine uniform or not.

"Eddie, you love your grandfather don't you?" Fred began.

"Yes, sir."

"You don't want to see him convicted, do you?"

"No, sir."

"Tell me, in the Marines do they teach you to follow orders?"

"Yes, sir. They do."

"As a Marine, you must obey the rules. Is that right?"

"Yes, sir."

"Why is that the case?"

"Because it's in the rules."

"But why is it in the rules?"

"Because that's the only way you can run an outfit. You can't have everybody making up his own rules."

"Exactly. It's the only way you can run the Marines. Everybody must follow the rules."

"Yes, sir."

"Nobody can make his own rules just because he disagrees with the rules. Isn't that right?"

"Yes, sir."

"Did you know it was against the rules for your grandfather to end Granna's life?"

"Yes, sir, I guess I did."

"You knew they had to have your mother's permission didn't you?"

"Yes, sir."

"And you knew she had refused, didn't you?"

"Yes, because she hates Grandfather so much."

"I'll repeat the question and I'd like you to listen carefully to it. And you knew your mother had refused permission, didn't you?"

"Yes, sir. I knew."

"Eddie, if your sergeant gave you an order, would you follow it?"

"Yes, sir."

"In the Marines, his word is the law?"

"Yes, sir."

"What if he gave an order that you disagreed with? Would you obey it?"

"Yes, sir."

"Even if he gave the order because he hated somebody, you'd still follow it, wouldn't you?"

"I'd have to."

"Because to do otherwise would be taking the law into your own hands. Isn't that right?"

"Because I'd be court martialled, sir."

Laughter broke out in the audience. Several of the jurors smiled.

"I assume someday you'll no longer be in the Marines."

"I've signed up for four years. I plan to go to college then. Maybe even Albion."

"And when you get out, you'll no longer have to do what the Marines tell you. Is that right?"

"Yes, sir."

"Will you be free to do anything that pleases you?"

"I don't understand, sir."

"After you leave the Marines will you still have to follow the rules of society?"

"Yes, sir."

"And the rules of society are commonly called the law, is that right?"

"I guess so, sir."

"So even when you get out of the Marines, you won't be free to take the law into your own hands. Isn't that right?"

"I think so, sir."

"So now, while you are in the Marines, you are not free to take the law into your own hands, and when you're no longer in the Marines the same will be true?"

"Objection," said Joseph. "He's arguing with the witness."

"Overruled," said Judge Hoskins. "This is cross examination."

"You'll not be free to take the law into your own hands even when you are out of the Marines. Isn't that correct?"

"Yes, sir."

"Do you think that principle applies to us all? No one can take the law into his own hands?"

"Yes, sir."

"We all must follow the law?"

"Yes, sir."

"Everyone, no matter how powerful, must follow the law?"

"Objection. The question has been asked and answered. Also argumentative."

"Overruled. You may answer."

"Yes, sir. I guess so."

"No matter how distraught the person is?"

"Yes, sir."

"Everyone? No exceptions?"

"Yes, sir."

"And *everyone* includes your grandfather, does it not Eddie?"

"Yes."

"So even though you love your grandfather and don't want to see him convicted, you will agree that he had no right to take the law into his own hands?"

Eddie did not answer. Instead he looked at the floor and swallowed hard. Fred knew that he had backed the young man into a corner, but he knew he had tread carefully. Juries didn't like lawyers to badger witnesses—especially sympathetic witnesses.

"That's all right, son." Fred said. "There's no need to answer. I think we all know the answer." Fred paused while Eddie looked up from the floor. "I have no further questions."

Cain returned to his chair at the counsel table. He was very pleased with his cross examination. He was confident he had demonstrated to the jury, through Eddie's own words, how vital it was that no one be allowed to ignore the rule of law.

"Mr. Jefferson. Redirect," said Judge Hoskins.

"Your Honor, may I approach the witness?" Joseph asked.

"You may."

Fred watched as Joseph walked to within six or eight feet of the witness. "Mr. Cain is very good at cross examination. That must have been very difficult for you."

"No, sir. It wasn't."

"And why is that?"

"All I did was what you told me to do."

"And what was that?'"

"I told the truth."

"Eddie, I have one last question of you. And this will be the last question I have in this trial."

Fred was apprehensive. He knew that Joseph was a worthy opponent and wondered what he was going to ask.

"If this whole nightmare were to happen all over again—your Granna had been in a 60 day coma, with no hope of recovery, but your mother wouldn't give permission—would you still tell your grandfather to go and do what he did?"

Fred decided not to object. The judge would probably uphold his objection, but Fred felt the jury would be annoyed at him if he prevented them from hearing what the young man had to say.

"Yes, I would sir. And if Grandfather couldn't bring himself to do it, *I would do it myself*."

"You would do it yourself. Thank you, Eddie. Your Honor, the defense rests."

Fred thought of asking one or two questions, but decided he already had demonstrated to the jury that Eddie's testimony was nothing more than an appeal to the emotions. After all, he had admitted what his grandfather had done was illegal.

"Ladies and gentlemen," said Judge Hoskins. "Mr. Jefferson, Mr. Cain and I will be in conference all afternoon, discussing legal matters. You are dismissed until tomorrow morning, when we'll have closing arguments. You are not to discuss this matter with anyone. We shall be in session at nine o'clock tomorrow morning."

When the judge left the courtroom through his back door, those in the courtroom began talking among themselves.

As Fred walked into the hallway headed for his first floor office, he entered the glare of the television lights.

"Mr. Cain, when do you think the case will go to the jury?" asked the television reporter.

"We are working on jury instructions this afternoon. I expect that closing arguments will take up most of tomorrow. The jury should have the case the day after that."

"Do you still feel confident about the verdict?"

"Yes, I do. I wouldn't have brought the charges in the first place, if I didn't think I could get a conviction. I still feel that way. Now, if you'll excuse me, I have work to do."

"That was Deputy Prosecutor Frederick Cain. As you know, Mr. Cain is a candidate for the chief prosecutor's post in the November election. His chances in that election may very well depend on the results of this case."

"Good-bye, Eddie. Thank you for coming," said David. The bailiff had allowed David to linger in the courtroom.

"I'm sorry I can't stay for the verdict, but the plane is waiting for me now." Eddie gave his grandfather a hug. "I hope the jury has some sense."

"It's compassion I'm hoping for," David replied. "But there's nothing more either of us can do now."

"Mr. Jefferson's secretary promised she'd call me as soon as the verdict comes in. Normally we're not allowed to take calls at the base, but she says Mr. Jefferson has some pull at the Pentagon. Well, I've got to go now."

"Good-bye, Eddie." David gave his grandson one last hug. "Remember, no matter what happens, I love you."

"I love you too, Grandfather. Good-bye." Eddie waved from the doorway.

As the bailiff took him to his cell, David wondered where he would be the next time he saw Eddie. Would it be in jail, or dare he hope that it would be someplace else?

-56-

Betty lingered outside the courtroom. She desperately wanted to talk to Eddie, who was ending a conversation with Joseph. As she had reflected on last night's dinner conversation with Eddie and listened to him testify, she had realized that unless she acted to prevent it, the rift between them would be permanent. She couldn't stand the thought of that.

"You did a good job, Eddie," commented Joseph, shaking Eddie's hand.

"What are Grandfather's chances with the jury?"

"One thing I've learned in 40 years is not to try to predict juries. It's going to be a tough one, though."

"Eddie, I need to talk with you," Betty interrupted.

"I've got to catch my plane."

"I know, but before you leave, I've got to explain," Betty said.

"Why don't you walk with me to the car?" Eddie suggested.

"Good-bye, Eddie." Joseph waved, pointedly ignoring Betty. "Good luck in the Marines."

The hall was blocked by a swarm of reporters and by the television equipment.

"Eddie, how do you feel about your grandfather's chances?" a reporter shouted.

"I'm sorry, but I've got to get back to San Diego," Eddie replied. "Could we get by, please?"

"Tell us how you feel about your grandfather taking your grandmother's life!" another reporter cried out.

"I would have done the same thing!" Eddie shouted back, breaking through the crowd. Betty struggled to follow him.

Outdoors, another television reporter spotted them as they neared the limousine, and rushed forward along with a mob of reporters. "Judge Neal, could we have your reaction to your son's testimony?" The reporter pushed a microphone at Betty.

"No comment," Betty snapped. "Can't you see I want to spend some time with him?"

Eddie and Betty finally were able to get into the car. The chauffeur closed the door behind them.

"Could the driver drop me off at my hotel?" Betty asked, catching her breath. "That way we can talk, away from this bedlam."

"Okay. Tell him where you want to go."

Betty told the driver the location of her hotel, and the car pulled away from the crowd of reporters.

"What do you want to talk about?" Eddie asked.

He seemed distant and anxious to get away from her.

"I want to apologize for what I said last night. I shouldn't have tried to get you to quit the Marines."

"Come on, Mom. Maybe it's time for us to be straight with each other for a change. You know very well as far as you're concerned the Marine Corps is for losers. You'd rather have me be in law school someplace."

Betty gulped. "Very well. I admit I've always wished you'd go to college and do something with your life, but every mother has to learn to let her children make their own decisions. Don't you see I love you? You're my son."

"Everybody can't be a judge, you know."

"You could be, if you wanted." Immediately, she knew what she had said had been a mistake.

"No, I couldn't. Don't you see? I just want to be a Marine. They want me just the way I am. That's something you could never do, as long as I can remember."

"I'm sorry. It's all been so difficult. You've grown up so fast. You're all I have left now."

"From what Mr. Jefferson tells me, it's your own fault."

"What do you mean? What did Jefferson tell you?"

"He thinks you put pressure on the prosecutor to take Grandfather to court. Is that true?" Eddie turned his head away from her.

"That's definitely not true!" Betty wondered if Eddie suspected she was lying, but she didn't dare tell him the truth. He would never forgive her.

"But you did go to see him, the prosecutor, didn't you?"

"Lasser wanted to see me. He asked me if I had consented to Granna's death. I had to tell him the truth." She disliked continuing with the falsehood, but there was no turning back now.

"I would have lied—to save Grandfather."

"Eddie, I was being considered by the President of the United States for a judicial appointment. Don't you understand? I couldn't go around lying to public officials."

"Well, you didn't have to testify against him."

"All I did was tell the truth on the witness stand—that I hadn't given my consent. He would have subpoenaed me." She had to convince Eddie that going to trial was not her fault.

"That's another thing," Eddie said. "Why didn't you give your okay in the first place? You saw Granna. You knew she was never going to get better." Eddie sat upright looking out the window, holding his hat in his hands. The car had come to a stop outside her hotel.

"Because I didn't want to lose Granna any more than I want to lose you. You two were the most important people in the world to me. I didn't believe in mercy killing. Especially when it came to my own mother. Surely, you can't blame me for that. Can't we disagree about something and still be mother and son?"

"I guess so," Eddie said hesitantly. "But I wish you hadn't done what you did."

"I'm sorry, Eddie. I was only doing what I thought was right."

Eddie let out a sigh and finally looked at Betty. "Okay, Mom. Thanks for telling me your side of things."

"Eddie?"

"Yes?"

"If I write you, will you write back?"

"Okay, but I don't have much time to write, you know."

"I'll write you. Please write when you can," Betty pleaded.

"Okay, Mom. You'd better get out now. I can't keep them waiting. This trip must be costing Mr. Jefferson more than I make in a whole year."

Betty got out of the car and then bent over for a last word. "Eddie, I don't want to lose you. You are very important to me."

"I understand. Good-bye, Mom."

Betty watched as the limousine headed for the expressway. She went to her hotel room. It was lunchtime, but she was too upset to be in the dining room. She felt she had not made much headway, and was worried that Eddie was only being polite to avoid a confrontation. She still knew she was right about the Marines. Joining the Marines was a waste of time, but from now on she had to keep those thoughts to herself.

Betty caught a glimpse of herself in the wall mirror as she went to her suitcase. Oh, God, she had to do something about her weight, but she'd have to wait until this trial was over. With Eddie and the trial, there was just too much tension in her life right now.

There in the bottom of her suitcase was the box of chocolates that had remained untouched since the trial began. She took off the cover and selected one of her favorites. Just one chocolate wouldn't hurt.

As she ate the piece of candy she knew that Eddie would never understand why she had pushed Lasser to prosecute. Her father had deliberately defied her and the law. Under the circumstances she had no alternative but to lie to Eddie about Lasser. Surely, no one could fault her for wanting to reconcile with her own son.

As she finished the caramel, she made a decision. There was no point in spending any more time in Marshall. She had a heavy case load waiting in Detroit. She would check out of the hotel and follow the case on the news.

As she began to pack her belongings, she reached for another chocolate. What possible difference would one more chocolate make?

-57-

In contrast to the courtroom, the setting of Judge Hoskins' book-lined chambers was one of easy informality. The windows displayed a tranquil scene of trees and lawn. This afternoon Hoskins would decide what instructions he would read to the jury when the attorneys' closing arguments were completed. All three men were in shirt sleeves, but wore ties. Joseph had been through hundreds of such jury instruction conferences in his long career. While the jury would decide which facts were true, it was the judge's role to instruct them as to the applicable law.

In Joseph's wide experience, even in the most dramatic cases, selecting jury instructions was not particularly difficult. In almost all criminal cases the applicable law was clear. Normally it was the facts that were in dispute, not the law. However, the law involving mercy killing was still filled with uncertainty and was in the process of being evolved by the legislature and the courts.

"Gentlemen, I've read your briefs," said Hoskins. "I commend you for your thoroughness. I've got some tough decisions to make, but first, let's take the easy ones. We'll go through the *CJIs* one at a time." Hoskins was referring to the official jury instruction loose-leaf book called *Michigan Criminal Jury Instructions*. "Let's see if we can agree I should give Instruction 16.1." He handed each attorney copies of a one-page printed sheet. *The defendant is charged with first-degree murder. The prosecutor must prove each of the following elements beyond a reasonable doubt.* "Standard instruction. Any problem?"

"No, Your Honor." Cain agreed.

"Joseph?"

"All right, so far."

Hoskins read the next instruction: *First, that the defendant caused the death of Lu Neal.*

"Here we have a major issue," Joseph said. "I'm going to contend that Fred hasn't met his burden on that point."

"What the hell are you talking about?" exclaimed Cain. "Neal turned off the respirator. He admitted it on the stand."

"He said he turned off the respirator. He didn't say he killed her!"

"You mean you're contending something else caused her death? Not your client?" asked the judge.

"Exactly." Joseph smiled. "You remember the coroner–what was his name?"

"Foley," Fred answered. "William Foley. He was called in from Lansing."

"He very clearly testified that Lu Neal could have died at any moment. She was a very sick woman. She might have already been dead when the respirator was shut off."

"For God's sake, Joseph, you're serious about this, aren't you?" Cain asked, incredulously.

"Go back and read the transcript," Joseph went on. "I intend to read it to the jury, if Your Honor will allow me. You'll find equivocation in his testimony about the cause of death. Sorry Fred, I didn't want to point it up too clearly on cross. I knew damn well if I did, you'd get him straightened out on redirect. I've got a shot at raising a reasonable doubt. All it takes is one juror and you don't get your conviction." Joseph loved the look on his opponent's face. It said, *You're one foxy son-of-a-bitch.*

"Come on, Joseph, you aren't going to have a prayer with that one", said Cain."

Joseph smiled. "We'll see. I've won them on less, Fred."

"Well, my job is easy on that issue," Hoskins said. "You two can argue to the jury until your hearts' content on the cause of death. All I do is read

Instruction 16.1–that the prosecution must prove the defendant caused the death."

"Beyond a reasonable doubt," Joseph added.

"So you really think you have a shot at hanging the jury on that theory?" Judge Hoskins asked. From his tone, Joseph knew the judge was skeptical.

"Any port in a storm, Your Honor. Dr. Neal is a very sympathetic figure. I think the jury will be looking for a reason to acquit him."

"It's your case, counselor," said the judge. "I wouldn't presume to tell you what to argue and what not to. It's an issue for the jury, not me."

"Then I'm entitled to an instruction that the defendant need not be the *sole* cause of death," said Cain.

"Of course," Hoskins agreed. "I'll tell the jury that to convict they only need find that turning off the respirator was a *contributing* cause of death, not the *sole* cause."

"I can hardly object to that," admitted Joseph. "That's basic law."

"Now let's move on with the rest of 16.1." The judge began reading again from the printed instruction. *Second, to convict the defendant, you must find that the defendant intended to kill Lu Neal.* "Either of you have difficulty with my giving that instruction?"

"No," said Fred.

"No," agreed Joseph. "It still leaves me with my basic argument that although he may have intended to kill her, she may have already been dead."

"I can't get over your arguing that," said Cain.

Hoskins held up his hand. "Please, gentlemen, save it for the jury. Now let's move on. *Third, that this intent to kill was premeditated; that is, thought-out beforehand.* Any objection? It's the standard instruction."

"I've no problem with it," said Cain.

"Agreed," Joseph said.

"And *Fourth, that the killing was deliberate, that the defendant considered the pros and cons and chose his actions.*"

"He even prayed about it beforehand, for God's sake," said Cain.

"Go ahead," Joseph agreed. "I've no objection to the instruction."

"Now part five of 16.1 is the problem," Hoskins went on. "It says a legal element of murder is whether *the killing was justified or excused.* This, of course is a key issue. *Was Lu Neal's death justified or excused?*"

"I think the jury is entitled to know more than what that simple canned instruction says," said Cain. "You can't just turn this jury loose without telling them under what circumstances, if any, so-called mercy killing is *justified* or *excused.*"

"I've no doubt about that." Judge Hoskins agreed. "Joseph, I've got to give them some kind of a special instruction that tells them the law on mercy killing. Fred's right. It wouldn't be fair to the People to tell the jury: 'Okay, you can acquit the defendant if you find the homicide *justified or excused.*' I've got to define for them what is and is not *justified or excused.*"

"I suppose I can't quarrel with that," said Joseph. "But beyond that the whole legal issue in this case is *What is the law?* What are you going to tell them, without the upper court's reversing you if you're wrong?"

"Gentlemen, I've read the cases you've cited." Hoskins held up their blue-covered legal briefs. "I don't mind telling you I spent all day Sunday in Ann Arbor at the Legal Research Building. I agree with most of what you say in your briefs, but the Michigan Supreme Court simply hasn't addressed the issue. Mercifully, we at least have the Michigan Appeals Court case you each cited..."

"*In re Rosebush,*" Cain said.

"Yes," said Hoskins. "Damn helpful case. Then too, we have all the cases from other states."

"But none really on point," Joseph said. "My researcher has worked around the clock since I took this case. I even consulted with Professor Thatcher over at the law school. The *Michigan Law Review* published an article of his a few months back. As far as I can determine, we've got legal issues here no high court has ever decided."

"Looks like I'm going to have to instruct the jury in some gray areas," said Hoskins. "No matter what I do, whichever one of you fellows loses is going to try to get me reversed on appeal. Ah, the perils of being a trial judge."

"We start with the *Quinlan* case 20 years ago in New Jersey. It's certainly the landmark case," said Joseph. "It established the basic proposition that it isn't necessarily murder to remove life support."

"But the Michigan Supreme court has never ruled on the issue," said Cain. "As far as we know our Supreme Court would hold that all mercy killing in Michigan is illegal."

"Oh, I think it would follow *Quinlan*," said the judge. It's a very widely accepted case."

"But even in *Quinlan* everybody involved–the entire family, the guardian, and the hospital ethics committee–all agreed to turning off the life support system. On top of that, they went to court and got advance permission to disconnect her," said Cain. "That didn't happen here. The daughter objected."

"True, but *Rosebush* is a Michigan case and it tells us a great deal," Hoskins said.

"I'd be leery of *Rosebush,* " Joseph pointed out. "It was only the Appeals Court–not the Supreme Court–and a split decision at that. I think we've still got a case of first impression here."

"I don't agree, Joseph." Judge Hoskins had stood and was looking out the window, his back turned to the others. "I've read *Rosebush* a dozen times. Surely I must follow it. Not only is it well reasoned, but, after all, it is a higher court, even if it isn't the Supreme Court. It addresses some of our legal issues. Others it does not."

Hoskins returned to his chair, opened a law book from the many piled on his desk and pointed to a page. "Here's what I think *Rosebush* tells us about our case and, unless you fellows can convince me I'm wrong, here's what I plan to instruct the jury."

Joseph's nerves tightened. David's chances with the jury depended immeasurably on Hoskins's decision on these vital fine distinctions in the law.

"First, I'm going to make it clear that under some circumstances mercy killing is legal," the judge continued. "I keep saying *mercy killing*, but I suppose it's really the withdrawal of a life support system."

"Understood," said Joseph.

"Many laymen think all mercy killing is illegal unless you have something in writing. I think I should straighten out that misimpression for the jury," said Hoskins. "The various cases make it clear you don't have to have something in writing."

"I have to concede that," Cain said.

Judge Hoskins leaned back in his chair, still looking at the law book in his hands. "The most important thing *Rosebush* tells us–I'm reading from page 687–is you don't need to get advance court approval to turn off the respirator unless, and I quote, 'the parties directly concerned disagree'...Now as far as I'm concerned that language makes it clear that Dr. Neal had no business turning off his wife's respirator when his daughter refused permission. I'm sorry, Joseph, but that's what I've decided to instruct the jury."

"I strongly disagree!" Joseph was looking at his own copy of the *Rosebush* decision. "The language you quoted says *the parties directly concerned*. The opinion does not say a child of the patient–Betty Neal–is *directly concerned*. I don't think she is."

"To the contrary," argued Cain. "Who could be more *concerned* than a daughter?"

"The language says *directly* concerned" Joseph argued. "To me that includes the doctor and the spouse, not the children. The opinion goes to great lengths to say mercy killing is a medical problem. It's the spouse and doctor who should decide, not a the children. The law is replete with instances where the spouse has priority over children–being administrator–being guardian– making burial arrangements. What's more what if the children were minors. Are you supposed to get kids consent?"

"That's a valiant argument, Joseph," Hoskins commented. "But I don't agree. I think the opinion was addressing itself to cases where the family disagrees–not just where the doctor and the spouse disagree."

"I couldn't agree more," said Cain. "If you're going to allow mercy killing, you've got to have proper safeguards. The law should not permit a spouse to take a life when a child disagrees. That's a safeguard we must have. Look, all Neal had to do was go to court and get permission."

"I think he's right, Joseph," said Judge Hoskins. "If your client is convicted, I'm sure you'll try to prove me wrong in the Supreme Court. In the meantime I'm going to tell the jury the daughter's consent was legally necessary."

Joseph did not reply. It was clear the judge had his mind made up. In his heart Joseph's knew the judge had a point. It could be dangerous to let a spouse override children in a case where there was a disagreement. Nevertheless, if David were convicted, he was going to do his damnedest to convince the Supreme Court to the contrary.

"That leaves us with one last issue–Lu Neal's alleged consent," said Hoskins. "Now, I fully expect you two to fight like cats and dogs about the factual issue, *Did she or did she not come out of her coma and consent?* But the issue I'm faced with is, what is the law on the subject?"

Joseph spoke first: "The law is simple; if the jury finds she consented, then they should acquit Dr. Neal."

"Now, just one minute!" said Cain. "The idea of her coming out of her coma in the nick of time to give him permission to do what he was going to do anyway is a total cock-and-bull story, if I ever heard one."

"That's for you to argue to the jury," commented Hoskins, "For all I know they could believe Neal."

"Let's assume for just a minute that it really happened as Neal said," Cain went on. "There isn't one case I know of that says it's okay to kill a patient when she says, *Okay, go ahead and kill me.* Especially when she's just come out of a coma, for God's sake."

"As far as I can find, this is a case of first impression," said Judge Hoskins. "It's one more point for the Supreme Court to decide on appeal, but I'm inclined to agree with Joseph. You know, gentlemen, as I sat on that bench when Dr. Neal was testifying, my mind went back to my stretch in Vietnam. A man in our company stepped on a mine. It was terrible. His legs were blown off. It was obvious he was going to die. He begged his buddy to shoot him. Finally his buddy did it. It never occurred to anyone to charge him with murder."

Cain was clearly perturbed. "Judge, we're talking real danger here. Maybe we put dogs out of their misery; but, for God's sake, not people, even when they beg for it. Even if it happened the way Neal says, which I don't concede for one minute, we don't know if she understood what he was asking her. The poor woman had been in a coma for 60 days, for crying out loud! No time to reflect! We don't even let someone make a will under such circumstances, let alone give permission to be killed."

"Juries decide issues like this every day," Joseph said. "These are all issues you should argue to the jury."

"You can't trust juries with issues like these," Cain argued. "They're too important. They won't understand them."

"You're really saying you don't believe in the jury system," Joseph said.

"I'm sorry, Fred. I think these issues are for the jury," said the judge, halting the discussion. "If those twelve find Mrs. Neal gave her permission and knew what she was doing, they can acquit, if they want. Frankly, I doubt if I would find she did, but I'm not the trier of fact here. The jury is."

"But Judge–" Fred protested.

"Fred, you're each going to have a dozen grounds for appeal. I don't mind tossing the whole mess into the collective lap of the Supreme Court, but I'd sure as hell be reversed if I didn't give Joseph a shot at convincing the jury Mrs. Neal gave permission."

"But–"

"No, I've made my decision. Anything else?"

"No, I guess all the rest of the instructions are standard. Degree of proof. Reasonable doubt. Credibility of witnesses," said Joseph. He was elated at Judge Hoskins' decision.

"Judge, can I ask you to think about your decision overnight?" Cain asked.

"Fred, this hasn't been an easy case for any of us." Hoskins closed the law book with a note of finality. "We'll start off with argument at nine o'clock. How long do you expect it to be, Fred?"

"I don't know. A couple of hours, maybe three."

"And you, Joseph?"

"Less than an hour. I always keep it short. They listen better if it's short."

"Gentlemen, see you in the morning."

That evening, as Joseph dined alone, he thought about his argument to the jury. From the beginning, his plan had been to provide at least one juror with some plausible grounds to find David not guilty. He was convinced that many of the jurors had liked David and were sympathetic to his plight. Joseph's task tomorrow was to show their minds a way to follow their hearts. He was not going to prepare much for argument. Long experience had taught him that his arguments were more convincing if he spoke extemporaneously.

Later that night Joseph visited David in the jail.

"David, there's something I want to tell you before tomorrow." Joseph said. "I've never tried a case I wanted to win more than yours, but all I can do is my best."

"Look, Joseph, no attorney could have done better. I never expected miracles." said David.

Both fell silent for a time, then Joseph spoke again. "I doubt if either of us will sleep much tonight. I seldom do before final argument."

David nodded his understanding.

Joseph felt an inexpressible kinship with David. The case they had so earnestly fought together would soon be in the hands of the jury. There would be nothing more to say or do. This was no television show where a favorable verdict was already scripted. The rest of David's life was at stake. It was as if a tornado were passing overhead and neither knew whether it would kill them, or leave them unscathed.

"Well, David. I'll say 'good night' now. I think I'll go for a long walk and do some thinking. Try to get some sleep."

Joseph reached to shake hands. Tears were in David's eyes as he took Joseph's hand and then hugged him. Joseph could feel his client's bony body trembling through his thin jailhouse clothing.

"Thanks, Joseph. Thanks for everything you've done."

As Joseph walked the dark streets, his resolve grew inside him. This was a case he simply had to win.

-58-

Marge watched with pride as Fred stood to make his closing argument to the jury. She had attended every day of the trial. Every evening they had worked together, going over the day's events and planning for tomorrow. She had seen him mature as a lawyer as the trial progressed. To her, Fred was destined to be a great trial lawyer. Sometimes as she lay next to him in her bed–he had slept over every night–she wondered if it wouldn't be best if he had not decided to run for prosecutor. Marge thought Fred had the talent to be one of the major trial lawyers of the country–handling famous clients like O. J. Simpson and Manuel Ortega, the deposed Panama dictator. That was where the money and the glory were. As the trial neared its close, she could see there was no longer any pretense in Fred's air of confidence. Now he radiated genuine self-assurance. Even when the young Marine, Eddie, made his shocking appearance, Fred had confidently taken it in stride. He had told her that night that she should not worry. There would be little harm done by the testimony, when he had dealt with it in final argument.

For Marge, her relationship with Fred had started out as an interesting diversion–a touch of adventure in the prosecutor's sleepy office. But in these last weeks she had come to love Fred. Working side by side with him had been the greatest thing to happen to her. She loved the power that she had seen develop in the man. Whatever his future, she wanted to share it.

Every night they had worked, trading ideas and testing theories until exhaustion had overcome them. But the strain had never diminished Fred's intense desire for sex with her. She had never had a lover like him, even when her other relationships had been fresh. She didn't know if it was something special about her or whether he would have wanted most any woman in the same circumstances, but she had dismissed the question. She wanted to follow Frederick Cain wherever it took her. She only hoped she would be invited to go along for the ride.

"Ladies and gentlemen," Fred began, as he walked from the counsel table toward the jury he maintained eye contact with one juror and then the next. "When this trial began I made a contract with you. I told you I would prove certain things, and, if I did, you would find the defendant guilty of first degree murder. I intend to enumerate the items that I have proved to fulfill that contract, but first I want to discuss what I believe to be the main issue in the case—the issue of emotion. You see, the facts and the law clearly require a conviction in this case. In my opinion, the only possible avenue left open to the defense is to play on your sympathy and emotion. Let us look these emotions straight in the eye right now.

"The defendant is a nice man. He is a likable man. He has never before committed a crime. He had been the pillar of the academic community. We all respect him. Second, we all feel compassion for the defendant. We are grateful that what happened to Lu Neal did not happen to our loved one. Each of us is aware that what happened to Lu Neal could happen in our own family—even to us. Next, we are not at all certain what we would do if the same circumstances were thrust upon us. Might not we do the same as the defendant? Lastly, I want to say that, with one major exception, I believe the defendant is telling the truth as he sees it. I suspect you do too. I believe that he genuinely loved his wife. I personally do not think he killed his wife for her money, although that is for you to decide. I believe that he genuinely was distressed by the decision he made to kill his wife. A sympathetic figure? Yes.

"However, I certainly do *not* have sympathy for his telling you that Lu Neal magically came out of her 60-day coma and agreed to her own murder. From the testimony of Dr. Jacobson and Dr. Foley we know that was medically impossible.

"Oh, some of you might speculate that the defendant *thought* she came out of her coma. To you I say *We do not deal in speculation; we deal in facts.* Furthermore, what Dr. Neal may have thought happened and what actually happened are two entirely different things. Are we to permit murders because a distraught killer tells a jury that he *thought* the victim said *Okay, go ahead and kill me?* Why, we don't even permit murders where the victim actually said *Go ahead and kill me.*"

"Now, I would like to return to our original contract–if I prove certain things, you will do your duty and convict the defendant. Remember, every one of you said on *voir dire* that you would not permit a person to take the law into his own hands."

Marge watched as Fred walked to the other end of the jury box and took out a marker to write on the board. She observed that the jury had been listening carefully. No one's attention had wandered and there had been no sign of disagreement on any juror's face.

"Now I would like to review the essential facts that clearly prove beyond a doubt that I am correct when I say that you have no alternative but to find Dr. Neal guilty of murder.

"When it comes down to it, this case is quite simple, factually. First, on the night of February 28, 1994, Lu Neal was alive." Fred wrote "Lu Neal alive" on the board.

"Second, Dr. Neal himself admits that he turned off the ventilator and that his wife died as a result." Marge watched the jury as Fred wrote "Defendant kills Lu Neal." Two jurors visibly nodded their heads in agreement.

"On cross examination of the coroner, Mr. Jefferson attempted to make an issue of whether it was somehow possible that Mrs. Neal had already died as a result of another stroke, moments before the ventilator was turned off. I don't blame Mr. Jefferson for raising this issue. I suppose any defense attorney faced with the desperate problem Mr. Jefferson has would make any conceivable argument. This is what defense attorneys do. But it is clear that this argument is totally at odds with the facts. There is not one scintilla of fact–not even reasonable speculation–that Lu Neal had another stroke at the last instant. It's as if Machine Gun Kelly argued his innocence because his victim might have died of a heart attack moments before Kelly pumped 50 bullets into him. I really don't think I need to spend any more time on that theory."

Fred had made the point well, Marge thought. They had decided last night that the defense theory was patently phony and that any detailed discussion of it might cause the jury to take it seriously.

"Next, let us turn to this inventive claim that Lu Neal regained consciousness. Ladies and gentlemen, I have prosecuted a great many criminal matters. It is common for defendants to try to figure out a way to beat the rap. What better way to beat this murder charge than to claim that somehow, miraculously, Lu Neal regained consciousness after 60 days in a hopeless coma, and told her the defendant 'All right, dear, if you think best, go ahead and kill me?' What nonsense. The defendant's only hope is that one of you will believe that is what happened. Remember, he never made that claim to the police. The first time we heard of it was in this courtroom. The story is an obvious concoction. I do not see how any reasonable person can believe it to be true. Dr. Neal himself admitted he thought it was a miracle. Some miracle, indeed. How convenient a miracle! How fanciful a tale." Sarcasm dripped from Cain's tone.

"By his own admission the defendant had planned to kill his wife, whether or not she agreed. He testified that he did not care whether or not the killing was illegal. That was not his concern. It also was not his concern that his daughter refused to give permission to what she deemed to be the murder of her mother. Remember he testified he would have committed the crime even if Lu Neal had not given her consent."

Fred returned to stand at the counsel table, letting the jury absorb the points he had made.

"Ladies and gentlemen, it doesn't take much imagination to know what happened next. The defendant sits in jail, waiting for trial. His wish for suicide passes, but he knows he stands to spend the rest of his life in jail.

He doesn't like that idea. There is only one plan that gives him a chance to avoid that fate. He decides to try to convince you that his wife consented to her killing. I've seen many cases where defendants have come to the point where they actually believe their own concocted alibis. A defendant can look us straight in the eye and appear to be telling the truth. We have to go by other factors. We have to ask, *What is plausible? What makes sense?* Ladies and gentlemen, it simply makes no sense at all to believe that Lu Neal came out of her coma and said, *Please kill me.*

"But let us assume just for the sake of discussion that she did come out of her coma. Mind you, just for the sake of discussion. Ladies and gentlemen, giving consent to your own murder is serious business. The very least we should demand is that the person know what she is doing–that she be given a chance to reflect on the fact she is going to die. After all, the decision is irrevocable. There will be no second chance. Consider this: The poor woman is unconscious for 60 days. She regains enough consciousness to open her eyes and look at her husband–so he claims. She can't speak. According to him, he tells her of his plan to end her life. 'If its okay with you, blink your eyes.' What kind of nonsense is this? Is this supposed to be informed consent? If a doctor so much as took out your appendix under such circumstances, you'd sue him and you'd collect. Agreeing to your own death under such circumstances? Nonsense. Absolute nonsense!

"Before I finish, I want to mention the appearance of Eddie Erickson. It was very dramatic, wasn't it? It couldn't have been done better if it had been in a New York stage play. I'm sure the young man loved his grandmother. I'm sure he loves his grandfather. I'm sure he will serve well in the Marines. But what possible relevance does his testimony have to this case? In a nutshell, he testified that he understood why his grandfather decided to take the law into his own hands. He even volunteered that he would have violated the law himself. And exactly what has that got to do with anything? Are juries suppose to let confessed killers go because their relatives love them? Are killers to go free because their grandchildren say they, too, would have been killers? To ask the question answers it. We cannot have such a system of justice.

"Lurking in the background of this case is a moral issue of gigantic proportions that society must face. It has been an issue since early times, but it has become much more pronounced with the ability of modern medicine to keep people alive under difficult circumstances. It is natural for you to wonder what you would do if tragedy struck one of your loved ones. It is natural for you to wonder what you would want done if you were stricken as Lu Neal was.

"As a society we ask, *Can it ever be moral for a life to be ended? And if so, under what circumstances?* These issues should be discussed and debated by judges, clergy, politicians, physicians, indeed by us all. But today you are not judges, politicians, physicians or even private citizens. In this case you are jurors. As you deliberate, remember it is not for you, as jurors, to worry about these moral issues. Under our system, we do not delegate to jurors what is moral and immoral. Under our system, we do not delegate to jurors what is legal and illegal. Juries decide facts and only facts. It is your sworn duty to do that and only that. Great complex moral and legal issues are for another day, for other people in other forums.

"When you retire to the jury room to commence your deliberations and concentrate on the facts of this one single case being tried in this courtroom in Marshall, Michigan, you will see there is only one remotely relevant fact that is in dispute–the desperate claim that Lu Neal consented to her own murder and that she was competent to do so. To pose the question answers it. Your inescapable choice under the law is clear. You must find the defendant guilty."

As Fred took his seat at the counsel table, Marge could feel her heart beat. The courtroom was totally and completely silent. Throughout the argument, the absolute attention of each juror had been riveted on Fred. To Marge, there was no doubt that the jury would give Fred the greatest victory of his career.

-59-

From her seat in the jury box, Billie Croft watched Frederick Cain take his seat and Joseph Jefferson stand to commence his final argument.

She had mixed feelings about Cain's argument. His logic and his personal force reminded her of her husband's. Logically, it was difficult to disagree with anything Cain said. But as John often did, Cain ignored the intangible, human side.

What would her sister and she do if their mother had a stroke, as Lu Neal had? Or—more like the Neal case—what would Billie do if her sister, Mickii, were to refuse to allow their mother's respirator to be turned off? Occasionally Mickii could be difficult, displaying that know-it-all streak of hers. Billie supposed she might turn off the respirator herself if Mickii pulled a stunt as Betty Neal had done. Billie was very ill-at-ease with the dilemma this case presented. A person should not be allowed to defy the law, yet she could imagine herself doing the very same thing Dr. Neal had done—especially if it were her own family.

"Well, Mr. Cain has this case wrapped up in a nice neat package for you doesn't he?" Jefferson began. "Your job is easy. Find Dr. Neal guilty of murdering his beloved wife. Lock him up. Throw away the key. Go home, turn on the television and forget about him. Don't worry about your conscience. After all, conscience is another department. That's what the prosecution would have you believe."

Billie was startled. It was almost as if Jefferson had read her mind. He had put his finger on exactly what bothered her about this case. It was not at all as cold and logical as Cain had made out. She leaned forward eagerly, wanting to hear Jefferson's argument.

"I suggest that Dr. Neal did nothing wrong. He acted no differently from the way you or I would have under the same circumstances. It is true that once he wanted to take his own life, along with Lu's. That is quite understandable. Wouldn't most of you have those same feelings?" Joseph looked Billie directly in the eye as he asked the question.

"It is also true that he later changed his mind and decided to live. He wants to write. He wants to contribute, as he always has. You saw his grandson on the witness stand. He wants to spend time with his grandson—to watch him develop and grow." Joseph continued speaking directly to Billie. "Isn't that, too, quite understandable—quite human? Any of us would want the same. Yet Mr. Cain tries to make something evil out of the fact that Dr. Neal changed his mind and wants to live as a free man.

"My wife died of cancer three years ago. I know what it's like to watch a loved one die an agonizing death. If you put Dr. Neal in jail, you threaten us all with jail, for many of us stand to face the same decision as Dr. Neal did.

"Mr. Cain tells you that you should have no part in deciding the issues of mercy killing. He tells you that people wiser than you should decide these great issues. I say nonsense! Who better to decide than the twelve men and women who heard the testimony of those involved? Who better than those who heard and saw Dr. Neal's agony as he faced those issues? Are these judgments supposed to be made by some wise men in Lansing who have never heard of Lu Neal? Wise men who don't know a thing about the love and compassion her husband of 51 years felt for her? I say no! I say you have a duty to seize the process. You have a responsibility to see to it that justice is done. I say that you cannot possibly put a man—a good man—a kindly man—in jail for what you yourself would have done!"

Billie watched as Jefferson walked to the end of the jury box and concentrated on another member of the jury.

"Judge Hoskins is going to instruct you that you must find Dr. Neal *not* guilty, unless the prosecutor has proved every fact essential to his theory of the case. Not only must each fact be proved, but it must be proved *beyond a reasonable doubt.* This means that if there is any reasonable interpretation of the testimony and facts which favor Dr. Neal, you must accept it as true and acquit him. Ladies and gentlemen, this time-honored principle is a cornerstone of our legal system. You cannot send Dr. Neal to jail if you think that any reasonable person could have such a doubt, even though you personally may not have that doubt."

Billie watched as Joseph moved his eyes to another juror.

"*Wait a minute*, you might say. *That is quite a burden. How could anyone ever be convicted?* The first answer to that question is, those are the rules. The judge will instruct you as to the rules and you must follow them. These rules were made over three hundred years ago so that juries could defy the crown and acquit people unfairly charged. As a society, we made the decision long ago that we would rather have a hundred guilty men and women be set free than have even one wrongly convicted. Juries cannot convict a person, because he *probably* is guilty. Persons who are only *probably* guilty are acquitted under our system. That is the law."

Jefferson's eyes moved to the next juror.

"Another point. You cannot vote for conviction just because all eleven others disagree with you and vote for conviction. If you think there is a reasonable doubt, then you must stand firm and vote for acquittal. Of course you will listen to what others have to say. But if that remains your belief, you must vote for acquittal, until the proverbial cows come home.

"Mr. Cain makes light of Eddie's testimony—that fine young man who is a credit to his grandparents. Mr. Cain obviously misses the whole point of Eddie's testimony. Eddie was there. Eddie saw this horrible drama unfold. He was a part of it. He loved his grandmother. She was his salvation. He never would have wanted her dead. Yet you heard him say that when his grandfather told him what he planned to do, he would have done the very same thing. How can you possibly ignore testimony like that? Can you dismiss it as sentimental drivel, as the prosecutor would have you do? Not on your life. In his youthful straightforward way, Eddie made us see that his grandfather took the brave course of action—that he did the right thing."

Every juror watched as Jefferson put his hands on the edge of the jury box and shifted his attention to a juror in the second row.

"There are two essential elements of the prosecution's case that have *not* been proved beyond a reasonable doubt. The first is whether Dr. Neal caused his wife's death. The second is whether Lu Neal came out of her coma and agreed with her husband's plan to end her life. If you think there is a reasonable doubt about the prosecutor's contentions on either of these points, you must acquit Dr. Neal.

"Let us examine whether Mr. Cain proved Dr. Neal caused his wife's death. First of all, I am certain that Dr. Neal *thought* he had caused his wife's death, but, ladies and gentlemen, that is not the issue. The issue is whether there is a reasonable doubt that he *actually* did so. If there is such a doubt, you must acquit Dr. Neal. The coroner's testimony on this point was sloppy, to say the least. You heard him. It is evident he *assumed* the turning off of the respirator caused the death and acted on that *assumption* from the beginning. Now I agree that it would be natural for us to assume the same thing, had we been in that hospital room, but the coroner is supposed to be a scientist, not a layman. He is not supposed to *assume* anything until it is scientifically proved. I suggest that he was in such a hurry to collect his fee and get back to Lansing that he did not do a proper scientific job. As Dr. Jacobson pointed out, Lu Neal could have died at any time from another stroke or other natural causes. It was a miracle that she had survived that long. When we are talking about whether a man is guilty of murdering his wife, we have no business making assumptions. We must require proof, and there is no such scientific proof."

Billie wasn't so sure. To her it seemed obvious that Dr. Neal had caused his wife's death. But Jefferson was right on one point. The coroner had been cocky and quick to judgment. Billie would give consideration to

Jefferson's argument, but she hoped his other points would be more convincing. She had come to the point where she was loath to send Dr. Neal to prison unless there was simply no alternative.

"Now, I would like to turn to the next issue. *Is there a reasonable possibility that Lu Neal did come out of her coma–that Dr. Neal disclosed his plan to her and that she blinked her eyes in agreement?* I say to you that what Dr. Neal says happened, did in fact happen. Again, I remind you that you must resolve reasonable doubt in his favor. You saw Dr. Neal on the witness stand. Do you believe him, as I do? You watched him as he testified. You cannot doubt that he is telling the truth.

"The prosecutor says that it is impossible for a woman near death to have made such a miraculous temporary recovery. *How convenient a story*, he says, as he mocks Dr. Neal's testimony. I think otherwise. I believe things like that happen. Dr. Neal had talked to his wife every day since her stroke. Perhaps she heard him. We don't know that she did not. Can you imagine her situation? Hearing her husband and yet not being able to tell him she heard? What a terrible plight. Yet we all have heard of stroke victims who have not been able to speak.

"Can you imagine the night she heard him reading from the Bible? She sensed the love her husband had for her. She wanted to respond, but could not. Then finally, in an extreme exertion of will, or perhaps through a God-given power, she opened her eyes. She heard her husband's plan, she understood what he wanted to do. Then, desiring to be released from life, perhaps, too, desiring to release her husband from his ordeal, she managed to blink her eyes, saying that, *yes*, she wanted the respirator turned off. I can certainly imagine that to be true. Can't you?

"And now her heroic efforts are for what? Are you going to disbelieve that she accomplished such a remarkable feat?" Jefferson glanced at Cain. "Is Lu Neal to be the victim of a prosecutor's skepticism born of seeing too many criminals trying to beat the rap?

"I can hear Mr. Cain and the skeptics say, *Nonsense. Just another desperate attempt by a slick attorney to get his client off.*"

Jefferson took a position near the witness stand, looking at the jury.

"Well, ladies and gentlemen, let me tell you a story. A story more incredible than the one you have heard. Yet a story that is true beyond a shadow of a doubt. A story chronicled in the very history of our country.

"My name is Joseph Thomas Jefferson. My father admired Thomas Jefferson, who, at 33 years of age, authored the Declaration of Independence. A man who later became our third president. I bear his name with pride. I try to live up to that name in everything I do. You may have heard of President John Kennedy's remark while entertaining a group of intellectuals in the White House. President Kennedy said there had never been so much brain power assembled in the White House since Thomas Jefferson dined alone. The story I'm going to tell you is about Thomas Jefferson.

"Jefferson completed the Declaration of Independence on the fourth of July, 1776–Independence Day. Half a century later, July 4, 1826, the fiftieth anniversary of the famous document was nearing. But now, at 83, Jefferson was near death in Monticello.

Miles away in Quincy, Massachusetts John Adams, the second president of the United States, an even older man, also neared death as the anniversary date approached.

"While the two had been hated political rivals, as old men they had reconciled and had written each other hundreds of letters. Both men were intellectuals–believers in the powers of logic–the rational mind. Neither believed in voodoo or magic.

"While the nation was preparing to celebrate the great fiftieth anniversary, Thomas Jefferson's doctors were certain that he would die before the day arrived. But Jefferson told his daughter and his doctors that he was determined to live until the anniversary of the historic document he had authored. All present thought his wish was impossible. Yet through sheer–it was not will power–I don't actually know what to call it–let us call it miraculous determination–Jefferson lived. He died at three o'clock in the morning on July 4th, expressing joy that he had survived.

"Meanwhile in Massachusetts, John Adams carried on the same struggle for life. It seemed unlikely, if not impossible, that he would survive to celebrate the anniversary. Yet he was determined to do so. Defying all logic, he too lived on. He died a few hours after Jefferson on July 4, 1826. Not knowing of Jefferson's death, Adams' last words were, 'At least Jefferson lives.'

"Unbelievable? Of course it is unbelievable. True? Yes, absolutely true. If John Adams could will himself to live a last few days, if Thomas Jefferson could defy all logic and appearances to live those last days so important to him, who among us could say that a determined Lu Neal could not regain consciousness long enough to signal her husband that she had had enough of life?"

Jefferson stopped and walked to the other end of the jury box. The jurors followed his every step.

"Lastly, Mr. Cain argues that if Lu Neal did agree with her husband's plan, she was not competent to do so. Thus her wishes must be ignored. Ladies and gentlemen, the effrontery of such an argument. Hearing the agony of her husband and defying all appearances, Lu Neal managed to blink her eyes. Now the prosecution says you are supposed to ignore her wishes because she might possibly have been incompetent. I say fie on such nonsense! Such an argument ought to be thrown in the trash can the same way this prosecution should have been thrown in the trash in the very beginning.

"I want to leave you with one last thought. A thought that has been with me throughout this trial. A thought that should guide you as you deliberate. What would Lu Neal have you do to her husband? How would Lu Neal vote if she were on the jury? I ask you to invite her into your deliberations. I ask you to make her a 13th juror. To give her a vote. Listen to what she says as you make up your minds. If you do that, I have no doubt you will acquit her husband. No doubt that you will allow him to be a grandparent to her grandson. No doubt that you will allow David

Neal to live out the rest of his days with at least some peace of mind and
to continue to be the productive person he has always been.

"I thank you very much."

Billie was stunned when Jefferson returned to his chair. She felt bound-
less compassion for Dr. Neal. She knew Jefferson was right. If Lu Neal
were on the jury, she would surely acquit her husband.

Billie knew that if the stroke had happened to her, she would have consented to John's removing the respirator. She would not have wanted to put
him through any more agony. Sixty days was enough for any human being.

Yet Billie was aware of a voice within her. It was the voice of her father,
dead these past years. It was at the family dinner table when she and
Mickii were girls. It was the time they had skipped class to go to the carni-
val. "You must follow the rules," her father had said. "We can't have people going around making up their own rules. I'm sorry girls, but I'm going
to have to punish you as soon as you've helped your mother with the
dishes. I hope I'll never have to do it again. Perhaps next time you'll not
ignore the rules just because it suits you." From that day on Billie had
always followed the rules. She had married a man who followed the rules
and she had taught her own children to do the same. How could she vote
to acquit Dr. Neal, no matter what her heart told her to do?

As Cain made his short rebuttal argument and Judge Hoskins read the
jury instructions, Billie knew it was that dilemma she must face once they
were in the jury room.

When the jury filed from the courtroom to deliberate, David felt
drained and empty. His emotions had been whipsawed by the closing arguments. Inexplicably, he felt both discouraged and encouraged at the same
time. He wondered how many sleepless nights he would spend in his jail
cell while the jury debated his fate. He knew only one thing with certainty.
If Lu could somehow be the 13th juror, he never would be convicted.

-60-

Billie had deliberately sat near Alvin Banning at lunch several times because he seemed more cultured than the others. Banning, about 50, owned a plastics business and wore a suit and tie. He had sat on one jury before. Billie was the one to nominate him to be foreman of the jury and his selection was unanimous.

"I'd like to start the discussion by going around the table and just talking," Banning began. "If you want to pass, you may. If you want to say how your vote is leaning, you may, but remember the judge cautioned us not to make up our minds until we've heard each other's viewpoints."

The first juror, a large black man named Louis Johnson, worked in one of the factories in Albion. "I'd like to pass. I've got my own ideas, but I want to hear what the rest of you have to say first."

Next was Alicia Phillips, a worker at a cereal plant in Battle Creek. She looked to be in her late 20s. "I don't mind telling you, I'm leaning for acquittal. Mercy killing goes on all the time, only it's just not broadcast. I think that doctor, I forget his name, should have done it a long time before. Why he even asked Dr. Neal for permission is beyond me, let alone asking that slob of a daughter."

"Oh, come on. Just because a woman is fat doesn't mean she doesn't have rights," said one of the jurors.

"Rights. Rights. That's all anyone ever talks about. Well, I have a right not to like a big fat slob," Alicia answered.

"Now, let's try to keep our discussion to the point," Banning interrupted. "Mr. Washington, it's your turn, if you like." Tom Washington was the second of the three African-Americans on the jury. He worked for the county at an office job.

"This case gives me all sorts of trouble. I've been a church-going man all my life. I know God is the only one who can take a life, yet I might have done the very same thing Dr. Neal did."

"Do you have any leaning so far that you'd like to tell us?"

"No," Washington answered. "Not yet. I'd like to listen to the rest of you."

"Mr. Page, you're next." Jim Page drove a forklift for a living.

"Well, I don't mind telling you how I'm leaning, because I'm not just leaning, I've decided how I'm going to vote. I don't need no deliberations. I think the guy's guilty as hell. All that stuff about trying to commit suicide is bullshit—pure bullshit. He brought his gun to the hospital to shoot her if she didn't die from the respirator. What Neal wanted was her dough! I'll bet that old son-of-a-bitch has got a woman stashed away someplace. I'll just bet you."

Billie could not contain herself. "How can you possibly decide just like that? Dr. Neal didn't need money. He lived very modestly. He wouldn't know what to do with a lot of money if he got it."

Page looked disgustedly at Billie. "Listen, lady we all could use a bunch of cash. Don't kid yourself. I still think he's got a girlfriend stashed away someplace. I know the type."

Billie felt like exploding. My God, she thought, they'd never reach a just verdict with someone like that on the jury.

"All right, next," said Banning.

The next juror was Reverend Harold Dempster. He was a young assistant pastor at a Christian church near Battle Creek. Dempster wore Levis and a tee shirt, showing his muscles. He was the last person you would expect to be a minister. "This case presents one of the issues of our time. People are living into their 90s and even 100s. I've visited them in those Godforsaken convalescent homes. I don't know what we're going to do with them, but we can't just kill them off."

"No, of course we can't," interrupted Sam Ameson, the owner of a men's clothing store. "But this case is different. She was unconscious for 60 days. What other recourse did the poor man have?"

Still another juror interrupted–Bill Gardner, the gas station owner. "Neal could have let her live. I'm sorry but I buy the argument that he was thinking of himself–not her. I agree with Cain. She wasn't doing anyone any harm by just lying there. He killed her because he wanted out of a bad situation, not because he felt sorry for her. I'm voting guilty."

Banning resumed control. "Now, let's try and be orderly. We'll have a general discussion later. "Next, Mrs. Croft? Do you want to talk?"

Billie took a deep breath. This was the moment of decision for her. Perhaps she was mistaken, but she sensed that what she said would have considerable influence on the others. "This has been a very difficult case for me. I know a person shouldn't take the law into his own hands. I had that drummed into me when I was growing up. But I don't see how I can vote to convict Dr. Neal. We all know–at least I certainly know–that if Lu Neal were in this room she would vote for acquittal. I heard her give a speech once at a club. That's the kind of woman she was."

"How many of you think Dr. Neal is telling the truth when he says his wife came out of her coma?" Banning asked. Four people, including Billie, raised their hands.

"I think you've got to put the question another way, if I understand the judge's instructions," said Billie. "How many of you believe *beyond a reasonable doubt* that Dr. Neal made up that whole story? How many of you are positive he's lying just to get off." This time only two people, then a third, raised their hands.

"Yes, Billie's right. I stand corrected," said Banning. "We must not lose sight of the fact that all reasonable doubts must be resolved in favor of Dr. Neal."

"I don't give a shit about all that stuff," said Page, waving his fist in the air. "That's just for smart defense lawyers like Jefferson to get their clients off the hook."

"I've been watching you, Page." It was the first juror, Louis Johnson, the African-American who had reserved what he had to say. Clearly he was angry. "I've heard what you've said about Mr. Jefferson when you thought none of us African-Americans were listening. You can't stand the thought of a black man being smart enough to be a good lawyer. A damn good one, I might add."

"Look, fella," Page answered, pointing his finger at Johnson. "I don't give a flying good goddamn if Jefferson is black or green. What I don't like is all this bleeding heart crap he's trying to feed us. You know damn well Jefferson is going to be the one ending up with all Lu Neal's dough. Win, lose or draw, he doesn't give a shit how he gets it. You saw those expensive suits of his. I saw the car he drove. He's got a chauffeur, for God's sake. I'll bet he defends drug peddlers when he's not trying to get some murderer off."

Billie was livid with anger, but before she could speak Banning interrupted. "Let's not get personal here, Mr. Page. We've got a case to decide."

"Well, that shyster is not going to get my vote. I know about people like that!"

"Mr. Page," Banning pleaded. "We've got to decide this case on a rational basis. I suggest we go over the evidence piece by piece. Are there any objections to that?" No one spoke. "But first, I promised I'd give everyone a chance to talk if they wanted."

"No, let's get to the actual evidence and try to keep our prejudices out of the case," said a juror who had not yet spoken. She was Millie Willis, an African-American woman who was a telephone company supervisor.

"Are you saying I'm prejudiced?" Page asked angrily. "Well, you're nuts if you are."

"I'm not saying any such thing. I just want to go over the evidence without getting personal," said Millie. "After all, that's what we're supposed to be doing."

"Good idea," Billie added. She hated this vitriolic bickering.

"I agree," said Banning. "Let's try to keep some order in our discussion. It seems to me that the first thing we have to decide is whether Dr. Neal actually caused his wife's death or whether she might have died from another stroke."

"Remember," said a juror who hadn't yet contributed. She was Julia Michaels, the retired supermarket supervisor who had said on *voir dire* examination that her father was a policeman who worried about possible wrongful convictions of suspects. "Reasonable doubt goes in favor of the defendant."

"Yes," agreed Banning. "We always must remember that. I have a suggestion to make on this point, if I may."

"Sure," agreed Harold Dempster, the young minister.

"Without actually deciding it, I suggest it's unlikely that she died from another stroke," said Banning. "But it's theoretically possible. I suggest we shelve this issue to see how we feel about the other points and then come back."

"Sounds sensible to me," said Sam Ameson, the clothier. "Why fight over it now?"

"All right, then," Banning continued. "It seems to me the main point is whether there is a reasonable likelihood that Lu Neal did in fact regain consciousness and agree to her own death, the way Dr. Neal testified."

"If I understood the judge's instructions, that's the only way out for Neal," commented Julia Michaels. "The only way he can be acquitted."

"Yes. I think he made it clear that Dr. Neal had no right to do what he did unless his wife consented," agreed Tom Washington, the county employee.

"I think we're missing the point," said Candice Laconte. She was the administrative assistant at a cereal plant who looked to be in her mid-thirties. This was the first time she had expressed an opinion.

"Why?" Washington asked.

"A person can't even consent to be helped to his own suicide, let alone consent to someone else's actually murdering her. We've got that new law."

"Yeah, but didn't they try Kevorkian under that law?" asked the gas station owner. "And he was acquitted, wasn't he?"

"Well, he was a doctor. Doctors can do things like that," said Louis Johnson, the first juror, a serious looking man nearing 60. "Besides, didn't he get off on some technicality?"

"Yeah, a technicality, like they're trying to do in this case," said Page.

"This case is entirely different," said the minister. "This isn't a physician-assisted suicide case like Kevorkian's. Dr. Neal is not a medical doctor. He had no right. Besides, Mrs. Neal didn't commit suicide. Dr. Neal killed her himself."

"But doctors do that all the time; don't tell me they don't," insisted Alicia Phillips. "If a doctor can do it, why can't the husband?"

"I doubt very much that doctors do it all the time," commented Sam Ameson.

"Yeah, they don't get paid any more if the patient is dead," said the gas station owner.

"Boy, are you the cynical one," observed Ms. Willis.

"Listen, have you ever been sick? Gas station operators don't get the big fat medical insurance like the telephone company gives you. Doctors will take you for plenty if you give them the chance."

"I'm bothered that the daughter didn't give her consent. Doesn't the daughter have to give consent?" Candice Laconte spoke again.

"That's what the judge said, for God's sake, unless you believe that cock-and-bull story about Mrs. Neal blinking her eyes," said Page. "I know I heard the judge say the daughter had to give her consent."

Billie was upset. They were all missing the point. "We're getting too far afield. The whole issue is, *Did Mrs. Neal give her consent?* If she did, Dr. Neal didn't need his daughter's consent. Isn't that right, Mr. Banning?"

"That's my understanding," the foreman answered.

"Well, I think Mrs. Neal could have blinked her eyes as Dr. Neal said," said Billie. "At first I sort of doubted his story, but now I certainly have a reasonable doubt. He could be telling the truth, you know."

Banning spoke next. "I'm going to ask the question again. A show of hands, please. How many believe Dr. Neal's story could be true? Remember reasonable doubt, now." Six people raised their hands.

"How many people definitely don't believe him?" Four raised their hands.

"I take it the others are uncertain."

"You know what I think? I think Dr. Neal imagined she opened her eyes and then blinked them," said the minister. "I don't think he was deliberately lying. I've studied a lot of psychology. I think he saw what he wanted to see, unconsciously I mean."

"That's a good point," agreed Julia Michaels. "Wasn't there some testimony about that?"

"I think so," said Millie Willis.

"Yes, what if Mrs. Neal didn't come to, but he *thought* she did?" asked Tom Washington.

"Good point," agreed another juror.

"Would that change any of your opinions? Would any of you acquit Dr. Neal if he *thought* his wife agreed, even though she actually did not?" asked Banning.

"Yeah, maybe it would change my mind," said Louis Johnson.

"Possibly," said another juror, nodding her head.

"I'll tell you what. It's after four o'clock. We've been deliberating all afternoon. Why don't we ask the judge?" Banning suggested.

"Can you do that?" Billie asked.

"In the other case I was on, we asked the judge. They call it *additional instructions*," Banning explained.

"Ask the judge what?" Candice Laconte looked questioningly at Banning.

"Ask him if we can acquit Dr. Neal if he *thought* Mrs. Neal agreed, even though he might have imagined it," Banning answered.

"I think you people are all nuts!" shouted Page. "Absolutely nuts! It's not going to change my mind no matter what the judge says. Can't you see

Neal's guilty as hell? But I'm tired of arguing. Go ahead and ask him. They're going to feed us. The bailiff told me they're going to put us up in a motel until we reach a verdict."

"Sure, we're not going to reach a verdict today anyway," agreed Sam Ameson.

"Or this month, for that matter," added the gas station owner.

"All right, I'll ask him for an additional instruction on the point. Then we can start fresh in the morning," said Banning.

Billie could see the puzzled looks on the faces in the courtroom as the jury filed into the jury box.

"Your Honor," Alvin Banning said. "We, the jury, have a question."

"Yes, Mr. Banning. I take it you've been selected as foreman."

"Yes, sir."

"And what is your question?"

"We want to know if we can acquit the defendant if we should find that even though Lu Neal may not have regained consciousness and given her consent to the removal of the respirator, Dr. Neal, in point of actual fact, *thought* she had done so. Perhaps through some kind of mental psychological trick or something like it?"

Billie saw surprise on Judge Hoskins' face.

"Thank you, ladies and gentlemen. You may be seated, Mr. Banning, while I confer with Counsel at the bench."

Billie watched as Hoskins and the two attorneys conferred animatedly out of the jury's hearing. After several minutes the attorneys left the bench and resumed their places.

"Ladies and gentlemen. I'm going to dismiss you for the night. As you know you will be sequestered until you have reached a verdict. You are not to watch television or listen to the radio, nor are you to discuss the case among yourselves except in the jury room. Your request has given the attorneys and me some work to do. In the morning I expect to have a decision for you. I will either give you additional instructions or announce that I will not. Thank you for your work, and I now remand you to the custody of the bailiff. We shall see you all at nine o'clock. No, make that ten o'clock tomorrow morning. We may have some additional work to do before we meet with you."

Billie was confused. The law must be clear on the point. Why did they need more time? Whatever the case, she was not looking forward to more deliberations nor to spending evening time with her fellow jurors. Everyone had such widely different points of view, she didn't see how they could agree on a verdict acceptable to her. So many seemed to be fixed in their opinions, especially that awful man, Page. Billie hoped that she could sit with Alvin Banning at dinner tonight. Alvin was the only one on the jury she could imagine she would want to continue knowing after the case was finally over.

-61-

"Well, gentlemen," commented Judge Hoskins, hanging up his robe as the opposing advocates took the chairs opposite his desk. "That was sure one hell of a surprise!" In his shirt sleeves, the judge leaned back in his chair, clasping his hands behind his head.

Joseph smiled inwardly. Experience with hundreds of jury trials told him that at least some members of the jury were trying to figure out a way to acquit his client. They never would have asked for the special instruction if they all were thinking conviction.

"It looks as if you may have a bit of a problem, Mr. Cain," Hoskins remarked, evidentially drawing the same conclusion.

"Not so fast, Judge," Cain quickly answered. "It's a dangerous game to speculate what's going on in any jury room."

"You're right, of course," agreed the judge. "But if I had to guess, I'd say they're taking a good look at Joseph's consent theory."

"It's a decent bet they're thinking acquittal," Joseph said. "At least some of them."

"Perhaps," said Hoskins. "But, as Fred says. *Who the hell knows what they are thinking?* But there's no point in speculating. The question I have to resolve is, *Am I going to give them the special instruction they asked for and, if so, what am I going to tell them?* Gentlemen, let's have your ideas on the subject."

Fred spoke first. "It would be ridiculous to let a man murder his wife because he can convince a jury that he mistakenly thought she blinked her eyes, *Yes, it's okay to murder me.*"

"He's got a point there, Joseph."

"Judge, every murder case turns on the state of mind of the defendant," said Joseph. "That's nothing new to the law. If a man kills his wife thinking she's a burglar breaking into the house, it's not murder. That's first-year-law-school."

"But Fred's right. It could be a clever way to murder your wife and get away with it," said the judge.

"You're damn right," Fred agreed.

"You're dismissing the jury system too quickly," Joseph protested. "It's a question of Dr. Neal's credibility. We ask juries to decide credibility issues every day."

"I can't believe what I'm hearing," protested Cain. "What you're saying is Neal can walk if he can convince a few sympathetic jurors he had an hallucination and *thought* the victim agreed to her own murder. Now I've heard everything. Why didn't you plead him insane, for God's sake?"

"Come on now, Fred. You're overreacting," Joseph asserted. "Juries are pretty good judges of who's telling the truth. Give them some credit. If they don't believe Dr. Neal acted under an honest belief about his wife, then they'll convict him." Joseph smiled. "Why, Fred, I'm beginning to think you don't believe in the jury system."

Judge Hoskins chuckled. "Show me a prosecutor who does. I'm reminded of something Lincoln said. 'The jury system is twelve people chosen at random to decide who's got the best lawyer.'"

All three laughed nervously. Joseph knew it was a kind of gallows humor that lawyers used to lessen the tension they faced in dealing with serious issues.

"Fred, I think Joseph is right," Hoskins continued. "Like it or not, the state of mind of the defendant is for the jury to decide. I'm going to tell them if Neal honestly believed his wife blinked her eyes, *Yes*, then that's enough." The judge turned to Joseph. "However, it's clear to me that Fred is entitled to one concession. That is, Neal must have been *reasonable* in his belief that she consented." Hoskins pushed his chair back. "Gentlemen, that will be what I'm going to instruct the jury tomorrow. *If Neal reasonably believed that she gave consent, then he's not guilty.* We'll meet here in chambers at nine o'clock tomorrow with the court reporter. You can make your objections for the record before we go out at 10. I'll see you then."

The attorneys gathered their papers to leave, but Hoskins continued speaking: "Gentlemen, I want to compliment you on the expertise you've shown in trying this case. Win or lose, each of you is to be congratulated. I'm sure you're going to appeal my rulings, no matter who wins. All three of us are just doing our jobs. That's the justice business for you."

At first Joseph was silent. He had seldom heard praise from the bench. "Thank you, Your Honor. I appreciate the compliment."

"Yes, Judge. Thank you," said Fred.

"Good luck to each of you."

Joseph stopped by the jail to talk with David before going to dinner. "What does it mean?" David asked. "I didn't know the jury could interrupt their deliberations that way." David sat nervously on the edge of his bed.

"It's dangerous to speculate about juries," Joseph answered. "At best it could mean some of them are looking for a way to acquit you. Or it could mean nothing more than they're being thorough."

"God, waiting like this, not knowing, is driving me crazy. They have my fate in the palms of their hands."

"I know. After all these years, I still get nervous and it's not my future they're debating."

David got up and walked the two steps to the end of the cell. "What's your best guess? Do you think I have a chance? Tell me the truth."

"My best guess is that at least some on the jury are taking seriously your testimony about Lu's regaining consciousness."

"I hope they do, because I told them the truth. I told them exactly what happened that night."

Joseph put his hand on David's bony shoulder. He noticed how very pale and thin his client had become. "I know, David, and I suspect some of the jury know, too."

As he walked down the corridor, Joseph thought to himself, "At least I sure as hell hope that's what the jury is doing."

-62-

B illie listened attentively as Judge Hoskins read the special instruction the jury had requested yesterday:

"Thus, if you found that the defendant believed that the deceased had consented to the removal of her life support system, and that he was reasonable in that belief, then you may acquit him."

Billie felt relieved. She had to admit that she had some doubt that Lu Neal had actually consented, but she had little doubt that Dr. Neal, in his troubled state of mind, had believed it to be so. Not only would the new instruction make it easier for her to vote for acquittal with a clear conscience, but it would make it more likely that some of the others would join her.

The twelve jurors sat around the large table in the jury room. Alvin Banning, still wearing his suit coat and tie, began the discussion. "I don't know about the rest of you, but I found the new jury instruction very enlightening. All it takes now is that the defendant *believed* his wife consented."

"But the judge said Dr. Neal must have been reasonable in that belief," interjected Millie Willis.

"Sure—he couldn't go off half-cocked," agreed Sam Ameson.

"How many think it would be helpful if we had a straw vote?" Banning asked.

A few muttered their assent. No one spoke out against the idea.

"I'm going to pass out these slips. I think it would help us see where we stand–at least initially. Understand now, we're just saying how we're leaning."

"I'm filling out no slip!" said Page disgustedly. "I'm voting guilty all the way and no one is changing *my* mind."

"You mean you're not going to listen to what the rest of us have to say?" asked Julia Michaels.

"Sure, I'll listen all right, but I'm warning you, you aren't going to change my mind!"

The jurors began the process of marking their slips.

"Oh, I just don't know," said one.

"It's a tough one," commented another.

"If you don't have a leaning, just put a question mark," Banning suggested.

After a few minutes they finished and passed their slips to the foreman–all except Page.

"Okay, here are the results," said Banning after checking the slips. "Five for not guilty, two for guilty and four question marks. With Mr. Page's vote, that makes three for guilty."

"That's closer than I thought," said Bill Gardner.

"Yeah," agreed another.

"I assume you all think that more deliberation might change your minds. Am I right?" Banning asked.

"Yes," several said.

"Not me," said Page. "I know the guy's guilty. You aren't going to change my mind."

Billie could stand it no longer. "Mr. Page, the judge told us we should listen to each other's reasons and be willing to change our minds."

"Oh, I'll listen all right. I'm not going to give you a chance to complain to the judge about that. I'll listen until you can't stand it no more."

Billie's frustration was overwhelming. Page seemed impossible. "Tell me this, Mr. Page," she said. "If all eleven of us voted not guilty, would you even consider voting along with us?"

"I guess the majority rules."

Billie was astonished at what seemed a complete turnabout for Page.

"Wait a minute," said Candice Laconte. "We all promised we'd stick to our opinions if we thought we were right. Don't you remember? You can't just go along with what the majority wants!" She looked at Page in amazement.

"You don't take that crap seriously, do you? I can vote any way I want."

Billie was dismayed. She wondered how could a man like Page ever have gotten on the jury in the first place.

"I think we should get to analyzing the evidence," said Banning. "After all, that's what we're supposed to be doing. Anyone want to tell the rest of us why they voted the way they did?"

"I doubt very much Lu Neal came to," said Bill Gardner. "I'm skeptical of Neal's whole story."

"Me too. He had no right to kill her," said Millie Willis. "I wouldn't want my husband having that kind of power over me. If I'm going to die, let me die. For God's sake don't get rid of me like some old dog."

Reverend Dempster spoke next: "I think we're dealing with dangerous ideas here. For all these hundreds of years we've just let people die natural deaths. They went when God took them. We're tinkering with God's natural law."

"Tell me this, Reverend. You're a moral man, right?" asked Tom Washington, who had told everyone he was a church-going person.

"I try to be."

"As a moral man, do you think we should send Dr. Neal to jail for the rest of his life just because he did what he did? Just because he disagrees with your idea of what is right?"

"As Mr. Cain says, you can't have people going around taking people's lives. That would be chaos," replied Dempster. "None of us would be safe."

"But that's why we have laws on the subject of mercy killing," Billie said.

"Yeah, but exactly what is the law anyway? It's all so confusing," said Millie Willis.

"The judge made it clear that mercy killing was legal under certain circumstances," Billie responded.

"The Neals should have made out powers of attorney. Then we wouldn't have this mess," commented a juror.

"But they didn't, and so we've got to solve the mess," another responded.

"The judge said a power of attorney isn't the only way for mercy killing to be legal," Billie said.

"It isn't mercy killing. It's just withdrawing artificial life support," commented Alicia Phillips. "I keep telling you, it goes on all the time, but some of you don't seem to listen."

"Well, I think it's murder. She was alive one minute and then because of what Dr. Neal did, she isn't alive," said Candice. "That's a murder if ever I heard of one."

"I don't care what you say, I can't vote to keep that old man in jail," said Julia Michaels. "I keep going back to what my father said. It's a terrible thing to convict an innocent man."

The discussion went on for the rest of the morning with the conflicting points of view becoming more, instead of less, pronounced.

"I think we should ask the judge to let us break for lunch," said Banning. "The other jury I served on wasn't making much progress at all. Then we went to lunch, and before we knew it we had a verdict."

When they returned from lunch Banning called for another straw vote. This time Page, who had been relatively silent, filled out a slip.

"I'd say we're making progress," announced Banning when he had canvassed the slips. "This time it's eight for not guilty, three for guilty and one question mark. Tell me, how many of you switched your votes from the first time? Raise your hands."

Five raised their hands.

"Good," Banning said. "That shows we're thinking and listening to each other. Anyone else want to express their opinion? Mr. Johnston, you haven't said much."

"That's my way, Mr. Banning. My wife always asks why I don't say much. I'm a good listener, though. I can tell we're all trying to do right. I'm voting not guilty and I'll tell you why. None of us was there. We didn't go through what Dr. Neal went through. I don't find it easy to judge a man when I haven't walked in his shoes. Isn't that what the Lord said? A long time ago I had an aunt. Aunt Maxine. Aunt Maxine had cancer, real bad. We didn't have money for no medicine to make her passing easy. Aunt Maxine had a tough time of it. I remember her asking my mother why she had to live. All my poor mother could say was, 'It's the will of the Lord.' I wasn't very old at the time, maybe twelve, but that, Will of the Lord, stuff didn't make sense to me. I don't think Aunt Maxine should have had to suffer that way." Johnston had tears in his eyes. "That's why I'm voting to let Dr. Neal go. He's suffered enough."

Billie was moved by what Johnston had said. He was right. No one should have to suffer the way his aunt had. And no one should have to go to jail for doing what was right.

Banning spoke. "Thank you, Mr. Johnston. You may not say much, but when you do, you do it well, sir. Anyone else want to say their piece?"

Billie decided to go next. "When I was first selected for this jury I felt very strongly that a person should not be permitted to take the law into his own hands. My God, I wouldn't go through a malfunctioning red light in the middle of the night with no one around. That's how strict I was. But I've changed my mind. My husband is never going to understand why I'm voting the way I am, but I'm like Mr. Johnston. I can't vote guilty. I can't have that on my conscience."

"Thank you, Mrs. Croft. Anyone else?"

Billie half expected Page to spout off, but it was Candice who spoke. "I'm sorry. I disagree. I don't want that happening in my family. I don't want to have to trust a man with my life. If I was too stupid not to make out one of those powers of attorney, then I just have to put up with the suffering. I'm sorry, but I'm voting guilty. I wish there were some other way–something more minor than murder maybe–but I can't vote not guilty."

"The judge said we're not supposed to take punishment into account," said Tom Washington.

"I don't see why, but I remember that's what he said," agreed another juror.

"Well, I don't care what he said. I'm not sending him to jail!" Julia Michaels resolutely clenching her fist.

"Anyone else want to speak?" Banning questioned.

"Mr. Banning, how about you? What do you think?" a juror asked.

"I'm voting not guilty. It would be like putting my own father in jail. Maybe he shouldn't have done it. Probably shouldn't have. But there are a lot worse people walking the street free. I don't think his daughter had any right to turn the doctor down. If she had been a decent human being, we wouldn't even be here."

"Yeah. She's the one who should be on trial, not Dr. Neal!" asserted the gas station owner.

"I'd like to see him be with his grandson," said Tom Washington.

"I can't help but remember what Mr. Jefferson said. 'How would Lu Neal vote if she were here right now? Here in the jury room.'" added

Johnston. "I know how my Aunt Maxine would have voted if she'd had the chance."

"I don't think there's any question," said Billie. "Mrs. Neal wouldn't want us to send her husband to jail any longer."

"I'd like to make a suggestion," began Reverend Dempster. "Would you mind if I prayed–prayed for us all?"

"You don't have to be religious to pray," observed Johnston.

"Go ahead, Reverend."

"Yes, go ahead."

"Our Father, please give us the wisdom to see what is right. You see things as we can never see them. Please guide us as we make this momentous decision. Amen."

"Thank you, Reverend."

"Thank you all for allowing me to pray."

"I think it's time to take another vote."

"Good idea," said Banning. "This time I'm going around the room one by one. Mr. Johnston, how do you vote?"

"Not guilty."

"Mrs. Phillips?"

"Not guilty."

"Reverend?"

"I've still got my misgivings, but I'll vote not guilty."

Banning continued until all had voted. Everyone voted not guilty, except Page and Candice.

"Tell me this. Do either of you think you might change your mind?"

"I'll tell you what," said Page. "If Candice, here, changes her mind, I'll go with the majority. Like I told you before, I believe in majority rule."

"That's very generous of you, Mr. Page," Banning commented.

"What do you say to that Candice…Miss Laconte?"

"What a terrible responsibility. You mean I've got to decide the whole case?" Billie felt sorry for Candice. The young woman seemed overwhelmed.

"You could just vote with the rest of us, and we could all go home," said a juror.

For nearly two hours more the discussion swirled around Candice. A few pushed, trying to get her to change her vote, but others were more respectful of her feelings. Over and over again they went over the case, discussing every conceivable angle.

"I'm sorry," Candice finally said. "I feel very guilty holding you up like this, but I have to stick by my conscience. I think it's wrong to have taken a human life, like Dr. Neal did. I can't vote not guilty. I just can't."

Billie felt sorry for Candice who was nearly in tears. "That's all right, Candice," Billie said. "I know how you feel. At first I felt the same way."

"Thank you, Mrs. Croft," Candice said. "I feel just terrible, but I'm afraid I cannot change my vote."

"Do you think if we waited until morning it would help?" Banning asked. "If you want I could tell the judge we need more time."

Candice had taken the tissue Billie had offered and was wiping her eyes. "No. You've all been so kind, but I can't change my mind. It wouldn't be right. More time isn't going to change me."

"You mean all this work and we're hung?" asked Bill Gardner, disgustedly.

"Candice has every right to disagree without us making her feel guilty," said Reverend Dempster.

"I agree," said Billie.

"Looks like we're deadlocked. What happens next?" asked Sam Ameson.

"Yeah, what happens when we're deadlocked?" asked Page.

"I guess they try him all over again."

"With us as the jury again?" Washington asked.

"No way," said another juror. "It would be with a brand new jury like that *Menendez* case in California."

"What a waste of money that will be," said Alicia Phillips.

"I feel so guilty," Candice said, dabbing at her eyes.

"I'll tell the bailiff we want to talk to the judge," said Banning. "I guess we're hung."

"I'm sorry Your Honor, but we find it impossible to reach a verdict," said Banning when the jury was seated in the jury box.

"Do you think more time would help you?" Hoskins asked.

"No, Your Honor, I do not. We've tried everything we can think of. We do not feel we can reach a verdict."

"I would like to know how the vote stands now. I don't want you to tell me whether it's for guilty or not guilty."

"Ten to two, Your Honor."

"Mr. Banning, I'm not ready to declare a mistrial. I'm going to ask the jury to make another attempt to reach a verdict. This Court has had many cases come before it over the years. While this case admittedly is difficult, there have been many more difficult cases where the jury has ultimately reached a verdict. We all have too much invested to give up at this relatively early point. Mr. Banning, you say you do not feel more time will help you?"

Banning was still standing in the jury box. "No, Your Honor, I do not."

"Nevertheless, I'm going to dismiss you for the evening. I will release you to the custody of the bailiff. Ladies and gentlemen, tomorrow morning I am going to ask you to resume your deliberations. I want you to make an additional effort at reaching a verdict. Do you understand, Mr. Banning?"

"Yes, Your Honor."

"Very well. Remember my admonition. You are not to discuss the case with anyone, including yourselves, and you are not to watch any television or read any newspapers."

Billie did not see how they could reach a verdict, but she supposed the judge was right. Perhaps they should make one last attempt in the morning. Billie tried to catch Dr. Neal's eye to give him some hint that she was on his side, but the bailiff took him away too fast. It would be terrible for the poor man to have to go through another trial. Perhaps by morning Candice would have changed her mind. Billie understood very well the dilemma that Candice faced, for when they had begun deliberations, she had been in the midst of the same dilemma.

-63-

"Gentlemen, you heard them. Ten to two," said Judge Hoskins. Fred and Joseph sat opposite him in chambers.

"Yes, but ten to two which way?" asked Fred.

Joseph smiled. He felt the odds were that the vote was in his favor.

"Look, Fred," Hoskins said. "You're the prosecutor, but don't you think it's apt to be ten to two for acquittal? They wouldn't have asked for the special instruction if it were the other way around."

"It could just as well be for conviction," said Fred.

Joseph thought he detected a trace of doubt in Fred's voice.

"Gentlemen, as I said yesterday, I respect you both. You've each done one hell of a job presenting your case, but sometimes it takes a third party to give you a different slant. The truth is, I think you both should be thinking compromise–a plea bargain. Shall I go on?"

"I'm always willing to listen to anything that makes sense," Joseph said. He would be reluctant to recommend a plea bargain to David–he wanted complete vindication–but there was a serious risk of conviction and he knew he should listen.

"Go ahead," responded Fred. "If Joseph is willing to listen, then I guess I should too."

"Okay, then, here's how I see it," Hoskins began. "It seems to me there's a very strong chance of a hung jury."

"If that happened, I would retry, without a doubt," Fred said quickly.

"Look, Fred." Hoskins glanced around as if he didn't want to be overheard. "Maybe this isn't my place to say, but you've announced you're running for Lasser's job. Word has it that Lasser didn't want you to prosecute in the first place, but you saw this case as your chance for his job." Hoskins held up his hand to stop Fred from answering. "I'm not asking you to admit it or deny it—that's not the point here, Fred. I don't care who wins the election. I want you to look at it this way. If you lose this prosecution, I'll bet you lose the election. If the jury stays hung and you retry, the trial isn't going to be until after the election and that does you no good."

Fred didn't answer the judge, but continued listening.

"If you make a plea bargain, you're a winner. You'd have your conviction and yet you're off the *heartless prosecution* charge. You could make it look as if you were upholding the law but were compassionate about it."

Fred started to speak.

"Just a minute. Let me finish my little speech. There would be no hung jury, no retrial and no appeals. If we go all the way with this, each of you is going to appeal, no matter what happens. A plea bargain gets rid of all that. Don't you see, you're both winners?"

"I'm sorry, Judge, but I can't go for it," Fred answered. "First of all, you're dead wrong about my bringing this case for political reasons. It was Lasser who didn't want to bring it, for his own damn political reasons. He thought prosecuting Neal would make him look bad. It was a loser for him, whether he won or lost. But more important, Lasser wouldn't let me enter into a plea bargain if I wanted. He wants to make me look like a loser. Don't you see, Lasser *wants* me to lose this sucker."

"I'll take care of Lasser," Hoskins interjected. "If you offer a plea bargain and Joseph accepts, we'd have a deal without Lasser. As far as I'm concerned, the trial deputy is the one in charge of a case—and that includes making plea bargains. I'd make Lasser come into open court and fire you. Am I making any headway, Fred?"

"Well, I'm listening."

"What about you, Joseph?"

"When the judge tells me to listen, I listen. But the worst I've got here is a hung jury, and I've got a decent chance for acquittal."

"Maybe, maybe not. Don't forget, if this jury convicts or if your client is convicted after a second trial, he goes to Jackson Prison. That would be a most unpleasant experience for a man 76 years of age."

"What kind of a plea bargain? What kind of a sentence are you talking about?" Joseph asked.

"I don't know," said the judge. "Maybe involuntary manslaughter. Maybe time served plus six months in the county jail. We'd have to talk about that."

"That's a long time at his age."

"Twenty or 30 years is a lot longer."

"I'll talk to him about it, but I don't think he'll go for it."

"Remember, Joseph–a hung jury–a retrial–would be a lot longer than six months, even if he were acquitted in the new trial. I'd tell him to think it over. I know damn well he'll do whatever you advise him."

"Maybe, maybe not."

"Tell you what," Hoskins continued. "You fellows think it over. Joseph, you talk with your client. We can talk more while the jury is deliberating in the morning. See you then, gentlemen."

As Joseph left the chambers, he had mixed feelings. He was a practical man, and from that viewpoint the plea bargain was attractive. But his old bones told him the worst he could do was a hung jury. And if those two holdouts changed their minds, he had an acquittal. He would discuss the dilemma with David tonight.

-64-

Fred waited until after dinner to tell Marge about Judge Hoskins' plea bargain suggestion.

"The judge figures the jury wouldn't have asked for that special instruction if weren't ten to two for acquittal."

"He could be right, but you're always telling me you can't predict what a jury is thinking, no matter what the clues. Remember the Colletti case last year?" Marge was referring to a drug pusher case where Fred had gotten a conviction when everybody in the courthouse was guessing the jury was hung. It turned out the jury was simply being extremely thorough in sifting through the evidence. "You sure did the right thing in not offering a plea bargain to that scum. He's doing 20 years because of you."

"I don't know, Marge. If the jury stays hung, I'd have to try the case all over again. The damn election would be over by then. Maybe I'd be better off taking a plea to involuntary manslaughter. I think I could put a spin on it to make it look as if I'd won."

"I think you're better off going for broke."

"I don't have to decide tonight. I'll sleep on it"

But Fred didn't get to sleep. At two a.m. he had gotten up and flipped on the television. Marge came downstairs wearing her robe. "Come back upstairs, sweetheart," she said. "You've got a big day tomorrow."

"Except for this plea bargain thing, all I can do now is wait. Waiting for the jury is the hardest part of any trial."

"Why don't you forget about a plea bargain? Then you can get some sleep. A plea bargain isn't your style."

"I think you're right, Marge. I've come this far. Gambled my whole damn career. I've got to see it through to the end. If I made a plea bargain, I'd always wonder what would have happened."

"Good. Now come back to bed with me. I've got just the ticket to make you relax."

Whether it was their having sex, or having made his decision or both, Fred had his first decent night's sleep since the trial began.

But in the Marshall jail, David could not sleep. Earlier, Joseph had come to his cell, where they had discussed the plea bargain.

"David, it's a tough one. First of all, I rather doubt if Cain is going to offer a plea bargain. He wants to win this election so badly he can taste it. I think it would take a win for him to do it. But we need to be thinking about what we'd do if it were offered. How do you feel about it?"

"My feelings have changed. At first I didn't even want you to defend me. Maybe it was guilt. Maybe I didn't think I could go on without Lu."

"But now?"

"Now, hearing all your arguments, I think I didn't do anything wrong. I'm sure most people don't believe me, but I'm telling the truth. Lu really did blink her eyes. Maybe you don't believe me either."

"What I believe or don't believe is not the issue here. The issue is what the jury believes, and the answer to that question remains unknown. That's our problem."

"I guess I have mixed feelings. I'd like to be vindicated. I don't look forward to being called a murderer. You say the judge would let me off with just a little bit more jail time?"

"Less than the time you'd spend in jail waiting for a retrial. With the time you've served, I suspect I could get him down to 60 days"

"I'd sure like to see Eddie graduate from Basic Training."

"But that isn't likely to happen unless we get an acquittal."

"And you think we might?"

"I think we might, but a hung jury is far more likely."

"Can I wait until morning to decide?"

"Of course, but remember, I wouldn't be half surprised if Cain doesn't even make the offer. I don't think compromise suits the man."

In Bloomfield Hills, Betty could not sleep. She had returned to her mansion late from giving a speech before the bar association. In her mail was an official communication from the Marine Corps. It was an invitation to Eddie's graduation from Basic Training next week.

Betty had known immediately that she wanted to attend. What kept her from falling asleep was Eddie's attitude toward her. She had thought that being a judge was going to make her happy, but she never had been more lonely. Although her friends and partners had not said so, she could tell they disapproved of her testifying against her father. There didn't seem to be anyone left to whom she could talk. She didn't want to go through the rest of her life estranged from Eddie–her situation with her father had taught her that much.

She'd go to the graduation in San Diego, of that much she was certain, but how could she make Eddie understand how desperately she wanted him to love her? If she had known how to do that, perhaps her problem with her father would have been healed years ago.

She decided to go to the kitchen. Perhaps some ice cream would help her relax.

-65-

The next morning's jury deliberations began with laughter and irrelevant chatter over the coffee and pastry that the bailiff had brought. It was obvious to Billie that no one wanted to say what was on their minds, "What had Candice decided?" Many were standing as they drank their coffee, as if to sit down would too quickly force the question.

Twenty minutes passed before the foreman spoke up. "All right, everyone, please take your places."

When they had quieted down, Banning continued. "I think it would be a good idea if I reviewed where we ended up yesterday. It seems to me that we have discussed the issues in this case until we're all blue in the face. I don't know whether or not any of you disagree with me, but I see no useful purpose in going over everything all over again. Do any of you disagree?"

No one spoke up.

"Okay, then. Mr. Page, you still will vote not guilty unless it turns out you're the only holdout?"

"Yeah. Sure. I wouldn't hold you up. You know, I've been thinking, Neal's already spent one hell of a lot of time in jail. No, I wouldn't hold you up if Candice changes her mind."

"Before I get to Candice, did anyone else change their mind overnight?"

Several shook their heads *no* and none indicated otherwise.

"Candice, I guess that leaves us where we left off yesterday. It looks as if it's up to you."

Billie felt sorry for Candice as she watched her fidget.

"As you can all imagine, I didn't sleep very well last night," said Candice. Her eyes were red, as if she had been crying.

"I prayed for you," said Reverend Dempster. "I know how you must feel. At first I found it very difficult to vote for acquittal."

"Thank you, Reverend." Candice paused, as if she did not want to go on. "I find this very difficult to say. I know how hard all of you have worked, but I'm afraid I can't go along with you. I just couldn't live with myself if I didn't do the right thing."

"But, dear, we all think we're doing the right thing," said Julia Michaels.

"I know. That's what makes it difficult. I'm sorry, but I have to vote guilty. I don't care what the circumstances, I just don't think one human being has the right to take the life of another human being."

"Is there anything we can say to change your mind?"

"No. I'm afraid not."

Billie could see that the young woman was about to break into tears. "I think we should all leave Candice alone."

"Thank you, Mrs. Croft." Candice wiped at her eyes.

"Is that it, then? Anyone have anything more to say?"

Judge Hoskins was conferring with Fred and Joseph in his chambers.

"Well, Fred," Hoskins said. "What do you say? Are you going to offer a plea bargain?"

"I'm sorry, Judge. I was up half the night thinking about what you said, but I just can't see my way clear to do it. I'm going all the way. If this jury hangs, I'll give it a shot before another jury. I didn't bring this case in the first place just to get a plea bargain. Mercy killing is too important an issue."

"You're the prosecutor, but I think you're making a hell of a mistake for all of the reasons I set forward yesterday." Hoskins turned to Joseph. "Sorry, Joseph, but I gave it my best."

"Don't be sorry, Judge. I doubt very much if my client would have accepted, even if the offer were made."

"That would have been an even worse decision than Fred just made," said Hoskins.

"Dr. Neal wants to be vindicated," Joseph said.

The judge shook his head. "A hung jury is not going to vindicate anyone. All right then, we'll let them continue deliberating. I want you to stay near the courthouse."

In the jury room, Reverend Dempster spoke up. "I have something I would like to say. It has been an honor to serve with each of you. If it wouldn't embarrass you, I'd like to propose that we all hold hands." The minister reached out and clasped the hands of those on either side. With a few moments of hesitation, the others did the same. "Let us be silent for a moment, knowing that we have done our best to serve justice."

Banning waited until they had dropped their hands. "Is that it, then? Shall I tell the judge we've been unable to reach a verdict?"

"I'm real sorry, everyone. I'm really very sorry," Candice kept her head down and avoided looking at the others.

"That's okay, my dear. I think there's probably a great deal of truth on each side," said Millie Willis.

"It takes courage to stand up against everyone else. We admire you for it," said Tom Washington.

"Thank you all very much." Billie handed Candice a tissue and watched with compassion as she wiped her eyes.

Joseph had just entered David's cell when the bailiff rushed up.

"The jury has told Judge Hoskins they want to come into the court-room. The judge wants you there immediately!" the bailiff said excitedly.

"Does that mean they have a verdict?" David asked nervously.

Joseph, put his hand on David's arm. "Not necessarily. They may want to say they're hung. Or they may have some question they want to ask the judge."

The bailiff hurriedly ushered David and Joseph along the hall toward the courtroom.

"What about the plea bargain?" David asked, nearly out of breath.

"Cain doesn't want a plea bargain. He wants you in jail, even if it takes another trial."

"Another trial?" David said. "I don't know if I could survive another trial." He was struck by a sudden wave of fear. As they crossed the bridge from the jail to the courtroom, his heart was pumping wildly and he felt faint. Last night he was positive he would not accept a plea bargain, but now that the moment of truth had arrived, he was not sure at all. "Is there any chance Cain will change his mind?"

"None at all, David. I'm afraid the die is cast."

"Ladies and gentlemen of the jury, have you reached a verdict?" asked Judge Hoskins.

Banning stood. He had written what he intended to say on a piece of paper.

Billie could see the tension on the faces of Dr. Neal and the attorneys. She only wished the jury could have been unanimous. She hated the idea of Dr. Neal's being put through the ordeal of another trial.

"We, the jury, are sorry, but we are unable to reach a verdict," Banning read. "We have deliberated in good faith. We have listened to all of our respective points of view and we simply cannot reach agreement. We

unanimously feel that no purpose would be served in further deliberations. We simply disagree."

"Mr. Banning, the Court thanks you and your fellow jurors for your
hard work and attentiveness in this matter. I'd like to ask you how you
stand. What was your last vote?"

"It was ten to two, Your Honor."

"For conviction or acquittal?"

"For acquittal Your Honor."

Billie could see the relief on Dr. Neal's face. At least he had him some
consolation.

"Normally when the vote is so one-sided, I would send you back for
even more deliberation," Hoskins said. "But, from what you say, the
prospects of reaching a verdict are nil."

"I'm afraid so, Your Honor."

"Let me ask you—are there any members of the jury who feel that further deliberation might result in a unanimous verdict? Remember, we all
have invested a great deal of time, money and energy in this case."

Billie watched as Judge Hoskins searched their faces vainly for an
answer. No one said anything.

"Very well, he continued. "I'm afraid I have no alternative but to
declare a mistrial. Ladies and gentlemen of the jury—"

"Your Honor!"

"Yes?" Judge Hoskins looked at the jury chart on his bench. "Miss
Laconte, is it? Candice Laconte?"

"Yes, Your Honor. I'm one of those who voted for a guilty verdict. I'm
sorry for doing this at the last minute like this, *but I'd like to change my vote.*"

The spectators broke into loud buzzing. "Oh, my God," said a woman
in the audience. Billie and each of the jurors looked at Candice in amazement. It took a few moments for Judge Hoskins to regain his composure.

"Well, Miss Laconte, I'm glad I asked. You cannot change your vote
here in open court. I think the best thing to do under the circumstances is
for me to order the jury to return for further deliberations. Mr. Banning, I

don't know if this will enable the jury to come to a verdict–apparently you have one more dissenter–but you may have all the time you need to see if you can reach a verdict."

After the judge left the courtroom, Billie could hear the crowd bursting with excitement as the jury filed out. She caught a glimpse of the television cameras through the open doors and wondered whether John were watching.

"I'm sorry! I'm sorry! I'm sorry!" Candice sobbed. "I just can't do it! I can't send that man to prison!" The jurors milled around the room without taking their seats.

"That's all right, dear. We understand. Don't you fret now," said Julia Michaels, putting her arm around Candice.

"I thought I could," Candice sobbed. "But I don't care what the people on the outside might think, they don't understand all the circumstances. I'm changing my vote."

Everyone was smiling–smiles of relief and happiness. Two more of the women put their arms around Candice, comforting her.

"Would everyone take their seats, please," said Banning. "Let's make this official, before anyone else changes their mind. Mr. Page, you're the crucial one now. I assume you're sticking by your decision. Are you going to vote for acquittal now?"

Page smiled broadly. "No matter what anybody says about me, Jim Page is a man of his word. Let's get the hell out of here and watch ourselves on television. I say *not guilty*."

Banning went around the table one by one. To Billie's relief, no one changed their mind. This time the vote was unanimous. Twelve in favor of not guilty.

Spontaneously the jurors let out cheers of relief. Some shook hands. Others hugged each other.

"I'm sorry. I'm sorry," continued Candice. "I didn't realize how I really felt until the last minute."

"Ladies and gentlemen, have you reached a verdict?" the judge asked when they had returned.

"We have Your Honor."

Joseph and David smiled broadly in anticipation. Fred looked more disgusted than dismayed.

"Would you pass the verdict to the clerk, please."

The clerk showed the form to the judge who read its brief contents.

"Would the clerk read the verdict please?"

"People of the *State of Michigan* vs. *David Neal.* We, the jury in the above entitled action find the defendant *not guilty* of the murder of Lu Neal."

"Ladies and gentlemen, is that the verdict of all of you?"

They all answered *yes* in unanimity.

"Mr. Cain, would you like the jury polled?

"No, Your Honor," said Fred, angrily shutting his briefcase and starting to rush from the courtroom. "I can see I've lost in this court. We'll see what the Supreme Court says when I file my appeal."

"Just one moment, Mr. Cain!" snapped Judge Hoskins. "You have every right to file an appeal, but you are still in my courtroom and you will not leave until I give you permission. You will please sit down!" Fred did as Hoskins had commanded.

"Dr. Neal, you have been adjudged not guilty. You are discharged from custody. You are now a free man. Mr. Cain, I order you to show respect for this jury and this Court by remaining where you are until the Court has left the courtroom and the jurors given an opportunity to leave first. Ladies and gentlemen, you are dismissed. You are now free to talk about this case with anyone if you wish. The Court thanks you for your service and wishes you well."

As the jury filed out of the courtroom, David threw his arms around Joseph who seemed embarrassed. Tears in her eyes, Billie shook David's hand. "Dr. Neal, I hope that you have many happy years."

"Thank you, Mrs. Croft. I wish I could find the words to properly thank you and the other jurors." David was near tears.

Billie walked into the glare of the television lights, which now invaded the courtroom as Candice and other jurors shook David's hand.

"Tell me ma'am, why did the jury vote for acquittal? What finally made the difference?" asked a commentator, pushing the microphone toward Billie.

"I don't know if I can properly explain it. I must confess in the beginning I thought I would vote guilty, but I changed my mind when I understood all the circumstances."

Billie brushed past the other waiting reporters ignoring their pleas that she comment. All she wanted now was to get home and return to a normal life.

-66-

Joseph and Ruby had picked up David at the jail and had driven him home to Albion. They were to pick him up at six o'clock for a celebratory dinner at Schuler's restaurant before Joseph returned to Detroit.

David bubbled with excitement. Tears of happiness formed as he walked from one room to another in the home he had almost forgotten. Joyously he touched everything in sight–his books–his bed–the clothes in his closet. He looked into Eddie's room. Graduation from Basic Training was next week. First thing tomorrow he'd make a plane reservation to San Diego–first class.

It was four o'clock in the afternoon. He had slept very little last night, but he felt exhilarated and energized. Sleep could wait until tomorrow. Before he got ready for dinner he wanted to go to the nature study. It had been a long time since he had stood by the river.

The joy and excitement of life flooded him as he crossed the bridge toward his spot by the Kalamazoo River. He stood watching the cool clear water passing by and thought of the agony he had known as he had stood there last winter. He recalled of the time he had resolved to kill himself. The time he had fired shots into the river. And the time he had decided to take Lu's life. Suddenly he was overcome with emotion–both joy at being free, and sadness that Lu was not there. He sat on the trunk of the fallen tree, as he had so many times. "Oh Lu," he said aloud. "I wish you were here with me, but I thank you for being in that jury room. I know you want me to be free. I know you want me to go on–to be the best I can be."

David looked up through an opening in the trees. An airliner heading west appeared from behind a large cloud. "I'm going to see Eddie graduate next week," he continued. "You'd be so proud of him in his Marine uniform. I'll tell him his Granna still loves him."

The three sipped their cocktails at the restaurant. Each had ordered prime rib–the specialty of the house. "Remember the first time I met you?" Joseph asked.

"I surely do," David answered. "I'm afraid I wasn't much of a potential client."

"You didn't want to live, let alone be defended," Ruby laughed.

On the way to Marshall in Joseph's limousine they had laughed uproariously at their silly wisecracks, but now the conversation turned more serious.

"What do you think you're going to do with the rest of your life?" Joseph asked. "How old are you now, anyway?"

"Yesterday I was a hundred. Today I'm only 30!" All three laughed at David's exuberance.

"Seriously, Dr. Neal, what do you think you'll do now?" Ruby asked.

"First I'm going to sleep about three days in my own bed!"

"And then what?" Joseph asked.

"I've got several ideas."

"Tell us about them," Ruby asked, with her typical enthusiasm.

"Whatever I do, I'm going full steam. A wise philosopher once told me life was for the living and he was going to keep living it until the day he died. Let me look around. Let me see. That wise philosopher ought to be here in the restaurant someplace." David laughed turning his head, as if to look.

Ruby turned her head too. "Here someplace? What does he look like?"

"Well he's old–about 66, I think. Worst of all, he's a criminal defense lawyer," David joked.

"You don't mean Uncle Joseph?" Ruby laughed, pointing her finger at her uncle. "Him, a wise old philosopher? You've got to be kidding."

"Hell, I'm no philosopher. I'm just a lawyer trying to do a job. You were pretty down that day in jail. You even got me to thinking that my life was supposed to have some grandiose purpose. I almost borrowed that gun of yours to use it on myself," Joseph wisecracked.

"Yes, until you remembered all the money you make," Ruby teased.

"You're right. That was grandiose purpose enough for me," Joseph joked.

Their prime rib dinner came, and the banter slowed down while they enjoyed their meal.

"Joseph, Ruby, I do want to be serious for a minute," said David. "I owe my life to you. I don't mean just my physical life. I mean my *real* life."

Joseph and Ruby stopped eating and gave David their attention.

"If it weren't for you, I'd be rotting away in Jackson Prison, trying to figure out a way to take my life," David continued. "Now I'm glad to be alive and a free man. As I say, I owe it all to you."

Joseph reached across the table and rested his hand on David's. "You don't know how much that means to me. Sometimes I feel like quitting the law, but it's cases like yours that make it worthwhile." A tear formed in the lawyer's eye.

"You never did finish telling us what you're going to do with yourself," said Ruby.

"First I'm going to see Eddie graduate from Basic Training."

"Sounds great!" Ruby said. "I wish I didn't have to work or I'd go with you. Congratulate him for me."

"Then I'm going to my cabin up North, while the weather is still good. I'm going to do some fishing and some thinking."

"Do I have an invitation to join you?" Joseph asked.

"Anytime. Maybe we could discuss the meaning of life as we did in my jail cell that day," David laughed.

"No thanks, that's too depressing," Joseph chuckled. "I'd just want to do some fishing."

"That would be fine with me."

"Then what are you going to do?" Ruby asked. "I hope you're going to keep living in Albion."

"Of course. Albion is my home. I may just write about mercy killing. It's a subject we haven't paid enough attention to. The moral issues. The psychological issues."

"The legal issues certainly need clarification," Joseph added.

"That too. Betty shouldn't have been able to block Ben from shutting down Lu's respirator. Maybe you'd help me write about the legal issues."

"You've got a deal," Joseph responded.

"That's what you should do," Ruby said. "Doctors and nurses all need legal guidance."

"First I want to see my grandson and do that fishing and thinking."

David thought he would sleep well that night, but he did not. It seemed strange to be in his own bed, his own house. It seemed as if Lu should be there. And he missed Eddie. He would have to give himself time to get used to his new life.

Before he fell asleep he resolved that when he went to his cabin up North he would take along his old typewriter–perhaps even get a new computer. Fishing and thinking would not be enough for him. He wanted to start on his new project right away. He had a new energy–the same energy as when he had first come to Albion College years ago.

-67-

David sat in the reviewing stand at the edge of the parade grounds of the Marine Corps Recruit Depot. Each graduating platoon had its separate section in the stands for parents, relatives and guests. Eddie's platoon was number 3073. David was the only person in his section wearing a suit jacket. He wanted to look his best for Eddie's big day.

David had arrived in San Diego the day before, but the rules did not permit Eddie to speak to him until after today's graduation ceremony. The new Marine would have a week off before being assigned his next duty. He planned to return to Michigan to visit.

As the Marine band played, David's emotions soared. He had not been near the military since his own Army service over 50 years ago. He was so proud of Eddie. There had been times past when he had been ready to give up on the youth's future, but Lu had always insisted that Eddie would straighten out. Now she had been proved right. On the telephone Eddie had sounded so mature. He was elated that David had been acquitted and was coming to the graduation.

Over the sound of the band, David could hear the Drill Instructors off in the distance, shouting marching orders to the newer recruits. "Hut-two-three-four," they shouted. Earlier this morning David had seen a group of recruits scale the obstacle courses that Eddie had mentioned in his letter. David could see the courage that was required—especially in jumping off the tall building-like structure while holding onto a rope. He was very impressed with the Marines.

After the invocation and the brief speech by the Commanding Officer, the thrill of the day occurred. From off in the distance some 300 smartly uniformed young men marched onto to the field in perfect precision. They formed intricate formations and ended up marching by the reviewing stands four abreast. Parents and guests strained to see their Marine.

Finally it was platoon 3073's turn to march past in absolute military precision–no doubt the result of endless training. David's old Army unit had never approached a performance such as he was witnessing.

Suddenly, he could see Eddie marching past! The third one in his row of four. Nearly indistinguishable from the others, but Eddie nevertheless. Tears of joy rolled down David's face. He was so very happy and proud to be there.

The 300 recruits, the buttons and shoes of their uniforms shining in the sun, stood in formation some 250 yards away, while the Commanding Officer spoke on the public address system.

"Ladies and gentlemen, I want to explain something about the Marines. For 13 weeks these young people have been addressed solely as recruits. It's been, Recruit Smith, this, and, Recruit Jones, that. Until this moment they have not earned the right to be called Marines. Today I have the privilege of being the first to call them Marines." Holding the microphone, the C.O. turned his attention to the distant group of recruits. "*Good morning, Marines!*" he said in a loud, strong voice.

"*Good morning, sir!*" shouted back 300 strong voices in absolute unison.

A chill went up the back of David's neck such as he had never felt before. Tears again flowed down his face. David had been so glad to get out of the service at the end of World War II that he had never wanted to see another uniform in his life, but today he was proud. Proud of his grandson and proud of the organization that had changed him so much.

The ceremony ended and the unit was dismissed. The new Marines began joyously congratulating one another. Many of the parents and girlfriends hurried out to their Marines. David waited at the edge of the stands, watching for Eddie to emerge from the crowd, knowing that Eddie would find him in the stands.

But the first person David recognized in the distance was not Eddie, it was Betty. He made out his daughter's large form, pushing her way toward the celebrating Marines. David had had no idea that Betty was coming to San Diego. She had not been in Eddie's section of the reviewing stand. She must not have told Eddie of her plans or he would have mentioned it on the telephone.

Then David saw that Betty had found Eddie. While they talked, Betty put her hand on her son's shoulder. After a few moments, Eddie pointed in David's direction. David assumed Eddie was pointing out that he was present. Good God, he thought. What would he say if Betty came over? He didn't know what to think about Betty. On the one hand he was pleased that she had cared enough to come to Eddie's graduation, but on the other hand he dreaded the possible confrontation that might ruin his big day.

But Betty walked away, toward the parking area. Eddie waved at her, then turned and ran full speed toward his grandfather.

Eddie hugged him so vigorously that David nearly lost his balance.

"Thanks for coming, Grandfather. I was afraid I'd never see you again outside of jail."

"Eddie. Eddie. I'm so proud of you." David hugged his grandson in return.

They held each other at arm's length for several moments, not saying anything.

"What about your mother?" David said. "Where is she going?"

"She's leaving for the airport. She said something about needing to get back to Detroit, but I think the truth is she's afraid to talk to you."

"Afraid to talk to me? Quick, Eddie, run and see if you can catch her. I don't want her to go off like that."

"Are you sure?"

"Yes, I'm sure. She's still my daughter. Now, hurry. See if you can catch her."

David waited while Eddie raced across the parade ground toward the parking lot, darting around the many small groups of proud relatives and friends. He had mixed feelings about Betty, but he wanted to at least speak to her.

In a few minutes David could see that Eddie had caught Betty. They were walking toward him from the parking area.

"Eddie says you want to talk with me," Betty said, puffing from the walk. The three stood in the now nearly deserted parade ground.

"I couldn't just let you go off that way, without speaking."

"I thought you would probably never want to speak to me again, after the trial and all," said Betty.

David started to reach out for her, but he could see her pull back. "I want you to know that I hold no grudge. I know you loved your mother."

"I loved her more than you could know, Father." Betty avoided looking directly at David.

"The same was true of me, Betty. I loved her more than you ever knew."

"Well, Father, I guess we had different ways of expressing it," said Betty, still not looking directly at David.

"Mother," said Eddie. "Grandfather did love Granna. You have no idea."

"I suppose I should congratulate you on your acquittal, Father, but I hope you don't expect an apology from me."

"No, Betty. I don't want your apology. I don't ever expect you to agree that what I did was right. I'm prepared to go to my grave knowing that. It's just that I didn't want you to leave San Diego without talking. You see, a father always loves his daughter, no matter what, and I've loved you from the moment Lu told me she was pregnant with you."

Betty looked up at David, blankly, saying nothing. David did not know if she didn't know how to answer, or if she still hated him but was holding back.

"I was going to ask Eddie to show me around the base and then have lunch someplace," said David. "Would you like to join us?"

"No, Father. My plane leaves in an hour. I think I'd better go," Betty responded.

"If you must. Maybe when Eddie comes home on leave you'll want to come to Albion for a visit. You could stay in your old room."

"Sure, Mom. Why don't you do that?" Eddie asked.

"I'm sorry, but I've got a very full calendar next week."

"I understand," said David.

"Eddie promised he'd stay with me a day or two," Betty said.

"That's great," said David.

"Well, I've got to go now."

"Do you mind if we walk you to your car?" David asked.

"Not if you want."

Eddie and David walked with Betty to her rental car.

"Good-bye, Mom," said Eddie. "I'll see you next week."

"Good-bye, Betty," David said. "Maybe by Christmas you'll want to visit me at Albion—especially if Eddie gets home for the holidays."

"Maybe, Father, but you have to realize that an awful lot has happened this past year. It's been very difficult. My divorce. Losing mother."

"I do realize, but I'd like you to realize something too," said David. "You see, before I die I'd like to know you don't hate me any more."

Betty's expression was pained, but impossible to read further.

"I've got to be going now," she said, avoiding her father's eyes.

Eddie and David watched silently as her car left the parking area toward the exit from the base.

"Mom's a tough one, Grandfather. Hard to understand."

"I know, Eddie. I wish there were something I could do."

"Come on, Grandfather, let me show you around."

Eddie proudly walked David around the base. "These are my bar-racks–I went out like a light every night at 21:00 hours and up at 05:00 hours. Sometimes I didn't think I could get out of bed."

David was still preoccupied with his conversation with Betty.

"This is the obstacle course." Eddie explained the difficulties involved with the various obstacles. David delighted in the pride the young man was showing for having succeeded with the Marines.

When Eddie's tour was completed they drove to a Mexican restaurant in San Diego's Old Town. The huge covered patio area had several newly graduated Marines and their happy families. A group of Mexican mari-achis roamed from table to table, playing requested tunes

"I'm sorry your mother doesn't get along with me," said David. "I hope it hasn't ruined your day."

"Mother is who she is, Grandfather. I just don't let her affect me the way I used to."

"You've grown wise beyond your years," said David, smiling as they ate their Mexican food.

"You know, I think she feels guilty about testifying and all."

"Maybe someday you can be a peacemaker between us. I meant what I said about a man not wanting to die still estranged from his children."

David and Eddie toured San Diego that afternoon, seeing Mission Bay and various sights. Several times David sensed Lu's spirit was with them. He hoped she knew that Eddie and he were together.

"I'll see you next week," said Eddie as David dropped him off at the base. "Northwest Flight 301 at 2:14."

"Do me a favor, will you, Eddie?"

"Sure, what?"

"Wear your dress uniform. I want everybody at the college to see my grandson, the United States Marine."

"Okay, if you want."
"You see, I love you, Eddie."
"I love you too, Grandfather."

-68-

Epilogue

It was Tuesday, November 8, 1994–Election Day in Calhoun County. Billie Croft and her husband had voted in the general election and were in their car headed for what would probably be their last round of the golf season.

"I guess I don't have to ask you how you voted in the prosecutor's race," said John.

"Actually my choice was not that easy. After all, Cain is a very good attorney."

"I read where Lasser said if he won the election he was going to drop the appeal in the Neal case."

"I read that too. That was the main reason I voted for Lasser today. I think we did justice in our case. It wouldn't be right to try Dr. Neal all over again."

"I still don't understand how you could vote for acquittal when you always believed so strongly in law and order."

"You had to be there to understand. You just had to be there."

Judge Betty Neal sat alone in the study of her Bloomfield Hills mansion, looking across the back lawn at the magnificent maple trees that were shedding their leaves. Her court was not in session on Election Day. The fall weather made her think of her mother. She'd give anything if her mother could be with her for just one more hour. She wished she could hear her mother tell her once again she was proud of her–proud of her being a federal judge–proud of her living in such a magnificent house–proud of her for having given her such a handsome grandchild.

When Eddie had visited her the week after graduation, Betty had taken him to downtown Detroit. She had been proud of him in his uniform as she had introduced him to her staff at the Federal Building, and as they had lunched at her old law firm. Although she still harbored a hope that one day Eddie would follow her into the legal profession, she had accepted that, for now, he was happy being a Marine.

Betty hadn't spoken to her father since San Diego. Perhaps one day she would see him; she was undecided. Maybe she'd feel differently when more time had passed. She knew she would not accept his invitation to return to Albion for Christmas. Last week she had booked a holiday cruise to the Caribbean. She wanted to get away. She needed to get a new perspective on her life.

Betty had brought home several legal papers she had to read for tomorrow's session. She looked at her watch. It was only 11:30 a.m., but she was hungry. There was some low fat yogurt in the refrigerator. She guessed she'd finish that off before lunch.

That night Fred Cain and Marge returned from election headquarters. The voting for prosecuting attorney had been very light compared to the congressional voting. There hadn't been as much interest in the prosecutor's race as Fred had hoped. He was losing by a margin of over two to one.

"It's just as well, darling," said Marge, consoling her crestfallen lover. "You don't belong in a jerkwater place like Battle Creek anyway."

After dinner Fred perked up. "You know, I learned something from the Neal case."

Marge looked up. "What, darling?"

"It's easier for the defense to win the big ones."

"I've been thinking for some time..." Marge said.

"What?"

"Look at Jefferson. He must make a ton of money and you're just as good a lawyer as he is."

Fred smiled. "Thanks. At least *you* think so."

"Who wants to be a prosecutor anyway?" she said. "You belong in Detroit, being a criminal defense lawyer like Jefferson. It might be slow at first. I'd go with you–if you want me to."

"Are you kidding?" he laughed. "A sexpot like you? I wouldn't go anyplace without you, but I think I have a better idea."

"What's that?"

"How would you like California? I could cash in my retirement and study for their bar exam."

"I'm all for it. Look at the kind of money they must be charging in the O. J. Simpson case."

Fred pulled Marge to her feet and hugged her. "Look out California. Here comes Mr. and Mrs. Frederick Cain!"

Eddie looked over the ship's rail. Yesterday he had added the Lance Corporal stripe to his uniform. In the distance he could see the mountain near Port-au-Prince. His battalion was there to replace the first group of Marines who had landed in Haiti in September.

He took out the letter he had just written to his grandfather.

Dear Grandfather,

I'm very excited about my duty in Haiti. I'm liking life in the Marines more each day. Maybe when I finish my hitch I could go to Albion College. What do you think? Mom offered to buy me a car to replace the one that was stolen, but I told her I'd rather earn it myself. I really appreciate having Granna's ring. I look at it every day.

Love,

Eddie.

He wished he could write a letter to Granna too, but he knew that
wherever she was she was happier now. He reached in his pocket and felt
her wedding ring. It made him feel close to her.

"All right, Marines!" a voice shouted. "Prepare to disembark!"

Joseph looked out his office window at the orange-colored freighter
going south on the Detroit River. It wouldn't be long before the river
would be frozen. He was going to try to get in a little more time in Florida
this winter.

Joseph had finished a three-week jury trial. The jury was still out deliberating. His client, an unlikable man worth about a hundred million dollars, had been charged with securities fraud. It was an almost routine case
for Joseph.

He thought back to the Neal case. He wondered how David was doing.
He recalled the time after the trial when David's grandson, Eddie, had
dropped by the office wearing his full dress uniform. He had been visiting
his mother over at the Federal Building. Joseph had enjoyed seeing the
young man. As much as any one thing, Eddie's testimony had helped win
his grandfather's freedom.

David had called him several times for legal points on the book David
was writing about mercy killing. David had invited Joseph up to his cabin
for fishing, but Joseph was too pushed for time, getting ready for the securities trial. Maybe someday when he wasn't so busy he'd take David up on
his offer. It was the occasional case like David's that made the practice of
law worthwhile.

The leaves on the trees outside David's Northern Michigan cabin were turning color. David had been busy these past weeks on the draft of his book. Tomorrow he would return to Albion for the winter.

The week Eddie had been home after graduation, the college had given David a festive reception at the Faculty Room. While the warm congratulations of his colleagues gave him great pleasure, his real triumph had been showing off Eddie, handsome and standing upright in his Marine dress uniform.

David reflected on the visit Eddie and he had made to Riverside Cemetery the week Eddie had been home. Together they had looked down on the grave marker that had just been placed on Lu's grave.

Lu Neal 1919-1994.

"Eddie," David had said. "I want you to have your grandmother's engagement ring. Here, I've been keeping it for you."

Tears had come to Eddie's eyes as he accepted the ring. "Thank you, Grandfather."

"Perhaps one day you'll want to use it, when you find a woman you love and decide to get married."

"I don't think so, Grandfather. I think I'll want to keep it for myself. I'll never forget her."

David remembered what he had said. "I'll never forget her either, Eddie, but it's time that I move on. It's time for me to build a new life."

David began packing for tomorrow's drive to Albion. He was due at Ruby's house for dinner tomorrow night and would have to leave early to make it on time.

In two weeks he was flying to New York to see his agent. His long-time publisher had expressed an interest in the book. He was excited about the trip. New York was fun in the fall. He hadn't been to the big city in a long time and there were several plays he wanted to see.

Maybe he'd fly over to London for a week or so. He hadn't been to Europe in over 20 years. He had also been thinking about a trip to Australia with some of the Albion faculty. The trip would be at Christmas time, but Eddie would still be in Haiti and there was little chance that Betty would want to be with him, so he might as well be away from home. There were so many things to do in life, he didn't know how he could fit them all in.

About the Author

In *Mercy On Trial* Wendell B. Will, an experienced trial lawyer, weaves an authentic page-turning thriller around a timely subject—mercy killing.

Will's first novel, *Not By Bread Alone*, also won critical acclaim. He is the winner of the Will Rogers short fiction contest. His work is character driven as well as driven by plot. Will may be contacted at: wbwill@earthlink.net.

0-595-21214-X